The Last Will of Moira Leahy

The Last Moira

Therese Walsh

Will of Leahy

A NOVEL

 SHAYE AREHEART BOOKS / NEW YORK

Copyright © 2009 by Therese Walsh

All rights reserved.
Published in the United States by Shaye Areheart Books, an imprint of the Crown Publishing Group, a division of Random House, Inc., New York.

www.crownpublishing.com

Shaye Areheart Books with colophon is a registered trademark of Random House, Inc.

6657

Library of Congress Cataloging-in-Publication Data
is available upon request.

ISBN 978-0-307-46157-5

Printed in the United States of America

10 9 8 7 6 5 4 3 2 1

First Edition   .

This book is dedicated to my Amelia.
Fly, my pretty bird, fly.

And to Sean, for nurturing my wings.

The First Will

THE KERIS

FOR THE JAVANESE . . . THE PURPOSE OF KNOWLEDGE (*KAWERUH*) IS LOVE, NOT AMBITION OR CLEVERNESS. KNOWLEDGE COMES FROM CARING ENOUGH TO SUFFER AND LEARN.

—PAWARTOS JAWI

CHAPTER ONE

lost my twin to a harsh November nine years ago. Ever since, I've felt the span of that month like no other, as if each of the calendar's thirty perfect little squares split in two on the page. I wished they'd just disappear. Bring on winter. I had bags of rock salt, a shovel, and a strong back. I wasn't afraid of ice and snow. November always lingered, though, crackling under the foot of my memory like dead leaves.

It was no wonder then that I gave in to impulse one November evening, left papers piled high on my desk and went to where I'd lost myself in the past with a friend. I thought I might evade memory for a while at the auction house, but I slammed into it anyhow. It was just November's way.

Only this time, November surprised me.

I HAD TO have it.

Just over a foot long, the wavy dagger looked ancient and as though it'd been carved from lava rock. The grooved base was a study in asymmetry, with one end swooping off in a jagged point and the other circling into itself like a tiny, self-protective tail or the crest of a wave. Gemstones filled a ring that bound metal to a cocked wood handle. Intricate engravings covered the silver sheath. If not for a small hole in the blade's center, it would've been flawless.

I leaned in to touch it but was jarred out of my study by a poke to the thigh. The poker, a little girl, almost capsized me, and not from the poking, either. I don't believe in ghosts, but if I did I might think I was looking at my sister from years past. My sister, a child. Eyes like the sea. Long, red hair like hers—and mine, before I snuffed out my pyrotechnics with several boxes of Platinum Snow and found a pair of scissors.

My vision grayed a little as I stared at her. She might've been seven or eight—a few years younger than Moira and me when we'd filched a sword like the one I intended to have and lost it in the bay. Well, I'd lost it, pretending to be Alvilda, Pirate Queen.

The girl poked me again.

"Can I help you, little one?" I asked. "Are you lost?"

She didn't answer, just pointed toward the far back of the viewing table. There wasn't much there: a bust of JFK, a pearlized candy jar, and an indigo bottle that might've been Depression-era glass. Noel would've been able to say for sure.

"Do you want that?" I took a guess and pointed at the candy jar. Maybe there was a secret stash of chocolate in there; who knew? But she shook her head. I looked again and saw a small black box slathered with pink roses, the buds as sweet as frosting. Of course. "The box?" She nodded.

I cradled it before her, and she reached out a hand pudgy with youth. "Careful," I said. I looked for parental figures but saw no one exhibiting missing-child panic—or with the right hair color. The girl didn't take the box, just left it in my hands and opened the lid.

Music swam up at me. "The Entertainer." The girl giggled.

"Do you—" My voice turned to rust. "Do you like music?"

"I love dancing to the music." Her voice was whisper-soft, as shy as her smile. She was so much like Moira, but whole, able to run and laugh. I missed my sister's laugh—maybe most of all.

"Do you play any instru—"

"Jillian! There you are!" A woman with dark hair strode toward us, her face a combination of annoyance and relief.

4

"I was looking at the music, Mommy," the girl said. "See how pretty?"

The mother bent before her daughter. "You scared me. Next time you want to look at something, we'll go together."

The girl nodded, serious, just as the lights flickered.

"Let's find a seat." The woman pulled her daughter behind her as the girl lifted her hand to me. Good-bye. They disappeared in the crowd.

I shook off my melancholy thoughts and turned back to the blade. My fingers itched to touch it, but just as I reached, an auction attendant pulled it off the table, sheathed it, and placed it in a cardboard box. "Viewing time's over," she said.

"But—"

"Fallen in love, have you?"

I'd never seen another blade like the one I'd lost to the sea, and the desire for it tugged at me as if a line were rooted in my mouth. "I have to have it."

The woman added items to her container: the blue bottle, the candy jar, the music box. "You'd better get out your checkbook, then. Old George thinks that sword will go for hundreds."

Fine, then. I had a checkbook.

After a few minutes of dodging elbows and purses, I registered as the temporary owner of one beat-up paddle (number 51). Snippets of conversation danced around me as I wedged my way between wide-shouldered men and women.

"John would love that old clock for Christmas."

"Let's get through Thanksgiving first."

"Thanksgiving's just a day. Christmas is an event. Besides, it's never too soon to buy for Christmas. Don't you think he'd love that clock?"

I veered away from them, closer to the stage. That stage and the old floor, pockmarked from where rows of shabby velvet seats used to reside, were all that remained of the theater that had once been a revered landmark in Betheny, New York. At least, that's what Noel had told me. I'd only been a resident since college.

I'd just reached the front when George Lansing, the owner of Lansing's Block, appeared center stage. There was a blur of activity—

the sale of someone's stamp collection, a worn set of stools, a mahogany china closet that would break backs. I saw the blue bottle poking out of its container at George's feet and knew the blade lay there as well. The bottle sold, and then George grasped the music box.

"Going once!" he said, after a token amount of haggling with the crowd. A middle-aged woman with a sour expression had raised her marker and placed a bid of $5.

Where was the girl? Wouldn't her mother buy the box for $6? I looked around but didn't see her.

"Going twice!"

My arm lifted almost of its own volition. "Ten dollars."

George didn't even look at me, probably just wrote the bidder off as a sucker. There were no further offers.

I didn't need a music box. I didn't want a music box. In fact, I'd hate that music box. But the child who looked so much like my sister should have it. I couldn't seek her out, though, because just then George held the sheathed dagger over his head, and the raucous room grew hushed. I leaned closer; everyone seemed to.

"Now here's something you don't see every day," Lansing said, his voice as gritty as his wares. "This here's a *keris*. It's a little roughed up with a hole through its middle, but not in bad shape when you consider it was made somewhere in Indonesia probably two centuries ago."

Somewhere in Indonesia. *Probably* two centuries ago. I smiled. Lansing had never been big on facts—something Noel had taken profitable advantage of in the past.

And then Lansing's pitch rose, and the chant began: "Who'll bid two hundred dollars, two hundred dollars, two hundred dollars?"

It seemed half the room's occupants held their markers high, and the price rose to $225, $250, $275. I gripped my marker with slick palms. Noel had taught me how to bide my time, to don a face as still as the water on a windless bay; the slightest ripple would attract Lansing's attention.

"This blade's worth at least double that last bid, and I won't sell it for anything less than $350!" He pounded the podium—a technique that probably wasn't in the Christie's handbook, even if it did work. I looked over my shoulder as number 36 grumbled his bid of $350.

How much was I willing to spend in honor of a memory?

"Going once for three hundred and fifty dollars, going twice!"

I raised my marker and hollered, "Four hundred dollars!"

George finally looked at me, and his speck-dark eyes grew wide. "It's Noel Ryan's friend, the little albino girl," he said with a smirk. He eyeballed the room, but Noel wouldn't be found here tonight. "He send you for this?"

"No," I said, "he didn't."

Little albino girl. Times like this I just wanted to shout out that I, Maeve Leahy, was in fact a professor and connoisseur of more languages than George Lansing could probably name. But I said nothing, just tried to skewer him with my most lethal stare as people turned to look at me and my hueless hair. He smiled as he waved the gilded carrot that was Noel's impeccable reputation and keen eye before the crowd, and didn't blink when the false bait drew bites and the bidding resumed.

My Irish kicked in when it was down to me and another persistent soul, someone who pressed on from the back of the room. I had to have the blade, so I would have it. I lifted my marker and tried not to think about the cost.

But the other bidder didn't relent, either.

"You?" George Lansing said with incredulity the first time number 12's marker was called out. After, he just glowered at whoever gave my checkbook and me such a run, which was curious in and of itself.

I craned my head to pierce my competitor with dagger eyes, to say, *Back off. This is mine.* But I couldn't stand tall enough to see a face, just the competing placard and an odd black hat on a short-statured body. I was no fashionista, but the hat looked like a pillbox wrapped in a scarf.

None of it mattered in the end. Once the price teetered up to $700, not even Lansing could coerce blood from the others' snapped-shut, firm-tucked, copper-pinching veins. So I won.

The tautness in my chest loosened as I made my way to the pay-and-pickup window. I might've forgotten about the music box, but the woman behind the counter quoted me $710, and handed it over straightaway once I'd written out the check.

"The other—that sword thingy—it's not here yet," she said.

I took the music box and returned to the jammed room. I spied the young mother right away, standing in line for hot dogs.

"Excuse me." I held the box out to her. "Your daughter admired this earlier, and I'd love for her to have it."

"Oh, no." The woman's painted brows knit tight. "We couldn't possibly. Thank you, but no," she repeated over my objections. "We can't accept that, can we, Jillian?"

Her daughter appeared by her side—or maybe she'd been there all along and I hadn't recognized her. Because her hair, it wasn't red at all; it was dark like her mother's.

"It's pretty," the girl said with a shrug. "You keep it."

"You must have another daughter," I said to the mother. "She's the one who liked the box."

The woman's expression turned wary. "No, I only have one." And then she laughed. "One's enough."

"No," I muttered. "One's not nearly enough." I took a last look at the girl before turning away.

I stood beneath the ratty paper-globe light at the pay-and-pickup window until the blade arrived. I couldn't wait to touch it, but when I did I felt a startling amount of disappointment. There was no internal tremor, no spark. Instead, my chest clogged with emotion. I held that blade and whispered in every language I knew, "*Bienvenue. Bem-vindo. Bienvenido. Salve. Benvenuto. Bine ai venit.* Welcome."

THE FIRST THING I noticed when I stepped into my apartment—besides the deafening silence that meant Kit was once again not at home—was the bright green face of my cell phone staring up at me from the entry table. I'd forgotten it again. And I'd missed a message. My thoughts leaped to Noel. I tossed the music box and the blade on the couch beside my sleeping cat, Sam, and checked for voice mail.

"Mayfly."

Daddy. My heart stuttered.

"We can't make it for Thanksgiving after all. Sorry, sweetheart. Well," he said, "wish you were there. Talk soon."

The Last Will of Moira Leahy

I stood static for a minute, then called Kit. It surprised me when she picked up.

"Miss your daily dose of harassment?"

At least she knew herself. "Yeah, my life's bland without your trademark aggravation peppered all over it."

She laughed. "I was just about to call you. I'll be home later, so don't freak if you hear the door open."

"They're letting you out for good behavior?" I walked to the window to stare out at the night. "Have they strapped one of those detection boxes to your ankle—you know, the kind they give to stay-at-home convicts?"

"Yep. It's called a pager." Kit, a first-year resident physician, worked far more hours than the law allowed, though it suited Betheny's floundering teaching hospital just fine.

I breathed on the glass, then put my finger against the film of condensation and made a tic-tac-toe grid. "My dad called. My parents won't be here for Thanksgiving after all."

"So go to them," she said without missing a beat. "It's not such a long drive, and you haven't been to Castine in years."

"I've been busy." I put an *X* in the center of my grid, then an *O* at the upper right.

"But it could be—"

"No." I imagined it for a second: seeing my parents and the old room I'd shared with Moira, walking over Maine's rock beaches and sailing the Penobscot. But as much as I missed the sea, Castine had become like quicksand for me. "No," I repeated. "I'll stay here. That means it's you and me and the cat."

"So we'll make our own Thanksgiving. Turkey, all the trimmings."

"They'll let you whip up garlic mashed potatoes in the ER?"

"Funny." She paused. "We still need to schedule your MRI."

I wished she'd let that go, but I guess it was my fault for making a big deal out of it once when the noises came—scattery disjointed sounds, a little like you'd hear trying to tune in to a distant radio station. We'd been eating one of our rare meals together when I'd covered my ears and growled, "Knock it off!"

She stopped twirling pasta to stare at me. "What the hell?"

"Nothing. Just my personal noise factory."

"You're hearing things?" Her cat eyes narrowed on me, and then she'd provided an encyclopedic listing of every freakish thing that could make a person imagine sounds. "I don't think it's schizophrenia."

"Thanks for that."

"But what about a brain tumor or—" A gasp. "It could be post-traumatic stress disorder! You're scatterbrained, you sleep for crap, you have zero sex drive—"

"Enough! I haven't been in a war, Kit."

"You have, kind of. It could be plain traumatic stress. That's like PTSD, just not as severe."

I understood the excitement of untangling a mystery and weaving a theory, but Kit was off the mark; I knew more about the noises than I'd let on. Those little immature sounds that wanted to bust free in my cranium were the remnants of a previous life, the parts that used to make up my sum. I'd moved on, and I wished the remnants would, too.

"Well, if I did have one of those diseases," I'd said, "could you prescribe something to stop the noises? Does such a drug exist?" Maybe not my best idea, but what good was it to have your best friend become a doctor if she couldn't whip out her prescription pad once in a while to simplify your life?

She'd just shaken her head and said, "You need to see a neurologist," which I wasn't about to do.

I tried harder after that to repress the sounds, though the effort stole my energy, and pretty soon Kit was saying I was too pale and my body temperature too low and that maybe I had chronic fatigue syndrome or a sleep disorder or needed to be tested for lupus and an array of other things. I thought she was the one with the clear diagnosis: medical residentitis.

"Hey, you there?" Kit said in real time. Me, I'd drawn my third tic-tac-toe board, and I hadn't won a single game.

"Only if you promise not to start in with me."

"Hallucinations can be serious, Maeve."

"Random noises don't count as hallucinations, just corroded brain joints." God, if I told her about the little girl with the not-red hair she'd have me admitted to the psych ward for sure.

"Well, I think you should see someone," she said.

"I know you do."

"I love you, you know?"

"I know. I'll leave a light on for you."

I shut my cell, then found the Windex. I squirted solution onto the window markings I'd made and cleared them all away—just in case playing tic-tac-toe with yourself could be used as evidence of insanity. And if there were any noises other than that of squeaky-clean glass, I pretended not to hear them.

THAT NIGHT, I had to force myself to read and grade half of the essays left on my desk. If not for Jim Shay's effort—*"C'è un'orrenda creatura nel mio brood"* (There's a gruesome creature in my soup)—the process would've been entirely unoccupying, which was odd, because I loved to teach, loved my students, loved to keep track of their progress and grade even the most Nytol-ish of papers. And I loved language—all those words with their own spin and dip, requiring their own special curl of the tongue: *ebullición, bellissimo, kyrielle, obcecação, labialização, babucha, l'Absolu, d'aria.*

I gave up on my work, sat on the couch, and unsheathed the dagger. My finger traveled the metal. God, it took me back.

Once upon a time, my parents liked to tell bedtime stories. My mother favored the parable of the Five Chinese Brothers, who were as identical as Moira and me, but whose different talents saved them from every imaginable catastrophe. One boy could hold an entire sea in his mouth, while each of the others could either go without air or survive fire unscathed, or had an iron neck or legs that could grow into stiltlike appendages.

But my father liked to tell Alvilda's tale. She'd escaped a prince who wanted to marry her to become a pirate and ruler of the seas instead. Funny, that very prince bested her in battle later and made her fall in love and settle down. She became the queen of Denmark. A story far more satisfying than your run-of-the-mill Cinderella romance.

At the fearsome and fearless age of ten, I decided to become the next Alvilda. All I needed was a boat, a sword, and the sea. I had plenty of boats at my command, since my father made them for a living, and there was sea all over the place in Castine. That left the sword. So one day, I put on my best Alvilda clothes—a red coat, black boots, and an eye patch fashioned out of black construction paper and a shoelace—and sketched a plan for pinching the wavy blade from the artifacts cabinet. There were all sorts of things in that cabinet that my grandfather, an anthropologist, had brought to us from all over the world. But the wavy dagger was my favorite and would make the perfect accessory for my adventure.

Moira was nervous—

"We'll get in trouble!"

"Shush, Moira, 'cause if Daddy comes now I'll tell him it was your idea."

—but she went along in the end. I found the key, opened the cabinet, grabbed the blade, and bolted with my reluctant shadow. We didn't stop until we reached the docks, and I barely waited for Moira to hop in before I started the motorboat.

We went pretty far out for us, and then I stood on a seat near the prow and acted my part as the mighty Alvilda.

"Bring it on, matey!" I crowed, waving the blade around until Moira squealed—

"Shark, shark!"

There weren't many words that could snuff out my bravado, but *shark* did it when we were in a tiny boat and far from Daddy's help. The blade and its sheath were lost in the water. I don't know if I dropped them in or if they slid from a precarious perch as I hovered over my twin. Regardless, by the time I realized the fin belonged to a whale—who lifted his harmless black head just once—they were gone.

My gut had ached more than my thwacked backside, knowing that beautiful blade lay at the bottom of the ocean, gone forever, thanks to me. But now I had one again.

Shadows drifted over the ceiling like a sorcerer's fingers, until my eyelids grew heavy and I gave in.

With sleep, though, came the nightmare.

Water seeped beneath the closed door as it always did. *Open the door!* the voice commanded as a growing stream drenched my shoes, socks, and skin. The pounding began. *Open the door!*

Then, something different: Tinny music, "The Entertainer," began to play on the other side of the wood.

I broke from the dream. My skin prickled with the icy-wash feeling I loathed, and my heartbeat thundered in my throat. The music box lay open on the floor, combing through its circular song with its many pins and pegs. I must've kicked it off the couch in my sleep. I shut the lid and "The Entertainer" stopped. But sound remained, intensified, then mutated.

My mind filled with its own music: Liszt's Hungarian Rhapsody no. 12, each hammered string tinkling through my memory like water torture. All in my head, yes, but far from a hallucination.

I tapped into an old skill and pressed back the sound until song became broken notes, and notes became a weak scatter of between-station noise. Why was it that whenever it snuck in, it was piano, like a knife scraping at the last of my nerves?

An owl hooted outside my window, and I thought with a mix of exhaustion and irony that perhaps I'd just been answered, but in a language I would never understand.

Out of Time

Castine, Maine
JULY 1995
Moira and Maeve are ten

Sounds eddied around her—of voices and her twin sister's music—
but still Moira kept her feet planted on the hot stone walk between
her home and the house that had been her grandparents' all her life.
Her gaze caught on the yellow moving truck in the drive. Everything had changed. First Grandpa had died, then Grandma three
months later. Daddy sold their house. Little by little, her grandparents' furniture and clothes were taken away, until a single solid item
remained: the piano.

She had to have it.

"Huh, she's good," said the bushy-haired woman who was their
new neighbor.

Moira's sister, Maeve, had just finished a busy phrase on her saxophone. Moira could picture the lost butterfly of the song, its journey through a wild storm before finding right-sided stability and
sunlight again.

"She is good," Mama responded, full of pride. "I taught her the
basics, but within a few months she was beyond my ability to teach.
She's studying with Ben Freeman now."

"Never heard of him."

"He's a pro just north of here," Mama said. "But Maeve's real talent is writing her own songs."

"That one there was putting puzzles together upside down when
she was three," the other woman said, motioning toward an elm
tree. A girl with two short blonde pigtails sat there, her hands busy
trying to clothe a fat gray cat in a doll's dress. Moira hadn't even
noticed her. "Smarter than me already. Mark my words, she'll get a
scholarship and go to college and make something of herself. Ian,
my older one, he's clever enough, but he'll stay and be a lobsterman
like his daddy. Ain't no shame in that. Come here, Kit," she called.

14

The girl uncrumpled herself and walked toward them. She stood as tall as Moira and Maeve, maybe even a little taller, and her eyes were like Daddy's—blue with a dash of algae, as Mama sometimes joked. The cat, half-clothed, followed the girl.

"We saw a show about a boy like your daughter, Mrs. Leahy—"

"Call me Abby."

"—but he played the violin. What did they call him, Kit?"

"A prodigy," the girl said.

"Prodigy, that's right. Four years old, he was, if you can believe. How a boy like that can play a violin when he can't probably even tie his shoes is beyond me." The neighbor woman snorted, then eyed Moira. "That one play, too?"

Mama smiled. "Moira plays the piano." She shouted for Maeve just as she started a new piece. "Come and be sociable."

Maeve's expression fell flat as she laid her sax in the grass. "But I'm making a song about seals, Mama. You can hear the Bagaduce in it."

"And the waves," added Moira.

"And the birds—"

"You can smell the fish in it!"

"Like the time we—"

"That's rude," Mama said as Maeve stepped up beside them. "You know no one but you two can understand when you do that." She stared until Moira stopped smiling. "This is Mrs. Bronya and her daughter, Kit. You girls are all in the same grade."

"You play real good," Mrs. Bronya told Maeve. She turned to Moira. "You make your own songs, too?"

"I'll teach her how," Maeve said.

"She'll teach me," Moira said. They both nodded.

The woman looked between them. "How do you know who's who?"

Mama laughed. "It's easy once you know them."

"I've never met twins before," the girl, Kit, said.

"I'm older by six minutes." Maeve's red hair blew into her mouth as a gust of wind drew up. "Mama says I was harder to push out and I've been harder ever since, but she's just teasing, because me and Moira are exactly identical."

"Ayuh!" Moira gave her ponytail a twist.

15

"You should've seen the twin convention in New York City a few years ago," Maeve said. "Twins everywhere! Some like us with their own language when they were little—"

"Your own language?" Kit asked.

Moira giggled. "It's called cryptophasia."

"I always called it *Trying Twin*," said Mama with a smile.

"Lots of twins have it," said Maeve. "But it's not the same for any-one but those two people before they forget it. I wish we remembered ours, because then me and Moira could say secret things at school and everybody would think we're aliens!"

"That's weird," Kit said.

"Nah, what's weird was that at the convention there was a pair of twins hooked together by their butts," said Maeve. "Mama said it was freakish, so we left after that."

"Maeve, that's not what I said." Mama glanced at Mrs. Bronya.

"There were twins with polka-dot dresses and a bunch with jeans and yellow T-shirts and even some dressed in matching suits, but Mama made Moira wear a skirt and I wore shorts, and we don't even have two of the same shirt"—Maeve pulled at her stained Smurfs shirt while Moira touched the sunflower on hers—"but Daddy said people would know we were twins anyway."

Mama sighed, but Kit laughed.

"One twin's brother died," Maeve said solemnly, and Kit leaned closer. "His wife said he felt it when it happened."

Moira remembered the man—how he'd rubbed his hand against his cheek and said he needed to sit, his eyes stumbling around. Moira thought he was looking for his brother, that he couldn't help it, even though his own twin boys swung from his arms.

"I've heard of that sort of thing, but I thought it was bunk," said Mrs. Bronya. "You girls read each other's minds?"

Just that morning, Mama had warned them about this stuff: *I want you to have friends, but it'll be hard unless you stop playing games. People don't understand you—not even me sometimes. There are five known senses, girls. Remember that.*

"We have the best card tricks," Maeve said. "I can be in a different room and still know what Moira's holding."

"Is that so?" Mrs. Bronya's eyes were as wide as Maeve's.

Moira tried not to look at Mama.

"And I swear I felt it on my big toe the time Moira stepped on a bee, even though I was with Daddy on—"

"Look, the piano!" said Mama in a loud voice.

They all turned to see Daddy walk out of the house backward, one end of the instrument in his grasp. His face, ruddy by nature, bloomed like a beet. He faltered a little on the walk, repositioned a squat cart of wood and wheels, and said, "A'right, one more push!"

The other end appeared with a man in tow—tall, plump, and bald but for some fringe around his ears. A blond-haired boy followed in their wake.

"Help your dad, Ian," said Mrs. Bronya. The boy scrunched a cheek up at her. He was tall like his father, but thin, and Moira thought he must be going into sixth grade at least. He stopped beside his sister, and they all watched as the men rolled the instrument across the walk, to the other door. And then—after another lift and shove, and a few more grunts—the piano disappeared inside the house.

"Is it your piano?" asked Mrs. Bronya, and Moira realized she'd let loose a gusty sigh.

"It was my grandma's." Moira looked at the yellow roses growing up the side of the old house and remembered soft, paper-thin-skin hands. "She wanted us to have it after she—"

"Did she die in our house?" the boy asked.

"Ian's afraid of ghosts," Kit said with a smile.

"Shut it, guano breath," he said. "What do you know?"

"More than you." Kit lifted the cat and stroked its head; its back legs were still stuck in the dress.

Mama used her patient voice. "She died in the hospital."

Moira remembered those last days, the liquid sound of every breath her grandmother took. Dying seemed a painful thing.

Ian kicked a rock in his sister's general direction before looking at his mother. "When are we going to eat? I'm starved."

"Let me make sandwiches for you." Mama ignored Mrs. Bronya's objections. "No, no, I insist." She shot a quick warning glance at Maeve and Moira, then strode into the house.

"That one's a fancy musician," Mrs. Bronya told Ian, jerking her head at Maeve. "At least I think it's that one."

"Oh yeah?" he said. "A strung-up lobster pot would sound better than that old piano."

"It just needs tuning," Maeve said. "Then Moira will be playing perfect piano and I'll be playing on my sax, and we can have duets like we had in Grandma's house. Grandma said we'd be famous someday and travel the world and play our music, so that's what we'll do." She nodded and patted Moira's shoulder.

Ian huffed. Moira thought he sounded like a horse. "Haven't you heard?" he said. "Nobody born in Maine ever leaves Maine."

"It's easier to leave Castine than come in new," Maeve said. "You're from away now, and you always will be."

"We're from flipping Bucksport. Throw a stone!"

"Watch that lip, boy," said Mrs. Bronya.

"Our grandparents came from Cape Breton when my daddy was just a baby and everyone here still says we're from away," said Maeve. "Course it didn't help that they spoke French or that we do."

"Sure you speak French," Ian said, and Kit giggled.

"Do too, best of all, and some Italian and Spanish, because my poppy's an anthropologist and he knows about different cultures. He's even eaten monkey brains before!"

"What a little liar you are."

"Am not."

"Prove it then, unless you don't have the balls," Ian said.

"Third strike," said his mother. "I'm telling your—"

"Tu peux me passer les dés s'il te plaît?" said Maeve. The Bronyas stared. Kit stopped laughing. *"C'est mon tour."*

"What did you say?" Ian asked, his voiced edged with surprise and annoyance.

"I said, 'I do have the balls,' in French." Maeve squared her shoulders. "And then I said, 'What's the matter?' in Spanish and 'Cat got your tongue?' in Italian."

Kit's face scrunched up, and Moira tried not to laugh. Maeve had asked Ian—entirely in French—if he would pass the dice because it was her turn to play. They'd played dice a lot with Grandma Leahy.

"Well, huh," said Mrs. Bronya. "A whiz at music and language both? What weird kids you are."

Ian snickered. "More like witches with your freaky hair and fat eyes."

Moira frowned as Mrs. Bronya thwacked Ian's arm. Daddy said their eyes looked big and beautiful: Maeve's like the sky before the rain, Moira's like the sea. They were the same shade, really, but Daddy swore he could tell them apart by their eyes.

"Ayuh, maybe we are witches," Maeve said, her mouth pressed in a line. "Better watch out or we'll cast a spell."

That's when Mama came out with a tray of sandwiches. Even Maeve knew to stop talking after that.

"I DON'T LIKE that boy," Moira said later that night. She and Maeve sat on the living-room floor together, hunched over *Webster's New World Dictionary.*

"But that Kit with the cat seemed okay," said Maeve.

"There." Moira pointed to an entry. "Is that it?"

prod|i·gy 1 [Rare] an extraordinary happening, thought to presage good or evil fortune 2 a person, thing, or act so extraordinary as to inspire wonder; specif., a child of highly unusual talent or genius

"Crap on a cracker," Maeve said. "Now we'll have to look up 'presage.' "

"No, it's number two: 'a child of highly unusual talent.' " Moira pursed her lips.

"Well, if I'm a prodigy, you're a prodigy," Maeve said.

Moira rose, then lay a hand on her grandmother's piano and ran a finger over the sharp edge of a chipped ivory key. "How do you make your music? Can you really teach me?"

Maeve looked through the opening to the kitchen, then moved beside her sister and sat on the piano bench. Moira sat as well. "I've told you, you have to be open to the sounds," Maeve said in a low voice. "The notes are in the air."

Moira closed her eyes tight and tried to hear the notes.

"It's like when I know things sometimes," Maeve said.

"But I can't do that."

"You could if you tried hard enough." Maeve sighed. "It's like when we block—that feeling of shutting everything up and going inside yourself. It's like that, but . . . more like going out."

Moira hated blocking, being separated from the pulse of her sister's energy and emotions. She thought again of the lost twin at the conference, his despair at being only one, and felt grateful she and Maeve never blocked for long—and only when one of them was sick or hurt.

Moira opened her eyes. "Okay, I'll practice."

"You can do it. I know you can." She paused. "Want to go build a ship out of that big box in the basement?"

"No, you go ahead."

Moira stayed at the keyboard for hours, her right hand splayed over the keys, her left clasped to the wooden seat. She tried to open herself to notes in the air but heard only the Bronya's noisy truck, their dog barking, and a motorboat. And she couldn't help but think about Grandma's roses. Maybe Moira would snip some, the way Grandma sometimes had when she'd seen pretty flowers in the neighborhood.

A little love is all you need, she'd said, *to make the flowers your own.*

Maybe it'd be that way with music, too. Moira just had to love it more, want it more. The notes were there, waiting for her, if only she tried hard enough to reach them.

CHAPTER TWO
UNDERSENSE

I missed my alarm the next morning, tired from bat-
tling back Liszt all night, and had to scramble or risk major late-
ness: shower, shove wet hair behind ears, forget the makeup, throw
on something clean, stuff all papers into battered briefcase for later
speed grading, tear in two the business card of one Dr. Stephen
Flett, neurologist, that Kit had left on the kitchen counter at some
point in the wee hours, feed Sam, and drive without coffee—which
was never a good idea, but you did what you had to do to make it to
Spanish Dialects on time.

I got my first real break just before noon and headed to my office,
weighing the likelihood of being able to sleep there and the reaction
my coworkers and students might have if they caught me. It'd make
the *Campus Times* for sure. *Dr. Leahy was discovered last week, snoring
and drooling over a stack of ungraded essays. Clearly, she needs naptime
built into her day, as might be expected for someone her age.* No, I'd never
live it down. Unless I locked my door . . .

On said door, though, an interoffice envelope hung from a nail
like a dictum. Papers and a half-eaten granola bar spilled from my
briefcase when I dropped it to wiggle free the nail, open the envelope. Huh. A pocket-sized book on weaponry lay in my hand. I

turned to a page bookmarked with a red scrap of silk, scanned, and found something interesting.

> The *keris* is another Javanese weapon made only after a great deal of preparation. First, the *empu* decides what he will craft. A *keris* may be made to protect against evil, preserve dignity or secure wealth, for example. The *empu* fasts, prays and makes ceremonial offerings sometimes days before crafting begins. Iron, nickel, steel and meteoric metals are heated. The *empu* layers and forges them together to form the *pamor* (design) of the *keris*. He then smiths the *dapur* (shape) by straightening the *keris* or creating an odd number of *luks* (curves) as desired. Finally, he chisels the base to form its many intricate details. A completed *keris* is filled with purpose. Some believe that humans easily succumb to its suggestive powers as inhibitions are stripped away.

A *keris*. That's what Lansing had called my new purchase, wasn't it? As a child, I'd never known the name of the wavy blade I loved. I flipped through the rest of the book but saw no other passages related to the *keris*.

I called Heather in the library to inquire about the book, but she said no such title existed within the university system. I checked the inner pages for stamp marks, any evidence that the volume had belonged to another institution or a particular individual. Nothing. The new interoffice envelope, barely creased and with nary a pen mark, was also devoid of clues.

I reached for the phone again, let my fingers dance over memorized digits.

"Time After Time. How may I help you?"

I smiled into the receiver. "I wondered if you have any of that amazing hot chocolate in your kitchen cupboard. You know, the stuff from Venezuela."

"My dear girl!" sang the lilting voice of Garrick Wareham, the owner of the antiques shop Time After Time—not to mention Noel's grandfather and my favorite Brit. "I've missed you!"

"I've missed you, too," I said, then added just as honestly, "And Noel. I've even been scoping Lansing's Block without him. How's that for crazy?"

Garrick laughed. "Have you made any buys he'd approve?"

"Good question," I said. Noel, whose business was finding valuable antiques in auction houses and estate sales throughout the country for Time After Time, would've taken the trouble to inspect the *keris* before leaping into a bidding war over it. Truth was, with Lansing's weak provenance for the blade and a hole going straight through the metal, Noel might not have approved of my purchase at all. "I bought something, but it was mostly for sentimental reasons," I said.

I told Garrick about the *keris*, and answered his questions about why I'd purchase such a thing—even if it embarrassed me to admit aloud that I'd once wanted to be a pirate queen. He took everything in stride and suggested I bring the blade by the shop for an appraisal. I thought about my packed schedule, my commitments with the university. No trip to Time After Time was ever brief.

"How 'bout I visit over Thanksgiving break?" I asked.

"Splendid! When does that begin?"

"Two days and four-and-a-half hours. Not that I'm counting." The break was a glorified long weekend, but it would be enough. I checked the clock, knew I'd be late for my intermediate Italian class, but had to ask, "Will Noel be home?"

"I'm afraid not," Garrick said just as the sound of the shop's entry bells drifted over the line. "Good God, my grandson must've shipped over half of Europe this week! I'll have to sign for all of this, my dear, but you're welcome to come by whenever you'd like. I have some Chuao cocoa on hand."

A NIGGLING SENSE of disquiet stalked me that night, as I drafted two tests, graded papers, then worked up a plan for helping a student on the edge of pass-fail. *Marilyn*, I wrote at the top of a note. Sighed, crumpled it up, tried again. *Marion.*

Kit might chide me about needing an MRI, but having a book anonymously nailed to your office door had a way of messing with your concentration. I couldn't deny wanting to learn more about the *keris*, and I knew Garrick would gladly pull up a chair with me tonight if I appeared at his door. Thanksgiving break was just two days out, though, and if I didn't focus, I'd never jump through all the university hoops. I could wait to learn about the blade—and my displaced friend.

Noel, my companion and ally since I'd arrived in Betheny eight years ago, had been in Europe for months, not just searching for antiques but for his only living parent: his mother. He hadn't seen her since she'd crushed his little-boy heart by leaving him with her father, Garrick, and disappearing from their lives. The only time he'd really talked about her, he'd said they thought she lived in Europe now and good riddance. But a few months ago, on a sweltering August day, he'd changed his mind, said he had to search.

How will you do it? You don't even know where to look.

I have some ideas, he'd said, evasive.

I didn't understand his sudden need, but I respected it, envied it even. At least some who were lost could be found.

It always made my day to receive one of his postcards, picturing cobbled streets, majestic castles, white-capped mountains, or balconies of cut stone. I imagined the rest—the people and language, even the music. Nearly a month had passed since I'd heard from him, and the silence was wearing on me. I had no way of contacting him at all; Noel didn't have a cell phone or an e-mail account, hated computers. In fact, he didn't like anything that verified he lived in the twenty-first century.

Is it me, Maeve? Or is it . . . just?

Just. Just.

Tension sprouted between us before he'd left. I'd pretended not to understand its root and then made a concerted effort not to think of it at all. I needed to do that again. Not think. Not miss him. Just wait. The Fifth Chinese Brother could hold his breath eternally, after all—though I wondered if his ribs ever cracked, if he ever longed to steal just a little air.

I pulled the book from my briefcase and touched the red silk marker, lifted it and breathed a spicy, exotic fragrance, the scent of a foreign land. It lingered with me for days.

I STOOD IN a park filled with decaying greenery. A hundred cranes flew overhead, but still I stared at the stone monument of a woman. Something seemed wrong with her, but I couldn't say what. Then she turned her head to stare at me, water trickling and words rumbling from her ancient mouth.

Nascer, nascer! she said. Rise. Get up.

I startled awake and rose, stumbled to my cell. The dream-world message continued to punch at me as I made the call.

Nascer, nascer, nascer!

Six rings, seven. I looked at the clock; God, only 5:10.

" 'Lo?" my father said in his sleep-scarred voice.

"Dad, sorry it's so early." I didn't sound much better than he did. I cleared my throat.

"Maeve? You okay?"

"I just wondered . . . Is everything all right?"

"Ayuh," he said, "same, you know." I let loose my breath. "Got the first snow last night. Wind's up. Your mother—she's not here or I'd put her on. Left for the day, I think."

Of course, at 5:10, she'd be off. Resentment pulsed in me, plain and ugly, though I wouldn't let it leak into my voice. Then I realized. "Dad, it's Thanksgiving."

"So it is. Forgot, just about." An uncomfortable moment passed. "Sorry we couldn't make it there, Mayfly. Sorry about all of it."

"I know. Me, too." The act seemed simple enough—visit me, share the holiday. But nothing was simple with my mother.

"You know," he said, "if you left now—"

"No, Dad." I tried to look forward. "At least there's Christmas, right? You'll come then."

Silence. My stomach sank.

"Your mother, she was going to call. She just doesn't want to travel right now, and—"

"But it's not right now! It's a month from now!"

"We hoped you'd come here for Christmas this year. Come home. We'd love to see you."

"Dad, you haven't been here since graduation, and Mom's never been to Betheny at all!" I'd never forget the look on President Stephenson's face when he'd asked to meet my mother at graduation and I'd told him she couldn't make it. His expression had transformed from respect into something I detested. *Her twenty-two-year-old daughter finishes a PhD program in record time, graduates with honors, is offered a position with the university, and she doesn't show up?* He pitied me. And it made me work that much harder—even now, nearly three years later.

I knew it was no use arguing or even pleading with my father. She would never come to me.

"If you don't want to drive, we can buy you a plane ticket," he said. "It'll cut your time in half."

"It's not that, Dad."

"Then drive, daughter. Get in the car and be with us. If not today, then for Christmas. Come home."

I shook my head, thinking of cranes and outstretched necks and chopped ones and Thanksgiving and Christmas dinner all at once, my mind a cornucopia of disjointed imagery. "I can't," I said.

He seemed to be similarly incapable of carrying on. "Well. We'll miss you, Mayfly. Good talking. I'll tell your mother."

I knew sleep wouldn't come again, but I stayed beneath my blankets for an hour anyway. I studied my room: the folded clothes, books stacked on my dresser, organized alphabetically. Neglect showed only in the slender mirror on the back of the door, dust-coated where there weren't course curricula taped to the glass. I rose and approached it as one might a sleeping giant, then lifted a single sheet and looked beneath. Wary eyes regarded me before I let the paper drop.

In the kitchen, I started coffee and pulled a carton of eggs from my refrigerator, along with some vegetables. I cross-sectioned a zucchini, then began slicing. Half-moon wedges puddled before me, as the noises started again.

"Leave me the hell alone," I said to my own head. Like a crazy person after all.

I SPENT THE day babying a small turkey and half a dozen side dishes. Finally, Kit called.

"It's a rarity," she said. "There's a pregnant woman here with two uteruses. Surgery's soon. I have to stay."

"Are you kidding? Where will you eat? The cafeteria?"

"It's not so bad, really. You could always . . ."

She let the thought trail off, as if realizing how dismal it was to eat Thanksgiving dinner—by choice—in a hospital.

"I'll bring a plate for you," I said.

"Aww, thanks. But I don't know how long this will go, and—"

"They're taking advantage of you. You work too hard."

"Pot calling kettle! Come in, kettle!"

"Whatever. Eat when you get home, all right?"

I hung up and poured myself a full glass of wine, sat by Sam on the couch. "Just you and me, bud." I took a gulp and stroked his fur. "Merry Thanksgiving." He snored faintly. "Sure, but you'll be wide awake when the turkey's finished."

I looked at the paperwork on my desk. I needed to plan the international outreach course I'd test online next summer. That's what I should do. But my eyes turned back, snagged on the *keris* I'd left abandoned on the table. I could still conjure the scent from that red scrap of silk, even over that of a roasted holiday. I touched the sheath and felt a tickle of heat. Maybe it was warm because of the meteoric metals I'd read about. Was that plausible? There had to be more to the *keris* than what I'd learned in that book.

I thought of Noel, touring European castles and museums, searching for dusty treasures and digging into a more personal kind of ancient history.

It'd been a long time since I'd had any sort of adventure.

Avventura.

How easily that word had rolled off my poppy's tongue, become the mantra for his life. I knew what he'd do with a mystery, no matter the size. Research. Dig. Figure it out.

Why not shun work tonight? It was a holiday, after all.

I turned on the computer and Googled, "What is a *keris*?" And when the screen lit with knowledge, I leaned in, took another swallow of wine, and gave thanks to technology.

Out of Time

Castine, Maine
OCTOBER 1995
Moira and Maeve are eleven

"No humming at the table, Maeve," Mama said as they sat down to Moira's favorite meal of crab salad and corn on the cob and mashed potatoes and salad with ranch dressing.

"It's a new song about a hungry fox," Maeve said as she reached for the corn.

Moira grabbed an ear, too. "It's sad, though."

"Yeah," said Maeve. "The fox is trying to get—"

"This had better not be about the baby again." Mama clutched her small round belly and made her neck tall and taut.

"No, it's about gooses," Maeve said. "The fox thinks they're tasty, so he's trying to get them all." She bit into her corn. Butter dripped down her chin.

"Geese." Mama shook her head. "I'm sorry for being so jumpy, Maeve. It's my hormones."

Daddy smiled but said nothing. Gorp, not as wise, barked. "Quiet, dog," he said, but Gorp kept howling and then ran out. Daddy stood, followed the dog. Maeve followed Daddy, the corn still in her hand.

Noise erupted—Gorp barking; the front door opening; Mama's chair scraping against the wood floor; Maeve whooping; Daddy saying, "John, what a surprise," as Mama exclaimed, "Dad! Why didn't you tell us—?"

Moira rounded the corner and landed beside her sister in their grandfather's open arms, his coat sleeves scented with the unfamiliar.

"Has my daughter been feeding you two magic growing beans again?" Poppy squeezed them, and they giggled and squeezed back.

"You've burned yourself." Mama touched his pink face. "Where did you come from?"

"Oh, just Cairo. I don't suppose anyone would be interested in having some real, ancient Egyptian papyrus?" He shrugged out of his coat, smiling, as Maeve and Moira squealed.

"You've made it in time for supper," Mama said. "I'll fix you a plate."

"I'll get your bags," Daddy told Poppy.

"Mama's having a baby. Just one this time," Moira said, when she and Maeve were alone with their grandfather.

"Yes, I've heard!" Poppy ruffled her hair with his big hands. "Are you excited?"

"Wicked excited!"

"And do you want a brother or a sister, Moira?"

"A sister."

"And you, Maeve? What would you like?"

"I don't know," Maeve said. "I think something's wrong with the baby."

Poppy's smile drooped. "Wrong? Abby didn't say—"

"Shh!" Moira poked her sister with her elbow, and Maeve's corn dropped to the ground. Gorp was out the door with it within seconds.

"Thanks a lot, Moira. That was good corn."

"Sorry, but you know Mom doesn't want you talking about your funny feelings anymore."

Poppy bent close to them and whispered, "Lucky for us those funny feelings don't always pan out. Last year, you thought something might be wrong with me!"

Maeve smiled. "I'm glad I was wrong about that."

THAT NIGHT, POPPY told stories of lost cities and found pyramids. He showed them photographs of rediscovered passageways and dark-skinned people and old paintings. Maeve asked a relentless stream of questions: "What did you eat? Did the natives dance and make sacrifices? Were there poisonous spiders? Snakes?" Poppy answered between frequent outbursts of laughter.

After dinner, while everyone recovered from big pieces of blueberry pie, Maeve played her saxophone. Moira closed her eyes and saw Egypt, felt it: the dance of a cobra in a minor-key melody; the whip of sand in a brief ascension; the persistent hot sun in a wavering high note; the tension of a dig and maybe a fall in a quick-drop scale.

Poppy applauded when she finished. "You never sounded like that, Abby." He winked at his daughter.

"No, all my squeaking probably sounded more like . . ."

"Gooses?" Maeve set down the instrument.

"Yes, Maeve," Mama said with a smile. "Geese."

Poppy leaned back in his chair. "I've missed the Atlantic," he said. "I hear you girls can handle the sails yourselves now."

They nodded in unison, said, "Yes, Poppy."

"Shall we go sailing tomorrow, bright and early?"

"Ayuh!" Maeve said without even asking Daddy. "We'll take you to a new spot on the island that has the best jasper ever!"

Moira stayed in Maeve's room that night, as she always did when Poppy came to visit. They cleared the floor of books and clothes and tapes, and made room for Moira's sleeping bag.

"You sure you don't want to stay up here with me?" Maeve peered over the side of her creaky bed to look at her twin.

"No, your bed's broke."

"Just broken in, like a baseball glove."

"Because you jump on it too much. I'll sleep here."

"Okay, but you're missing a good bed."

Moira read *Jane Eyre* by moonlight until her eyes hurt, then fell into a fitful sleep as dream pythons squeezed her middle. She woke to her sister's moan.

"You're sick," Moira whispered. "You shouldn't have had two pieces of pie."

Maeve groaned again, clasped her stomach.

"Should I get Mama?"

"No, if she finds out, she won't let me have pie tomorrow. You go back to sleep. I'll block."

"Don't block. It's not that bad." Worse than pain's shadowpart would be feeling cut off from her sister. The effort of blocking would make Maeve extra tired, too.

Moira curled beside her twin, and slept until she felt a tap on her shoulder. Mama, rimmed in faint yellow, stood over them with a question in her eyes. Moira looked at Maeve, whose cheeks were two red splotches in a pale face. She no longer felt an undercurrent of pain but knew from the tight, hollow feeling in her chest that Maeve had blocked after all. It felt, almost, like hunger. "Maeve's sick," she explained.

Mama touched Maeve's forehead, frowned. "Go on down and have some eggs," she said. "Daddy has to work on Dan Brooks's windjammer today, but you and Pops go have fun on the boat." She left, taking wide steps to avoid shuffled piles of room rubble and muttering something about the thermometer.

"Feel better," Moira whispered, and kissed her sister on the head.

THE SUN HADN'T yet cleared the mist when Moira and Poppy set out twenty minutes later. Moira's anxiety over Maeve lingered as well, though it unfurled some when the first gust of crisp, salted wind filled their sails. Poppy managed the mainsail and tiller, while Moira kept her hand on the small jib sheet and monitored the wind vane Daddy had put on top of the mast. *Always know where the wind is coming from*, he'd said. *It's the first lesson for sailors and the most important.* Moira watched the wind vane.

"What did the Atlantic Ocean say to the Indian Ocean?" Poppy asked once they'd been sailing awhile.

"What?"

"Can you be more Pacific?"

Moira giggled.

"Do you know what the Indian Ocean said in response?"

"No."

"Nothing, he just waved."

She had another fit of laughter and he chuckled along with her, as they adjusted their sails at a change in the wind.

"So tell me how school has been. Do you like your teacher?"

"She's very nice." Moira chatted about Mrs. Keeler and her classmates for a while, then adjusted the jib again and stopped to listen to the irregular cadence of rippling sails.

The wind had picked up as they'd sailed farther into the heart of the bay and closer to the mouth of the open sea. Waves had grown larger and the fog thicker, like a blanket over the whole of the sky, a clot over the sun. Moira shivered. She could see no landmarks. Hear no other sailors.

"Poppy, should we should go back? Maybe a storm's coming."

Poppy didn't answer. His face looked funny, like it was coated in chalk. Moira watched, horrified, as he slumped against the side of the boat, then fell, headfirst, into the sea. The boat lurched on a splash.

"Poppy!" she screamed, as his body bobbed to the surface, his face framed in the sun-faded life preserver she'd teased him into wearing. His eyes were closed. He didn't speak, didn't move except with the waves. Moira's mind felt suspended, too, as she drifted away from him.

She had to turn, or Poppy would be lost to fog and sea.

Her hands had just begun to follow her brain's orders when a strong gust hit. The boom moved, the boat leaned, her hair flew into her eyes. She grabbed the jib sheet, uncleated it. It luffed, blaring in the wind, but the boat stabilized.

"Poppy! Wake up!" His shape grew smaller behind her as panic beat hard and painful in her chest.

She lunged for the tiller. This had never been her job, but she'd seen it done, knew the steps: *Haul in the jib, cleat it tight, push the tiller, haul in on the mainsheet.* The boat began to turn and tip slightly. She muttered steps—"turn into the current, adjust the mainsheet"—and tried to keep her eyes on the wind vane and Poppy both.

He lay far to the left of her. She couldn't get to him in a straight line; she'd pull closer in one direction and move farther away in another as minutes lapsed. She battled frustration as she worked. *Imagine the line between you, pull as close as you can this way, uncleat the jib.* It seemed to take forever, and when she thought she was close, she braced herself to come about. *Push the tiller away*—she ducked under the boom—*trim the main sheet, move the jib, cleat it.* The boat turned for the last time.

Poppy floated in front of her now, and the boat moved forward, closer . . . closer. A wave covered her gloved fingers as she leaned, reached beyond the boat—

"Poppy!" She grabbed his life jacket, but it caught halfway down his arms, the straps unfastened. She made fists in his shirt and hair instead, and pulled his body against the boat. With a glance back at the wind vane, she maneuvered them enough to point the boat into the wind. The sails stalled. The jib flapped deafeningly as it lost air. The liberated lines jumped and pinged against the mast, and the boat stilled.

Moira hugged Poppy's body and sobbed. His chest moved—he breathed—but his skin felt like ice and his lips were blue. She knew she had to get him out of the water, but his heavy body, covered in layers of soaked clothes, lifted only a little when she tucked her arms under his and pulled. The boat leaned when she tried again, straining as hard as she could, but he barely moved with her efforts. She stopped, panting, and the boat settled back into the sea.

"Help! Can anyone hear me?" she shouted. "Is anyone there?" Only the wind shrieked in response, and the boat pitched dangerously with the hard gust. Moira reached a hand toward the sail but wasn't fast enough. The vessel tipped.

Her lungs seemed to deflate as she hit the frigid water. She gasped in shallow breaths, coughed, kicked. Somehow her hands found what they needed: her grandfather, the boat. Her fingers slid on the slimy underside of the craft as she tried to right it. Failed. She grabbed some floating line, managed to wrap it around Poppy and her own wrist to make a clumsy knot.

"Help! Please, someone, help us!" Her voice jangled like bones in their sockets as the sea slapped and sucked against the inside of the boat. She'd never felt more alone.

Time slurred until she heard a noise that was not the sea. *Help.* She could not holler or even raise her arm to wave. She tried to pinpoint the source and couldn't. She no longer felt the cold; her body no longer shivered. She tried to open her eyes, but they felt heavy with the sting of salt as she drifted in the dark space behind her eyelids.

SHE WOKE IN an unfamiliar bed, covered in blankets.

"Can you hear me, sweetie?"

Was that Mama? Moira fell back asleep.

She woke briefly to the sound of her parents' voices: *incapacitated, therapy, recovery.* The words were indecipherable to her. Again, she slept.

At some point she became aware of a thin tube along her arm. Her eyelids felt like anchors as she pulled them partway up. Darkness filled the room.

"Poppy?"

The word came from her raw throat as a rasp. Glass pressed

against her lips. She sipped water, then sunk back into the void, still feeling the greedy surge of the sea in every breath.

Then it was day once more. Moira noticed white walls, a green curtain over a wide window, a machine with red lights. Maeve sat beside her, the pale skin beneath her eyes lined in shadow. Moira didn't need to ask the question.

"I felt it somehow," Maeve said, "even with the block. It was terrible, cold, the worst feeling ever. Mama said it was the sickness, but I knew it wasn't, so I ran and found Daddy getting ready to leave, and he believed me and we found you."

Moira learned more later—about Maeve pointing the way as unerringly as a wind vane through chowder-thick fog until they were found, floating in the sea like fishing buoys.

"Poppy had a heart attack in his brain. He's going to live with us now," Maeve said. "I think this is what I felt last year about him. What if I'm right about the baby, too, and—"

"Stop it!" Mama stood in the doorway, looking furious and wild, like a stranger. She rushed at Maeve and, for the first time, slapped her across the face. The sting of her assault spread through Moira's flesh as well.

Daddy seemed to come from nowhere, and pressed his hand over Mama's mouth. He pulled her away, his lips pale and flat. "I'm sorry, sweetheart," he muttered, and Moira didn't know to whom he spoke, since he looked at all of them in turn.

Mama never mentioned the incident after that. She all but lived at the hospital until Poppy's release three weeks later, then made a place for her father in their home and spent most of her time caring for his needs.

"You saved my life," Moira said one night, lying beside her twin. She didn't mind about the droopy bed now.

"No," Maeve insisted, "you saved your own. You're like a goose on the water."

"Goose brain."

"Goose butt."

They slept together after that like goslings—huddled for warmth and hoping the foxes stayed away.

CHAPTER THREE

CRIMSON STAIN

he day after Thanksgiving, I finally made my way to Betheny's biggest and best antiques shop, Time After Time. Like most retailers across the country, it would be a huge sale day for Garrick, so I arrived before the shop officially opened for business. Excitement hit as I pulled into the empty lot. I'd missed this sight. Three stories tall, perfectly white, with a peaked tower and twin chimneys, the old Victorian looked like something out of a Norman Rockwell Christmas village.

I strode across the stone walk with the *keris* in hand, and was greeted with the rich scents of cinnamon and pine when I opened the heavy wooden door. As always, my eyes couldn't pick a focus in this place that seemed like Oz to me, like Willy Wonka's chocolate factory. Every nook and cranny beckoned with some new treasure— *come, look, touch, buy.* There were Japanese woodblock prints, stained-glass lamps, ornately carved pieces of furniture, African masks and Indian headdresses my poppy would've loved. A huge blue spruce stood in the center of the room, bedecked with multicolored glass ornaments, miniature lamps, real tin tinsel, and a crystal star.

Scads of fascinating old books lay everywhere, including one I'd been tempted to buy after a particularly bad run of nightmares: *Old*

Gypsy Madge's Fortune Teller and the Witches Key to Lucky Dreams. Inside were instructions for making talismans against love, enemies, war, and trouble in general. TO BE WORN AROUND THE NECK, it read. Turned out I wasn't that desperate.

Artwork decorated every wall, including one area near the front that was dedicated to Noel's paintings. His specialty: irony. True love between a fly and a cow's tail. A pregnant old man. A squirrel chasing a dog up a tree.

Come on, Maeve, pose for me. Just once.

Don't be stupid, I'm no model, are you blind?

Who's being stupid? And who's looking at you? Let me.

Sorry, too shy, I'd lied with a saucy grin. Truth was, I'd never be able to sit for that long with Noel staring at me, even if he did have a pencil or brush in his hand.

A proper English accent sated my hungry ears—"My dear girl, it's wonderful to see you!"—and there before me stood Garrick Wareham, dressed for tea in a green shirt, striped wool vest, and gray trousers. He looked like a Hobbit: short in stature (we are actually the same height—5'3"), with a mop of curly white hair and a pair of blue eyes that sparked with intellect and steadfast good humor. A Hobbit, except for that snowy white mustache of his, tipped up at the ends.

I hugged him. He smelled of lemon drops.

He led me down a familiar hall off the main room—the one that also led to Noel's studio. *How's Noel? Where is he? When will he be back? Did he find his mother? Has he asked about me?*

These questions stalled on my tongue as we turned into the weapons room—a formidable place lined with locked glass cabinets full of machetes and bayonets and spearheads and other things I couldn't name but wouldn't want to meet up against in a dark alley. Various showcase pedestals dotted the floor, including one that displayed a pyramid of musket balls and another that featured the navy cap of a Civil War officer.

"Now," Garrick said, stopping at a workstation, "let's have a look at that *keris.*" I handed it over, and then he unsheathed it and whistled long and low. "Fly me over the moon. It's perfect."

"Well, not quite. There's a hole."

"That's not a flaw." He turned the *keris*, brought it close to his face. "You're supposed to be able to see the future through those. It's good luck."

I wasn't surprised I hadn't read about good-luck holes during my Internet search; Garrick prided himself on obscure information. While he might call his knowledge factual, though, Noel probably would've said otherwise.

"Let's see what we have after I give it a bath." He unlocked an opaque cabinet, and pulled down half a dozen bottles covered in warning labels. Toxic cleansers. "Make yourself at home, Maeve. There's cocoa in the kitchen if you'd like."

"You're too good to me," I said, though my taste buds didn't jolt as they should have. I loitered. Strolled the room. Watched Garrick. Finally, I stepped before a pedestal displaying a Revolutionary War bugle, and my thoughts drifted to Castine's own legendary Revolutionary War musician.

According to the story, Castine's drummer-boy ghost died during a skirmish in my hometown. He'd haunted the battlefield for a while, then moved into a tiny nearby dungeon. I'd always wondered why. Maybe he'd grown tired of the field. Or maybe he'd wanted to escape the memory of trumpet call. I could relate to that. Mozart's Piano Concerto no. 20 in D Minor had been with me since the previous night, as ceaseless as a haunted music box.

"How's the music?"

I nearly knocked the bugle over. "What?"

"Is it too loud, not loud enough? I swear, my hearing . . ."

I became aware of Bing Crosby's crooning for a white Christmas coming in through the shop's speakers. "Oh, it's perfect." I needed to hold it together.

"There's a resting snake in the last case on the left if you'd like to look," Garrick said, still scrubbing at the blade.

"Snake?"

"A straight *keris* is sometimes called a resting snake, and a wavy blade is active. It comes from *naga*, a mythical reptile. Do you know Sanskrit?"

"No," I admitted, walking toward the back. "But I did find out that the word *keris* comes from the Javanese *ngeris*, which means 'to pierce.' I did a little research last night." Eating cold turkey with my fingers and fighting the effects of tryptophan for as long as I could.

"Did you? And what did you learn?"

"That I shouldn't believe half of what I read."

He chuckled. "Well, what did you read?"

"That some *kerises* bring good luck and some bad."

"Yours will certainly bring good. What else?"

"They come in different wave lengths and patterns. Let's see if I can remember the names—they were in the book, too." I stopped before the last case. "The number of waves are called the *luks* and the pattern is called the *pamor.*"

"Very good. Look at the *pamor* on that one," he said, and I swiveled around to face the glass. I recognized the *keris* right away by the unique cut of the metal near the handle—an area I now knew bore a long list of specific features, like *ganja* and *tang.* In fact, the *keris* had more labeled parts than most unassembled toys imported from China. Otherwise, there was little resemblance between this particular *keris* and mine.

"It's very nice," I said, noting the scattering of bold ovals along its straight length. No need to tell Garrick that *that* blade wouldn't have caught my attention at Lansing's Block.

"*Kerises* may well be manufactured by machine nowadays," Garrick said wistfully, "but it used to be that *empus* made them, layering metals to create perfect patterns by following something like a blueprint. Each design was supposed to bring the owner a specific gift— like wealth or inner strength.

"But sometimes the *empu* would allow the blade to be made however it wanted to be made. When that happened, it was said the gods had a hand in crafting the *keris* because they had plans for it. Your *keris,*" he said, "is fated."

"Hmm." Another hole in my education.

"The details in your blade's *pamor* have darkened over time, but I believe they're clearer than they were. Come and see."

I stepped up. Though still near black with age, the *keris* now shimmered bronze and silver, like the skin of a serpent in intense sunlight. Thin veins ran from one end to the other, swirling harmonically in some places and eddying off in others. No intentional design. Fated—or fluked—into being.

"It's beautiful," I said.

"It's positively brilliant!" Garrick's mustache convulsed.

I took the proffered blade and balanced it on my palms. A citrusy fragrance emanated from the warm metal.

"Do you see the man in the blade?" he asked.

"Man?" I felt a subtle pressure against my palms when he touched the *keris*.

"There's the head," he said, indicating a dark metallic pond toward the handle, "and there's the chest, arms, and legs. It's a bloke, and it makes your blade more powerful. Magical. And, I suspect, worth quite a bit of money."

I squinted, but these supposed body parts still looked like random blobs to me. "What about the waves, the *luks*? How many are there?"

"Well, let's see." He traced the length. "Hmm." He started over, his brows bunched together. "Eleven."

"What does that—"

"Or thirteen." He nodded and scowled simultaneously.

"It matters how many, to know what it was made for, right?" Not that I believed in that mumbo-jumbo-gobbledygook stew, but it was interesting. On a hypothetical level.

"Yes, that's part of the equation. I'm sorry to say I can't be sure about it, though it must be an odd number of *luks*."

"Why must it? What if it isn't?"

"It always is, otherwise it would be unlucky."

"Unlucky *luks*. That doesn't sound good." I smiled even as his frown deepened; Garrick took his lore seriously.

"Some *kerises* are luckier than others," he said, "depending on the *pamor* and the shape. Even the blade's length is important. You know," he said in his big-eyed, silky-voiced way, "you can tell a blade's intention by putting it under your pillow. If you have a nightmare, the *keris* is bad."

"I'll keep that in mind," I said, though I had no intention of snuggling up to objects that might lead to my accidental impalement or doing anything—regardless of my skepticism—to court more nightmares. "Let's consider a hypothetical. Say my *keris* had eleven *luks*. What would that mean?"

"I'm afraid I don't know," he said, replacing caps on bottles. "There are about one hundred and fifty shapes and as many as two dozen patterns possible on a blade. Think of the combinations. It's a real science!"

"So, if I wanted to know more about it . . . ?" I prompted.

"Hmm." He stilled, thoughtful. "I suppose there are books dedicated to the *keris*. Or you might look for an *empu*—though I believe they are exceedingly rare nowadays."

"Oh," I said, as if I'd cracked opened a fortune cookie and found it empty. What an unfulfilling *avventura* to be left with so many unanswered questions. Disappointment must've shown on my face.

"Don't be disheartened, my dear. Every *keris* is imbued with magic. Did you know meteoric metals were used to create the *pamor*? *Empus* believed meteors were metal of the gods, coming straight from heaven." I opened my mouth to reply, but he went right on. "It doesn't matter where the magic comes from, I suppose—only that it exists. There are old stories of *kerises* flying from their sheaths to defend their owners, and there are still towns in Malaysia and Java that fear some notorious blades possessed by evil spirits. And there *is* some evidence . . ."

I could just imagine Noel standing beyond his grandfather, the roll of his eyes, the sardonic grin. *Humor him,* he'd mouth.

"It's too bad Noel isn't here to look at your *keris*," Garrick said, like he'd read my thoughts. "He's quite a talent at estimating age and value. Ah, well. He'll return one day."

My toes curled. "Soon, I'm sure, for Christmas."

"I've been kindly asked not to count on it." He said it with a hint of melancholy, but then he looked straight at me and the ends of his mustache tipped toward his nose. "You know how he detests flying. He'll never need to ride another aeroplane again if he stays in Europe. He'll just use the rail!"

I was too numb to smile back at him. Maybe that's why I asked the question so artlessly.

"Did he find her?"

"Who's that, dear?"

"Um . . ." Hadn't Noel told Garrick about the search for his mother, Garrick's daughter? Was it supposed to be some sort of surprise?

Garrick seemed oblivious to my confusion, though. His mustache had drooped again. "Ah, well. I get the feeling he's preparing me for something. I fear he may never come home."

Never? My fingers curled as tightly as my toes. Too bad I'd forgotten about what lay in my hands. The pain shocked me; I couldn't swallow my gasp. I heard Garrick's voice as if in a tunnel—"What have you done?"—as blood oozed from my sliced palm.

He brought me a damp washcloth and something to kill germs.

"Be careful with the *keris*," he said as I cleaned the cut. "It's a true weapon." He sheathed the blade, but even with my flesh aching, I wanted it back in my hand.

"The metal's so warm," I said. "Why is that? I never found the answer online."

"Warm?" He slid me a knowing look. "A *keris* can do that. Bewitch a person. It has its own will."

Humor him.

"Have a care, dear Maeve. The little man in the blade may have plans for you."

He left the *keris* on the counter when bells announced the arrival of his first customer. I don't know what made me do it. I picked up the blade and spoke directly to the bleary man in the metal. "Don't try to change me."

An unwonted shiver slithered down my spine when the words filled my head: *There will be no going back.*

SLEEP WOULDN'T THROW its prickly comfort over me that night, thanks in part to Fauré's "Sicilienne." Like it had been in the past, music was just *there*, ever present. With one exception. Those old songs had been mine. Not the piano. Not even the sax. Just pure tone. And every major, minor, augmented, diminished sound had given me joy. This music just pissed me off. Mostly because the hammered keys in my forehead resisted the usual shutdown. I had a strong urge to reach below my mattress and dive right in. *If you can't beat 'em* . . . But I knew better than to disturb the boogeyman under my bed.

Instead, I unsheathed the *keris* and touched it, felt energy swim through my fingertips again. I peered through the aperture, hoping for some future glimpse—

—and noticed a trickle of blood on the metal. I knew where that had come from; I looked at my hand.

41

My efforts at scrubbing out the stain met with failure. The line merely grew long and thin. The sweet scent of citrus disappeared. I called Garrick the following day. He could fix it, he said, and invited me to bring it by when I could.

I should've been reassured, and maybe I would've been if things hadn't seemed so strange lately. If the music stopped, would let me stop it. If Noel would come home. If I could get a decent night's sleep. If the stain didn't look so much like a strand of red hair.

Out of Time

Castine, Maine
NOVEMBER 1995
Moira and Maeve are eleven

"What do you see?"

Moira lay on a golden sea of elm leaves beside her sister. She thought all of the clouds looked like birds today, but she knew Maeve would think that was Pure Boring, so she lied a little. "I see a dragon and a great big ship. I think the dragon's at war with the people on the ship."

"What's the dragon's name?"

"Alfred."

"That's a horrible name!" Maeve grabbed a handful of leaves and tossed it at Moira with a laugh.

"Hey, who's telling this story?"

Maeve stifled another giggle. "Okay. What's Alfred doing trying to be fierce, anyway?"

"Maybe he wants to try something new. Would that be bad?"

"Nope. That's why we're going to explore the world."

"What if I don't want to explore the world?" Moira asked, testing, but Maeve's face seemed untroubled, her eyes back on the sky.

"Of course you want to," she said.

"I do most of the time." But Moira liked the crunch of elm leaves, too. She liked her roses. She liked Castine. She'd miss their family. "What should we name the baby if it's a boy?"

"Alfred."

They stopped laughing when Ian Bronya and his friend Michael burst through the clearing.

"Look, it's the witches," Ian said with a mocking smile. "Catching frogs for your brew?"

"Maybe we are," said Moira.

Maeve stood when the boys stopped before them. "Hold still and we'll cut out your tongues," she said.

43

"Try it." Ian reached into his pocket and pulled out a closed jack-knife. He tossed it toward Maeve, but she didn't reach for it, so it fell in the grass. He sneered at her. "Which one are you anyway?"

Maeve tilted her head to the side and her face softened, just a little. "Guess."

Moira felt her sister's wish to fool Ian and decided to go along with it. They'd tried this game a few times before. Two years ago, Moira had pretended to be her sister for an entire day at school, but when Miss Haskell had teased her about being in control of herself for once, Moira had felt oddly dispirited. She didn't mind fooling Ian, though. She leaned back and twirled hair around her finger, knowing it would look like her sister's today—unbound and littered with sticks and leaves. As an added touch, she sharpened her eyes on Ian and didn't blink when he looked hard at her. It made her a little nervous, that looking.

Finally, Ian turned to Maeve and said, "You're Moira, but you're not usually such a bitch."

Michael laughed.

"You have a nasty mouth, Ian Bronya," Moira said, then looked at her sister. Maeve didn't speak, but her eyes had taken on their usual edge, and Moira felt her anger along with a surprising amount of hurt.

Ian scrunched up his face and looked at them both again. "Which witch is which?" He took a step nearer, and Maeve met it until their noses all but collided.

"I once saw a horse's behind that looked a lot like you," she said. "Smelled better, though."

He laughed. "I was wrong. This one's Maeve."

"Who cares about them?" Michael said. "C'mon. Let's move."

"Where're you two going?" Maeve asked.

"Come find out." Ian picked up his jackknife, then started with Michael out of the clearing. He turned and walked backward—toe to heel—a few steps, long enough to taunt, "Unless you don't have the balls."

"Let them go. They're jerks!" Moira said. But Maeve shook her head and followed without her.

That afternoon, as Moira trimmed back her roses for winter, she felt Maeve's curiosity and fascination. She became curious herself when she heard the screen door slam and saw her sister leap off the back porch in a cloud of dirt.

"Follow me," Maeve said in a hushed voice.

Moira brushed off her hands, then followed her sister across the yard and into their small shed. Maeve closed the door behind them.

"Give me your finger," Maeve said, Daddy's best jackknife slipping out of her long sleeve to land in her palm.

Moira hid her hands behind her back. "Why?"

"Ian and Michael went to Hearse House and made each other blood brothers. Everyone in their club's done it as a sign of bravery and allegiance. They said we wouldn't have the guts—well, balls—to do it, but I told him we would, so let's."

"But we're already blood *sisters*." Moira stared disbelievingly at her twin, who opened the knife with little regard for its sharpened edge. "What if you cut your fingers off? What if you cut mine off and I can't play piano anymore?"

Maeve sighed. "Do you have a scab?" she asked, opening the jackknife.

"I have scabs from working with the roses, but Maeve . . ."

Moira watched, fascinated, as Maeve pushed the tip of the knife into the fleshy part of her finger, until a small crimson bead appeared.

Maeve looked up at her. "It's okay, Moira. Just scratch a scab off. That'll be good enough."

Moira ran a finger over a rough bump near her wrist. Maybe it was the story of Fierce Alfred and the dragons or the fact that she hadn't blinked at Ian earlier, but she didn't want to settle for *good enough*. She held out her finger. "Here. Just be careful." She closed her eyes.

It happened quickly: some pressure, a quick sting. When she looked again, her finger bore a deep red bead, just like Maeve's. "It looks like a ladybug." Moira giggled, excited and a little troubled at what they'd done.

Maeve let the knife fall where they stood. "Now we'll always be joined, no matter what," she said, and pressed the twin incisions together—lifeblood mating with lifeblood.

"We're sisters, gooseball, of course we'll always be joined!" Moira tried to retrieve her hand, but Maeve held tight.

"Wait, we have to say the words."

"What? Till death do us part? This is silly!"

"No, it's not good enough." Maeve gnawed her lower lip for a moment, then gripped Moira's hand with fresh enthusiasm. "I know! 'Even if I die, I'll be with you for always.' Say it." She ground their fingers closer.

A little shiver ran through Moira as she said the words: "Even if I die, I'll be with you for always."

CHAPTER FOUR
ELING

*D*ecember arrived, and I tried to forget about the *keris*. Soon the semester would end, followed by a lengthy break, but for now I needed to concentrate on my job. Exam preparations and handholding for my most grade-anxious students always took top priority those last weeks of class.

I felt distracted though, my days full of incessant mind music, my nights littered with dreams of gushing water and that omnipresent door. In odd moments, I found myself researching crazy things, like "*Empu* for hire," only to come up empty-handed. I unearthed one possibly relevant and interesting book online, but it was out of stock. Maybe I'd ask Heather about finding it, or another like it, through an interlibrary loan over the break. More than once, I peered through the aperture in the blade—the one Garrick said could foretell my future—but only ever saw what was right before my eyes.

I had to stop. I was becoming obsessed.

It first happened in early December, as I sat hunched over my work during office hours. My skin felt stretched, like it was pulling away from my muscles and bone. Someone was watching me. I turned around, but no one stood in the doorway. Neither was there

47

a soul in the hall. Plenty of times after that, I felt as though someone was following me, but I never saw anything suspicious.

The sensation struck again the final week of lectures, where naturally many eyes (two or three pairs, anyway) were upon me. I stopped midsentence to scan the tiered hall, just in time to see a door shut. That afternoon, I found a slip of paper nailed to my office door, bearing a single word.

Eling

Foreign, and I didn't know it.

I hoped Google's "I'm Feeling Lucky" search would give me immediate gratification, but it just landed me on the Totton and Eling town council page. After several minutes of scanning similar pages—and just as I considered siccing one of the department's TAs on the mystery—I typed in the phrase "eling means." *Javanese Mysticism* appeared in several links. I clicked, skimmed one of the pages.

```
Eling means remember.
```

The site spoke of awareness, self-control, things experienced with the spirit. Nothing sensible. Nothing about the *keris*.

Another link sent me to a site called *Joglosemar* and a page that read something like a prayer.

```
I eling to my life . . . I love the life of soul, the
real life, the life of light, the life of Atma (the
place of life), which are eternal, which could guide me
to reality.
```

I didn't understand this, either, but my eyes fixed on certain things.

```
If I come back to where I belong, it will be a per-
fect life. I 'eling' to both of my parents, mother and
father; I 'eling' to all my spiritual sisters and
brothers. I 'eling' to true knowledge.
```

Breathe during your prayer, it said. Breathe like a pregnant woman. Fill your stomach with air.

```
You are going to be spiritually more sensitive and
stronger. Some say you start to have the 6 sense.
```

```
Eling means remember.
```

Languages jumbled up in my mind as I did what I didn't want to do: I remembered. My mother upset when Moira and I refused to sit for Candy Land, when we told her we only wanted to play outside alone. My father's boat-building hands, holding our family together as well as he could. Poppy's smile. His short lessons in Italian and Spanish, all before the stroke. My mother again, breathing like a pregnant woman, happy with the promise of a new life. Castine: the hill, the lighthouse, the dark, the wind and rain. Ian. Moira. Moira. Moira. In my mirror. Under my bed.

I got in my car and called Kit, my foot heavy on the accelerator, and felt a gush of relief when she answered.

"What's going on?" she asked. "Are you sick?"

"No, I'm not sick! Do you have some time? I'm practically in the parking lot of Betheny General."

"Go straight to the cafeteria. I'll meet you."

A SMALL MIRACLE, Kit was sitting at a table in the cafeteria when I arrived. I gave her a hug, registering an antiseptic scent in her hair, then sat across from her.

"What's up? You okay?" She offered me her dinner—a plastic-wrapped burger with sweet-potato fries and applesauce.

I wrinkled my nose. "I'm being followed."

"What do you mean, followed?"

I told her what I'd felt, and about the *keris* and the book and the note. "Do you think I'm paranoid? Wait—if paranoia's a symptom of something horrible, I don't want to know."

She gave me wry smile, then dipped a potato chunk into a puddle of ketchup. "I don't know, Maeve, your feelings are usually spot on.

Maybe you have an admirer. Don't act like it's impossible," she said when I sneered at her. "You're beautiful."

"Stop," I said.

"What?"

"You know I don't put out the *gimme-a-man* vibe." I'd learned years ago how to avoid too-long eye contact and other forms of flirtation. If not for an absolute lack of connection with religion, I might make an excellent nun. Somehow I found myself with a fry in hand.

"Yeah, but any interesting offers?"

I wiggled the fry at her. "A grad student asked me out in September."

"And you went out, and after eating a meal of oysters and cheap beer, you had wild monkey sex in the backseat of his—"

"I don't date students."

"Or other professors."

"I don't want to mix business and . . ."

She stared at me. "The word that escapes you is *pleasure*. Where exactly are you going to find it? You don't leave the apartment to go anywhere but school or the grocery store. I've never heard of a love match made while weighing olives in the deli section."

"Why weigh olives? Besides, how would you know where I go? When's the last time you stayed in our apartment for more than a three-hour stretch? When's the last time *you* had a date or wild monkey sex? Kettle calling pot! Come in, pot!"

"For God's sake, eat the fry."

I stuffed it in my mouth. "Oh, I forgot someone," I said, midchew. "A colleague asked me out before Thanksgiving. You'll enjoy this. He asked if I was a lesbian when I turned him down."

Kit coughed into her napkin.

"Heimlich?" I offered, but she shook her head.

"And you said . . . ?"

" 'I wish!' "

She chortled. "I know a few, you know. Really nice women. I can introduce you if you'd—"

"I am *not* a lesbian!" I slouched low when a few faces turned our way.

Kit glanced at a group of hunky physicians, then back at me. "So now the whole cafeteria understands you're a heterosexual and thinks I may not be—"

"Sorry."

"—tell me, how's Noel?"

I guess I deserved this. "He's still in Europe. He's not even coming home for Christmas. Garrick wonders if he'll ever come back."

"Stop torturing him and he'll come back."

"Stop torturing *me!* I have nothing to do with it," I said. "God. He's trying to find his mother. Can we talk about my stalker already, before you're paged away or something?"

She leaned forward. "You haven't seen anyone? This is all based on feelings?"

"Yeah, feelings." My thumbnails picked together metronomically. "Your brother's not in town, is he?"

"No, Ian's off a coast somewhere." She threw her crumpled napkin on her plate. "Won't you tell me what happened with you two? Did it have something to do with Moira?"

"Kit, don't." She knew the rules. No discussing the past, period. "I have to admit, though . . ."

"What?"

"I've thought a lot about home lately. Memories."

"Aw, Maeve. Regression isn't such a bad thing, you know." She covered my hands with her chapped ones. I hated when she acted like this—as if it was her personal calling to be my protector—about as much as I appreciated it.

"Don't use psychobabble on me, Kit."

"Regression means you revert back a little."

Revert back? Like being attracted to things you had as a kid, buying the tool of a wannabe pirate? I'd admit nothing.

"I'm not reverting," I said. "And I don't want to go back."

"Sometimes regression comes before you take a big leap forward," she said, just as her pager went off.

IT WAS A roller-coaster ride to the end of term. I rushed right along with my students: grade the finals, tally the marks, post them.

And just like that—whiplash—the semester was over. This always brought on a mild case of the blues, probably because I had a like-hate relationship with free time. I forced myself to lie on the couch and watch two hours of TV that first weekend night—a behavior that felt more foreign than any language I taught.

Sleep became more difficult, too. Sunday night was particularly bad; apprehension swelled in the back of my throat like a beached whale. Sometime around 1:00 a.m., the phone rang.

"Dad?" I waited a beat. "Mom? Is it you?"

No answer, but I knew someone was there. Long seconds passed before the line went dead.

I wouldn't think about Ian. I wouldn't *eling*.

I went back to bed, and tried to relax my muscles and my mind, sleep. I imagined her so clearly, though. Moira in the grass with her keyboard, chewing the end of her ponytail. Gliding her fingers through sun-cooked water on the seat of our boat as we planned our future.

I tried to picture my saxophone, my fingers over its cold neck, but just as I managed it, it turned into Noel's warm one. My second attempt was no better: I stood naked in a field of brown grass with my sax, blowing soundlessly through the mouthpiece. Noel was there, too, fully clothed and flipping through his passport. I threw down my saxophone and covered my chest when he looked at me. They all changed into something . . . other. Noel, the sax, and the passport grew forked tongues and coiled at my feet. I ran away, blades of dead grass catching between my toes, but I knew it was only a matter of time before one of them caught me.

Out of Time

Castine, Maine
NOVEMBER 1995
Moira and Maeve are eleven

Moira woke in the middle of the night, though she didn't understand why right away.

"It's happening." Maeve was sitting upright in bed.

Moira sat, too. "What's wrong? Poppy?"

Their mother's howl splintered the night.

"No, Moira, don't—"

But Moira leaped up and ran to her parents' room. Mama writhed in their bed, and Daddy had his arms braced over her, his face close to hers.

"Oh, sweetheart." He made a noise—sibilant—a let of air. "Honey, it's all right."

"Oh, God!" Mama howled again. "Jack, no!"

Moira felt a tug on her arm and looked back at her sister.

"Come away."

"No." Moira spied the crimson stain on the sheet, watched, rapt and frightened as it spread, ate up the white. "No."

The baby was lost.

CHAPTER FIVE
SIGMUND'S SECRETS

wove my way down the familiar halls of Time After Time until I stood before a closed entry. I cracked the door, hoping to see Noel absorbed in his work. Instead of finding him as I often had—at an easel, barefoot on bleached tarps beside the long bank of windows—I discovered him asleep on his bench, slumped over a table streaked with colored paint and heaped with old palettes, tools and glues, an assortment of pigments. A sketchpad sat open beside him, and his fingers barely held to a teetering pencil.

I stepped inside. Every barrier I'd erected toward the opposite sex, toward Noel, sighed away as if napping was the order of the day. A beautiful man, asleep and unaware. My eyes wandered over him like an eager adventurer. I scaled a cheekbone, skied his nose, and glided over the curve of a full bottom lip. I ran wild through a thatch of black hair, then lay in the hammock of his ear, the pinna, the little wing. I moved closer. Slid down his neck and loped across one broad shoulder and the curved part of his back. Dallied over a length of bare arm and lingered for ages on a hand—what gorgeous skin he had, how strong his musculature, how long his fingers.

Then the fingers moved, and my reverie shattered. His eyes opened and fixed on mine. He lifted his head slowly.

"I'm sorry," I stuttered. "I never should have—" I spun around and faced a windowless wall, like I'd caught him naked or some-thing. I repressed the urge to walk to a corner and press my nose into its seam. "Sorry."

"Maeve," he said, "turn around."

But I ran out, closed and locked the door from the hall. Water spurted from beneath it. The wood shook as Noel pounded on it from the other side.

"Open the door!"

I sat up in bed, gasping, drenched in sweat, and saw that it was just after 4:00 a.m. I heard more pounding. Real. This was not Kit forgetting her key.

I grabbed my robe, flung limbs where they belonged. I looked out the peephole and saw him, though I hardly believed it was true until I opened the door and met his eyes. And then I threw myself into my father's arms.

ALL THE SCENTS that were Castine hugged around my dad's body like a net; he couldn't escape them if he tried. He seemed thinner, his body and his salted hair, but his smile looked just the same. I didn't ask why he hadn't called to say he was coming or waited to travel during the day. My guess was that he'd finished his weekend chores and decided right then to make the trip, and hit the road.

"It's so great you're here," I told him. "What made you come?"

"Well, you know how I love my girls," he said, and I smiled what felt like the first honest smile in a decade. "I even brought one of them along."

My jaw slackened, but when I looked out at the blue pickup on the road I saw only a little fur face in the window. I didn't have to ask to know my mother wasn't hunkered down beneath the tarp-covered bulge in back, waiting for her moment to surprise me. The last time we'd met, over two years ago at a halfway mark in Boston, she'd barely offered a word.

"That's Sparky. I hope you don't mind I brought her."

"No, she'll be fine. Cute."

"Your mother wants me to bring you home for Christmas."

"No, Dad." I didn't believe him, but even if it was true, it was only so she could ignore me a little more directly.

He looked past me and into my living room—the sparse walls, squared-off piles of paper on the oak desk in the corner, uncluttered stone fireplace, single denim sofa, and entertainment unit with a television and no CD player. "No Christmas tree?"

"My landlady doesn't like trees," I said. "Fire hazard."

The dog, a little thing with a white body and brown head, curled up on my couch when my father brought her in. Sam must've found a good hiding spot.

"The couch is a pullout," I said as he set down his duffel. "So you'll have a place to sleep, if your dog will share with you. I'd offer you Kit's bed, but I never know when she might actually use it, and I think you'd give her a heart attack if she found you under her sheets. I doubt even she could perform CPR on herself."

He smiled. "I can sleep anywhere."

"Are you tired?" It was, after all, still four-something in the morning. "Or are you hungry?"

This was a rhetorical question with my father. I poached three eggs, firm, the way he liked them, brewed coffee. We made careful small talk in my kitchen. Ned Baker—a hellion I'd gone to school with—got married last month, Dad said. I told him about a student of mine also named Ned Baker who was just as troublesome as the Ned back home.

"Must be the name," he said. I agreed, and then we fell into a silence that felt necessary but a little uncomfortable—like a straw bed when you're just too exhausted to care about the bits and pieces sticking into your side.

"How long can you stay?" I asked as he scraped up the last of his eggs.

"Like I said, your mother wants me to bring you—"

"I can't go home with you, Dad. If Mom really wanted to see me, she could've gotten in the truck with you and come." I didn't mean to sound so sharp. I swallowed guilt when he turned and looked out the kitchen window.

"There's lightning," he said. "Storm's coming."

"Lightning in late December? It's been a little warm, but—"

Thunder like cannon fire rattled my windows, and that was all it took. Adrenaline tore through me. *It's just a storm, Jesus Christ, don't be a freak.* I couldn't control my response, though I tried to hide it. I wanted my dad to see I'd become a well-adjusted adult after all, to tell my mother so.

He waited until another bolt of lightning flashed, and then he pushed back his chair. "I'll stay through the weekend," he said. "Your mother, she can't do it all herself."

I regretted the words right away but couldn't stop them. "No, she can't, but she'll still try."

I GATHERED SHEETS, a pillow, and a quilt, and put them beside Sparky's prone form on the couch. "Lazy dog," I said, and scratched her head. She stretched, but kept her eyes closed.

"You going to sing, Mayfly?" My father leaned against the doorway to the kitchen. "Sing a bedtime song?"

Like I was fourteen again, and he was in the hammock with a lemonade cradled between his hip and hand as Moira and I played for him—*sang* in the only way we could. Neither of us could carry a tune with our own vocal chords.

My best naps I owe to you, he'd say, and ruffle our hair.

"Sorry, but my landlady lives upstairs and she doesn't like music." This detail may or may not have been true, but it served the moment well enough. "I could recite a French poem, though. Italian. Latin. Spanish. Portuguese. Even Romanian, if you don't mind a bad accent."

"No music?" This was the real foreign concept to my father, the thing I couldn't put words to. The sky rumbled again.

"Should we take the dog out before this hits?"

We stumbled into another uncomfortable moment outside. As Sparky did her business, my father looked back at my apartment and grunted. The blinking lights of my landlady's Christmas tree illuminated a second-floor window. I pretended not to notice.

"Looks like less sky out here, eh?" he said.

I couldn't see any sky at the moment, just dark, but I agreed. It had taken me a long time to get over the feeling of claustrophobia here. Less sky, too much land. I felt the draw of the sea, too, a force as ancient and enduring as a siren call.

"Some things never change," my father said. I thought he'd go on about storms and how they smell and sound and feel on the skin before the first spill—he was a Castinian, after all—but he surprised me. "Stars are up there, Mayfly, above the clouds. Can't see 'em all the time, but they're there, day and night, fair weather or gale."

He kept his face slanted upward as if he hadn't meant anything more than what he'd said. I knew better. But so what if I didn't have pictures on my wall or a tree covered in lights. So what if everything was neat and I had a nearly empty bottle of Windex. So what if I had no music in my home and couldn't sing to my father. It had nothing to do with stars and constancy. It was just . . . *just*. And I had a lot, had done so much with my life. I was a great teacher, I—

Thunder split the air again, and this time I flinched.

"It's a good storm, Mayfly," my father said, as the first rain hit my cheek.

Good storm. Heel. Roll over. Don't stay.

I left man and dog to their pseudonight, and crawled back into bed. I listened as clouds labored over drops of water, as the after-birth of every storm known to man seemed to fall. The noises were there, too, riled up in my head like positive and negative charges, wanting to write themselves into a song about a storm out of time.

Daylight filtered through the seams of my shade when I finally gave in to temptation. I pulled my dusty saxophone case out from under my bed and stared at it, perhaps the way an alcoholic looks at a bottle of Scotch. My hands shook as I opened the latches, lifted the cover.

Vivid scent hit me first—dusky brass and bittersweet cane. My mouth watered, but no instrument lay atop the matted-plush insides. Instead, there were folded notes, mementos, my passport, a few reeds from my old sax, and some stones from Castine. I stared at it all for a moment, then opened one of the notes.

Maevy Gravy,
Guess what number I'm thinking of. Come on, guess!

Oh, God. Nauseous. Bleeding memories. I hated *eling*.

I tucked some rocks into the pocket of my pajamas, then put Noel's postcards into the case with my sister's note and closed the lid. And then I shut my eyes and let myself sway with the turbulence, feeling like the First Chinese Brother—my mouth filled with water, the ocean pressed against my ribs.

Out of Time

Castine, Maine
JUNE 1999
Moira and Maeve are fourteen

Kit had requested a personal concert, so Moira and Maeve set out one day with their instruments in the lobster boat—a vessel that was sturdy and long and had decent coverage. No clouds roamed the sky, but because Moira had a keen and personal appreciation for how weather conditions changed in the bay, she took care to drape an orange rubber coat around the edges of her keyboard.

Maeve warmed up with a series of arpeggios as Kit made her requests: "Don't Speak," "Nothing Compares 2 U," "My Heart Will Go On" (Maeve pulled away from her sax and made a retching noise), "Sowing the Seeds of Love."

When Maeve smiled, Moira set her keyboard to Reverse Gurgle, put her right thumb on D, and began. The brass of Maeve's sax caught and threw sunlight, and her clear tone rang out. Moira knew her sister was a true talent, the prodigy she'd been labeled years before. Ben Freeman said he'd see to it that she made an album someday.

If I do, so will you, Maeve always said.

Sometimes, alone with her thoughts as her sister slept, Moira wondered what might've been if she'd tried the sax first. She might've been a prodigy, too. Then she remembered the things she liked best—her piano, her roses, *Jane Eyre*, and solitude—and knew she wouldn't have liked the attention so well as Maeve.

Later, as Maeve played a piece she'd written herself, Moira noticed a lone boat lingering nearby. She pointed it out to Kit, whose lips twisted into a parody of a smile.

"It's my brother," she said.

"Ian?"

"Well, yeah, I only have one brother, thank God. See the little red cat on the mainsail? That's Michael's boat." Kit leaned close, whispered in her ear, "I think Ian likes Maeve."

59

"He does not!"

Maeve's cadence faltered.

"Shh! He always talks about her."

"That's not a good thing. He probably has a voodoo doll with red hair and pins sticking out of it."

Kit giggled quietly as Moira studied the boat. It was Ian, all right. He was hard to miss. Though just a grade ahead of them, he was more than a year older and had sprouted taller than anyone in his class. He looked dusk-gilded and windblown, like a storybook hero with a kind heart. Moira knew better, even if he did look softer, more mortal somehow, surrounded by so much sea.

"When Maeve plays in your living room, Ian takes out his telescope and watches her," Kit said.

"He doesn't!"

"The first time I saw, he said he'd give me ten bucks not to tell anyone. I told him to keep his money, and then he told me he'd break my legs if I said anything."

"Maybe he just likes the saxophone?"

"Maybe, but whenever Maeve's over he gets all googly-eyed and dopier than usual."

Moira dredged up a smile for that. Everyone knew Ian was wicked smart. Almost as smart as Kit.

"You don't have to tell Maeve, do you?" Kit asked. "I mean, it'll make her uncomfortable, and, I mean, Ian wouldn't really break my legs"—she paused for a moment as if considering the legitimacy of this statement, then continued—"but I'll have a miserable summer if he's mad at me."

"Uh, I can try." Already, Moira felt the pulse of her twin's curiosity. Maeve's last notes still hung in the air when she turned to Moira.

"What's going on?"

"Ian and Michael boated out," Moira said, hoping Maeve would be satisfied with that. She nodded toward Michael's craft, now turned landward.

"And?" Maeve prompted.

Moira shrugged at Kit, who looked between them with exasperation. "How do you two do that?"

"It's because we're witches, according to your creepy brother." Maeve smirked. "What did he want?"

"He likes you," Kit said, then added hastily, "but please, please don't ever tell him I said so."

Maeve's mouth fell open.

"Tell her the rest."

Kit glared at Moira for a second. "And he watches you sometimes when you play the saxophone."

"All of it," Moira said.

"Through the window." Pause. "With a telescope."

Maeve's tongue hung from her mouth as if she'd eaten something shockingly bitter. She coughed and danced in circles as the girls choked with laughter, and then she spouted various things in French that Moira understood but Kit did not—that Maeve would be forever scarred by the knowledge and would never play near a window again for the rest of her life—all of which made Moira laugh until her sides ached. Finally, Maeve said something Kit could understand: "That's disgustipatingly horriflable!"

They giggled for several minutes more as the concert came to an official—if not dignified—end.

THE NEXT DAY began with their regular morning order: "Girls, go find something to do."

"We can help with Pops—"

"No."

"We can watch a movie. Daddy rented *The Wizard of*—"

"No." Their mother held an empty plate in one hand and dirty laundry in the other. Beneath her eyes lay dark creases that looked to Moira like crescent moons, dead on their backs. "Go on," she said. "Do something *outside*."

Moira waved to Maeve, and together they walked downstairs. "Let's practice at the picnic table."

"No." Maeve bowed her head. "I thought we could practice in the basement today."

"Mom said outside, and the basement's gross." The cellar air tasted stale and clogged Moira's nostrils. They didn't even have chairs down there, just a few bones Maeve thought belonged to a dinosaur, the prow of a wrecked boat, some line Daddy had called *the shittiest piece of lash I've ever been sold* . . . and spiders. "Forget it. Why would you even want to?"

Maeve rubbed her arms, bit her lip. And then Moira knew.

"You can't avoid Ian forever!"

"I don't want him to watch me. How would you feel?"

Moira thought she might not mind so much, but she didn't want Maeve to know that. "We'll wait until his driver's lesson," she suggested. "He should leave soon."

"We should take his telescope when he's gone and break it."

"You'll be cranky later if you don't use your Ian-free time to practice."

Maeve's hands danced around her. "Fine. I don't want to spend my summer in jail for stealing someone's telescope anyway, especially when that someone isn't worth jail time and is the one who should really be in jail for peeking around and making girls younger than him so wicked uncomfortable." She paused. "Unless the jail is air-conditioned."

Maeve snorted. Moira laughed.

"Plenty of people will be looking at you if we travel the world like gypsies," Moira said. "You'll have plenty of admirers." She tried to leer the way she'd seen a man leer at a woman once in a movie—mouth open a little, eyes piercing—and then she threw in a wink.

Another snort, another giggle.

They waited until they heard the Bronyas' rumbly old truck heading down the road, then went outside with their instruments. Lilac trees snowed blossoms along the pebbled path in the backyard, and even though the picnic table was in the shade of one of those trees, it was still unseasonably hot.

"Let's go," Maeve said, and soon they were in the thick of a classical piece, *Trois Romances sans Paroles*. But even though Maeve's line in the first part should've been a clean bit of melody, she stumbled through it.

Daddy, who'd emerged from the docks, tapped his fingers against the table, and when Maeve paused after a run of errors in part two, he spoke up. "You okay, Mayfly? Need a break?"

"No, Daddy," she said. "I'm just sloppy today, and we didn't warm up." She squinted at the sky. "Or maybe we're too warmed up."

"Ayuh, it's hot." A bead of sweat trailed down his cheek as he glanced at Moira. "How 'bout you, squirt?"

"I'm good. There's lemonade in the fridge," she said. "I made it how you like with extra sugar. Don't tell Mom."

"Good girl." He tousled her hair and went into the house.

Maeve blew out a gusty sigh. "Pick it up from part two?"

They were just about to start their fifth piece when Maeve abruptly dropped her sax and sprinted inside. The porch door slapped shut behind her.

"What the heck's wrong with you?" Moira yelled, just before she heard another slam, a car door. Ian and his dad were back. She left her keyboard and followed her sister into the house.

Maeve stood with her back against the kitchen wall, twisting a strand of hair. "Can you grab my saxophone for me?"

"You're so weird about him that you can't get it yourself? Are you going to be like this all summer?" When Maeve gave her hair another twist, Moira locked her jaw and strode back into the sunshine. Her hand had just gripped the sax's hot brass when a voice behind her said, "You sounded good the other night."

Ian sat in the grass with Gorp, their wandering mongrel. The dog writhed with pleasure as Ian scratched his stomach.

Maybe it was because of her rare edgy mood that Moira didn't startle or even think it odd that he spoke to her civilly. "Thanks," she said. "I saw you there."

He dipped his chin, and his blue eyes grabbed at her as he smiled slow and warm. She half-wondered if he'd open his mouth a little and wink, but those things never came. The effect was better his way. Maeve would've passed out. A nervous giggle caught in her throat.

"You're good," he said. "Really talented."

"Thanks." She almost uttered, *So are you.* That would've been embarrassing—though not insensible. He was talented at math and blood brothering and taunting them all, and at making Moira nervous and curious with his so-blue-stay-here eyes.

"I almost forgot." Ian stood as Gorp whined for another scratch.

He reached into his pocket, and a moment later revealed something small and white on his outstretched palm. "It's a rock I found inside a mussel shell that looks like . . . you'll see."

The tiny curved bit of stone was about the size of two pencil erasers but shaped like an irregular *Z*, fat on one end and tapered on the other. "What's it supposed to be?"

"Forget it. It's stupid." He closed his palm and made to throw the stone, but Moira grabbed his arm before he could.

"Show me again. I'll figure it out." She slid her fingers to his fist, worked it open, and removed the stone. She stared at it with as much imagination as she could muster. A snake, she thought, a second before he said—

"It's a sax. See it?"

"Oh—oh yeah! That's cool!"

She was about to ask him if he'd seen a keyboard on the beach as well when he said, "It reminded me of you. Keep it."

When it hit her, she felt number than a pounded thumb: *I'm holding Maeve's sax. He thinks I'm Maeve.*

"Your dad could maybe put it on a chain or something for you, you know? There's already a little hole on one side."

She looked away. She had to tell him—

"Or just chuck it. I don't care," he added gruffly. The Ian she knew.

"No, I wouldn't." He'd be mortified now if she revealed herself. It would be kinder not to. And what harm could it do to let him think she was Maeve for just a moment? Decided, Moira said what she would if the gift had been meant for her. "That was nice of you to think of me. I'll take it, if that's okay." She smiled as warm a smile as she had to give.

"Sure," he said, though the word sounded as slow and muggy as the day. He bent to pat Gorp on the head one last time, then took a step toward his house. "Me and Michael are going to the island later if you want to come."

"We're pretty much grounded. But thanks."

He took another step. "Sure. Seeyaround."

"Okay," Moira said. "See ya." She didn't laugh when he tripped on his own porch stair, and she turned quickly away when he looked back to see if she'd noticed.

The Last Will of Moira Leahy

Alone in the kitchen, she set Maeve's saxophone on the table and looked again at the rock in her hand. A gift from Ian. Holy heck. Maeve wouldn't play anywhere but the basement again if she knew. So Moira wouldn't tell her; there was no need. But she couldn't throw the gift out, either. With a rush of guilt, she tucked the tiny charm into her pocket, where it burned for the rest of the day with all the weight of a stolen sun.

CHAPTER SIX

ALLUREMENT

o what do you do for fun around here?" My father leaned back in his chair and sipped coffee after our lunch of turkey on rye and chicken noodle soup from a can. Sparky sat on his lap. I still hadn't seen any part of Sam.

"Oh, I have a lot of fun. I could show you the exciting cupboard that is my office." We exchanged smiles.

"Do you see much of Kit?"

"Not very, but she's become a good cell mate."

"Cellmate?"

"Cell-phone mate. She's very busy, Dad. I left her a message that you were here and invited her to dinner. Maybe we'll hear back, but probably not."

He tapped his thumb against the rim of his mug. "How about other friends?"

I thought of Noel, and of Garrick and the shop. I even thought of Peter Link, the colleague who'd asked me, straight-faced, if I was a lesbian. "I keep pretty busy, too."

"Yes, I know," he said. "But what do you do when you're off the clock?"

"Well . . . there's Lansing's Block."

The Last Will of Moira Leahy

He made a noise that meant *Tell me more.*

"It's an auction house here, and—" The *keris* would be something my father would appreciate, maybe as much as I did. "Hold on," I said, brightening.

I made a beeline for the coffee table, expecting to find the blade in its usual spot, but it wasn't there. Hmm. I must've moved it when my father came in last night. I spun on my heels. Not on my desk or the top of the entertainment center. In my bedroom, I scanned dressers, the chair and table in the corner. I returned to the kitchen and double-checked the countertops. I swore in several languages.

"You all right?"

My father followed me back into the living room as I felt under the desk and entertainment center, and between couch cushions I'd replaced an hour before. I was about to start searching stupid places—the inside of the stove, the cereal cabinet—when the music began. I stopped, disbelieving. For the first time in a nearly a decade, it wasn't piano. Saxophone tones raced through me like a chorus of trilling bees.

Check. The place you store your memories.

I tracked back to the bedroom. There wasn't a single reason to believe it, but I sat on the floor, pulled the sax case out from the shadowed space beneath my bed, opened the latches. There, half-buried beneath Noel's postcards, was the *keris.* The music ebbed, *ritardando.*

I lay my throbbing head in my hands. *Think.* I'd had the case open, but I didn't put the *keris* inside, just the postcards.

Cognitive impairment, Kit would say. *Time to scan your brain.*

Well, right. Something was clearly wrong, wasn't it? Sheets of music scattered around me like dry pine as I jerked the *keris* from the case. I took a minute to compose myself, put on my game face.

"You've had it all these years, then?" my father asked when I presented him with the blade.

"No, I bought this *keris* at an auction last month." I sat beside him on the couch, my pulse still so loud in my ears that I wondered if he could hear it.

"Looks just like the old one, except for this hole here." He touched the cavity in the metal.

At least my memory hadn't turned completely unreliable. "Do you remember anything about the old *keris*?"

"Well . . ." He rubbed a scruffy cheek with his free hand. "Your poppy brought it back from one of his trips. I think he got it for rescuing someone."

"He rescued someone?"

"Or so he said! Your poppy had a story for everything, Maeve. This one had something to do with a volcano that erupted unexpectedly. The dagger was a gift of thanks."

"Can you remember anything else?"

"Not at the moment," he said. "Does it matter?"

"Probably not, but . . . Did it ever act funny?"

"What do you mean?" One of his eyes half shut when I shrugged. "Did anything weird ever happen with it?"

"My daughters took it and lost it in the bay." He chuckled and turned the blade over in his hand. "Well, this is a nice piece," he said. "A beautiful thing."

"I thought you might like it. I have a book about the *keris* and other foreign weapons, if you'd like to see it."

He stood a little straighter. "Ayuh, I would."

"It's at my office."

"Oh." Were my eyes playing tricks on me, or was he reluctant to leave the blade, too?

"We'll bring the *keris*," I said, to assuage us both. "You know I just want to show off the awards on my wall, right?" I delivered a faux-smug smile. "And prove to you that the administration has stuffed me inside a veritable suitcase?"

"This office gets smaller every time you talk about it."

"It gets smaller every time I step into it."

Sparky wasn't pleased about our leaving. She stood at the door and cried.

"She'll be fine," my father said. "Just close the door."

I did, feeling guilty, but putting my faith in her decided love of naps—and Sam's hiding place.

"HEY, DOC LEAHY," someone called as my father and I neared the language department's main office, on the way to my shoe box.

"Hello," I called back. Jordan Somers and—wouldn't you know—Ned Baker were examining a list of final grades. Jordan should be pleased with his standing, though Ned, the troublemaker, might not be. Still, he didn't look upset; he smiled at my dad and me.

"Going away for break, Doc?" Ned asked, glancing with fleeting interest at the *keris* in my father's hand.

"Not me. You?"

"Going to Cancún." He howled the last like wolfsong, his cheeks flushed and hair a curtain over his eyes. Ian came strongly to mind.

"And you, Jordan?" I said. "Big plans?"

"Cancún, too. We're going to"—he paused, looked meaningfully at Ned—"practice our Spanish." They laughed, smacked hands, and headed down the hall. "See ya!"

"Have fun," I said as we passed one another.

"Seem like nice boys," my father said.

"Do they? I think their practice starts and ends with Dos Equis, but maybe I'm wrong."

"Hmm?"

"It's a beer, Dad."

"Right, right. I think I've heard of it," he said. Dad was a Moosehead man, through and through.

I stalled to paw through my pockets and briefcase. I refused to believe I'd left my keys in the car, that I was that far gone.

"Nice posters," he said. "Sure sets the atmosphere."

I continued rummaging blindly as I looked up at the artwork and photos in the hall. A woman pinned clothes on a line from a high window; boys stood barelegged in a fountain; a mandolin player's likeness covered brick somewhere in Vieux Lille.

Sometimes these scenes made me itch with longing for all my old dreams, but only one piece bothered me consistently: a sepia print of a woman cowering over a desk as owls and bats swooped low behind her. The desk bore the words *El sueño de la razón produce monstrous* (The sleep of reason brings forth monsters). I'd removed the picture once, but Will Holmes, the chair of my department and a closet philosopher, insisted it remain. I'd stood my ground. "The woman seems tortured."

"It's a masterpiece," he'd said. "And that's not a woman." I stared at what looked to me like a skirt and bare woman's legs as he speculated over the work's meaning. "What if dreams and reason aren't so different and monsters ride the line between the worlds?"

It might've made for fascinating debate, but I'd never be in the mood to discuss dream monsters or the line between the worlds. It still looked like a woman to me.

"Aha!" I said, finding my keys as my father and I turned down the short hall that housed my office. There, on my door, was another note, impaled with another nail.

"That's not good for the wood," he said.

"I know. I'll probably be charged for it one day: one abused utilitarian door, $300." I ripped down the note.

> Visit with me in the New Year.
> There is much I wish to tell you.
> Via della Scala ___, No. 47
> Trastevere

"Ned! Ned Baker!" My shout echoed down the hall. No reply.

"What's going on?" my father asked.

"Someone's been leaving notes," I said as I unlocked the door. "This time it's an address." A single fluorescent light sparked to life when I hit the switch. I sat in my chair.

"Those boys?"

"I doubt it. It's not for Cancún. It's for Rome."

Squares and churches with ancient architecture, statuesque fountains, medieval homes on tiny streets, women kneading bread, bistros filled with artists, the Tiber River sidling through it all—my mind buzzed with what I knew of Trastevere.

"Maybe it's for work?"

I laughed. "You think the department would send me to Rome?"

"Why not? Bring back a picture for your hall."

"Because Will Holmes doesn't send anyone anywhere, and he wouldn't drive a nail into one of his precious doors, even to an office the size of a wallet. I doubt he even owns a hammer," I muttered, as my father studied said office. I looked, too, at things I'd seen often but never through his eyes: a clear and dust-free desktop, shelves full of alphabetized books, three framed awards, my degrees, a calendar with days x-ed out in neat lines. Where was a toppled stack of papers or pile of crumbs when you needed one?

"Here, Dad," I said, and pulled the weaponry book from the shelf. I'd just handed it to him when Ned peered around my father in the doorway.

"Did you holler, Doc? Jordan thought—"

"Ned! Yes, come here." My father backed away as Ned stepped in. I held up the note. "Did you leave this on my door?"

"No!" he said, so emphatically that I believed him. And then he surprised me. "Some guy did. A little weird."

"Weird?" I stood. "Tell me what you saw. What did he look like?"

"I dunno, he looked like a guy. Hey, will I get extra credit for this?" Ned's lips cocked into a half-smile as my father's muted chuckle trickled in from the hall. I just glared at my student until he flinched, a skill purloined from my mother's bag of tricks.

Ned reached into his jacket pocket. "He gave me this."

I recognized the antique book and its tea-colored cover right away: *Old Gypsy Madge's Fortune Teller and the Witches Key to Lucky Dreams*. Had my note-leaving visitor been watching me? Had he followed me to the shop? I couldn't deny a thread of apprehension.

"The guy made it sound pretty lame but said I might dig the love spells. You want it, Doc?" Ned waved the book in my face, smirking like the scamp he was.

"Keep it," I told him, locking my office door behind me. "Maybe it'll make Cancún more interesting."

"Oh, and he had an accent, if that's—"

"British?"

"No, like—" He shrugged.

"Like what, Ned? Spanish, French, Italian, Chinese, Scandinavian?" Still his face was blank. "Oh, forget it."

I herded my father back down the hall. "I want to show you something else, Dad. A great shop. You'll love it, I swear you will."

"Ayuh," he said, keeping pace with me, "if you promise we'll stay long enough to see it."

Out of Time

Castine, Maine
JANUARY–JUNE 2000
Moira and Maeve are fifteen

It took Moira many months to admit she had a crush on the fearsome Ian Bronya. She watched him in odd moments, like when he shoveled the walk or petted Gorp in the yard. She looked for his long-legged gait at school, and noticed he always bought chocolate milk for lunch and ate two sandwiches instead of one.

She didn't want Ian to mistake her for her sister again, but she wasn't sure how to be distinctive. For a few days, she wore skirts, but this wasn't very practical for life as a boat-maker's daughter. Though she could cut her hair, she loved it long and wavy. In the end, she opted to wear a headband at all times; it helped her to see the world with clear eyes, even if she often felt on the edge of a headache.

When spring arrived, she took daily walks to The Breeze, a dockside eatery, and to the lighthouse—Ian's favorite haunts. She'd wave and carry on as if they'd magically run into each other . . . again.

It wasn't until Ian turned seventeen in June that Moira took a bold step. Her mother had long since relinquished head chef duties to care for Poppy full-time, so when Moira threw herself into cooking one day it drew only grateful comments. A casserole, salad, even dessert were all ready for the evening meal. She waited until Maeve left for her lesson with Ben Freeman, then uncovered a second pan of brownies.

Her legs were wobbly, but she walked past snapdragons and yellow roses, and knocked on the Bronyas' door anyway. Seconds passed as she stood there, mentally rehearsing her words, but no one answered. Only then did she realize that the Bronyas' car wasn't in the driveway.

Disappointed but also relieved, she placed the brownies and card she'd made for Ian in front of the door, and had walked halfway home again when she heard a scrape of wood and—

"Hey!"

Moira spun back around. "Hi," she said in a squeaky voice.

Ian stood in the doorway in jeans and bare feet, his shirt unbuttoned to reveal a fit chest. He picked up the brownies—"What's this?"—then, to her mortification, read the card aloud. "Happy Birthday, Ian. Your friend, Moira." He looked at her, his eyes bright and lip quirked at a funny angle. "Moira."

She'd die if he laughed.

"Hey, whereja go?" Paula Dunlop, a girl from Ian's grade, stuck her face under the crook of his arm. She giggled when she saw Moira, then snaked her hand onto Ian's chest, and pulled him and the brownies inside. The door closed.

I'm so stupid, Moira told herself as she trudged back home. *He's cute and smart and older. Of course he has a girlfriend.*

A wretched reminder of her gift appeared in friendlier hands on the back porch the next day. Moira took the empty pan from Kit, and waved her into the kitchen.

"Your brownies were wicked. We all loved them," Kit said. "Especially Ian."

Moira shushed her, though everyone was either upstairs or out. "Don't say anything, okay? Not even to Maeve." Kit's eyes widened, but Moira extended her pinkie and they shook on it.

That evening, Moira sat on the walk beside her garden, as the setting sun coated the sky in shades of watermelon and amber. *Red sky at night, sailor's delight*, she reminded herself. Tomorrow would be a better day.

"Ian, we go now or we don't go." Mrs. Bronya's voice rang out, just before a car door slammed. Moira turned to find Ian a few feet away, staring at her.

He smiled. "See ya."

"See ya," she said.

Who cared that she'd forgotten her headband or that her hair blew around her face in a Maeve-like way? Paula couldn't be that important to Ian if he still looked at other girls.

It'll grow, Moira thought to herself. *It'll grow if I nurture it right.* She pinched off a rose bloom, then breathed in its sweet essence and smiled.

CHAPTER SEVEN

FORSAKEN

had to park on the street a block away from Time
After Time. I hadn't once thought, *It's four days before Christmas, it'll
be busy*, but I doubt it would've stopped me if I had. I counted eight
people in the front room alone. One part-time assistant spoke to a
woman near the pottery while another rang out customers. No sign
of Garrick.

In the wide main hall, long tables sat stocked with platefuls of
gingerbread cookies and cheese-square towers and crackers and
grapes. Two children ran past us and into the raspberry room,
home to Nattie the carousel horse and half a dozen trunks piled with
dolls and down-filled bears.

My father's head swiveled all over the place as he filched a cookie.
"How big is this store?"

"This is Narnia, Dad." Something like pride surged in me as I motioned him forward. "Come on. I know something you'll like."

I led the way to the weapons room, but stopped short of entering.
Something else had captured my attention.

"Go on. There's a World War II bazooka in there somewhere," I
told my father, leaving him with my *keris* and a hundred other
weapons, a mesmerized expression on his face.

I dashed to the end of the hall where light filtered out from another familiar room. The studio. Scent escaped through the cracked door—oil paint and clay and other things I couldn't name but always thought of as promise. Noel could be in there. He could be home.

My hope withered and died the second I pushed open the door. No Noel. Not only that, but the twin easels stood bare. Tarps were folded. A box on the paint-stained worktable sat closed, and the benches had been tucked away. Paintings and sketches that had once dotted the walls now leaned against one another in a corner like guilty lovers. Maybe Noel had asked Garrick to pack up his things for good. Maybe he'd become so enraptured with European antiques that he didn't miss home at all. Or me. Maybe he'd decided against stepping on another plane for a truly noble reason: He'd found his mother and decided to stay with her.

I couldn't help myself. I reached for the paintbrushes—spotless and stored inside an old biscuit jar, not strewn about the room or soaking in turpentine as they should be—and spilled some over his desk. Pushed aside the bench, tossed down a tarp, opened the box on the worktable, and pulled out a handful of pastels. Then I grabbed a large pad off the shelf and put it on a paint-speckled easel. The empty white seemed to taunt me—*Feeling blank?*—so I let my frustration out on it with smears of blue and purple and red, mashing hues together with my fingers. When no white remained for me to cover, I flung the paper up and over to continue my madness. But madness already claimed the next page.

It was me; I stared at myself.

The work, only half painted, showed my eyes luminescent, my cheeks flushed with laughter. I'd never posed for Noel; he must've drawn me from memory. *Who's looking at you?* Though I knew he'd looked on occasion, I'd never before had to face the evidence of that in strokes of black on white, never had to think about what he'd truly seen. My throat closed.

"He cares for you, my dear. You know this."

I flinched as Garrick stepped up beside me, but I couldn't make my mouth move to apologize for my bizarre act. He seemed all right with that, just patted my back as we stared at my one-dimensional likeness. I felt the threat of salt behind my eyes.

Why hadn't Noel finished it? Why had he left me half done?

"Maeve Leahy, you've made a mess of yourself. Good." My father stood in the doorway, looking at me like he'd just discovered Atlantis under the tin top of a trash can.

I couldn't find my voice, just scrubbed at my face, glad to feel no sign of tears.

"Ah, wait," Garrick said. He lifted my hand and showed me the rainbow mess I had all over my fingers.

Watercolors. The word chimed in my brain just as a single tear squeezed its way out and slid down my cheek.

GARRICK LED US into the kitchen. My father's eyes bugged again as he took in the cavernous space—the Italian marble console with its ivy-covered mantelpiece and cherub statuettes, the medieval chairs and long mahogany table.

"Please, sit." Garrick motioned to two leather chairs before the inglenook's hearth, where a fire crackled warm and homey, and hickory-bark notes filled the air.

"We shouldn't take you away from your customers," I said, struck finally with some guilt.

"If I'm needed, I'll be found." He turned to my father. "Coffee, Jack?"

"Ayuh, thanks." The men had obviously made their own introductions when I'd left to clean myself up.

We sat as Garrick walked into the kitchen's heart and poured coffee, then pulled a copper pot off a carefully disordered arrangement of cookery hung from an old ladder.

"Don't go to any trouble for me," I said when I recognized cocoa preparations, though my mouth watered. Garrick really did make a mean mug of hot chocolate.

"No trouble at all. And I have something extraordinary to share with you!" He hurried back, gave my father his coffee, then sat on a nearby bench. "Someone came to Time After Time yesterday," he said in his best storyteller's voice. "I spoke with him. A Javanese *empu.*"

"An *empu*? God, really? An *empu*!" My mind spun.

"What's an *empu*?"

"A *keris* blacksmith," Garrick told my father. "Maeve's *keris* was made hundreds of years ago by such a man. But there are very few *empus* still around today. You should've seen him. Simply regal in his black cloak and hat, somewhat short and—"

"Wait!" Something clicked. A short person with a black hat. "Did the hat look like a pillbox wrapped in a scarf?"

"Why, I suppose so!" Garrick said. "You've met him?"

"No, but I think he was at the auction the night I won the *keris*. I think he bid on it."

"Well, of course!" Garrick said. "He would have!"

"Where is he now?"

"Over the Atlantic, I suspect. He's flying home today."

"I don't suppose he lives in Italy?" I asked. "Rome? Trastevere?"

"Temporarily, I believe. Let me find his card."

"Wait, I have a note," I said as Garrick made to stand. I dug out the Trastevere address as he plucked a pair of reading glasses off a side table and settled them onto his face.

His eyes widened as he read. "You have met him!"

"I haven't, but"—I bowed to instinct—"I think he's been following me."

"Following you?" my father asked, but I pressed on.

"And I think he might've left that book for me, and later some notes. What's up with this guy? Is he crazy?"

"Well, no." Lines on Garrick's forehead deepened. "He seemed very honorable, polite, learned. We spoke at length. He hopes to teach at university."

"That's why he was at Betheny U? Looking for a job?"

"He didn't say, but that makes sense."

"What was he doing here at the shop?"

"Shopping." The ends of Garrick's mustache peaked. "He purchased the straight *keris* I showed you. He said it, eh . . ."

"What?"

"My memory, my dear, I'm trying to recall—it was so interesting how he put it." Garrick stared into the fire as an ember leaped onto the marble floor. "He said it was a shame to see a snake with a dead will. That's what he said."

"What's this about, Maeve?"

"Hold on, Dad. Did he mention me, Garrick, or my *keris*?"

"No, though I said I'd seen a stunning blade recently that I wished he could examine. I even tried to call you, but there was no answer." He shrugged. I'd been home yesterday, torturing myself with relaxation. Why hadn't I heard my cell? Maybe I'd left it in the car. Lost it. Let it molder in its usual blind spot by the front door with a dead battery. "He just asked if you were happy with the *keris*," he continued, "and I told him you were. He seemed pleased to know that."

"Can I see the business card? Unless he nailed it to your hand?"

"Nailed it?" Garrick blinked.

I smiled. "Just kidding. I'd love to see that card."

My father hunched forward after Garrick left, his forearms on his thighs, the *keris* still in his hands. "So this blacksmith guy's the nailer?"

"I think so, Dad. For some reason this *empu* took an interest in my *keris* and left me a book and a bunch of notes. Now I find out he lives in Trastevere." I drummed my fingers on the chair's leather arm, heard a corresponding play of notes in my head and didn't even care. "And now I might never find out what this guy knows and why he wanted the *keris*, or even if he *did* want it—but of course he did because he's the one who bid against me in the first place."

"Seems he'd be interested if he makes them, right?"

"Well, right, but what did he want with *me*? Why'd he leave all those notes, and why does he live in Rome?"

"Why does anyone?" my father asked. "I don't see the attraction, personally."

"You're kidding, right? I mean, the Pantheon's there and the Forum, the Colosseum, Michelangelo's dome. It's Rome!" My hands flew all around me as I spoke. "The city's oozing with culture, and the food! There's pizza all over the place, tiramisu, gelato—"

"What's that?"

"Gelato? Just the best ice cream in the world," I said, but he wrinkled his nose. "And Trastevere is this amazing artists' community. Lots of, you know, hippies and art shops and quaint restaurants and mangy dogs and laundry hanging from windows."

"Laundry. Like the picture in your hall?"

"Yeah, yeah, like that. *Empus* aren't supposed to live in Rome, though, they're supposed to live in Malaysia or Java. What if this guy is some quack *empu* impersonator?"

"What if he is?" He shrugged. "Does it matter?"

"It does matter. It matters because if he's real, then he knows things about *kerises* that no one else knows, and I want to know all of that."

"Why? You going to start making blades? Is this about Alvilda?"

"Alvilda? No, the here and now, Dad, because suddenly I buy this sword and things start happening. Aren't you listening?"

He scratched his head, but before he could respond, Garrick returned with the business card.

"Check both sides," he said, handing it to me so that the first thing I read was the familiar handwritten address of Via della Scala in Trastevere.

"It's the same address," I said, then flipped the card. Here, a symbol like a snake coiled alongside the script, indicating an address in Java and the man's name:

Empu Sri Putra

"No phone number, no e-mail. Why don't any of the men in my life live in this century?" I looked at Garrick. "No offense."

"Oh, none taken," he said cheerily. "But not all answers can be found with the click of a rat. Some need to be uncovered the old-fashioned way."

"Mouse," I said.

"What's that, dear?"

"It's a mouse. Not a rat."

"Ah, well. Vermin all the same."

I stood and stared at the fire, the flames licking the brick.

"Maybe it doesn't matter," my father said. "No school until January, right?"

"Late January, right."

"And you know the language."

I faced him, incredulous. "You don't mean—"

"You have his name and address. Go find him. You've done crazier things. Think about it, Mayfly—all the hanging laundry and gelato you could handle."

"Right." I laughed. It sounded a little maniacal.

"You always wanted to travel," he said. "You've got a passport you never used."

"The passport's probably expired." I thrummed my fingers against my leg, made more notes. This time they bothered me.

"They last for ten years," chimed Garrick, scooping cocoa into a pot by the stove.

"Ten years," my father said. I waited for him to puzzle it out, though I knew damn well when it expired. "Sixteen when you got it, twenty-five now. Just enough time for a trip."

"I don't think so."

"Why not? Name one good reason."

"I can name several. One: I don't look like the same person"—I grabbed a handful of my choppy achromatic hair—"which means I'm probably breaking some passport rule."

"I don't think—"

"Two: What if the guy's crazy? I just told you he's been following me around. You want to send me off to chase after a potentially insane person? What if I end up hacked into little bits and left in a suitcase somewhere?"

"He really did seem like a good man," Garrick said.

"See there, Maeve. I don't think—"

"Three: I don't care enough about this to uproot myself."

"Now there's crazy." He stood. "You used to yammer on about all the places you'd go, but now here you are, a full-grown woman, and you've never even stepped on a plane. Look how fired up you are over this thing you say you don't care about. I haven't seen that storm in your eyes in ages."

"Chops away soul bonds, lets a person live how they should— that's how a *keris* works." Garrick stepped close and handed me a mug. I hugged it to my chest as chocolate steam rose into my nostrils. His voice lowered to lore-telling levels. "That *keris*, with its little man and the hole in the blade, is full of power. I knew it from the start."

My dad couldn't have had a clue what Garrick meant, but he nodded anyway. "It's a good blade. Proving itself already."

It seemed a conspiracy I'd have to shut down hermetically.

"I won't give up my winter break and spend all my money to run off to a foreign country over some nutjob"—I held my hand up to my father when I saw his mouth open—"or for any other reason. I've already made plans."

"What plans?" my dad asked.

"I have a course to prepare. It'll take a lot of time and—"

"So you'll hole up here alone. How's that living?"

Garrick wandered casually back to the sink.

My father lay the *keris* on the chair, then put his hands on my shoulders. "Maeve, what do you want? What makes you happy?"

I tried to focus on the spit of wood and the distant hum of people around us—gorging on ginger cookies, laughing—but my voice broke when I answered. "My work. I love my work."

"Work is not life. Work is work. What about your dreams, daughter. Do you still have them?"

Eling. The word seemed to strike at me from out of nowhere.

"Did you know Maeve plays the saxophone, Garrick?"

My lungs deflated. "Dad—"

"Is that true, my dear?"

"A long time ago," I said. "A very long time ago."

My father stared at the fire. "She was supposed to make a record. Well, a CD, right?"

"You must be quite a talent," Garrick said.

"She is."

"I'll have to look into a saxophone for the music room. We'll have a concert!"

I said nothing, just set down my mug and walked. Out of the kitchen, down the hall, past a group of people at the register. There was an alcove near the entrance, deserted. I ducked into it. Here, tiny houses sat on a dais covered with reams of snow-white cloth. Pinpricks of radiance emanated from a hundred wee panes of glass, like a vast sea of earthbound stars.

I cradled my face in my hands and listened. To the wind outside. To conversation in the main room. To children playing with the old

Lionel under the tree. We'd had a train like that once. Moira and I used to lie together on our bellies and watch its click-clackety journey under the Fraser fir my father brought home every Christmas.

Maeve, let's travel someday on a train.

Yes, maybe it'll come off the track, and then we can go wherever we want, drive it across the sea and over to Europe and then to Africa and Australia and—

You goose. Daddy's never going to let you drive anywhere!

Solid, even footsteps approached. I felt my father beside me.

"You lie when you say you're okay. When's the last time you played your sax?"

I shook my head.

"When?"

"Before it happened." It. I couldn't say the words.

He paused for such a length of time, I thought he'd left. Then he said, "Maybe it's for the best you won't come home. You think your mother can handle seeing how you've let go of everything you are? You think that's what she needs?"

My head shot up. "Don't blame me for her. Don't do that."

"It's not about blame. It's about doing and it's about being. Do you think we want this for you? You think Moira would've wanted this for you?"

"Stop."

He brushed his hands over my hair, grasped my face, forced me to look at him. "I see you, Maeve. You're still in there in eyes full of sky. Still stubborn as your mother."

"I'm not like her."

"More than you know," he said. "It's not that you can't go. It's that you won't."

Rome again. "Right," I said. "I won't."

"Even if you need to?"

"Why do I need to? Because I once wanted to travel? Because my childhood dreams didn't come true? That makes me like 99 percent of the rest of the world. I'm not unique, Dad."

"You're wrong there."

"Because of music?" I straightened my spine, hardened my tone. "Do you know how sick I am of people defining me by that? Everyone did—even Moira, thanks to Mom."

"Don't blame your mother—"

"How can I not when she manipulated every critical decision in our lives growing up? You know how it was for us. You know what came of it. Why do you defend her constantly?"

"Jesus H," he said with a fractured look, then walked away.

Bells jangled on the front door. Gone.

Out of Time

Castine, Maine
JULY–SEPTEMBER 2000
Moira and Maeve turn sixteen

Summertime passed in a rush, as Mom stayed busy with Poppy, and Dad with work. Maeve had more lessons than ever with Ben Freeman, who was helping her make a tape for an agent. On his advice, she even met with the high-school counselor to see about graduating early—something supersmart Kit planned to do, too. Moira busied herself in the garden, planning meals and playing the piano; and when she found out that Ian had broken up with Paula, she managed to bump into him a lot more often. Sometimes he'd lift his hand in a half wave, which always made her day.

A few weeks after school began, Moira and Maeve celebrated their sixteenth birthdays. Mom made a cake smothered in buttercream frosting with two large "16" candles on top, and the girls each blew out their half. Daddy hauled two huge suitcases into the kitchen—powder blue for Moira and dark blue for Maeve. They didn't fully understand the significance until Poppy gave them his gift: passport applications.

"We'll get your pictures taken and go down to the post office tomorrow after school," Dad said. "Poppy wanted you to have this much today, though."

"You t-t-two go," Poppy stuttered. *"Avven-t-t."* He slumped a little farther in his wheelchair.

"Don't upset yourself, Dad," their mother said. "We all understand, right, girls?"

The twins responded at the same time: "Yes, Poppy. *Avventura.*"

Later that afternoon, Moira walked to the docks, her cheeks wind-washed. Sixteen! Real adventure might be just around the corner. Someday soon, she'd travel with Maeve, but until then there were lots of adventures to be found in Castine—maybe as many as she'd ever want. She hoped to catch Ian, to get a birthday smile from him. Anything seemed possible now. Everything did.

She'd walked halfway down the hill, near Michael's house, when the peal of Maeve's laughter made her stop. Maeve and Michael? A secret boyfriend?

"Get it, Maeve!" Michael yelled.

Moira stood just close enough to see Maeve catch a football and run with it hugged to her chest for a few yards.

"Oh, no, you don't!" said another voice, and like a lion claiming its prey, Ian came out of nowhere and tackled her.

For a second Moira admired how his blond hair complemented her twin's sundown strands. *That's how we'd look together*, she thought. But Ian stayed on top of Maeve, laughing with her, not struggling too hard to steal the football. He stayed there, in fact, until Michael shouted, "Get a room already!"

They're together, really together. The words became Moira's cadence as she ran back home. Had Ian kissed Maeve? If he had and Maeve had kept that secret, Moira would never forgive her. Why was Maeve always the lucky one? Why couldn't Moira have anything for herself?

Once in her room, Moira opened her desk drawer and unearthed the stone saxophone Ian had given and she had taken. There was only one critical way she and her sister were different. And that, Moira thought as she clutched the token, could be remedied.

MOIRA FOUND THE saxophone case leaning against the piano in the living room. When she flipped its latches, the hard snap of metal seemed to reverberate like an alarm in the otherwise quiet house: *Wrong sister, go away.* She assembled the sax easily enough. The next step proved harder; Maeve had once tried to teach her about positioning, but the lesson was long forgotten.

It should just come to me, Moira thought. *It should come to me the way it came to her.* She set her fingers on the keys with hope. *Listen for the notes, find them in the air, breathe and—*

A warbling squawk erupted from the instrument.

Try again. Fingers down, take a breath—

Hobbled notes poured from the horn.

"What's that horrible noise?"

Moira felt a hot blood in her cheeks, but she lowered the sax and turned to face the woman who had the power to change her life. "I want to take saxophone lessons."

Her mother rubbed her hands on her apron and stepped farther into the room. "Why would you want to do that?"

"I could be as good as Maeve. I'd like to try."

"Hmm," she said, staring out the window. Seconds passed.

"Mom?"

"Did you know your name was supposed to be Chelsea?"

This wasn't what Moira had expected. She shook her head.

"It's true, after Grandma Chelsea. But your father decided that his redheaded girls needed Irish names. Maeve and Moira, after his mother and grandmother. He said that Chelsea was the name of a London borough and his ancestors would turn over in their graves if we named you that. So I gave in, even though they sounded like twin names to me."

"I don't get it, Mom. You don't like my name?"

"I love your name, and it fits you. What I mean is that I've tried to differentiate you girls from the beginning, and it's been like fighting"—she looked up, toward heaven, maybe, and her voice softened—"like fighting the tide. But I keep at it, because I know it's important for the two of you to have separate identities." Her eyes found Moira's and her voice rang clear again. "You'll have your room back once Poppy's better, you know."

"I know." She had to admit she didn't want to share a room with Maeve right now. She didn't want to share anything, except the sax. "I want saxophone lessons," she said again.

"You're a good pianist, Moira."

"But I'm not a prodigy like Maeve, am I?" The distinguishing word she'd heard so long ago. Prodigy. Special. Gifted. Magnetic. Attractive.

"You're both talented young women."

"I'm not a prodigy. You can't say it, can you?"

Her mother rubbed her forehead. "You've grown into a terrific player, Moira. I didn't mean to imply that—"

"She always gets the best of everything! Everyone likes her! Everyone loves her! Everyone—"

"Ah, I see," said her mother. "You want to impress someone. A boy, maybe?"

"No one." Moira met her mother's suspicious gaze, tried to deflect it. "Please, just let me try it. Let me be myself."

"You are yourself. Of course you're yourself. What you need to understand is that being separate is healthy."

"Healthy?" Moira knew then her mother would not relent—not with this tone of voice, this unwavering brand of speech, and a smile so sharp it seemed to cut through skin and muscle and bone. She should give up. She would, normally. But then she remembered Ian. Words to persuade, and emotions—fear, frustration—tumbled over themselves in her mind. She grasped at half a thought. "But isn't it healthy to feel . . ."

"What? To feel what?"

"Whole." Moira's vision blurred. Her eyes stung. "I don't feel whole." Truth. She swallowed. "Can't you try to understand? Can't you help instead of fighting me?"

"Oh, Moira"—she shook her head—"I *am* helping. You need to find your true self. You won't always be joined at the hip to Maeve. You won't always be together. Stretch out a bit. Don't search for space inside your sister's shadow."

Moira battled a wave of potent humiliation as panic swelled in her. *I'll never have him, never be good enough.*

"I'm not worth a try, even if it means so much to me?"

"Worth? You're worth everything, but Moira—" Her mother stepped closer. Moira thought maybe she'd reach out, hug her, even yield. Instead, she brushed the piano with her hand. "Maybe some extra piano lessons will make you feel better."

Moira didn't speak as she disassembled the saxophone and put it back in its case. Then she regarded the piano. "I should be grateful you let me take Grandma Leahy's piano and have lessons," she said evenly. "I should take some more lessons and I'll be happy, right?"

"If that's what you want."

"It's not what I want! I'm trying to tell you what I want, and you won't listen!" She crashed her hand over the black keys with one

hand and slapped at a sheaf of music with the other. "Clair de Lune"
fluttered to the floor.

"Moira Leahy!"

Moira ran out of the house and across the lawn. When she
reached the shoreline, she sat on stones as gray and chill as her
thoughts. Would she never affect anything in her life? Would she
never prove herself to be . . . essential?

"Moira?" Maeve stood beside her. Though her face was drawn
and serious, her cheeks were pink—scrubbed fresh with air and
laughter and maybe Ian's kisses. Sweet sixteen. "I felt something
bad. What's wrong?"

"Go away. I can't be near you right now." Moira's chest felt wire-
bound, but she ignored the hurt in her twin's eyes.

After Maeve left, Moira looked across the Penobscot at the bur-
geoning clouds on the horizon. She wished her arms would grow
long enough to reach into them, that she could somehow move their
dark shapes where she wanted, make it rain and thunder, make the
air jump with lightning. Fly. But she was second born and earthbound and not meant for such things.

CHAPTER EIGHT
JOURNEYS

Hours passed as I waited for my father's return. I helped Garrick and his assistants stack dishes and gather cups, sweep gingerbread crumbs into dustpans in the hall. I went through the small rooms, too, straightening bears and books, setting chairs back in their places.

Once, I peered inside the music room and saw the Steinway. I could easily picture Moira behind it, playing one of her favorites, something from *The Sound of Music* or *Pippin.* Or Liszt. Struggling over the difficult measures, perhaps, but injecting each phrase with heartfelt emotion. I felt a prickle, turned, and saw Garrick at the end of the hall, looking at me. Neither of us spoke.

I picked at the simple meal he prepared for us, and the third white plate on the table was so brilliant with emptiness that it nearly hurt my eyes. I spent the rest of my time in the front room, my face all but pressed against one of the cold windows as the sky spit sleet on the walks and the season changed before me.

Walking was my dad's way of processing anger, releasing it peacefully. He must be furious with me to be away for so long. I wondered if I should go out looking for him; this wasn't his town. Still, I couldn't believe he'd be lost with his sense of direction.

Maybe he'd made the state line by now. Or maybe he'd walked back to my apartment and his truck, and left for Maine.

I'd just reached for the shop phone, intent on calling my landlady to verify whether my father's truck was there or gone, when Garrick approached. The *keris* lay unsheathed in his hand.

"I tried to remove that stain," he said. "I used all of my cleansers, but . . ." The mark was still there, long and thin like a vein. "It blends with the *pamor* and shouldn't reduce the value. You needn't worry." We shared a look; we both knew I had other things to worry about.

When I called my landlady, she said my dad's truck was there all right. And so was his dog. Running around the yard, barking, spawning all sorts of complaints. Had been for nearly five hours. The dog seemed rabid, she said.

"A little brown and white dog?" I clarified.

"That's the one. Cujo." There was a tremor in her voice. Her fear of dogs was legendary, but Sparky? Menacing? "I'm surprised no one's called the police," she added. "I was nearly ready to do it myself."

What the—?

"I've got to go," I told Garrick, gathering my things. "If my father comes back . . ." Icy rain beat against the window.

"I'll get him to you."

SPARKY NEARLY BIT off my nose when I got out of my car and rounded her up. Shivering. Bits of ice stuck to her fur. Not rabid, but frenzied. Frenzied as only a frightened, freezing animal could be. Five hours, oh, my God, what a horrible person I was for completely forgetting about her.

The mystery of how it happened was solved at the front door. Closed but not quite latched.

Kit was a dead woman.

I'd thought her cured of this particular bad habit. In her first weeks as a resident physician, she'd often left our apartment open in her rush to get back to the hospital. I'd had to remind her repeatedly to lock up, which was usually her cue to joke that my forgetfulness was rubbing off on her. But this—now—was no laughing matter, and there were not enough miles for me to walk to dissolve my anger.

I bathed Sparky in warm water, apologizing to her with my human words, but I was still livid when I found my missing cell (in my car, beneath the seat) and called Kit. *Be gentle*, I thought, taking deep and calming breaths as the phone rang. *Tell her you love her.* Voice mail picked up. I waited for the beep.

"You're such an ass. You left the door unlocked again and my father's dog got outside and nearly died from hypothermia. Isn't 'first, do no wrong' part of some sacred doctor code or something? Maybe you should read up on it." I hung up and brushed my hand over Sparky's warm, dry coat, as she burrowed more closely against my leg. "I think I handled that pretty well," I told her. "All things considered."

I FELT THE slow pulse of time that night as I had just once before. My father's truck still sat outside of my house and his dog on my couch, but I saw no sign of the man himself. I reached for my old senses, the ones I used to rely on, but I couldn't sort my anxiety from any possible omen of disaster.

Only the dark seemed comfortable, as I stepped out into my backyard. Cold air rolled over me as long minutes passed. The multicolored glow from my landlady's window disappeared as she turned her tree off, went to bed. Sleet came again and pelted against my hood, until a song evolved from the rhythm of nature. Tribal. Compelling. I breathed it in. Swayed with my hands over my head. Moved my limbs to it. But I'd never been graceful on my feet. I slid, fell. Sudden laughter burbled up in me as I lay there on my back, staring up at night.

"Mayfly. Sorry, didn't mean to scare you," my father said, when I nearly leaped out of my skin.

"Dad, I was so worried." Felt my heartbeat, strong and hard beneath my hand. But thank God. He was here. Whole and well and . . . here. Muscles I hadn't even realized were clenched relaxed as I followed him inside, back into the living room.

"I have something for you," he said, just as I saw it. Beside my couch sat a miniature boat, made into a coffee table—the wood burled and polished to a high sheen, a generous loop of lanyard on either end, twin seats under a pane of glass.

It took a second for me to find my voice. "Did you make that?"

"Christmas present," he said sheepishly.

So that's what had been under the tarp in his truck. "You knew I wouldn't go back with you."

He didn't answer, just wrinkled his lips—a man sorry to be right.

"You're leaving now, aren't you? I can tell."

"In the morning," he said. "Right after you." He held out an envelope, waggled it at me. I took it, tucked my finger beneath its seam, and tore. Inside was a plane ticket for a trip that would begin in less than ten hours. Destination: Rome.

"I can't take this." I set it on the table. "Dad, I'm sorry for everything. We should talk about—"

"I'm tired of talk." He did look tired, the creases around his eyes as deep as I'd ever seen them. "You have time off now. You want to learn about that sword, and the man who can tell you what you want to know is on the other end of that ride," he said, picking the ticket back up, holding it out to me again.

"How did you get that?"

"Found your airport. Small thing, but it'll get you a plane to Newark, and from there to Rome." The airport. No wonder he'd been away for so long. "So you'll go," he said, like it was a done deal.

Excuses reared up like students with their hands raised high, but when I gave them their chance they lacked spine.

"I don't have time to pack."

"There's time enough."

"I can't take a *keris* on a plane—not after 9/11."

"I asked about that," he said. "You won't be able to take it in your carry-on, but you can pack it in that big blue suitcase of yours. About time you used it properly."

"I can't leave Sam."

"Kit said she'd take care of Sam."

"That's a good one. Kit nearly killed your dog this afternoon leaving the door open. Sparky was outside for hours."

He glanced at his dog, asleep on the couch. "No harm done.

She checked Sparky out, even took her temperature. Everything's normal."

"Kit was here?"

"Not five minutes ago. Just took off."

"See that? She's avoiding me," I said. "Plagued with guilt."

"Nah, she just said she had to go back to work, grabbed a few things, and left. You're alike, aren't you? All work, no play. We're going to change that. She mentioned a place a surgeon friend of hers likes in Rome, a nice hotel, and said she'd make a reservation. And your ticket back is open, so you can stay as long as you'd like."

This was his talent: making the stiff limber, bending it to his will, reinforcing weaknesses.

"You asked why I stand by your mother."

"I shouldn't have said those things." I forced my eyes to stay on his. "I'm sorry."

"She's hard sometimes, Maeve, but strong and steadfast like a shore. My shore. I love her for that. I don't believe she ever meant to hurt you girls—not in any way. She did her best. I know your sister was your shore."

"Dad—"

"Let me finish. Moira was your shore, and now she's gone. Maybe you don't want another shore, maybe you don't need one, so you've decided not to bother looking. But what I'm seeing in you is some-one who's afraid to move at all, someone who's decided to play it safe. That's not living. The Maeve I used to know would take this ticket—which, by the way, is nonrefundable. Better not waste my money, or I'll be pissed like you've never seen."

What did I want to say? *Don't make me do this.* But my hand reached forward anyway, and then the ticket that would change my life lay on my palm. My throat clogged. "Thanks."

YOU'D THINK MY head would've been full of Italian music that night—"O Sole Mio" or even plainchant. "Harlem Nocturne" stalked through me instead, along with the image of a detective with a pillbox hat searching Rome for an *empu.*

Earlier, I'd pulled my passport from my saxophone case and

leaned it against the lamp on my dresser. Looking at it now from my bed, in the shadow of night, its cover seemed black as a raven's wing, though I knew it was navy. *What am I doing? What am I doing?*

My phone rang at five of six. Kit.

"Still feeling bad about the dog? You've called, finally, to face my wrath?"

She ignored me. "You're going this morning, right?"

"I'm not sure," I said, staring at the mound of clothes on my bed. The suitcase yawned open on my floor, and I'd yet to offer it even a pair of socks.

"What could possibly be holding you back?"

I knew what was holding me back: good, old-fashioned panic. I said something different. "I have a few appointments."

"What appointments?"

"I need a haircut and I'm due for some color—"

"Color? Color would be nice!" she said. "And that's the lamest of all lame-ass excuses in the history of the world. Don't think I don't know you cut your own hair or that I haven't seen your stash of bleach under the sink. Don't think I haven't been tempted to toss every last box." Foiled at every turn. "I can't believe you're not jumping at the opportunity to take this trip. You hate the break! Just think about all the hours of rest you'll avoid by trekking around Rome." This was a good point. "In fact, the only possible downside of this trip is that we won't have a chance to exchange gifts, which means your chocolate won't be around when you come back. I apologize in advance for my lack of willpower."

Somehow she got a laugh out of me.

"Maeve! How can you even think about not going?" I felt her mental shake through the phone. "Here's your chance to take that big leap forward!"

"Oh, stop with all that leap crap already, will you? You know how I hate it when you get all motherly on me."

"Where do you land, and when?"

I sighed. "Fiumicino Airport, 7:45 a.m. Roman time tomorrow. You figure it out. Kit, Dad mentioned a hotel—"

"I'm totally on it."

"You don't have to—"

"Shut up, I already ate two of your chocolates. Give me your flight info," she said, and I gave her the specifics. "All right. I'll meet you at the airport. I want to see you off."

"You want to strap me to the wing of the plane."

She denied it, but we both knew I'd spoken truth.

"IF YOU FORGOT to pack something, you'll buy it there." My father stood beside me as I waited to check my luggage, studying my face. I realized I'd been frowning.

"It's not that," I told him. I glanced at the woman before us, at the sleeping child over her shoulder. "I should call Mom."

"It's late. She'll be off. What do you need to say?"

"I don't know."

He nodded. "You can't know what your mother thinks or what she'd say. Sometimes even I don't. You just have to do for you."

"Yeah, I know." I looked again at the little boy.

"Hey, I thought maybe I'd missed you!" Kit strode toward us, a small gift bag in her hand and a scowl on her face. "What in Godiva's name are you wearing?" she asked me.

"What?" I looked down at myself, but there weren't any holes in my sweater—a billowy blue comfort—or my jeans. No stains and not too much cat fur on my coat, either.

"You're going to Rome!" she said. "You look like you're off to a ball game! Tell me you packed some decent clothes. Something with sparkle. Something with color. Something fitted."

I blinked at her. Who cared about clothes?

"You're hopeless." She turned and smiled at my father, who'd been smiling ever since she'd arrived. Their faces had collusion written all over them. "You're looking fine this morning, Mr. Leahy."

"As are you, Kit. All set with the hotel?"

"It's in the bag." She patted said bag and handed it to me. "But no peeks until after takeoff," she warned. "You're going to love it!"

I tried to tamp down my concern when I saw her eyes light with a hint of the devious. "Thanks," I said, then returned her wicked smile. "I left your present at home. I'm sure you'll find it without any problem."

There wasn't much fuss over the *keris* after all. The woman at the counter said it would go through a security check. I watched my big bag and its blade disappear down a conveyor belt, and then I turned to Kit. "You'll remember to feed Sam?"

"Who's Sam? Just kidding!" she said when my eyes bugged. "Yes, I promise to take care of your cat."

"You'll have to actually go home to feed him. Don't set him up with a tube and some gross liquid food. Don't let him wander out of any wide-open front doors. And don't stuff him into any dresses, either. His girlfriends wouldn't like it."

She surprised me with a hard hug. "Love you," she whispered. "Get the hell out of the country already."

I turned to Dad and hugged him.

"Have fun, Mayfly."

Oh, Daddy.

Everything became a blur of waiting until, finally, I boarded the plane, and, finally, it lifted into the sky. Clouds lay outside my window, beside me and then under me as sunlight streamed in my eyes. Other people closed their shades, but I couldn't bring myself to surrender a second of the experience.

When a flight attendant came by with snacks, I remembered Kit's present, the details about the hotel. Inside the bag were a box of chocolates and a sepia print card picturing a woman taking a leap. I opened the card and found a scrawled note with the name of a hotel and these cryptic words:

Tall, dark, and handsome will meet you at baggage claim. Smile pretty.

My heart skipped several beats as I realized just what she meant. And then I ate all of the chocolate.

Out of Time

Castine, Maine
SEPTEMBER–OCTOBER 2000
Moira and Maeve are sixteen

A chill settled over Castine in late September. The winds blew harsh, and Daddy banned boating until spring. The cold bit through the old walls of their home in new ways as well. Poppy's health deteriorated; he seemed unable to recognize any of them. Daddy worked more than ever, traveling to find new business as their medical bills increased. Mom cried a lot. Both Maeve and Moira took part-time jobs to help—Maeve with a boating-supply store and Moira at a bookshop.

It was through the bookstore's owner that Moira discovered Franz Liszt, a composer and pianist who injected his music with romance and humanity. At home, she struggled with his difficult sheet music, slowly keying notes for right hand alone.

"I can play the melody on the sax if you want," Maeve said one evening as Moira struggled with "Liebestraum No. 3."

"I'd rather do it alone, thanks."

"What's wrong?"

"Nothing."

Moira kept a close watch on her sister, but only once did she spy Maeve walking with Ian near the docks. After, she felt so hurt, so angry, and so unwilling to discuss those feelings that she blocked Maeve. Weird, but the sense of isolation she'd once loathed felt to her now like a cocoon of safety.

That night, their mother begged them to try a card trick for Poppy—something that had always made him smile. They tried, and failed.

"I was holding a three of clubs, didn't you know?" Maeve asked.

"No."

"Why are you blocking me?"

"I don't want to talk about it."

Kit approached her the next day at school. "Why are you mad at Maeve?"

"It's private."

"Is it because of my brother?"

"No," she lied and walked away.

At night, Moira sometimes saw Ian's shadow through the shade covering his window; he paced a lot. At school, too, he seemed restless. If only she had a single, golden opportunity, she could make him happy. *She* had liked Ian long before Maeve had taken him seriously, after all. Shouldn't she have a chance with him first?

She opened *Jane Eyre* and read the passage she felt so intimately now: *Do you think, because I am poor, obscure, plain, and little, I am soulless and heartless? You think wrong!—I have as much soul as you,—and full as much heart!* She would prove it. She had to prove it. Somehow she would.

Two weeks later, she slipped a note into Ian's locker.

I need to see you. Meet me outside at midnight when my parents and sister have gone to sleep. Don't tell anyone, and don't try to talk to me about it before then. I'll just play dumb if you do. Just meet me.

—Maeve

The Second Will

NOEL

YOU DO NOT TRAVEL IF YOU ARE AFRAID OF THE UNKNOWN,
YOU TRAVEL FOR THE UNKNOWN, THAT REVEALS YOU WITH
YOURSELF.

—ELLA MAILLART

CHAPTER NINE
FAR AND AWAY

*O*ne stop in Newark and more than a dozen hours later, I stepped off the airplane to a frenzy of shouts and hand gestures. Around me, people scattered, to the turnstile or down brightly lit corridors teeming with other travelers. Overhead, announcements made in Italian—about planes boarding, planes delayed, planes arriving—flooded my ears, and even I had trouble understanding because the words spilled so fast. A group of giggling Americans clasped their translation dictionaries and clunkered through a phrase about ordering pizza as a couple ran by— *"Su, sbrigati, perderemo il volo di coincidenza!"*—late for their flight.

Great Zeus—err, Jupiter! I pinched myself. Rome!

For a second, I thought I saw a little girl with red hair standing beside a revolving door. Then she was gone.

Think about where you are. Don't do this now.

Right. I inserted my Visa into a nearby machine, and it spit out euros so colorful they felt like play money in my hand. I dashed into a gift shop to pick up a tourist's guidebook and some other essentials, then took my purchases and stood—well, paced—beside the turnstile to wait for my luggage . . . and Mr. Tall, Dark, and Handsome.

After so many months, I would see Noel. Noel, who'd been weirdly out of touch. Noel, who'd been a touchstone for me since my undergrad years at Betheny U. Back then, Kit and I were fresh escapees of Maine, entrenched in school and needing to prove we could make it alone. Noel sat beside me one day in French class, and I swear we recognized something in each other from moment one— some invisible badge that attracted others who'd had their hearts trampled early and utterly. He'd accepted me as I was and taken only what I could offer. At first, it wasn't much. Smiles. Jokes. A walk. The occasional movie when I couldn't study anymore. Hot chocolate at the shop. Someone who grew to know me well, who didn't know me from Before.

What a blessed relief to keep everything so neatly compartmentalized. The After Maeve without music could still function and make friends. She excelled in school and didn't think much about her former plans or even have time for that. She was so much better off grounded.

I reset my watch to 8:30 a.m., though it felt like the middle of the night to my body. Noel was forty-five minutes late. It struck me then that I'd assumed a lot: that Kit's note meant she'd actually spoken with him, that she'd told him the right time and place to meet me, and that he'd find me.

I tried to calm my nerves by perusing the new guidebook. Small squares lay spread across the city—Piazza Barberini, Piazza della Rotonda, Piazza delle Coppelle—and so many museums, cathedrals, places to eat. The muted sounds of "Harlem Nocturne" kicked up a notch as I scanned a map of Trastevere, home to Empu Sri Putra. Why had he followed me, given me that book, asked me to remember? *Eling.* What did he know about my *keris*?

"*Scusi,*" a woman said, brushing past me.

The bags were in; I spied my blue beast on the conveyor. I made to grab it, but another hand got there first.

"Hey!" I spun around, and there was Noel, smiling at me. He set my bag down beside us.

"Rome's full of relics," he said with his hint-of-British voice. "You didn't have to bring your own."

Memories of a night so many months ago rushed back at me: opening a second bottle of Shiraz; me calling him a ninny, explaining that the word was derived from the Latin *innocens;* his hilariously garbled expression as he called me sozzled; me denying it, announcing that I was high on life; snugging my cheek against him to say good night; the almost kiss.

Is it me, Maeve? Or is it . . . just?

Just. Just.

"You're really here," I said.

"I really am. And so are you." He kissed me, quick on the mouth, then laughed at my speechlessness. "My chariot awaits," he said, with a little jerk of his head. "Unless you'd like to go and stand outside for a while, maybe work up a good taxi-fume high."

"Tempting," I said, recovering myself, "but I think I'd like to get out of here."

We settled my luggage in the trunk of a white car with an official-looking light on top, and got inside. The cab lurched onto the roadway.

"Sorry I was late," he said in a low voice. "Cabbie went to the wrong airport. Not the brightest bulb on top of this heap."

We laughed almost giddily. The whole situation seemed surreal. We were together, in Rome! I looked him over, took in his dark jeans and coffee-colored sports coat. Had I ever seen him look so comfortable? "You look great!"

"Well you look *bloody* great," he said.

I remembered my baggy sweater, the faded jeans, and tucked wayward strands of hair behind my ears. "No, I'm a wreck."

"Who's looking at you?"

He was, all right—until the cab bucked and nearly sent us both through the windshield.

"Told you," Noel mouthed. "No seat belts, either."

I gripped the vinyl. "Where are you coming from?" I asked. "Tell me everything."

"Paris. Hang on." He leaned forward and spoke to the cabbie, gave him the address of my hotel. I interrupted him.

"Would you mind if we stopped at Sri Putra's first? I'm anxious to see him. Sorry, I thought Kit would've said," I explained, when his thick brows bunched. "I'm here to take a *keris* to see an *empu*. Sri Putra."

"An *empu* here in Rome? A Roman *empu*. You came for a *keris*?"

"What did you think?" I asked, hyperaware that our darting cab had become the vehicular equivalent of a hummingbird.

"My grandfather called yesterday with a message from Kit and the name of a hotel. 'Merry Christmas. Maeve needs you. Meet her in Rome, 7:45 a.m., Fiumicino Airport.' Over and out."

"Well, I do need you. You can help me." It was the wrong thing to say—that was clear from the quick retreat of his every expression. "And of course I'm happy to see you again! C'mon!"

I pulled Sri Putra's card from my pocket and read it to the driver, and he spun us onto a roadway we'd nearly passed. I bumped into Noel as I slid across the seat.

"So," I said, inching back to my side. "You were in Paris?"

"Yes," he said. "Paris."

"Did you find her? Is your mother in Paris?"

"No." He laughed humorlessly and turned to stare out the window. "At least I don't think so."

"I thought maybe you'd been out of touch because you'd been with her, you know, catching up or—"

"I've been busy, Maeve. Scouting antiques, taking day trips."

"No luck at all then?"

"No. No luck."

And then I stopped pushing, because our driver turned into a sui-cidal-homicidal maniac. Alarm spindled through me as he weaved ever faster between cars. I tried to say, "Slow down!"—*Rallenti, per carità!*—but my tongue was too busy cowering in the back of my mouth to form words.

MY KNUCKLES LOOKED as bleached as my hair by the time we jerked to a stop alongside a gold-washed building with black shut-ters. Beside the entrance, a flag bearing basil, ripe tomato, and moz-zarella-cheese stripes rippled from a long pole.

"Let's have him wait for us," Noel suggested, after the cabbie stepped out to remove our luggage.

"Let's not," I replied, opening the door. I pulled the smaller of my bags from the trunk as the cabbie dragged out Goliath. Before he could retrieve Noel's sleek black valise, though, my friend stopped him.

"Wait for us," Noel said. A scar near one of the cabbie's eyes puckered in confusion, but then Noel handed him a wad of bills and the driver smiled. *"Per favore."*

I tried logic. "We might be a while." Lowered my voice. "What if he takes off with your stuff?"

"He didn't at the airport. Come on, Maeve. What if we can't find another cab? I don't want to carry that thing around the city." He glanced at my bag. I grunted as I hoisted it onto my shoulder, grabbed my smaller case, too. "You're being a little paranoid," he said, which shut me right up.

We stepped inside, into a foyer that smelled of stale bread. I spied two narrow halls, a broken light, and a stairwell that led to darkness.

"Exactly how I'd expect an *empu* to live," Noel muttered.

I ignored him, though admittedly this interior didn't jive with what I knew of the artsy and well-kept homes in Trastevere. "Look for apartment forty-seven. It should be on this level."

It didn't take long. We turned a corner and found a door bearing three nails, a few notes, and more wood scars than I could count. Number 47. I knocked, waited. When I knocked again, the door creaked opened. I heard a tinkling noise, bells or chimes. "Empu Putra?" I called. "Hello?"

"The lock's dead," Noel said, indicating severe damage to the wooden frame near the handle and around the latch. "We should go."

"Maybe." Scent made me do it, a rich spice that drifted from the room, a fragrant match to my silk bookmark. I pushed at the door, stepped across the threshold as Noel tried to grab my arm, missed.

Inside, dozens of puppets made of golden metal, leather, and wood hung from the high ceiling, their bodies cloaked in tribal costumes—painted skirts, headgear, and thick collars dotted with red and blue faux gems. Skinny brass tubes dangled from the figures' thin hands like ski poles.

"We can't stay here," Noel said behind me, but I knew by his awed tone that he wasn't eager to leave, either.

In one corner, a foot-long bronze lion sat beside a large metallic bell and a miniature temple. Along the wall, a triad of shelves bowed, overstuffed with a variety of wooden human figures—small, large, regal, and wild.

A curtain of hot air poured from a ceiling vent, tickling strands of wooden and metallic spheres into music. I walked through it, and into another room covered in relief panels—carved pictures depicting kings and queens and forest animals, wide-eyed villains, battles and victories. Propped against one of the panels stood an instrument with a long, slender neck, three strings, and a skinny pot at its end. I leaned toward it, curious over its sound, but stopped short.

There, on a carved armchair, lay the straight *keris* whose bold oval pattern I'd last observed in a case at Time After Time. *Jackpot,* I thought, just before a reverberating crash sounded out in the other room.

"Christ!" Noel said. "Are you the *empu?*"

"*Empu?*" Deep sardonic laughter filled the air. "*No. No. Non sono empu. Eppure, questo è il mio edifizio. Lei trapassa!*"

The landlord, not the *empu*. And yes, *trapassa*, we were trespassing.

"Sorry, then. *Scusi*. We'll go." Though I doubted Noel had understood every word, he'd comprehended enough: time to leave.

I crossed, tentatively, back into the room to find Noel restoring a tipped bronze gong. A man, tall and with a thick head of unruly black hair, stood beside him in a posture of intimidation, and when he turned his head, his eyes laser-focused on me. Handsome. Dark. Ageless as a Roman god.

"*Non bastano mai.*" A grimace formed around his lips. I noticed he gripped a small sledgehammer, that his fingers were tightening around it. "*La velocità non basta mai. Non basta mai la buona sorte.*" Never enough speed, never enough luck.

I spoke quickly in Italian, told him we were looking for Sri Putra, the *empu*.

"*Lei dovrebbe cercare me.*" His eyes tracked my body, my face, my bag. "*Non lui. Me.*" You should be looking for me. Not him. Me.

"What did he say? Translate." Noel's eyes fixed on the man whose words had confused me into silence, and his voice carried a rare edge when he spoke, made me think not much had been lost on him. "Do you speak English? Does Putra live here or doesn't he?"

"He does," I said, thinking of the *keris*. "I just found—"

"I understand your language." The Italian seemed to hover over Noel, though he was only an inch taller. "You do not know mine? That is too bad. *Chi va dicendo che io non sono Putra?*"

"Who says you're not Putra?" I repeated his question for Noel's benefit, then answered it. "*You* said you weren't the *empu*."

The man bowed grandly at the waist, tucking in one arm but lifting the other so high behind him that the sledge struck the gong and filled the room with a hollow peal. "It is true. I am no *empu*. Merely a man and a fool. *Il tempo dirà quant'è scemo. Il tempo dirà quant'è bravo.*" Time will tell how big a fool. Time will tell how big a man.

I didn't know what to say to that, was too busy trying to figure the guy out. Beautiful as Noel, but bizarre, a puzzle. He seemed to enjoy my confusion, smiling to reveal a line of straight, white teeth.

"We're looking for Sri Putra," I repeated, handing him the *empu's* business card. "Do you know when he'll be back?"

"Did you bring a *keris*?" he asked, his eyes brightening.

"Yes!" I said. "All the way from America."

The man tapped the card in his closed palm. When he opened his hand again, it was empty.

"I'd like that back," I said.

"*Mi dispiace.* It's gone." He showed me his sleeves.

"Let's go, Maeve," Noel said, urging me toward the door. "We don't need it."

True, but I still felt irritated as we returned to the musty hall.

"Why not leave a message for him?" the man asked me, trailing behind us. "Yes, yes, you should. Leave an address where you can be found in Roma. I'm sure he will want to meet you. *Certo che mi piacerebbe!*"

I turned away from him and his subtle innuendo—*I know I would*—as Noel found a pen. He wrote on the back of one of his business cards.

About the keris from Betheny. Contact Maeve Leahy at

"Not my cell. I forgot it." It probably wouldn't have worked overseas, anyway. "I'm staying at—"

"We're staying at the same place."

"Oh, good." I nodded, distracted, but still a question registered: Exactly how far would Kit go to play matchmaker? No. Even she wouldn't cross *that* line.

When Noel finished writing, the Italian snatched the card from his hand and speared it over a nail on the door. Another paper fluttered to the ground.

"Thanks for the help, friend," Noel said.

The landlord genuflected in a way that seemed just as sarcastic while I stooped to pick up the dislodged piece of folded paper. My last name, Leahy, was scrawled on the front. I opened it—

Visit Santa Maria in Cosmedin

—then, before the Italian might see, stuffed the note into my pocket. Too fast. My luggage strap free-fell from my shoulder to the crook of my arm with bruising force.

My groan must've caught the stranger's attention. He stood erect, reached forward, and replaced the bag onto my shoulder with a lingering hand. "Be sure to come back again when you are less"— he looked at Noel— "*carica.*" Burdened.

Noel pushed the man's hand aside, took my bag. "Let's go." He trailed me down the hall, out onto the street. The flag snapped over our heads. "What an ass!" he said. "What did he say, at the end?"

I was trying to figure out a diplomatic way of telling him when I noticed . . . "Noel, where's your cab?" But it was gone, had left us— and Noel's bag on the stoop—in a cloud of Roman dust.

IT WAS LOVE at first step—winding cobblestone streets, the scent of baked bread and sauce permeating the air. Never had a stereotype been so welcome. My stomach rumbled in time with our luggage wheels as we walked by a wall of homes and businesses—a hodgepodge collection of ancient architecture and newer structures, melding together to create a seamless passage of time. The weather was an unexpected pleasure. Though overcast, it had to have been about sixty degrees, reminiscent of a New York autumn or spring, and a vast improvement on the sleet I'd left behind.

Noel stopped and my bag slid from his shoulder. "We've been here before."

"I don't think so." I looked at the map.

"I remember this shop and that marble bust in the window. And we've seen that tower, that church."

Maybe they did look familiar.

"You're reading the map, right?"

I nodded, mentally crossing my fingers; I knew I'd been slacking off, making some guesses. I used to have a good nose for this sort of thing.

He looked over my shoulder. "Where do we think we are?"

I pointed to a dot that was a church and hoped for the best.

"And where do we need to go?" he asked.

I pointed at what I hoped was the vicinity of our hotel.

"Let's turn around then." He hoisted my bag back onto his shoulder and grabbed for his wheeled one. "What did you pack, anyway? Rocks?"

"Only a few," I said. "Look, I told you I'd carry that—or at least pull your bag along with mine. Which do you want?"

"What I want is a bloody cab."

We redirected ourselves. The slender paths were surprisingly free of cars, though motorbikes in every conceivable color zoomed all around us. My heart marked time with the city as I took in the scents, the sights, the sounds.

We were following behind two women who were joking about the shape of their boss's derriere when we stepped before the same marble bust in the window.

Noel dropped my bag again, his face sporting a thin trickle of sweat, and squinted at me. "Time to ask for directions."

"Wow, I didn't think men did that."

"Let's see. One of us speaks like a local," he said darkly, "and it isn't me."

Right. Not the ideal time for jokes. I ducked into a nearby shop and learned our hotel was, in fact, just around the corner.

"I thought so," Noel said when I told him.

"Sure you did."

And that time, I know I caught the edge of a smile.

Out of Time

Castine, Maine
OCTOBER 2000
Moira and Maeve are sixteen

"Can you wash the dishes tonight, Moira?"

Moira looked up from the table, where she had ostensibly been reading *Jane Eyre* but was in truth thinking about what she'd say later to Ian. "Sure, Mom," she said. "You look tired."

Hair hung in her mother's face, and her cheeks were flushed. "It's been a hard day with Pops. No words." The fine lines around her eyes wrinkled in misery even as her jaw hardened, and Moira knew she'd work twice as hard tomorrow.

"You should take a bath. That'll make you feel better."

Her mother nodded and left the room. Moira closed her book.

"I'll wash."

Moira turned to find her sister standing near the stove. How long had she been there? "I'll do it," Moira said. "I told Mom I would."

"You can dry."

I don't want you here. Go away. The words almost spilled from her mouth, but she shored up her thoughts and retrieved a towel as Maeve filled the sink. It would be stupid to make her sister suspicious tonight. She would meet Ian in just over two hours, at midnight.

Midnight. That had been when Cinderella's ruse fell apart. Moira shouldn't have chosen such a doomed hour. She should never have sent that note. Now she would have to face the consequences as *her* ruse fell apart, when she told Ian the truth.

It's what she had to do.

Deception made her feel like an outsider in her own skin and made her stomach ache—as did the question of how to explain it all now that she'd sent the invitation. She'd considered just not showing up, letting the note become an anomaly. But what if Ian asked Maeve about it? If he showed her the note, Maeve would recognize the writing, so much like her own, as Moira's. That would be the worst. No, tempting as it

110

was to forget everything, she had to come clean. Maybe things would work out. Prince Charming found the right sister eventually, despite her threadbare appearance. Moira would tell Ian how she felt, and maybe he'd see she was as good as Maeve, even if she was less outgoing.

Maeve shut off the water and leaned against the counter. "What's going on?"

"Stop it," Moira said. She could feel Maeve's attempt to probe her thoughts.

"Why do you block all the time now?"

Moira didn't know how to answer that. She stared at the sill, at the young dieffenbachia she'd started in a pot. "I just want my thoughts to stay private. Are you going to wash or not?"

"Daddy told me, you know."

Moira's head snapped back around. "Told you what?"

"That you asked Mom for sax lessons," Maeve said, watching her closely. "Why didn't you tell me you wanted to learn?"

"Because I knew it wouldn't matter. You won't teach me."

"Why won't I? Besides, you're as good on the piano as—"

"Are you deaf? Maybe if I'd had a chance with the sax I could've been as good as you, but we'll never know, will we?" Moira yanked a string from the towel's fringed edge as Maeve cocked her head.

"Why do you act like you have no choice? If you want to learn, then learn. Who says you can't? If you want me to help, ask. Or have Ben Freeman teach you."

"As you already know, Mom won't let me learn."

"What are you, five?"

Moira flung the towel and accidentally hit her young plant. The dieffenbachia landed in the sink. She pulled it out as quickly as she could, but the soil—what remained of it—glistened with suds. "Happy now?" she snapped, then marched away.

Maeve followed her to the living room. "What's wrong with you? Why won't you just ask me for help if you want it?"

"You can't teach, Maeve. You never could. Besides, if there's not enough room for me inside your shadow, then there's not enough room inside your spotlight, either." A bitter tang rose in Moira's throat, shame over her own resentment.

"What's that supposed to mean? Are you jealous? I never thought you cared about—"

"Shut up, Maeve. Leave me alone and stay out of my mind!"

Moira left her there and walked back to the kitchen, but when she heard Maeve run up the stairs, her eyes burned with injustice and regret. She'd never felt such dissonance with her sister. It tipped the world upside down, made everything wrong-footed. But Moira couldn't afford to think about that just now.

She washed and dried the dishes alone, then sat on the couch. No clock had ever moved so slowly; it had to be broken. Could it really be just after eleven? How would she ever live through another hour? Maybe time would move faster under the stars. She pulled on her jacket and shoes, then went outside, careful not to let the back door slam behind her.

"Maeve!"

Ian's voice. Moira froze; she wasn't ready for this. Why had she thought she'd be ready for this? Somehow she heard him speak again over the surge of blood in her ears.

"Here," he said.

Something moved in front of her as she tried to adjust to the darkness. All at once she felt his hand on her cheek and his lips on her mouth, soft and pliant. She let out a soft *Oh* of surprise, then wrapped her arms around his neck and kissed him back until brightness permeated her shut eyelids.

Light from Poppy's room streamed out at them.

"I have to go," she whispered.

"Come back later," he said and grabbed her hand.

She shook her head. "I can't."

"Tomorrow then. At eleven. Everyone's asleep by then."

It would give her time. Time to think and decide. She touched her hand to her lips and nodded.

Back inside, she shrugged off her jacket, and heard a creak of wood. Her mother stood at the top of the stairs, frowning down at her. Moira expected questions about the hour, why her feet were covered in shoes—shoes that felt light, made of magic glass—but that's not what she heard.

"I need to change Poppy's sheets. Can you help?"

Moira nodded and looked at the clock. *It's not midnight yet*, she thought. *It's not midnight.*

CHAPTER TEN

EROSION

The hotel appeared welcoming from the outside, with a sandstone exterior, birdbath, and porch, and little tables set on a cobblestone drive. It was as convivial within: wood floors, bold prints, and urns full of fresh flowers, and a fireplace to rival Garrick's in an expansive entry.

"*Buon giorno!*" said the clerk, a twentysomething man with short curly black hair. A large wreath with a frosting of white lights adorned the wall behind him.

"*Buon giorno! La signora Maeve Leahy e il signor Ryan,*" I said, and he immediately responded with "Welcome to Roma!"—in English.

"I am Giovanni Benedetto Chioli." He slapped his hand over the breast of his red hotel jacket. "Please tell me if you find something not to your liking. I am here, as you Americans say, twenty-four over seven." He leaned close, whispered, "My mama is the boss."

"*Grazie, Signor Chioli—*"

"No, please. You speak English, and I will get my practice." I smiled. So much for applying my Italian. "And it is Giovanni. Your pleasure is my greatest wish." He managed to sound sincere when he said this, and to include both Noel and me in his pledge. He set a key on the counter along with a big purple box wrapped with a bow. "Panettone," he said. "For a happy Christmas."

"Thank you." I accepted the key and the panettone—an Italian brandied bread full of raisins and nuts—then moved aside as Noel stepped up to the counter.

"*Sì?* I mean, yes?"

I leaned forward.

"I'd also like to check in," Noel said.

"I thought—" The clerk looked down at a computer screen, hit buttons. "There is just one room in order. Are you not—?"

"I *knew* it!" I practically shouted. "Kit did this. I'll kill her." Noel stared at me blankly. "I'm sorry," I told the clerk, who wore a similarly bemused expression. "We'll need two rooms, if you have them."

"*Mi dispiace!*" He set a silver box on the counter this time. "For you," he said, motioning to Noel. "I will fix it. You can . . . sit."

He moved with a lithe grace around to the front of the counter, then waved for us to follow. We did—into a small room with a bar in the corner and several tables, each topped with a red flowered cloth and miniature lamp. He said something I didn't catch to the man behind the bar, then turned back to us and set a generous plate of bread, oil, and olives on a table. "You will relax and have wine. It is on the . . . how do you say?"

"On the house?"

He smiled widely. "*Sì!* And you would like rooms that join? Is that, ah, good?"

"That would be perfect," I said, and Giovanni gave a brisk nod and left. I dropped my bag, set my panettone on the table, and sat, but Noel remained standing with his silver box. "Leg cramp? Come on, sit."

He did. Uncomfortable seconds passed.

"I'm sorry about all that," I started. "Kit made the arrangements. I would never—"

"I know, Maeve."

There it was again—that tension. But Noel knew that wasn't what we were, it wasn't what we were, it wasn't.

"You said I could help you. What can I do for you?" he asked, and I felt no closer to him than a stranger who'd jingled the bells on the front door of Time After Time.

"You're mad at me, aren't you? My little adventure took you from far more important things. I'm sorry."

"No, it's—" He pushed his hands through his hair on a long in-hale. "I'm tired. I'm hungry." Exhale. He grabbed a hunk of bread, dredged it through a pool of herbed oil, and took a bite.

I looked at my watch: one o'clock. Fatigue must've eclipsed my hunger, and I hadn't even considered his. Now I noticed the dull sheen of exhaustion in his eyes and that his cheeks, chin, and upper lip were roughed with dark pine-needle stubble. How many hours had he traveled on a rail to get to me? What had he been through before he'd trekked with me, lost, carrying my bag? And all I could focus on was a piece of metal.

We ate in silence, as a soap opera played out on a small-screen TV in the corner. I doubt Noel understood much, but then again, some things defied translation. I studied my hands when a half-clothed couple began making love on a kitchen table.

"All right," he said, pushing aside the plate. "Let's see your *keris*."

"That's okay. You don't have to—"

"Maeve, come on. I'm here. Ready, willing. Able."

I glanced up, but the show had gone to commercial.

I burrowed into my bag, handed Noel the *keris*. And then I sat back and watched as he focused his keen eyes on the sheath. As he traced intricacies with his fingers. As the little mark, his thinking line, formed between his brows. God, I'd missed that. I'd missed him. I wanted the tension between us to go away. I wanted normal back.

"I know you took this to the shop," he said. "What did my grand-father have to say?"

"He said the *keris* is beautiful, probably worth a lot, and in good shape, but he couldn't date it."

Noel nodded. "How is he?"

"Great. The shop's been kicking this month."

"But how's *he* doing?" He looked up, and I noticed his eyes had softened, carried now a warmth reminiscent of melted chocolate. Ah, normal. There it was.

"Really, he's great." I hesitated. "He misses you, though."

"Well," he said. "I miss him."

The barman appeared. He regarded the *keris* with vague interest,

then left us with full glasses of red wine. I took a sip as Noel un-sheathed the blade. He turned it over once. Twice. "What made you fly all the way to Europe for this thing?"

"The *empu* . . . he was following me around Betheny and—"

"Hold on." He leaned forward. "Following you? In Betheny?"

"Around the university. He nailed a book about Javanese weapons to my office door after I won the *keris* at the Block."

"Did you call the police, have him checked out?"

"No, it didn't make me *that* nervous. I felt more intrigued than anything. Besides, Garrick likes him."

"They met?"

"Yep. Sri Putra visited the shop." I'd leave out the possibility that he might've followed me there. "I've never seen him, though. Just his weird black hat at the auction. He bid on the *keris*, too," I explained. "My guess is that he left that book for me afterward to teach me something about the blade."

"Why would he?"

"I don't know," I said. "To be helpful? That's partly why I'm here, to understand all of that. And the notes."

"What notes?"

"Two notes at my office. The second one invited me here."

"So, the one you found today makes three?"

I paused in the act of ripping off another hunk of bread. "You saw that? And here I thought I was quick."

"You were. *He* didn't notice." He smirked. "Did you bring those notes with you, by any chance?"

"Sure," I said, my hand already rummaging through my coat pocket. I handed him all three notes, then watched as he considered them in turn.

"So you didn't have this *empu* meeting set up? You weren't in touch with him about coming?"

"Nope. It was all pretty last minute."

"Guy makes a lot of assumptions."

"I guess so." Noel, I noticed, liked green olives. I chose a black one, popped it in my mouth.

"Don't you think it's a little reckless, flying over here to meet up with someone who's been following you around?"

"Well, it's not like I wanted to at first."

"But you did."

"I did. My father bought the ticket."

"What if I hadn't been here? What if you'd run into that Italian ass without me?"

I rolled the olive pit around in my mouth. "What if I had?"

"Not all men are nice."

I knew he meant this word, *nice*, as a reference to us, because I often said that he was one of the nicest men I'd ever met—a compliment that was both true and safe. But the use of the term now made me bristle—as if I were a naive five-year-old who needed a warning about men with candy.

"Didn't you find it odd that he was in that apartment, acting like he belonged there?" he asked. "*Empus* don't generally live in Italy. Maybe that guy's some con artist, *empu* posing—"

I laughed, and because I was still irritated with him, it erupted from me as a rude guffaw. "If you'd taken more than a semester of Italian you might have understood that guy when he told you he's the landlord," I said. "Besides, your own grandfather met the man. The *empu* is Javanese. And I saw the *keris* Sri Putra bought at Time After Time inside his apartment—an apartment overstuffed with Indonesian culture, I might add."

"I don't like this," he said.

"I think you're overreacting."

"I think I'm underreacting."

He studied me for a minute, then pulled out a magnifying glass and bent over the blade. I breathed, slow and silent. It was Noel's skill at centered observation that made him so adept at finding treasures and conveying details in his art, but I always felt a little itchy when he turned those eyes on me.

"I know why my grandfather couldn't tell you much," he said after a while.

"Why?"

"The *luks*, first of all. *Luks* are the—"

"Curves of the blade, I know. I learned that all on my own. The Internet, see, isn't such an evil thing."

"You're entitled to your opinion," he said with a crooked smile.

"Did you read, on your Internet, that the *luks* are always an odd number?"

"Yes. Garrick said this one has eleven or thirteen."

"The *luks* are ambiguous here at the end," he said, marking the blade's length with his fingers, rounding the tip. "It looks like it has twelve. That can kill the value."

"I don't really care about its value. I won't sell it."

"But you'll travel thousands of miles to learn more about it. I don't get that. Why?" He leaned back, and then he laughed. "Don't tell me—he talked up magic and stardust, didn't he?"

I pursed my lips.

"And you believed it!"

I tapped my foot on the floor, counted to ten.

"Come on. What did the proprietor and chief storyteller of Time After Time tell you about the myths and legends of the mysterious *keris*?" he asked in a mock-spooky voice.

I leaned close. "He said the *keris* can decrease inhibitions, make a person not call the police when they should, fly off to Rome at a moment's notice and—most nonsensical of all—endure their friend's insinuations that they're an idiot incapable of separating fact from fantasy."

"I didn't say that."

"You didn't have to." I pushed the plate back at him. "Maybe you're still hungry. The olives are particularly . . . *nice* . . . don't you think?"

"Huh." He took an olive. I watched him chew and refused to blink when he watched me right back. "Did he tell you to sleep with it under your pillow? That a nightmare tells you if the *keris* is good or bad?"

"No," I lied.

"What did he plant in your head? Did he find a man in the blade?"

I said nothing.

"Did he mention the hole?"

"He said the hole makes the *keris* powerful," I conceded. "Like a window for future events or—"

He snorted. "Thought so."

"All right, Boy Wonder," I said. "What do you think?"

"Batman, please. Boy Wonder was just a tool," he said, and I smiled despite myself. "Expert opinion? The aperture doesn't look man-made. See the blemishes?" He passed me his looking glass, and I peered through it at my blade. The streaks looked exaggerated, and the hole seemed rough edged and marred with flecks of rust. "That reads like neglect, not *empu* intention."

"How old is it?"

He tapped his fingers on the table. "I'd say seventeenth century."

"What else? Why's it always warm?"

"Because the room's warm. Look, whatever he told you, it's not magic metal. It'll be room temperature."

"It feels warm to me."

"Then you're imagining it."

"What about the stain?" I turned the blade over, pointed to the skid of my own blood married to the metal. "I cut myself. That's a blood mark that won't come out." ·

"How did you clean it?"

"Soap and water. Then Garrick used something at the shop."

Again, he examined the blade with the glass. "I don't think that's blood."

"Trust me on this, it is," I said.

"It looks like part of the design to me."

"It's not."

He chuckled and tucked away his magnifying glass. "Is there anything more I can tell you in my professional capacity, or are you through with me?"

"I'm through with you. Want me to buy your ticket back to Paris?" My gut knotted when his expression blanked. Ah, hell. Over the line. Damn line. I never knew for sure where it lay.

I tucked the *keris* back where it belonged, then found the plastic sack. I'd bought more than a guidebook at the airport shop. It wasn't wrapped, but did that matter at a time like this? I set the small bag between us. It gaped open. "For you," I said. "Plastic-bag wrap is in vogue this year, you know."

"What's this?"

"Santa time."

He shook his head. "I don't think so."

"It's okay that you don't have anything for me. Come on."

"I do have something for you." He tossed his napkin on the table. "It's buried under a heap of clothes."

I pushed the bag closer, persisted until he reached in and pulled out a leather-covered book. He looked through the pages, some lined, some blank. My muscles tensed when he said nothing.

"It's an art journal," I said.

"Thank you." His smile seemed . . . sad. "I haven't been drawing."

My mood wilted a little more. "Oh. Bad gift."

"No," he said. "Perfect gift. I haven't drawn, but I want to. I will."

"No time?"

"Something like that." He reached out and brushed his hand over my cheek. "You had a hair near your mouth," he explained. "Friends help friends prevent hairballs, you know."

I turned my head, and noticed that the television couple still writhed together on the table.

A WIDE WINDOW and pair of rose curtains framed a segment of the city in my suite, a plush sage settee sprawled before it. The unconventional bed—two doubles separated by an inch or two but united by a single headboard—boasted a lavish display of pillows. The air carried a hint of lemon, a fan's quiet purr. Kit had done well. I'd bring her back some good chocolate, enough to keep her blood sugar humming into the new year.

It finally hit me as I unpacked. I was sleepy. Dorothy-through-the-poppies sleepy. I attempted to calculate how long it had been since I'd had even a nap, and gave up, sinking into the delectable comfort offered by my mattress. All of my muscles cooed and sighed, *Yes, more.*

The phone rang. I growled at it. It rang again.

"Noel?" The door between our rooms stood ajar. "Do you need something?" He didn't respond. I picked up the receiver. "Hello?" A long pause, then,

"Maeve Amelia Leahy, is that you?"

My insides went tight. "Mom? Everything okay? Did Dad make it home?"

"I just spent an hour on this phone trying to find you, because I wouldn't believe what your father told me," she said. "You left the country, but you wouldn't come home? How much more untouchable can you become?"

My father shushed in the background: "Abby, don't."

Don't listen to her.

"Mom, I just—"

"I'm disappointed in you. In your choices," she said, and I could almost detect honest letdown in her tone, simmering alongside her irritation. Of course she'd expect me to be in Maine, even if she'd spend her time ignoring me and the reasons I'd left. There was so much she'd never forgive. That she was wrong about nearly everything had probably never occurred to her, and I'd never bothered to set her straight—at first too stunned and hurt, and finally too proud to do so.

"Hey, did you say something?" Noel came through the doorway, but stopped when he saw the phone. "Sorry, I'll go."

"No, you don't have to go anywhere," I told him.

"Is that a man?" My mother's voice cracked like thunder and brought with it a flash from my past:

A man? You disgrace this family. You've all left me, left me with—Find her! You have to find her!

Sometimes I still felt the sting of her palm on my cheek.

"Are you all right?" Noel again, and then my father. "Stop it, Abby! She went alone. Let me talk to her."

"You've done enough, Jack! And she's not alone, are you, Maeve?" More guilt. "How could you choose a man over your family at Christmas? How could you?"

It sounded like the phone knocked against something. I thought she'd hung up on me, until . . .

"Sweetheart?"

"Daddy?"

"I'm sorry, Mayfly. Is someone there? Noel?"

"Yes, Dad. Kit set it up. I didn't know, but—"

Pots and pans banged in the background. I heard my father's voice through a muffled phone. "Abby, go sit while I talk," he said, then to me, "Did you get to your *empu?*"

"Not yet, no."

"Well. Go on and see Rome. Do whatever you'd like. Enjoy your time with Noel. Don't worry about the rest of it."

Stupidly, I nodded. "Good-bye, Dad."

"All right, Mayfly. Bye now."

Noel still stood before me. I couldn't hold his gaze for more than a few seconds. All of me felt numb.

"I need some time before we go out," I told him. "A nap."

He nodded and left. The door between our rooms closed.

I hoped for a dreamless sleep.

I STOOD ON a grassy knoll somewhere in Rome as cars battled for supremacy, and raced between statues of black and gray and red. I was not afraid. The *keris* lay across my back, and I knew what I had to do.

Find her, find her, you have to find her!

Find her, before time ran out.

"Moira! Moira!"

A huge bird hovered overhead, like a raven, but monstrous and deformed. It saw her when I did: the little girl with red hair atop a distant hill. Not Moira, but somehow, in this dream, she was. I ran hard, swerved around honking cars and frowning statues. Out of nowhere, a bus accelerated past me, headed for the crest.

"Moira!" I screamed. "Moira!" The *keris* on my back rattled in its sheath, and I pulled it free, ready to war with the bus.

I should've watched the bird. In one swoop, it seized the girl, clasped her in its hooked talons. I shouted Moira's name again as the black-blood speck dissolved into the horizon, and everything—the cars, the bus, even the grass—vanished.

I stood alone in a void with a long, blue shadow. My own, I knew, but sickly somehow. I don't know why I did it. I held the blade in both hands, pointed its tip toward the shadow, lifted my arms, and—

"Maeve? You all right?"

I opened my eyes. My throat felt raw.

"Hey, there." Noel hovered close. "Have a nightmare?"

"Yeah." I grasped at the edges of a lingering dreamworld. "I was just about to slay my shadow with the *keris*."

He chuckled. "The *keris* and the shadow. A Wareham favorite."

I pushed myself upright. "What are you talking about? Garrick never said anything about shadows."

"It's an old belief," he said. "Stab the shadow of an enemy and he'll die."

"Oh." Maybe I was still dreaming. "That's true?"

"That stabbing shadows kills people? Of course it's not true. It's a myth, like all the other stories he told you."

"I would've remembered if he'd told that one."

"Maybe you read about it in that book or on your Internet."

"I didn't." Questions about the *keris* mounded atop one another in my mind; I hoped I remembered them all when I met with the *empu*.

"It's late now," he said, "and it's the middle of the night back in New York. Let's sleep and start over in the morning." I wondered who he'd be in the morning—who we'd be. "Good night."

"Good night. Noel?" He turned back to me. I twisted the sheet in my hand. "You think I'm crazy to come here, don't you?"

"A little crazy." He nodded. "But I think I'm glad."

I swore he mumbled something about inhibitions as he walked back to his room. Whether he meant his or mine, I couldn't say.

Out of Time

Castine, Maine
OCTOBER 2000
Moira and Maeve are sixteen

⸙

The next day moved more slowly than even the one before, but eleven o'clock finally arrived. Moira waited again until the upstairs turned dark and quiet, then stepped outside. Ian didn't say anything this time, just touched her hand. Not hearing Maeve's name made it easier, somehow.

"I thought about you all day," he said.

Moira staved off the impulse to bow her head; instead, she met his eyes, shadowed and intense. "I thought about you, too." Some of those thoughts had lead to guilt, but everything—even her worst self-recriminations—faded at the memory of Ian's kiss.

"So?" he said. "What are we doing?"

It would be easiest to show him her decision. Moira stood high on her toes and kissed Ian for long seconds. "My sister can't know about this," she said when she pulled back. "She'd be jealous."

"No, she wouldn't." He kissed her neck. His lips felt warm.

Moira remembered the words she had to say. "I know her best. If this is going to happen, it stays secret. Never in front of my sister. I won't hurt her that way." She let the stranger within form these words and funnel them out of her mouth, and then followed the same alien instinct and pressed her hips against Ian's. She felt only a little alarmed when he pulled her closer with his hands on her backside.

"We can meet every night after dark," she said, eager to spill all the conditions. "But you can't tell anyone, not even Michael. And when you see me any other time—at school or anywhere else during the day—you have to pretend we're just friends."

She missed the warmth of his mouth when he pulled back. "We've never been friends. And why not during the day? You don't want to be seen with me? You embarrassed of me?"

"No. Oh, no. You're perfect. You're . . . charming."

Ian laughed. "I'm not," he said when Moira shushed him.

"You are to me."

He didn't argue further when she kissed him again.

Later, she snuck into bed, careful not to wake Maeve. She settled under her blankets and glanced out the window at a perfect full moon. Just as beautiful as her sister, the sun, but more . . . welcoming. Touchable. And the moon never burned the eyes of people who looked at her.

Moira slept as the moon shone on in her borrowed light.

CHAPTER ELEVEN

MOUTH OF TRUTH

I knocked on Noel's door the following morning to
no response, and then I tried the handle. It turned, but the only
thing inside his suite was his suitcase. Maybe he'd gone for coffee.

Back in my room, I opened the map, lay it on the mattress. I hovered over it, lazily stroking the *keris* with one hand and sketching a
path to Sri Putra's with the other. Noel might not want to join me,
but I intended to make my way back to the *empu's* apartment and get
answers to my growing list of questions ASAP.

What about pizza and gelato and mangy dogs and sheets on the line?
What about getting a picture for your hall? What about culture and
avventura*? What about*—

My eyes stumbled over the familiar: *Santa Maria in Cosmedin.*
Why had Putra wanted me to see that place? Could it be that he
worked there? Or maybe the place held answers and I'd have to puzzle them out like my own personal da Vinci code.

With a quiver of excitement, I grabbed my guidebook and looked
up *Santa Maria in Cosmedin.* A church. Featured in the film *Roman*
Holiday. A fountain and some temples sat across the street. The
church had a famous drain cover shaped like a god's face—*Bocca*
della Verità, the Mouth of Truth. Well, there went my workplace

126

theory; it seemed unlikely that a Javanese *empu* would choose to work in a Catholic church.

I read on, hoping to stumble over some form of illumination, until the phone rang.

"How's the country?"

"Kit!" I smiled into the receiver. "How are you?"

"*Buena!* That means 'good,' right?"

I laughed, sat on the bed by my map. "You got it."

"Did Noel meet you?"

"Yes, and remind me to kill you."

"Whatever do you mean?"

"The single room. Not a good plan."

"The hotel dude said there were two beds to a room. I just thought . . . well, never mind."

"Exactly." I looked at the bed beside mine—so close but still distinct—and wondered if I'd overreacted. "How are things there? Did you find your present?"

"Love the massage certificate, thanks!" she said. "Clever leaving it under Sam's food. Don't you trust me?"

"Nope. Are you going home to feed him?"

"Well," she said, "I left a really big pile of food."

"He's going to leave you a really big pile of—"

"All right, all right. What about you? What have you seen?"

A comely Italian wielding a sledgehammer, I thought, but Kit's response to that would've been all too predictable. "Took a tour of Trastevere," I said instead. "Lots of delicious smells and old buildings and people kissing on cheeks and all that."

"And Noel? How is he?"

"Good."

"Just good?"

"He's . . . distant." I flopped down on my back. "This whole thing caught him by surprise."

"So go and buy something decent to wear. God knows your wardrobe couldn't entice a man out of gentlemandom."

"Who says I want to entice anyone?"

"I do, but you won't do it with your clothes."

She'd been such a polite, quiet girl growing up. No hint of the rottweiler she'd become. "All those long hours without sleep have turned you mean."

"It's called tough love, sweetie. Seriously, do you own anything that might not have been purloined from the closet of a ten-year-old boy? Or purchased at Unisex-R-Us?"

"Do we have one of those in Betheny? Cool," I said, glancing down at my prone torso. Sure, today's oversized cotton top was figure filtering, but I had a nice set of breasts in there somewhere. Thankfully, she changed the subject.

"How are you doing? Any weird noises?"

"Nothing weird." I hadn't even been aware of the music looping through me until she'd asked. Quiet, smoky blues.

"I found another neurologist for you. Hotter than the last one, just in case things don't work out with Noel."

"Kit—"

"Oops, gotta book. *Buenas noches!*"

"That's Spanish! For good night!"

My smile lingered even after I heard the dial tone, until I heard Noel's phone ring.

"Oh no, you don't." I leaped from the bed, and ran to his room. I couldn't give my matchmaking friend the chance to leave even a five-second message. "Kit—"

"Sorry, must have the wrong room," said an unfamiliar male voice. English.

"This is Noel Ryan's room," I said.

"That's who I'm looking for. Is he there?"

"No. No, I'm sorry. Can I tell him who called?"

"Jakes. He can reach me at—"

"Hold on." I opened the desk drawer. Inside, a FedEx envelope bearing Garrick's familiar bold penmanship seized my attention. Unopened. Unopened? I moved it aside, found paper and pen, jotted a phone number.

"It's important he call me back," the man said.

"I'll be sure he does, Jake."

"Jakes. As in *Mister*. But Jakes is fine."

"Okay, Jakes. Mister. I'll give him the message."

I hung up and touched the envelope. Addressed to Noel in Paris. Sent weeks ago. Why hadn't he opened it?

There was a knock at my door—a fervent one. "Maeve. Maeve, you there?"

Noel. I opened his door and peered down the hall at him.

"What's up?" I asked, when relief flooded his face.

"Nothing."

"Where were you?"

"Nowhere," he said with a strolling tone as he stepped into his room. "Why are you in here?"

I squinted at him, not buying his sudden nonchalance but distracted by that FedEx package.

"I was here playing secretary. You just missed a call from a guy named Jakes." I handed him the note, which he took and crumpled without even a glance. "Hey, he wants you—"

"I know what he wants."

I put my hand on my hip. "What does he want?"

"For me to call him. I have his number. He knows it."

"Who was he?"

"My bloody investigator. How the hell did he find me?"

A dozen questions leaped to mind, but Noel's stone-cold expression warned I shouldn't ask any of them. Besides, I didn't like anyone prying into my secrets, so I'd try to honor his. I couldn't deny wanting to pry a little, though. Okay, a lot.

I tried for levity. "Well, he *is* an investigator."

"Remind me to fire him, will you?"

"He sounded nice enough."

Noel grunted. "Enough about Jakes. Let's forage for food. Breakfast or lunch."

"You didn't eat?"

"Nope, and I'm starved."

"Then where did you—"

"You must be hungry, too," he said. Getting better at evasion.

"Food first," I agreed, "then let's go to Putra's. I think I've figured out a shortcut and—"

"Maeve."

"What?"

"I thought you were going to wait to hear from him."

"I'm impatient."

"You're also in Rome, and not Rome, New York. Rome flipping

Italy. Go see some of it." He paused. "Unless you're a fraud. Maybe your Italian's not as good as you say."

I delivered him a long Italian monologue about his everlasting snit, and promised that if he didn't get over it soon, I'd out him to his investigator and throw him into a Roman cab. I knew he didn't understand a word of it.

"You can't spend all your time chasing after that guy, and that's the truth," he said when I finished.

Truth. A Machiavellian thought took shape. All right, I told him. I knew just where I wanted to go.

WE STOPPED AT a bistro filled with tall tables and stools, and gorged ourselves with chicken *panino*, roasted red pepper, mozzarella, and pesto sandwiches. It would be an understatement to say that Noel seemed distracted.

"Sorry?" he said for the fifth time during our conversation. I'd never had to repeat myself so much or had a companion look so often out the window. It wasn't lost on me, either, that I should be pleased he wasn't using his X-ray vision on me today, but that I wasn't.

I rapped the table with a sugar packet, aggravated with us both. "What's up? Worried your investigator will find you?"

"Jakes?" He made a face. All right, so that wasn't it.

"Worried about wasting your time today? You have somewhere else to be? Maybe you don't want to hang out."

"Sure I do." His eyes darted to the sugar packet, back to the window.

"Worried about letting me guide us through Rome? How about we hit a few antiques shops first?"

"What?"

I sighed—"C'mon"—and prodded him off his stool. "Let's go."

He perked up a little in the shops. One, spanned with brick columns and arches, looked like an extreme makeover of a former aqueduct. Gilded frames held tight to paintings hung on columns; and tables of all shapes and varieties were home to small vases, books, miniature statues, and silver pieces. There were wood-framed couches, children's rockers and large dressers, standing mirrors and lamps. He was lost to it all, gathering finds and arranging to have them sent to Betheny. He came back to reality eventually, seemed to notice my twitchy legs and me.

"Sorry," he said. "This isn't exactly seeing Rome, is it?"

"No, not really." I looked at him through the lattice framework of an old folding screen. "But I have a cure for that, if you trust me." He was quiet for so long that I thought I'd have to repeat myself again. "Noel?"

"Should've brought my sketchbook," he muttered, and I took a big step back from the screen. He shook his head. "All right, Maeve. Cure away."

WITH THE MAP in my hand and a fledgling's confidence, I led us to Aventine Hill, where I was steeped in surreality. Here stood republican temples and kids tossing pebbles into the Tiber. I lay back in yellowing grass atop one of Rome's seven hearts and admired riverbank trees—pines with sprigs just on top, pointing toward the sky as if paying homage to a sun god. Helios? No, he was Greek.

"Who's the Roman sun god?"

Noel shrugged, his face framed in the long rays of some god whose name neither of us knew. Still distant. Still different. Maybe he'd understood my Italian diatribe after all.

"Come on." I nudged him with my knee. "You're Garrick Wareham's grandson. Don't tell me he didn't make you take a class or two in mythology." I thought I remembered him studying this at Betheny U, along with ancient civilizations and art history. Thinking back to those days always took me too close to the edge, though. Too close to Before, to the days of plenty and daydreams and hope and wholeness, when I'd pretended to be Alvilda, daughter of the king of Gotland.

"Why haven't you done this before?" Noel asked, and I felt momentarily disoriented. I ran my palm over the grass.

"What?"

"Come to Rome. Gone anywhere. You speak so many languages, so why not?"

"I don't know." Clouds drifted in flocks today, and I found myself hunting for Alfred, the dragon who always eluded me. Maybe he only came out in Castine, for believers like Moira. "I guess I didn't want to go it alone."

A pause, then: "Sol."

"What's that?"

"The Roman sun god."

I stood along with him, though I felt a little thrown, like a pebble skipped over the Tiber. "Thanks."

We walked in silence until I knew my sense of direction hadn't failed me again. There stood a fountain, a high bell tower, a church lined with archways and medieval windows. *Santa Maria in Cosmedin.* I knew *cosmedin* meant "decorative," ornamental like cosmetics, but Santa Maria looked rather plain to me.

"Let's stop here," I said, trying for casual.

"Where's here?"

"Let's find out." I led us past a sophisticated nativity scene to a portico and columned walk. There, at the end of it, sat a large, round, ancient face. *"Bocca della Verità,"* I said, like an introduction. "The Mouth of Truth."

"Hmm," he said.

I smiled. "Anyone who puts his hand into the mouth and tells a lie will have it snapped off by marble jaws."

"Hmm."

"Talkative today."

"I never should've gotten out of bed this morning. I see that now."

"So, go stick a hand in."

"For what? I'm an open book."

I clucked at him when he pocketed his hands.

"That's mature."

But it worked, because he stepped up to the mask, shot me a doleful look, then placed his hand inside the mouth. I wanted to know so much. Why was he ignoring his investigator? Why didn't he open that FedEx? Why had he stopped sending me postcards?

"Why didn't you finish my painting?" I asked.

"Your painting?"

"The one in your studio. Why didn't you finish it?"

His jaw slackened. His hand fell.

"Hand in." Good heavenly Sol, I couldn't believe I'd asked about that. Still, now that I had, I would have my answer. I recalled the half-finished work, my frustration over finding it abandoned. "You're speechless."

"Just about."

"That's not an answer, you know."

He hesitated. "I needed more material."

"More paper? More paint?"

"More knowledge."

"What—"

"Uh-uh." He withdrew his hand. "You've had two questions already. My turn." His smile expanded and drew up on one side—a man who knew the game now and wanted to play.

The mask's hollow eyes and nostrils looked ominous, lined with the dark veins of time, but I put my hand inside the cold marble and waited.

"How did you find that painting?"

"I—uh . . ." There was nothing more backward-of-brilliant than stumbling into your own trap.

"Speechless?"

I said it, fast. "I thought you were in your studio because of the light, so I went in and saw you weren't there, but everything was picked up so neat, and everything was off the walls, and I kind of freaked out and decided to mess things up a bit, to pretend like you were there, and so I took some paper down and started to paint, and after I filled one page, I turned to another, and that's when I saw it. Me. There I was."

He stayed still as stone himself—probably because he couldn't process what I'd said or imagine the scene. Because it was so unlike me. I still didn't know why I'd done it.

"The *keris*," I said. "The *keris* made me do it."

"I thought you didn't believe in the *keris*."

"I don't."

He dragged a hand over his face. Maybe I'd finally confounded him. "Did you feel better?" he asked. "After?"

"After what?"

"After you'd played in the paint."

"Yes." I pulled my hand from the mouth. "Now you."

"But—"

"That was three questions. You owe me one."

He groaned, but put his hand inside the marble. "Interrogate away."

I felt less concerned now, since I'd humiliated myself already, about delving into the personal. "Truth. Why have you been out of touch? Were you planning to stay in Europe forever?"

He dipped his chin. "I haven't met my goal."

His mother. I nodded. "You're no closer to finding her?"

"Maybe."

"That's not much of an answer."

"It's the best I can give right now."

"And what about Garrick?"

"What about him?"

"He doesn't know why you came here, does he?"

"He didn't, no."

I knew the answer this time but asked the question anyway. "He knows because of me and my big mouth over Thanksgiving, right? I didn't know you hadn't told him, Noel. I didn't think asking about her would—"

"It's fine," he said. "I never asked you not to talk about it. You didn't know."

Had Garrick made the investigation difficult? Maybe this was why Noel had been so remote. I was reconsidering asking about that unopened FedEx when he stepped back, his eyes black beneath the shaded portico.

"Your turn again," he said.

What had started as a game of sorts had evolved into a battle. I needed a white flag. I put my hand inside the marble.

"What are you afraid of?"

"Pain," I answered without thinking, the word rising up and out from some inner wellspring of truth. I cringed, hating the implication of it: that I was weak, that I couldn't take a bruise or bump or cut. That wasn't truth. It wasn't that sort of pain. I closed my eyes, saw the water behind the door, and felt, for a second, what it would be like to be naked in the crosscurrent.

"What kind of pain?"

I would've been glad for a chance to take the answer back, refine it, if only it led to light.

Tell him.

"What should I say?" I asked.

"The truth, Maeve."

"The pain of regret." I shivered, exhausted. "Loneliness." My voice became a shadow of itself. Noel moved closer.

"Who's Moira?"

He might've punched me.

"Who's Moira?" he repeated.

Truth.

"My sister."

"The sister you lost?"

"Yes."

I'd told him that much—that I'd had a sister once, but I'd said no more. I wouldn't linger in the past. He got that. It was like an unspoken deal between us, not to prod into those parts of one another's lives, the secret pains. His mother. My sister. A golden hush we'd shattered in minutes with mouths of truth.

"You know her name. How?" This, I'd never shared.

"You shouted it last night."

The dream. The malformed bird. The bus. The little girl with the red hair. My hand slipped from the Mouth, landed against my thigh.

" 'The pain of regret.' Is Moira why you regret?" he asked, and I felt jerked under his magnifying glass against my will. "Is Moira why you haven't traveled, because you're going it alone, without her? Is Moira why you work all the time, why you won't let anyone in?"

I clutched at my shirt, the thin cotton over my heart. "Stop saying her name."

"I can't believe she'd want that for her sister."

"You didn't know her! You don't know what the hell you're talking about!" I struck his chest—once, twice. But instead of pushing me off, he touched my face. My hands calmed as reflexively as they'd knotted. "I'm sorry." Mortified.

"It's all right, Maeve." His eyes softened. "Thank you."

"Thank me? For hitting you? I'm sorry I hit you, I didn't mean to hit you, I was just, just—"

"Thanks for giving me a little more material."

I understood then why he hadn't finished the painting, just how much of myself I'd withheld. But that was then. Truth had torn something open in me and more of it surged out.

"I missed you, Noel. So much."

He winced, and it was like his eyes cleared of some horrible cataract. He looked at me—really looked at me—and my Chinese Brother mouth smiled, my lungs filled completely for the first time in months. It was then, enfolded in his tight hug and with my face buried in his coat, when the angels began to sing. At least they sounded like angels.

Noel and I stepped through the church entrance and inside a sanctuary lit with candles. There, atop a mosaic floor, stood a choir garbed in rich yellow robes. I thought about Sri Putra for the first time in hours, wondered if he could be up there, trying to tell me something in a song. But there was no sign of a short Javanese man or a pillbox hat.

The question of what Sri Putra had intended for me here faded as harmony meshed with melody, as voices rose and fell, as soft tones gave way to boisterous ones.

Christmas Eve. I'd nearly forgotten.

Another song began, a lone bagpiper's reedy chant that droned solemnly outside of the church. These different concerts might have been cacophonous, yet they were not. Somehow, each remained rich and beautiful, and became all the more poignant for its place in the crosscurrent.

Out of Time

Autumn took hold of Castine. The wind whipped, the leaves dropped, and the sea churned gray. Moira tried not to think about Maeve or their rift. She worked to keep her mind sealed. But though her time with Ian—full of kisses and whispers in the hammock at night—fed a yawning need within her, her deception cost.

Her appetite abandoned her, and her head hurt more often than not. She dreamed of discovery. Once naked in a tree with the entire town and Ian below chanting, *Witch, witch, witch.* Once called out before the whole school, made to take up the saxophone, and blow through a broken mouthpiece until frogs leaped from the bell.

One night she dreamed dogs and men with guns chased her. She ran all the way to a foreign sea to escape them, and swam until her muscles screamed agony. Somehow, Maeve's hands found her and lifted her up each time she thought she'd drown. But when Moira found a lone island and safety, Maeve didn't emerge beside her. Instead, her twin's body bobbed facedown in the deep, her head enwreathed in sodden strands of flame.

Moira shrieked when she woke to Maeve hovering over her.

"Are you all right?" Maeve asked.

"No, I'm not all right! You scared the crap out of me!"

"It's your fault. You called my name."

Moira wrestled with the covers. "I'm fine. Just go."

"Why don't you tell me what you're doing? I know something's going on, you know."

"Don't be a drama queen."

"Well, I do feel a little like a queen lately." Maeve tipped her head. "I thought maybe I'd ask Ian on a date."

Moira's chest felt thrust into her throat. "Maybe you shouldn't. Maybe he already has a girlfriend."

"I don't know," Maeve said. "He seems to like me pretty well. At school or at The Breeze, he smiles at me in a way I don't see him do with other girls. That says something, right?"

This couldn't be happening, Moira thought. It wasn't possible. Did Maeve know? Was she taunting her, or was she serious about making a play for Ian? "I thought you hated him!"

"Everyone can change. Right, Moira?"

It took a lot of effort, but Moira didn't swallow the pool of saliva in the back of her throat. "Don't do it. Mom wouldn't like it."

"Oh, I think there are probably ways to sneak out if I had to. Mom doesn't need to know a thing. But I'd have to be careful about the moonlight. It reveals so much." Maeve's shrewd gaze pinned her, and Moira couldn't help but swallow then. "Tell me what you're doing," Maeve demanded. "Are you in trouble?"

I've kidnapped you, and bound your mouth and wrists! Moira thought. *Can't you feel the cuts on your skin? Stop me!*

But Moira's words, when they came, sounded calm and cold. "It's none of your business if I'm in trouble. Stay out of it and leave me alone. I might call for you in my dreams, but I don't need you. I'm fine without your help."

The pain in Moira's stomach intensified when Maeve took her pillow and a blanket from her bed, and left the room without another word. This couldn't go on forever, yet she couldn't imagine its end. Couldn't bring herself to apologize for her words or actions, either. Not yet. Not with so much at stake.

INTERMEZZO

*V*isions of home danced relentlessly in my head on Christmas morning. Moira's music was back, too—the song about twinkling stars she'd always played on this day. I couldn't handle that. *Good-bye, song,* I thought, surprised and a little disappointed when it receded easily. A mild headache took its place.

"Damn *eling*," I muttered, but I picked up the phone and dialed anyway.

"We're not here right now. Leave a message and we'll get back to you," said my father's timeworn voice on the machine. I waited for the beep.

"I just wanted to say Merry Christmas." That I miss you. Love you. Wish you were here. "Merry Christmas." It wasn't until after I hung up that I remembered it was 2:00 a.m. in Maine. Idiot.

My phone rang a short while later, and I surged for it. No one answered my greeting, though. Like the night before my father's arrival in Betheny, I sensed someone on the other end, waiting, listening. Breathing.

"Mom? Dad?"

The phone went dead; I left it off the hook.

Christmas Day continued with a whimper. Noel had left a note under my door.

Merry Christmas, sleepyhead. My caffeine addiction had less patience for you than I did, so I left to satisfy it. Will bring back something appropriately festive for breakfast.

-N

Maybe I should head to Trastevere before he got back. The *empu* had yet to reach out to me; I'd called the front desk frequently to check for messages. This, however, could be the perfect day to reach him. It seemed unlikely that *empus* would celebrate Christmas, and nearly everything that wasn't a church would be closed for the holiday.

The more I thought about it, the more convinced I became that Putra would be home, and so that's how Noel found me upon his return—my feet stuffed into shoes and the *keris* in my hand.

"No. It's Christmas," he said, easily reading my intent.

"But—" I started, and he lifted a big white bag. The scent of warm pastry and coffee had me wavering on the threshold. "Later then. After breakfast."

Without answering, Noel set up a little table for us near a window in his room. From the bag, he produced napkins, paper plates, and something wrapped in wax paper that left a sigh of powdered sugar in the air, dancing like dust motes.

"I could use a little break," he said when we sat. "I didn't sleep well last night."

"I'm sorry. I can go alone, though. I was planning on it."

"What do you say we take it easy today? I know we're in Rome, I know you're anxious to see the *empu*. But it's Christmas. A rest day. Can't we have that?" Something showed briefly in his expression, made me swallow the leap-ready words on my tongue. Distress? Alarm?

"Where did you go this morning? What happened?" I asked.

"I went to the bakery and bought naughty things. And *those* are the only two questions you're allowed today."

I caught a whiff of warm-cherry scent. "All right. Today, an *intermezzo*, but tomorrow it's back to Putra's. Tomorrow," I repeated firmly. "No matter what."

"Tomorrow," he said, producing two Styrofoam cups bleeding coffee at the lip. "No matter what."

I was only halfway through my tart when Moira's song surged in me again, and again I pushed it back. My headache worsened. My appetite disappeared. I pinched a piece of my pastry and watched as filling oozed out in a gruesome cherry death.

"You all right?" Noel asked. I wasn't one to let confection go to waste, and he knew it.

"Just feeling a little far-flung today."

"Sorry. You know you didn't have to come here for that *keris*."

"Well, I—"

"You could've had it appraised by an expert in the States—"

"But—"

"—or sent it to Java and found a real *empu*."

I pointed a cherry-coated finger at him. "Putra *is* a real *empu*. Besides, I can't put the *keris* in the mail. What if it's lost?" I asked, then licked my finger clean.

He sighed as he deposited a small wrapped box with a looping red bow on the table before me.

"What's this?"

"A Maeve Leahy tactic. When things get tense, give a gift."

"What a good student you are." I lifted the present, gave it a shake. "Could it be a tiny, rectangular panettone?"

"No. Go on."

I unwrapped the box, opened the lid. Made a sound, inarticulate. Draped over a quilt of cotton lay a necklace coated with deep red gems.

"They're garnets," he said.

"Holy extravagance, Batman! Noel, I gave you paper!" If I'd been home, if he had, if I'd been prepared to see him, I would've given him something better than a blank book from an airport gift shop, surely, but nothing close to the level of gems.

"I love my journal. I've been using it."

"Really? Do tell." I leaned forward. So did he.

"Tell me what you think," he said. "*The Impotent Artist*. Some poor guy holding a limp paintbrush."

"Oh, uh-huh."

Noel's smile vanished. "It's not . . . me. I mean, I can . . ."

I looked down, around, anywhere but at Noel.

He snorted first, and then we broke down into paroxysms of laughter. "Bloody hell." He wiped his eyes and stood. "Let's see that."

I handed him the necklace. He moved behind me, and then the chain hung before my eyes and bounced twice on my chest.

"Garnets are good for preventing nightmares. So says my grandfather—and the storekeeper in Paris."

"Paris? You bought this before you knew about my nightmares?"

"Must be fate. A Maeve Leahyesque mannequin wore it just a toss from where I stayed. I had to have it. And now, let's see."

He turned me around. I studied his eyes as he studied me. "Well?"

"Much better than the mannequin." He reached forward and trailed his fingers over gems near my collarbone.

Avventura, something in me whispered.

"I love it, thank you," I said. Was that my voice, sounding all breathless? "You shouldn't have." And a cliché. God.

I had a hard time keeping the smile off my face that morning, even though my headache didn't improve. Noel made an educated guess about the pain when he caught me with my head thrown back in a chair, rubbing my temples.

He grabbed his coat. "I'll run out. There has to be an open pharmacy somewhere. People get sick on holidays all the time."

"Don't bother," I said. "Drugs won't touch it."

"I'll pick up lunch, too. Maybe you're hungry," he said, patting the coat with his hands before throwing it down again. I sat up, watched with a growing suspicion as he looked under the bed, behind the table. I stood beside him as he opened drawer after drawer of his desk and dresser. I spied a blue-gray check, pajamas maybe.

"You lost your wallet," I said as he checked his coat for the third time. "When's the last time you had it?"

"The tarts."

"And you came right back?"

He cursed. "I walked through a crowd of artists, kids, beggars. One of them knocked into me."

"Stolen?"

"Must be. Shit." He tallied his losses as church bells tolled in the distance. "Credit cards, traveler's checks, euros, photographs, the key to my place in Paris. I'll have to call Ellen."

"Ellen?"

"I'm renting part of her house."

"You have your own place?" I sat on the bed, dizzy. "How long are you planning to stay?"

"I don't know." He opened a drawer, pulled out a piece of paper and pen, started writing. "Oh, a debit card, too."

"Noel," I said, louder. "Are you staying in Paris indefinitely?"

"What?" he said, then, "I don't know. Paris is the best. Amazing antiques, wine, interesting people. Ellen's great." A noise came from my throat, part grunt, part growl. He seemed oblivious. "No one ever stole my wallet in Paris, and everyone seems to know a little English."

"I thought the French hated Americans," I argued.

"Oh, they do, but one of the benefits to being homeschooled by an Englishman is I can pass as a Brit when I want," he said with a thickened accent. "The French hate the English just slightly less than the Americans. And I can always tell someone to bugger off."

God, I loved that accent.

"So, this Ellen—Ellen, the great," I said, unable to help myself. "She's the reason you're staying in Paris?"

He cocked his head, and then he had the audacity to laugh. "If I didn't know better, I'd swear you're jealous!"

I tightened my lips, which only made him laugh harder.

"Maeve Leahy, jealous? Of Ellen Dubois?"

"I'm not."

"Come on, make my day. I've been robbed, after all, and it is Christmas." He hunched his back, took on a conspiratorial whisper. "Be just a little jealous."

"No."

"C'mon." He winked.

"Maybe just a little."

His grin widened. "Pinch me, I'm dreaming."

And because he sounded cocky, I reached across the table, aimed for his arm, and obliged his request.

"Hey, ow."

"I'm not jealous-jealous," I said.

"Good." He rubbed his arm. "Because she's eighty-three. Though I'll admit she looks cute in her running shorts."

"You're horrible."

Ink swept over the page as he made notes about who to call, steps he'd have to take. I wandered into my room and lounged on the settee, traced my necklace, and thought of eighty-three-year-old Ellen, who'd been born a few generations too late.

"Feeling better?" he asked, looking at me from the doorway.

I thought about it, nodded; my headache was gone.

"Thought so. What's that song?"

Only then did I hear the melody sprung from my throat— hummed notes that carried an air of joviality, of Parisian necklaces, cherry tarts, and handsome men. "I don't know," I said. "Too merry? Not postrobbery enough?"

"Nah, it's nice," he said. "What is it?"

"I don't know. I'm making it up as I go."

His eyes honed in on something beyond me. "Maeve."

"Hmm?"

"Your phone's off the hook. What—"

"It's nothing," I said. "Just didn't want to talk to anyone today." A small fib, but worth it. The query on his face smoothed over.

"Why talk when you can hum, right?" he said.

My eyes stung a bit as I matched his smile and started up again, consciously this time, welcoming my new-old gift back, unwrapping its song, inviting it to stay awhile.

CHAPTER TWELVE

DARK NOTES

*S*unshine streamed through the window the next morning, and a melody played itself in my head. The hummed bit I'd made up the day before had evolved into something more complex. I didn't shut it down, just left it to whatever sustenance it might find within me. What a relief that these sounds were not piano. They weren't sax, either. Just pure tone, the way it used to be. I couldn't think what it meant, to be rejoined with this long-gone part of myself, but I felt more refreshed than I had in years and my blood seemed to fizz, effervescent, a restless brew in my veins.

I plotted my day. I'd have to call Kit and tell her just how fine I was and that Noel was back to his old self. But before that, I wanted to explore. And before *that*, I meant to find Sri Putra. I had my persuasive speech prepared for Noel but didn't need it in the end. He'd stuck a note under my door.

I have to deal with my bloody wallet this morning, but I'll be back to hunt empus with you after lunch. Be my date? ps. If you go out, you may want to put your keris in the safe.

Noel was humoring me, I knew; he'd hate having to dedicate any part of what remained of his day to my *keris* obsession. So I'd spare him and go by myself.

I showered and dressed, and eventually slunk over to the mirror for a cursory check. It was still impossible to see anything but her in the looking glass, even after draining my color and hacking my strands. I spied a hint of red roots, then tousled my hair to hide them. That fix would have to wait.

Traffic or no traffic, I would have *avventura* today.

WALKING THROUGH ROME with a weapon in hand sounded like a ticket to trouble, so I did something I'd never done before. I bought a purse—a big one, with room enough for the *keris*. I probably should've just tucked the blade down a pant leg and secured it with a shoelace, Alvilda-style. Whatever, at least now I could tote it around without drawing attention to myself, and, I thought wryly, I'd have some defense against pickpockets.

Though I knew it worked out on paper, I still impressed myself when I located Sri Putra's place. I'd nearly forgotten about the sledge-wielding landlord until I stepped through the door and saw him walking up the stairs.

"You're back," he said, stopping to tip his head. "Unencumbered."

Three things happened in close succession.

I gasped as a static charge radiated through my bag-wielding arm, raising gooseflesh all over my body.

The Italian bolted down the stairs. "It will always be a struggle for you!" he said. "Why not let me have it? I can care for such things."

"Wha—What are you talking about?" I leaned away, took a step, but he followed each movement, inch for inch.

"Don't be alarmed. You have the *keris* with you, yes? I know why you fear it!"

"I don't fear it!"

"You should, it is too much for you." So close now I could smell his breath, a strong, sweet mint. "Let me take it. I will even buy it. It will be very fair."

"I don't want to sell it! Back off—"

146

"Why not be reasonable? Let me see it." His fingers had somehow slithered inside my purse.

That's when the third thing happened, just as I yanked my arm back, a hundred blue curses crystallizing on my tongue: A woman walked into the apartment building behind me, carrying groceries. She was old, weathered as a Castinian, but with sharp Italian eyes that spied the man's hand resettling on my purse.

"Cosa sta facendo?" she asked him. What are you doing?

He lifted both hands in the air, took a step away from me. *"Sto cercando d'aiutare la signora."* Just helping the lady.

"I don't need help," I retorted, tucking the purse tightly beneath my arm again. It no longer tingled.

"Ah." He nodded. "We will see."

"No," I said. "We won't."

He smiled at me, then addressed the woman. "Now, Mrs. Fiori," he said in Italian. "Don't work yourself up again, remember your heart. You know I wouldn't harm a hair on her head, anymore than I would harm a hair on yours."

Pears tumbled out onto the peeling linoleum when she dropped her bag. Chuckling, the landlord disappeared up the steps. She stared after him, her olive flesh pallid; maybe she did have a heart condition. I retrieved her pears, some with torn skins, and stuffed them back inside the bag, then offered to help carry her groceries.

"Mi segua, prego!" she agreed, and led us down the hall with a limp. From her belt loop, she produced a key on a crocheted band, and unlocked a door a few feet from Putra's apartment, on the opposite side of the hall. The smell of onions wafted out at us as she set her bag inside. I handed her the bag I'd carried as she regarded me.

She asked if I knew who that man was.

The landlord, I replied.

She clicked her teeth. *"Come si chiama?"*

Though unused to strangers asking me, flat out, for my name, I told her: *"Mi chiamo* Maeve Leahy." I was here to visit with Sri Putra, the *empu,* I said. Did she know where he was?

He's dealing with an illness, she said.

What illness? I wanted to know.

She scrunched up her face, asked if I was a troublemaker.

No, I told her. I just wanted to see Sri Putra.

"Why do you?" she asked in her tongue.

I hesitated, then pulled the *keris* from my bag. Her eyes bulged as she backed into her apartment.

"Wait!" I said. "I'm not going to hurt you. It's just a—"

"I know what it is," she said, hiding behind the door. *"Magia nera."*

"Black magic? You're joking."

She looked at me sternly, said it was no joke.

"I'm sorry," I told her, "but I don't believe in those things—curses and spells and voodoo dolls."

"Maeve Leahy." My Irish name distorted in her mouth. "You look like a good girl. You should not be here. You should not have that . . . thing." Again, her eyes dipped to the blade. "And you should stay away from Ermanno."

"Ermanno? Is that the landlord? What's wrong with him?"

She lowered her voice. "They hate one another. They will destroy one another. The woman will be hurt—always the woman. You will be, if you don't get rid of that."

I didn't understand, and told her so.

"It is true that Ermanno is the man you met, but he is not a land-lord," she said. "Only the landlady's son. He is taking over tem-porarily. He has always done crazy things but not had such power to match his skeleton-key fingers. Now, I fear he will creep in at night and pluck at my hair for his spells if the rent is late." She crossed herself.

"He's just trying to intimidate you," I said. "Like a schoolyard bully."

"No, he tries to summon evil spirits." *Demone* was the word she used. "He tries to conjure the magic his brother brings from the east. I thought that was all behind us, but now that the *empu* brother is back—"

"Fratelli?" They're brothers?

"Fratellastri." Half brothers. Sri Putra's mother had been Asian, she explained, and Ermanno's Italian. They shared a father. "Now go and never return. There is no good here." She shut the door.

At least now I understood why Sri Putra lived in Rome. He and Ermanno were brothers. Half brothers. One short and clearly Javanese, as Garrick had confirmed; the other tall and seemingly a purebred Italian.

I took a few steps and knocked on Sri Putra's door, hoping Mrs. Fiori was mistaken as to his whereabouts. No response. I breathed a little quicker, though, when I spied another note addressed to me. I tore it free of a nail, read.

Visit Il Sotto Abbasso

Taken literally, that meant "the under down." Was I meant to search under something? Was there a trapdoor in Putra's apartment? A basement of some sort?

My hand hovered over the doorknob as I considered trying my luck again with the weak lock, but then I noticed Ermanno standing with his eyes on me—no, on the *keris* in my hand—from the wrong end of the hall. The building must have two sets of stairs. How long had he been there, what had he heard?

I didn't wait to find out. I bolted down the hall the way I'd come, my head full of demon spirits and my nose the stench of onions.

I DIDN'T LIKE to admit that Ermanno had bent any of my steel nerves, but I looked behind me more than a dozen times as I traced my path back to the hotel. It didn't help that I felt the lift of my skin, the sense that someone's eyes were all over me. Then I realized that *everyone's* eyes were on me and that I still held the *keris*, and so I tucked it back into my bag.

It must be very powerful or he wouldn't want it so badly.

Hadn't Glinda said something like that to Dorothy about her red shoes? Though I didn't believe there was anything otherwordly about the *keris*, I had to admit that shock had been curious. Maybe the threat of black magic had been enough to make even a *keris* flinch. Or—I smiled—maybe that zap was the universe's way of telling me I shouldn't carry a purse.

I'd nearly reached the hotel when a mime's street performance caught my attention. Dressed all in black, with a spade painted over one eye, the man entertained a small crowd with a deck of cards.

Choose one, he'd indicate with a sweep of a gloved hand, and someone would. *Now, tuck it back in the deck.*

I knew the trick, the way he marked the chosen card with another so that he could find it again in a flash. Moira and I had awed our friends with that exact illusion countless times; it was one of the allowables. Harder to explain were the times we'd be separated and know what the other was holding—or what the other was feeling. But that wasn't magic. That was just . . . *just.*

The mime did a quick shuffle, then lifted the two of diamonds before a young boy, who giggled and clapped along with the others. A good trick. The man caught my eye, offered me the deck, but I shook my head and kept walking.

My skin rose up again, but I didn't look back. I wouldn't fear Ermanno. He was just a man, as he'd said. A man and perhaps a fool, for trying to appear more than he was, for making others like Mrs. Fiori with her bruised pears afraid of him over something as phony as *magia nera.*

Phony or not, though, there was no reason for Noel to know about today's adventure. What would he have done if he'd seen Ermanno's hand in my bag? I imagined heated words. Dagger-eyed stares. Pistols at dawn. A sword fight. I grinned, despite myself. The beautiful, noble Englishman versus the beautiful, twisted Italian. I knew whose cravat I'd have tied around my arm, the scent of it faint with turpentine.

THOUGH MY ITCH to explore never lessened, Putra's latest note took priority. Visiting Santa Maria in Cosmedin and the Mouth of Truth—though I hadn't a clue why he'd wanted me to go there— had brought good things. I was beginning to think that Il Sotto Abbasso must be a Roman attraction, too, since Putra must've known that my gaining entry to his apartment with Ermanno lurking would be unlikely. This was a disappointment; finding a trapdoor would've been fun.

I was passing through the hotel lobby on the way to my room when I ran into Giovanni. "You weren't kidding when you said you work all the time."

"I told you, my mamma is the owner. But what can I do? She makes fantastic cannoli." He winked at me.

Ah, Italians.

"Any messages?" I asked.

"One. Your friend, Noel, wanted me to tell you that he is at the shops."

Oh, well. Hearing from Sri Putra would've been more surprising than not at this point, anyway. I pictured Noel appraising antiques throughout the city and wondered if he'd remember our lunch date; the lost scepter of Romulus would trump his appetite any day of the week.

"He needed clothes," Giovanni said, rupturing the image.

"Clothes? Noel needed clothes? You're kidding."

"Does this look like kidding?" He pointed to himself, his sober expression. "It is why his wallet was stolen from him—wearing blue jeans on Christmas." He tsk-tsked.

"But he just went for pastries!"

"He knows now he must look his best for *passeggiata*."

I'd heard of *passeggiata*—when families went out to stroll the town in their finest clothes, confident they looked better than the neighbors.

"You two will have not a euro left if you are not careful. 'When in Rome' does not come from nothing." His hands flew; God only knew what they said. "You look like tourists."

"We are tourists."

"You look like . . . a red spot."

I scrunched my face to match his. "We look like pimples?"

"Targets." The word burst from him. "They will crush your grapes and make you wine if they see you are tourists!"

I repressed a laugh. "Do we look that bad?"

His eyebrows did a funny dance—up with one, down with the other and switch—as he scowled at my faded Bugs Bunny sweatshirt. I covered Bugs in a protective gesture with my right hand. Moira and I had bought two of these tops when we were fifteen. Oversized. Perfect. Obviously long lasting. Exactly identical. Our mother had hated them. But, okay, maybe I was underdressed.

"All right, name a nice shop with reasonable prices." I wasn't tenured, after all. Yet.

"Mariella's shop is close. You give her my name and she will turn you . . ." He kissed his fingers.

"And what if I don't want to be—?" I made a rain shower of kissing sounds.

"*Passeggiata,*" he repeated, a grave wisdom in his voice.

I lifted my hands in a gesture of defeat. "I'll go, but I have a mystery to solve first. I don't suppose 'Il Sotto Abbasso' means anything to you?"

He looked around, lowered his voice. "It is secret place, in the underground."

"Harlem Nocturne" kicked in again.

"What is it, exactly?" I asked.

"A place to dance and drink and—"

"A club?"

"Yes, a club under the ground. It is, how you say, hot."

A club, huh. Sri Putra wanted me to go to a club? "I'd like to go there sometime, with Noel," I said. "How do I get there?"

"It is only open on Sunday night—tomorrow. It is good luck that Mama let me have the night off. I can take you two. You would not find it without me. But first you will visit Mariella," he continued. "You cannot wear bunny man to Il Sotto Abbasso."

It was my turn to raise a brow. "I have some nice pants—"

"We will dance."

"If you think I'm going to buy some sort of flowy skirt—"

"Flowy? Like flow-in-the-dark?"

I covered my mouth, but laughter burbled out.

"Go to Mariella's," he said. "She will fix you."

"And you're sure about the bunnies? Maybe just a little one?" I couldn't help myself.

He scowled. "No bunnies."

KEEPING NOEL'S ROBBERY and his sensible advice in mind, I left the blade in the safe in my closet, then made my way to Mariella's. A saleswoman in a bronze-toned belted suit and pointy shoes approached as soon as I stepped through the door (Mariella herself, as it turned out). I needed an outfit, I explained. Pants and a top. For dancing.

She threw me in a dressing room and poured me into something scandalous. Not a pant leg or cartoon character in sight. I couldn't wear it.

"The flower is in full bloom." *In piena fioritura.* "You have nice breasts," she said. "Why not show them off a little?" She sounded like Kit. Maybe that's why I let her bully me into buying what I did.

I was standing at the counter, my credit card still smoking in my hand, when I saw him. Turned away from me, but close by, lurking in a corner. Tall. Dark. Ageless as Romulus himself. I would've felt better about it with the *keris* in my bag, but I called his name anyhow.

"Ermanno."

He turned, perplexed. This was not Ermanno's face, but I thought, for a crazed second, that it still might've been him. *Magia nera.*

The man smiled, asked if I'd mistaken him for someone. I was losing it.

I apologized to the stranger, grabbed my stuff, and left before I changed my mind again.

Out of Time

Castine, Maine
LATE OCTOBER 2000
Moira and Maeve are sixteen

The lighthouse became Moira's favorite place to meet Ian, though there was nothing light about it; it'd been defunct for as long as she could recall. Still, he always brought a flashlight, and they walked up together, kissing, laughing, ducking when a car door slammed nearby.

One Saturday they met earlier than usual, the sun just shy of a spectacular sunset. They found a secluded nook on the side of a hill, with a scatter of crisp leaves they covered with a blanket, and then they sat and watched the sky.

"They think I'm seeing a movie with Ann," Moira explained when Ian asked how she'd managed the early getaway.

"Ann Houghton? She's as boring as your sister."

He laughed as Moira hid her hurt. Next time she'd lie about a girl more exciting than bookish Ann. It was so hard to constantly re-member how Maeve would do things. It was exhausting.

"Come here, Maeve," he said, and her stomach tipped as it always did at the sound of her twin's name. She moved until they were face-to-face, thinking he wanted a kiss. Then all at once he laughed and grabbed her, turned her so she sat on his lap.

The first time she'd felt his arousal, it frightened her. But boys couldn't help things like that when they kissed girls. It was natural, harmless. At least that's what Ian said when he'd seen the look on her face. She didn't mind it at all now. In fact, she knew she could give him a little pleasure, and herself, by sinking into him when he pressed against her.

"Play a song for me." He tucked his hand beneath her shirt and stroked her belly.

"Ian."

"I won't do anything you don't want," he said, stretching his free arm out before her. "C'mon. Play for me."

"You think I pack a saxophone in my hip pocket?" she asked with forced levity.

"I'd love to be your saxophone, have your hands all over me and your mouth on mine all of the time." He made a deep noise that sounded like he'd just eaten a spoonful of caramel.

Moira swallowed hard. Twice. "You would?"

"Oh, yeah," he said, and nuzzled his face into her neck. "C'mon, one song. Unless you're not who I think you are." She went stock-still. "Maybe that's a recording I hear from inside your house and not you at all."

"Right." Her breath felt shallow and sharp. "Or maybe I'm really my sister?"

"She could never be you."

"Why not?"

"She's not like you."

"We're twins. Exactly the same genetically."

He dropped his arm. "Which just proves there's a lot more to a person than genes. You've got balls. You've always had them. That's why you won't be stuck here for the rest of your life."

He looked seaward with the same longing she'd seen in him before—when he stared at the enormous ship stationed in the Penobscot, where trainees from all over the country came for education in ship handling. She felt his restless desire for more in a hundred ways. He and Maeve were so alike that way.

"You can leave, too," Moira said. "Join the Maritime Academy. You can travel all—"

"Not if my old man has his way with my life."

She stared where he did, at the black water and its dusky golden highlights. "I think you can make anything happen if you believe in it. You can convince your father and become a merchant marine. And Moira has a lot more to offer than you're giving her credit for," she couldn't help adding. "She's had different opportunities than . . . than I have. She plays the piano very well and—"

Ian feigned a yawn. "Sorry, I'm sure you love her and all that, but I can't stand the piano."

"She knows Liszt."

"What's Liszt?"

"The composer, Franz Liszt. He's difficult to master."

"Yeah? From what I've heard she hasn't mastered him yet."

Moira couldn't hide her splintered expression that time.

"I like *you*," he said. "*You're* the one who's fun to be with. I don't want you to be your sister. C'mon. Play me."

Moira put her cold fingers on Ian's arm, moved them around a little.

"That's not a song," he said. "That's a fidget."

She closed her eyes against a blurred and watery vision, and played for him. The fleshy notes she touched were for piano, but she held herself as if she played the sax; and the song was Liszt's *Liebesträume, notturno No. 3*, a piece about love, holding onto it for as long as you're able—for lost love is wretched. She doubted Ian would ever appreciate it.

"You're amazing," he said when she stopped. "The most amazing girl in the world. Let's go all the way."

She turned to look him in the eye. The sun cast long orange fingers over his cheekbones and made a mask of his face. He pressed himself against her again, clasped her to him.

"I hope it's not too soon, but I need a real girlfriend. I'm a man, you know, not a boy anymore."

"But—"

"You thought I was a virgin?" He smiled.

Moira nodded. "Who—?"

"If you're not ready," he said, "then maybe *we're* not."

"You mean you'd break up with me?"

"Break up from what? You won't even hold my hand in the hall." His gaze grabbed at her; it hurt. "Maybe that's the game, huh, Maeve?"

"There's no game."

"You want to keep me at a distance. Other girls wouldn't."

Moira thought of Paula, the day Ian had been with her without his shirt. And then she thought of her sister. Maeve, she knew, wouldn't think so much. She'd live in the moment, let passion decide. Moira wanted to believe she had passion, too.

Do you think, because I am poor, obscure, plain, and little, I am soulless and heartless? You think wrong!—I have as much soul as you,—and full as much heart!

"Can I think about it?"

Ian wrapped a finger around the saxophone stone necklace and pulled her close, then kissed her until her body hummed with possibility.

"Just don't think about it for too long," he said, as breathless as she was. "You'll love sex, Maeve. You'll be a natural. You'll see."

CHAPTER THIRTEEN
DECLENSION

When I arrived back at the hotel, I carried four bags of clothes and quite a bit more debt. I changed into one of my new outfits—a pair of gray trousers and a tangerine-toned silk blouse Mariella said made my eyes look *elettrizzante*. She'd somehow noticed my hair as well, my roots. *Why have you taken away your color? You are young. Be beautiful.* But in this, I was resolved; I bought a blue hat and stuck it on my head.

"Hello, gorgeous," Noel said after he stepped through my door a little later.

I wrinkled my nose at him. "How did it go today?"

"Remind me never to take the bus again."

"That good?"

"Better. And I'm sure my wallet's history. Working with the law was a challenge, even with Giovanni's help, but at least I learned a lot about *passeggiata*."

"Silly, isn't it?"

"Silly. Effing insane. Whatever."

"Where'd he send you?"

"A leather shop. Do you want lunch?"

My mouth fell open, and then I laughed so hard that I sent myself into a coughing fit. "I'd pay to see you in leather pants! Seriously, oh, my God—"

"Go on. Murder my self-respect."

I gasped for breath. "It's just so not you. Noel Ryan in leather pants, riding a Harley."

"We're in Rome. How about a Vespa?"

I laughed harder.

"First, I didn't buy any pants. Second, I did own a motorcycle once. Third, I'm hungry, so let's go." He tossed my coat to me, a curveball I barely caught.

"What? When did you have a bike?"

"Oh, you know, when I was a pain in the ass adolescent, around the time I grew my hair long. The girls loved long hair."

"Did they?"

"Definitely," he said, and winked at me. His hair was still on the long side, sleek and dark like mink. "But it wasn't something my grandfather thought was appropriate for life at the shop. I exploded. Told him I didn't want to run the bloody shop my entire life. I wasn't his son, why did he care what my hair looked like?"

"Wow." I found the whole scene hard to imagine—arguments between two of the most gentle men I'd ever met.

"He gave me the bike the next day. I knew I didn't deserve it, but I took it anyway. I just wanted the choice to be mine, you know— stay or go." He shrugged. "Things got better after that. Truth was, I did want to be his son. I was just pissed I wasn't."

I nodded. Moira and I had struggled just as hard over our identity. Identi*ties*, rather; my mother made sure they were separate. Skirts and books and gardening and piano for Moira. Jeans and comic books and football and saxophone for me. How different things might've been for us if we'd had a Garrick in our lives to offer what we didn't know we craved—freedom of choice. Especially Moira. Especially her.

I stirred from my musings to find Noel excavating me with his gaze. I suggested pizza, and we headed for the elevators.

"Let's try a club tomorrow night," he said as he pushed the button to the lobby. "Giovanni said he'd take us, even got his mother to give him the night off. It's underground—sounds interesting. You up for it?"

"Yeah, it's intriguing," I said. "The idea to go to Il Sotto Abbasso came from me, actually."

Silence, then, "You've been to Putra's, haven't you?"

How had he known? He pulled a piece of paper from his jacket pocket, exactly like mine; "Visit Il Sotto Abbasso," it read. We spoke over each other.

"You didn't tell me about a note with my name on it?"

"You went back after what happened with that landlord?"

"Yes." I hardened my jaw. "And he's not the landlord, smarty; he's the landlady's son—and Sri Putra's brother. "

"Brother?"

"Half brother. Ermanno's weird, granted, but—"

"You know his name? Did you talk to him? Did—"

"Stop! It doesn't matter!" My fingers made ten exclamation points between us. "You're missing the point."

"No, you are. The note you found—let me see it."

"Why, starting a collection?"

The elevator stopped. The door opened. Neither of us moved.

He spoke intensely. "There are things you don't know, Maeve, things I've learned about that guy—"

"You mean his love of black magic?" I laughed humorlessly when he reared back. "This response from the man who doesn't believe in myths!"

"I don't," he said. "But you shouldn't go anywhere near that guy alone. He's a whack job. He could be dangerous."

"I've done plenty of things in my life alone, Noel. I've faced danger. Whatever delusion you have that I'm a weakling woman is wrong. I won't let you lie to me."

"I've never lied to you."

"Not telling the truth then. Dissembling. Whatever you want to call it. That note was meant for me. This is my journey."

"Then why am I here?" The door closed again.

"How many times have you gone back there?" I asked.

"A few. How many times have you gone by yourself?"

"Just once. Today."

Noel continued looking at me like I'd let him down. I hated feeling like a scolded child; it made me angry. "Any other notes with my name on them? Did you take anything else?"

He didn't answer right away, but then he pulled a slip of paper from his other pocket. I took it.

Visit Villa Borghese

"Any more?"

"No," he said, with just as much snap. He punched a button and the doors reopened. I matched him step for step when he strode out.

"I'm not the bad guy here," I said.

"Guess that means I am. I'll stop trying to protect you."

"Jesus, God, there's no reason to protect me! Do I seem like some fragile little wisp of a girl to you? Nothing I own is pink! I didn't even own a purse before today!"

We rounded the bend, the front desk in sight. Giovanni waved to us.

"I tried to ring you in your room," he told Noel. "A thing *rimarchevole* has happened. Your wallet has been returned. It was left by someone unanimously."

"How—?" Noel took the bag Giovanni held out to him, and pulled out a wallet.

"Yours?"

He opened it. "Christ. It really is mine." He dumped the bag's contents on the counter: traveler's checks, cards, a key, and several golden coins fell out; yellow, blue, red, and gray euro notes drifted to the floor. "Unbelievable," he said. "What the bloody hell?"

Within the rubble, I spied a picture of Garrick snoozing in a chair at Time After Time, his glasses teetering on his nose. "What a great shot," I said, pointing to it, trying to put the bad feelings behind us.

My words triggered something in Noel. He pulled the photo from the rubble with unseeing eyes, then began searching through the pile with new vigor. Bills scattered across the counter. Business cards fell to the floor. I asked what he was looking for, if I could help, but he ignored me. Finally, he stopped.

"He stole it," he said in a voice that struck me as dangerously calm, placid as the water in the eye of a storm.

"What? Who?"

"Your photograph—the one I took last year at the maple festival. It's gone. That bastard."

"Who are you talking about?"

"Your new buddy, Ermanno. He stole my wallet."

"Wait, wait, back up. You saw him at the apartment? He was there when you took the note? What happened?"

"I went to the apartment after I bought the tarts," he said, hard-focused on the counter. "I'll bet he followed me when I left. Or maybe he took it right there, in the hall."

"Did you two argue?"

"No, I never saw him. But the hall was full of people, kids showing off their presents, that sort of thing. He could've been anywhere. He seems to be everywhere at once."

I wanted to shake him. "Seriously, Noel, do you hear yourself? You were in a hall full of kids and maybe one of them did take your wallet, yet you blame Ermanno—someone you didn't see. Why? Because he can appear out of thin air, thanks to his astounding skill in dark magic?"

Giovanni made a sign of the cross.

"Listen." Noel gripped my shoulders. "Who knew we were staying here? Kit, my grandfather, and him—this Ermanno."

I remembered the information Noel left on Putra's door that first day, the information Ermanno had seen. Maybe Ermanno *had* taken it. But there were a hundred better, more rational explanations. "You probably had a card in your wallet with the hotel's address."

"No. I kept details about your flight and the hotel information in an inside pocket. Here." He opened his jacket, pulled out a paper, and waved it in my face.

I tried reasoning with him. "You probably dropped your wallet just outside the hotel and someone brought it back in."

"After sitting on it for two days? No. Everything was returned. My cards. The key to my flat in Paris. My euros and traveler's checks. The only thing missing is your photograph. How many co-incidences can there be?"

"I think you're a little obsessed over trying to find fault with the *keris* and with Sri Putra and Ermanno. Really," I said when he glared at me. "It's not healthy. In fact, it's a little paranoid." He deserved the dig.

I turned to Giovanni, who'd just placed a handful of fallen euros on the counter. "Giovanni, how far is Villa Borghese?"

"Christ all-freaking mighty," Noel said. "Now?"

"Yes," I said. "Villa Borghese now, and tomorrow night Il Sotto Abbasso. I'll go with or without you."

His eyes lost a little of their spark. Despite everything—my anger and his questionable behavior—I knew he meant well. I gentled my tone.

"I read about a gallery in Villa Borghese. Let's go look at beautiful things and try to unravel this mystery. It's not like Ermanno will be hiding out behind a painting with his sledge."

Giovanni looked between us. "There is the gallery and also a museum. There is much to see."

"Can we walk?" I asked. "I have a thing against cabbies who try to match the speed of light."

Giovanni shot Noel an apologetic look. "There is the bus."

THE CLOUDLESS DAY seemed ideal for a visit to Borghese Park, and it would've been if not for the tension between Noel and me. We ate pizza in near silence. Walked to the bus in absolute silence. Took our seats among people who chatted about the holiday and the museum and where they would eat dinner. The couple before us kissed.

I leaned against a rattling window and stared out. We traveled a grand avenue, past headless statues, and some who'd kept their heads over hundreds of years. When we arrived, we debarked and purchased admission into the gallery for later that day. There was time, we were told by an attendant, to visit the National Etruscan Museum if we so desired. Noel said he'd like to go, which I took for progress.

A bunch of us headed up hills, then down again to reach Villa Giulia and the National Etruscan Museum. I couldn't contain my excitement. I don't know if my poppy ever went to Rome, but his enthusiasm for artifacts had rubbed off on me as I grew, and I wanted to see what the Etruscans—who predated the Romans and whose language predated Latin—had left behind.

Once inside, our group divided, some going straightaway to see the reconstructed temple and famous *Nymphaeum* on display in the courtyard, while others decided to walk the halls first, as Noel and I did. We stopped to take in the various coffers, vases and terra-cotta sculptures, even a surprisingly well-preserved sarcophagus of a married couple—their facial features clear and smiles broad, despite being over twenty-six hundred years old.

"I wonder if they'll ever decipher it," Noel said when we stepped before a display of three golden tablets. The writings, Etruscan and Phoenician, provided one of the rare clues in existence about the Etruscan language. The lettering had always looked backward to me, though, like words viewed in a mirror.

"I doubt it," I said. "That language died over two thousand years ago, and there are so many variables—regional dialects, phonetic spellings, abbreviations."

"A lost language." Noel's tone was thoughtful. I would've asked what was on his mind, but my head filled just then with long-buried sounds.

Vinah way pleshee myna.

I flashed to a time barely within memory's grasp—a day when I stumbled with pudge-toddle feet over rocks on the beach beside my sister. I could hear my mother call behind us, "Slow down, girls. Be careful." Moira tittered in her hand and I held tight to her other one. We ran.

Vinah way pleshee myna.

I could not recall what the words meant, but I knew without doubt they were from our language, the language my mother had called Trying Twin. We'd forgotten it by age six.

I suppose I had more knowledge than most about lost languages, and lost people. But that day in Villa Borghese marked the first time that I seriously wondered if I'd lost myself—not just my music or my sister or a mother who'd call on Christmas. Me. I feared I'd lost my essence, that it was so far gone in the wrong direction that I'd never get it back.

WE ARRIVED AT the Borghese Gallery at our appointed time and went inside. I appreciated the vivid artwork, the sculptures, the essential dedication needed to accrue all of that splendor in one place. Noel, though, was enraptured. I couldn't tear my eyes from him as he touched, examined, even sketched in the book I'd given him. His brows crushed and lips pursed as he honed in on particulars. I thought his eyes might've misted once.

He was a beautiful man, I acknowledged, as sculpted as anything around us. I don't know why I found it so difficult to admit that I was simply and strongly attracted to him, and probably always had been. For that moment it was enough to know that I admired his spirit and liked being with him—maybe because he was an artist, as I'd once been, maybe because I fed off his passion in some nameless way. Or maybe just because he was fine.

"Christ, here's a classic. Look at that press of flesh. So bloody real."

I turned toward the statue he admired. A man's hand on a woman's thigh, dug deep in her flesh. Yes, that did seem real. But the woman didn't want his attentions. She fought him. Suddenly, my lungs felt heavy. Like marble.

"Maeve, you okay?" I'm not sure what he saw in my face, but the joy in his eyes vanished as, somewhere, a crow cawed.

I ran. People stared at me, scowled at such improper conduct inside a renowned art gallery. I kept on, escaped out the door, down the stairs, onto the pavement. The cawing bird flew above me. The bus drew near.

A dream, I realized, almost with relief; I was dreaming again. I didn't remember falling asleep or where I'd lain my head, but I knew the *keris* would be in my hand soon, ready for a fight. I looked for the little girl with the red hair.

Another bleat, another caw, and then a force hit and my lungs emptied as I landed on the grass. I opened my eyes to Noel, his body pinned over mine. I felt the heat of him, his hard breath as he clasped me close, and a chill air where my silk blouse had opened.

"Get off me!" I pounded at his chest. "Get off!"

"What the hell's wrong with you?" he hollered into my face. His was red, raging. "You almost died just now! You almost died!"

I heard, as if from a great distance, the fading sound of a horn and realized the bus had just passed, that I had—truly, not just in some dream world—almost been killed. That I'd almost let it happen.

And just beyond Noel's shoulder, I saw the wave of a black wing as the bird flew away.

I CALLED KIT that night and left a message on her voice mail. Something incoherent. I needed a doctor, needed my brain checked because something was very, very wrong with me, because I'd started dreaming during the day with open eyes fastened against reality.

I stared at the mirror after I hung up. "I'm not crazy," I informed my reflection. "I refuse to be crazy." The woman in the glass nodded in agreement.

I couldn't bring myself to answer Kit's call hours later, just listened to the message once the light on my room phone blinked. "The doctor I told you about can get you in as soon as you're back," she said. "I wish you'd told me more about what happened. Was it a flashback? I told you it could be PTSD, I told you that might be it." I heard the frantic worry in her voice. "You should come home now. Call me back."

The sun set and still I sat alone in my room, sustained by panettone and Italian soap operas. Noel knocked on my door with less frequency as the hours passed—"Come on, Maeve, I know you're there"—but I didn't answer. How could I explain my actions when even I didn't understand them?

Instead, I retrieved the *keris* from the safe and did something that might seem truly mad. I placed the blade on the other side of my bed—on the other bed, really—then crawled under the covers on my side and turned off the light.

That moment marked a turning point for me, though I wouldn't know it until later. Still, ramshackle as I felt then, I sensed an unloosing as the part of me that should've been keeping guard, looking out for my best interests, suddenly disappeared. Poof. Like magic.

A NEW SONG debuted the next morning. Very, well, piratey. Alvilda would've approved. And it became the perfect antidote to the gale that had whipped my emotions around the previous day.

I called Kit and left a message: "Sorry about the confusion. I feel fine. Better than fine. It was just a bad day. Don't worry." If self-determination counted for anything, I would make those words true. I grabbed my coat and left before she could phone back and yell at me.

The heavy drape of yeast and sweet spice enticed me into a nearby eatery, where I sat at a table for two. I devoured a Danish and three cups of espresso, and read a newspaper full of articles on football scandals and fashion and commerce, soaking up culture as my sister would've a good passage of *Jane Eyre*.

Moira.

The thought of her steeped in me, and I let it. She would've loved Rome. The people. The language. She would've noticed things like plants and the color of people's front doors. She would've noticed babies in carriages and stopped to coo at them. She would've enjoyed gelato.

After breakfast, I purchased a disposable camera and took pictures. Of plants and babies and front doors, and a woman hanging laundry on a line.

I RETURNED THAT afternoon to find a note taped to my door.

Where are you?!?
-N

I pulled it off and knocked on Noel's door there in the hall. "You're behind the times," I bellowed through the wood. "Nails are the latest rage."

No response. Maybe he'd left for dinner.

Back in my room, I pulled off my coat, set it on the bed. Stared at the other side. Realized. The *keris* wasn't there. Had I seen it that morning as I'd swaggered around to Alvilda music? Worst-case scenarios stampeded into my imagination—a greedy maid, the bartender who'd noticed it that first day, Noel trying to prove a point. But when I rounded the end of the bed, I found the *keris* on the floor, in the slight gap between my two mattresses. Warmth traveled my arm when I picked it up.

Room temperature, my ass.

That's when I heard something in the other room. Shuffling sounds. People noises. Noel. Ignoring me. I knocked on his door.

"I hear you breathing."

"I'll be there in a minute," he called back. "Just wait."

Wait? I squared my shoulders, the *keris* still in my hand. Alvilda wouldn't wait for some guy. In fact, Alvilda wouldn't knock. I turned the handle between our rooms. It gave way. And there, with a towel around his waist, stood my bonny friend.

"Christ," he said. Water rivulets streamed down his face. "I said 'wait,' not 'come in.' "

"Oops. Sorry." Every bit of me went hot, and I knew it had nothing to do with the *keris* or the temperature of the room. I stared at his eyes, tried to pretend he wore more than a scrap of cotton terry, though my peripheral vision took comprehensive notes on his toned body and scatter of chest hair. If I'd had any functioning brain cells, I would've slunk back into my room. As it was, it took a vast effort to pull my gaze off him. That's when I saw the big envelope on the floor near his door. "Look!" I picked it up. "Another FedEx from Garrick!"

"Another?"

Ah, hell. "That time Jakes called, I needed something to write with so I opened your drawer and saw the FedEx, and I noticed that it was from Garrick, but I didn't open it even though it might've been important. Have you opened it yet?"

"No." He stepped so close I could smell the soap on his skin, and then he took the envelope from me and tossed it onto his bed.

My non-*keris*-holding hand jangled in his face. "But . . . but, what are they?"

"Packages from my grandfather."

"We've established that. Why haven't you opened them?"

"Let's say I won't grasp the language. It's lost to me."

"I don't understand."

"There's no reason you should. Now are you going to let me get dressed?"

"I don't think I will. Frankly, I've had enough of your bad moods." And then, because three cups of espresso does things to a person, I lifted the sheathed *keris* and put my hand on my hip. "*En guard*, scurvy dog!"

"You have me at a disadvantage," he said, right before reaching behind him at lightning speed. I barely registered a flash of white when the pillow hit me in the face and dropped artlessly to the floor.

"Grab your sketchbook. There's an inspiration for you." I looked at the *keris*, which now pointed toward the floor as well. "The impotent sparrist." I snorted. He chuckled. "Not that I don't know how to wield this thing," I continued, waving the *keris*. "I mean, let's be clear."

"Cute."

"I am, aren't I? So cute you'll explain those packages."

"Persistent as a bloodthirsty mosquito." He pushed wet hair out of his face.

I made a high-pitched mosquitoesque sound.

"After you told my grandfather that I came here to find my mother—"

"I didn't exactly tell him—"

"—he sent some of her old letters. He thought there might be a clue in them to help an investigation. Problem was, I didn't have an investigator. So he hired Jakes."

"But why didn't you have—"

"Now Jakes is harassing me to turn over the letters so he can analyze the hell out of them," he said. "But I won't give them to him until I've read them. And I won't read them."

"Why not read them? Why not give them to the investigator?"

He crossed his arms over his chest. I thought his towel might fall, but it must've been superglued in place.

"You know why this is crap? I don't need her. I don't even think about her."

None of this made sense.

"Then what's all this for?" I asked. "Why come so far, spend all this time and money on finding someone you don't even think about?" He didn't answer, just turned his wet back on me. Any respectable person would give him some privacy, leave him alone to dry off and dress. I stepped a little closer. "You've become a real stub of companionability, you know."

"You almost died." He struck at the last word like a gong.

I wanted to reach out and touch him, but didn't. "It was a mistake. Can't you just let it go?"

"What? The image of you nearly flattened by a bus?"

"A bloody bus," I said, trying to lighten the moment.

"It would've been bloody."

"I lost my head for a second."

"You might've lost it forever. Christ."

"Noel, I—" I strode around his still form, looked him in the eye. "It was like a dream," I said. "I was out of it."

"If that's true—" He grunted. "You should see a doctor."

"Now you sound like Kit."

"Good. Kit's a smart woman. Listen to her."

"I feel great today." I tried for a smile, but his glower sapped the will from my lips.

"You walked in front of a bus," he said. "Tell me how this is a good thing."

"Right. And you saved my life."

"Not that you need rescuing. Isn't that how it is?"

"Not that I do, generally speaking, but you came in handy just then." My voice softened. "Thank you for being there."

He regarded me for a long moment. "Giovanni wants us ready around eleven."

I'd forgotten. The club. My outfit. "We don't have to go," I said. "If you'd rather—"

"He took the night off to help us." Words spoken slowly, enunciated crisply.

"All right, all right," I said.

I'd just crossed the threshold to my room when I was struck in the back of the head with a damp towel. The door thumped closed behind me.

I turned, put my hand to the door, and envisioned Noel on the other side. The *keris* flared hot in my hand. My vision blurred. I leaned against the settee, let the blade fall onto a pillow.

Color and focus came back slowly as a fine film of sweat formed on my upper lip. There was risk and then there was stupidity. I wouldn't wear that outfit. I just wouldn't.

Out of Time

Castine, Maine
LATE OCTOBER 2000
Moira and Maeve are sixteen

Moira nearly slammed into Maeve as she stepped out of the bathroom.

"Don't go," Maeve said. Just that.

Moira had been a wreck of nerves all day, but she'd made a decision: Tonight would be the night with Ian. Making love would bond them completely. She'd have time, after, to explain things. For now, she was obsessed over the details of the moment: What would she wear? How should she behave? Would it hurt?

She'd found an outfit—a black stretchy top, a nice pair of jeans— and she'd applied just a little of Mama's perfume, some of her lipstick. She'd left her hair loose and mussed it into a semiwild state. And just when she felt satisfied with her reflection, Maeve stood in her way and asked her not to go.

Moira walked around her and into their bedroom. She kept her voice low. "What's the matter with you? I'm going to Ann's."

"No, you're not."

"Are you calling me a liar?"

Maeve rounded on her to barricade Moira from their closet. "I know you didn't go out with her last week. I know because I saw her in school and asked about the movie. She said there wasn't a movie."

"Stop butting into my business!" Moira tried to push past her twin, but Maeve grabbed her arms.

"I have a bad feeling. Don't go."

Moira stiffened. "Your feelings aren't always right."

"They're right most of the time."

"Not this time."

"Stay here tonight." The storm in Maeve's eyes softened. "I have a new piece, and I think it'd be easy to adapt to piano—"

"I don't need your charity." Moira felt the words land like a blow to her sister and regretted it. Still, this was her night with Ian. The only time she'd give away her virginity. Nothing was going to stop her, not even Maeve and her bad feelings. She tried again to dodge her twin and succeeded this time in snatching her sneakers.

"Why would you say that? You know I love to play with you."

"I'm not in your league, and we both know it. You're too busy with your Hollywood stuff for me now." She stuffed her feet inside the leather.

"It's not Hollywood stuff."

"New York, whatever." Moira hated her jealousy, the way it heaved in her like a sickness, but she couldn't seem to stop it.

"Why are you doing this to us?"

"I didn't do this to us! You did this!" she said before she could stop herself.

"I did? How did I?"

By being perfect and always so sure of yourself. By flying high while I stood on the ground and watched. By not helping me learn to fly, too. By making Ian love you.

"By making my life impossible!" Moira made for the door.

Maeve grasped her arm again—"Please, don't go, please"—and again Moira pulled away.

"I will go. I don't believe in your feeling," she said, already down the hall and at least three steps ahead.

CHAPTER FOURTEEN

IL SOTTO
ABBASSO

Something about Rome stimulated contact and inti-
macy; maybe the fountain water everyone sipped was laced with
pheromones. People held hands, embraced, kissed. Even the statues
twined around one another. So it was easy to blame the great city's
power of suggestion for my ogling Noel, which began the moment I
appeared back in his room. *Perfectly tailored pants the color of rich
espresso. Midnight blue silk shirt fitted like a skin, open at the neck.* My
eyes roamed him as he chatted with Giovanni. *Abdomen, shoulders,
thighs, mouth.*

I thought Noel caught me once or twice, but I always looked
away, then.

"You will change, yes?" Giovanni asked me at one point. I still
wore the outfit I'd had on that day.

"I thought maybe this would—"

He tsk-tsked. "No," he said. He looked sinful himself in black
pants and a leopard-print shirt with an overlay of bold orange
stripes. "Where is your flow-in-the-dark?"

I glanced at Noel, who raised a brow.

"I . . . I don't—"

"Mariella said you have a new and beautiful thing. You go. Go
now and change."

Before I could respond, Giovanni began a twisty little dance. "Sunday night and I ain got no body! I got some money 'cause I just got paid! Mama let me have someone to talk to, and there will be jazz tonight." He continued to sing and dance while my thoughts snagged on just one word.

"Jazz?"

"Music," Noel said. "It's a jazz club."

Ah, hell. Jazz almost always meant the sax. Though I hadn't managed to evade all sax music over the last decade, I'd done my best. I imagined it was like seeing an old lover, happy without you; hearing the live sound of a reed's voice made me ache. It had ever since my instrument drowned in the Penobscot, met up somewhere on the sea's rock-and-silt floor with my family's old *keris*. Time to pull out my Chinese Brother skills and take a long drag of air; I wouldn't let Noel down again.

Back in my room, I closeted up with my new clothes, my old concerns, and finally my resolutions. And when I finished with my transformation, I stared at the woman in the glass. Her wisp-of-smoke skirt showed the curve of slender hips. Her sheer black top revealed a dimple belly button, and its elaborate silver threading concealed only the most intimate parts of her breasts. There was something medieval about her sleeves—the way they hugged tight to her forearms and flared at her wrists. Her cheeks and lips looked ruby-kissed, her eyes dramatic, and her hair held a flock of butterfly clips. A pair of red heels made miraculous work of her calves.

"Who are you?" I asked the mirror.

You are Alvilda. You are Maeve. You fear nothing.

Right, then. I would go. I would face Noel as I faced the glass. And I would face the music.

I REPLACED THE *keris* in my safe before I left. "Stay," I told it. I knew I was stalling.

I donned a silver wrap, then took a deep breath and opened the door. Noel and Giovanni looked staggered, and I had to admit to a thrill of feminine power.

"My girlfriend will kill me for saying so"—when the words came, Giovanni Benedetto Chioli sounded as American as Billy Crystal— "but you look marvelous!"

"That's the magnum opus of understatement," Noel said.

I smiled and wondered if I might glow in the dark after all.

NOEL SETTLED HIS jacket over my shoulders as we walked a short but chilly distance to the outskirts of Trastevere. When Giovanni announced that we'd reached our destination, I thought he'd lost his mind; we stood before what looked like a long shed. He opened a door marked with nothing but a thin growth of moss, and in we stepped. We traveled a dim hall, then a long flight of stairs, before passing through another door and down more steps.

I hadn't known places like Il Sotto Abbasso existed—a club beneath modern-day Rome, where a buried city sprawled in mute glory. Shops and homes, streets and aqueducts—there were many such places, even under people's houses, Giovanni said, and owners hid them away to maintain their peace. It fascinated me, the idea of a secret world beneath the surface.

Before the final door was even opened, I heard the din of holler-talk along with strains of Louis Armstrong's "Nobody Knows the Trouble I've Seen." Relief. Recorded trumpeting I could handle.

Giovanni left us to visit with friends while we took in the room. Tall tables dotted the floor, amid a throng of swaying bodies. I turned to Noel, ready to let loose a comment about the likelihood of me going out to dance, but he stopped me.

"You look delicious," he said.

I shook my head. *Delicious* wasn't a label I could own.

"You make it hard sometimes, Maeve Leahy, to be a gentleman."

"But you are one."

"An effing inconvenient reputation," he said with a grimace. "But I know the rules. I'll be good."

I realized then, in that under-down place, why I'd kept Noel in my life when I'd shunned others. Because he was, at heart, an old-world chap like his grandfather. A man who might've stepped from the pages of *Jane Eyre*. Safe. And maybe I'd wanted him close because I knew he genuinely cared for and admired me as a woman, and I craved that rush, even if I took nothing else. Not kisses or sweet words. Not a body to hold at night. Noel Ryan was my not-mate mate. My not-lover love. My gentleman who didn't always want to be a gentleman.

What a selfish bitch I'd been. To both of us.

I let my wrap slide down to the crook of my arms and held out my hand. "Let's dance."

He regarded me with hooded eyes, then joined his palm with mine. Not at all awkward, just . . . *just.*

I pressed my face against his chest as we melded in to become two more people on the dance floor. "You know something? I missed your smell."

He laughed. "My smell? God, do I smell?"

His scent was rich with complex notes—like air, earth, water, and fire, distilled and woven into his DNA. Like a seasoned shore, maybe, one that had endured some bad times and survived. "You smell good."

The song changed, became "Dream a Little Dream of Me." I spoke in time with the tune, mimicked Louis' words: "Say nighty-night and kiss me. Just hold me tight and tell me you'll miss me . . ."

He stilled, swayed again.

When the next verse began, with talk of craving kisses and lingering till dawn, I switched to Italian. *"S'affievoliscono le stelle, ma io, tesoro, indugio con l'anelito tenace, bramante per il tuo bacio. Con l'ardore languisco . . . E già è l'alba! Tesoro, che posso dirti?"*

He sang the next words in my ear. I don't think I'd ever heard him sing before, but his voice was a rich, clear tenor. "Sweet dreams till sunbeams find you. Sweet dreams that leave all worries behind you. But in your dreams whatever they be, dream a little dream of me."

His fingers splayed over my bare back, and I leaned into him, held tight. Here we were again, like the night I'd had too much to drink and called him a ninny. Like then, but different.

"God, Maeve, it's worse and worse," he said in a soft-serious mutter. "You have no idea."

"Yes, I do." My hand dipped to his hip, flexed there.

176

He pulled back, and the expression on his face—like I was it for him, the only woman in the room—filled me with rapture. I realized in that honey-covered moment, as he tucked a finger under my chin, that I'd kissed Noel a thousand times in my dreams. But this was no dream. His lips were warm and gentle. They didn't ask much, just to be still with mine. Not nearly enough for my resurrected yearnings. Just as I'd begun to brush my mouth over his, though, Louis' song stopped abruptly—

—and was replaced by the squeal of a microphone. I jerked my head back as a stew of live sounds thickened the room. The pluck of a bass, the steady tap-tap of the cymbals, a beat on drums, and an ivory-key melody. *Oh, Moira*. And there, not quite on key, the sax.

MY JOY SOURED as the player sustained his bad start. Strident notes sounded out with a hiss—the clear protest of a harassed instrument. I put my hands to my lips, my ears, set them down again.

A black curtain lifted in a dark corner, revealing a stage and a group of musicians. A woman with black hair and red lips at the piano. A thin man plucking a bass. A bald drummer who married stick to metal with his eyes closed. And a guy with hair whiter than mine who completed a flat run on an airy nonnote, his fingers wrapped around a sax.

"Are you all right?" The man I'd just kissed looked at me with a reasonable question in his eyes, as my eyes stung.

"Sorry. I'm just . . ."

Noel shook his head in question, and I shook mine back in response. The tale of my music, of my sax, was one of a long-lost love. Intimate. Over.

Cymbals crashed. I turned to see metal disks fluttering on their stands as the sax player righted himself, squealed out another note. He had to be drunk or high. Plenty of people laughed. My fingers itched to steal his instrument.

Remember the taste of reeds?

My tongue watered and curled. I had to get out of there.

I opened my mouth to offer an excuse. Headache. Fatigue. The urge to kill. That's when I noticed a high shelf loaded with skulls just beyond Noel, a Jolly Roger pinned to the wall. The sight of those disembodied heads took my anxiety up a significant notch. I would gladly have sunk into the floor to escape, but deep in Il Sotto Abbasso, there was nowhere to go but up.

I pushed my way through the crowd and to the exit, and had run halfway up the first set of stairs when Noel called. I waited as he followed me up, reached the step just below mine. We stood almost nose to nose.

"Was it that bad?" Pride and hurt warred in his eyes.

Comprehension dawned. "It's not about the kiss. It's personal."

"How much more personal—"

"Later, all right?" I took a step backward, upward. I still heard the lush's massacre too well.

"What about now? Now sounds pretty damned good to me." Frustration threaded through his voice. It rushed through me, too—like water in my lungs, through the heart of my sax—as more laughter rose from below. "Why can't you open a little, Maeve? Say what's in your head. Trust me."

"Like you trust me?"

"What do mean by—"

"Just what I said—you don't trust me." I clung to this line, desperate, and pursued it, let anger fill me up as I took another step back. "You don't contact me for months, you say nothing! Why don't you send those letters to the investigator? Why won't you read them? Why don't you want to find your mother?"

"What has this got to do with that?"

"You're avoiding talking about it or taking any action."

"*I'm* avoiding?"

"You still hate her," I said, four steps away now. "Maybe you don't want to hear what she has to say, but you might be able to fix things! Don't be a coward!"

His chin jerked as if struck, but it was too late now to call the words back. "Tell me you've never run from anything, Maeve. Christ, you're running now, look at you go!"

"Maybe I am. But you . . . you don't even know what you're running from. You don't know what your mother ran from."

"She ran from me."

"And now you're running from her!"

"No, I'm running from you!"

My foot froze midair. From me? The possibility exploded in me, fused together incongruent bits and settled them into sense: Noel's lack of contact over so many months, his distant behavior since my arrival in Rome, the sense that I'd hampered him with my *keris* business. He didn't want me here. He didn't want me because—

"You didn't leave Betheny to find your mother at all." My voice was a rasp. "You left to get away from me."

His jaw worked.

"Tell me. Tell me the truth!"

"Fine, the truth! I needed solid ground, and you're anything but that. What would you have me believe? The look in your eyes when you think I'm not paying attention or your body language when you know I am?" He laughed without humor. "I wanted an affair with a beautiful woman to get you out of my blood, but I couldn't even do that. And then you came here, across an ocean, like a ghost on the trail of her favorite tormentee!"

His expression grew cracked and raw. And then he took the steps, two at a time, near me, past me. I ran after him, tangled my fingers in his shirt until he stopped. He emanated heat.

"Let go, Maeve," he said, quiet now. "You're just another woman who doesn't give a damn."

"That's not true."

He turned, looming over me. "It bloody well is true. I want you exorcised." Long dark strands stuck out between his fingers as he snatched at his hair, and I thought of the skeletons near the ceiling, thought of them falling on my head. "I want to be free of this. And I don't want to love you anymore, Maeve Leahy," he said, quiet and solemn like a prayer.

Love me? I couldn't quite wrap my brain around it. Love me? My fingers loosened. I tried to make words and couldn't.

Stop. Stop him.

Noel had pulled away and disappeared up the stairs, while below sounds of torture seemed to grow louder by the second. I put my hands over my ears and still the noise thrummed in my veins and kicked my heart offbeat.

Take control.

I couldn't stand it anymore.

Fix that much.

I hovered with my foot in the air for several seconds before I followed the impulse and returned to the under down.

DO IT.

I had no desire to resist the summons, and I had a great need for release, for communion. I found my way to the stage. The pianist's eyes widened. Was I a maniac? Definitely.

I approached the sax player, his eyes red and bleary, his cheeks puffed like an obese squirrel's. He was also huge, much taller than he'd looked from the floor. But I felt tall myself just then, in my red spiked heels.

"Don't drink and jive," I said, and stripped him of his sax. "You obviously don't have a permit to play that thing."

"Sc–c–cusi?" he bumbled back.

"Sleep it off," I said, and he chose that moment to pass out on the floor. I spied a case full of fresh reeds.

The other instrumentalists faltered to a halt.

"Grazie a Dio," muttered the bass player in thanks.

"Yeah." The drummer squinted up at me. "You a player?"

Me, I'd just comprehended that I had a sax in my hands and a reed in my mouth. Oh, good heavenly danger. What should I do?

You know what to do.

Reed in place. Tighten ligature. I committed my lips to a musician's kiss I'd missed more than I'd realized. I bent my knees, arched my back, and let loose all my frustrated desires. Though I should've been cautious after nearly a decade of abstinence, my fingers bounded over the keys with all the assuredness I'd ever possessed.

And it felt like home.

I LOST MYSELF to the music for long and blissful minutes. Applause filled the room in the end, which you might think would've filled me, too, but it didn't. Less than two beats after I lowered my arms, I recognized a familiar face in the crowd.

Ermanno. Ermanno, there at Il Sotto Abbasso.

I remembered the last time I'd seen him, staring at me from the dark end of the hall as I stood before Sri Putra's door. Of course he'd read the note I'd found, too. It couldn't have been hard to guess when I'd come, with the club open only on Sunday nights. Did he think I'd have the *keris* with me here of all places? What did he want?

"Ne suona un'altra?" the pianist asked.

I remembered myself and where I was, what I wore. Though part of me ached to play another song, I could never do it now. Not with that man boring holes into me, drifting closer to the stage, his smile widening as my questions mounted.

"Non posso." I set the sax on the piano and shook my head. *"Grazie, grazie, grazie!"*

Most people made room for me when I stepped down. I tried to be gracious, thank the strangers who spoke words of gratitude and praise, but I had only one thing on my mind.

Ermanno bowed in mocking surprise when I stopped before him. "What luck to see you!" he said. "I have wanted to talk with you again about the *keris*. I must say, you look lovely." He acknowledged my outfit with two theatrically unfurling hands—a jester's gesture. Maybe he'd been hiding behind a painting at Borghese Gallery after all.

"This has nothing to do with luck and you know it. I don't know what your game is, but I thought you should know that the *keris* is gone."

His mask cracked. "Gone?"

"Yes," I said, deciding in that moment the exact words I'd need to speak to put an unequivocal end to his interest in me and my blade. "I sold it."

I'd seen anger before, but never anything like the metamorphosis of Ermanno's expression. He bared his teeth, clamped them together. His lips paled and brows formed a stark black line. His face turned the color a person devoid of oxygen might turn just before death, a sickly purple. Black eyes grew larger as he craned close, his animated hands balled into fists.

Move.

My fight-or-flight instinct kicked in, and flight won; I bolted, losing myself in the crowd, heading for the door. When someone grabbed my shoulder, I spun around, ready to defend myself. Not Ermanno. Noel. I threw my arms around him, scanning the crowd, but the Italian had disappeared. This was no credit to magic, just the cunning skill of a stalker, a sneaker, and a schemer; no doubt Ermanno knew how to use shadow to his best advantage. And whether my certainty was normal human instinct or not, I knew that—even as enraged as he'd been—Ermanno wouldn't show himself again in this place, not with my friend near.

"You're shaking," Noel said.

"Jacked on adrenaline," I told him, which was true enough.

I didn't question his fortuitous reappearance, just let him lead me out, up the stairs and through the doors, his hand secure over mine. He hadn't seen the Italian, that much was clear, and I didn't want to get into another argument about my safety. Not now, when Noel and I had a chance to resolve our angry words. Not when he'd seen me with the saxophone, stripped bare in a way he could never have anticipated. He'd have questions, and I was ready for them. What a surprise to be so relieved that he knew the truth.

The promise of rain pricked my Castinian senses when we stepped outside. "I want to explain this to you," I began.

"Let's just walk," Noel said, his expression an incomprehensible muddle.

"All right."

"I can write backward and upside down," he said a minute later. "Have I ever mentioned that?"

"No. No, I don't think so."

The sky let loose on us then, and by the time we reached our hotel, we were beyond drenched. I was grateful the lobby was empty when we stepped inside, because I couldn't imagine what I looked like in Noel's sopping coat and my skimpy outfit. I'd known wearing it would invite disaster, just not a hundred shades of it.

I crossed my arms over my chest as the elevator began its ascent. "I really do want to talk about this," I said through my shivers. "Tonight."

"Hot shower first," he said. "Then talk." He pulled his drenched silk shirt away from his chest.

I wanted to say something about sweet dreams and kisses, but before I could form the words, the door opened and Noel stepped out without looking back. I knew then my worries were anything but behind me.

Out of Time

Castine, Maine
LATE OCTOBER 2000
Moira and Maeve are sixteen

Soon it will be over, Moira thought. *It will be done.* Her body stiffened as Ian kissed her neck and put his hand under her shirt to feel a breast.

"You sure you want to do this?"

"Yes," she said.

He kissed her, but her lips felt tight and hard; she couldn't seem to help it. *Hurry.*

Leaves crackled under the blanket when he rolled onto his back. The half-moon leaked enough light to reveal his scowl.

"I'm sorry." She rearranged her shirt and sat up.

"You're just not into it."

Fear of Maeve sensing her emotions would ruin this experience, Moira knew; she'd blocked so much and so hard that she wouldn't let herself feel anything at all. And that was wrong. Because for all she felt anxious about this night and how it would change her and her life, she wanted to make love with Ian. She wanted to do this for him and for herself. She touched his cheek. "Sorry, I'm just nervous."

"Maeve Leahy is never nervous."

The words broke her. She stretched out and lay atop him. "You're right. I forgot, for a second, who I was."

She opened, felt all: his hands on her, his mouth, the rush of emotion at her core, the rise of desire.

"Touch me," he said, and she put her hand along the seam of his jeans. He moaned and unzipped them himself, then kicked them off as Moira stripped her own clothes.

They were two naked people then, on a blanket in the leaves in the woods. Ian's face hovered over her as he kissed her mouth. There was pain as he pushed inside. When he stopped and rested his lips on hers, Moira felt they shared the same breath.

"I lied." He lifted his face so that their eyes locked as tightly as their bodies. "I've never done this before."

Moira smiled and her eyes teared.

"Are you okay? Does it hurt?"

"A little," she said. "But I'm still glad."

"I love you, Maeve."

"I love you, Ian."

The reality of her situation pierced Moira like never before. She loved Ian Bronya. She, sixteen and a virgin until that moment; she, of Liszt and *Jane Eyre* and the garden; she, Moira Leahy. And he loved Her of the pirate dreams and golden notes; Her of bravery and risk, of football tackling and blood-sister making and *avventura*; Her, Maeve.

Moira couldn't compete with that. She never could.

But maybe she didn't have to. Other things bound people together. What could possibly unite them more than making love? Maybe, someday, they'd even become a family.

She gripped Ian's shoulders and closed her eyes. She thought of sperm, of eggs splitting into equal parts; of ham cooking on a Sunday morning and eggs breaking over a bowl, their yolks dripping thick and sizzling in the pan; of eggs in a robin's nest, blue and speckled and full of hatchlings who'd pecked away at the hard curve of their existence, hoping for just a glimpse of sky.

CHAPTER FIFTEEN

APPRENTICE

don't know why I went back, but there I was in Il Sotto Abbasso, the under down. I must've died somewhere along the way, because I was just a skull, all bone and eyeholes, sitting on a shelf beside a fleet of other heads. While my cranium comrades had bright lights flickering in their open mouths, though, my closed one held only a weakling flame.

Water flowed like a river beneath a door bearing the bloodstained X mark of a Jolly Roger. There was death here. There was death. The *keris* appeared below me in the swirl, and then Ermanno was there, staring up at me with his flawless smile. I understood his intent: to destroy my *keris* himself if the water didn't do it first.

I struggled until my skull tipped into the subterranean sea. Bone cracked against blade. My flame all but extinguished. The other skulls popped and jumped above me, their candlelight scorching the ceiling. One by one, they disappeared, until I was left alone with my paltry light and the bull-like sound of Ermanno's breathing.

My light would go out soon. I would go out soon. And then the world shifted, the scene changed.

My skull rolled down a hill, hit hard against compacted mud. I heard the spatter of water above me, the swirl of it below, then a strident horn. I screamed.

The moon stared at me through my Roman window as I sat up in bed. Life. Real. I hoped so, anyway.

The door between my room and Noel's opened and light flooded in.

"Christ! Are you all right?" he asked. "Are you being murdered or something?"

"No."

"No, you're not all right?"

I squinted up at him and tried to think sense. "I mean, no, I'm not being murdered, and yes, I'm all right. Just another dream. What happened?"

"No idea. I just got out of the shower a while ago."

That's right. Noel and I were going to talk. I remembered showering, then thinking I'd lie down for just a minute. I felt my hair, still wet, and knew I hadn't been out for long. I wish I'd been under the covers, though. My teeth chattered.

"Are you sick?" he asked.

"Just cold." Chilled to the bone. "I owe you an apology."

"Let's sort it out tomorrow. Sleep now."

"I can't. Tonight was a disaster."

"No." He shook his head. "It wasn't. I know something now, for sure. You're the red woman, Maeve Leahy. I thought you were, deep down."

The red woman. The flesh along the back of my throat tickled.

"You were amazing," he said. "Why do you hide your talent?"

"I'm not hiding it. I just don't play anymore." I pulled the blanket up and over my legs. "Music is part of another life. Another Maeve." The Before Maeve.

"What happened?"

"It's complicated." How much more of my lack of disclosure would he take? What, exactly, did I owe him? "Come here," I said. "There's a glare."

He stepped up so I could look him in the eye. He'd changed into jeans and a soft blue sweater.

"Noel, I really am sorry. I said a lot I shouldn't have, especially about you and your mom. I'm not one to judge in that area. My mother and I barely speak."

"All right," he said. "I'm sorry if what I said hurt you, too, but I'm not sorry tonight happened. It was . . . liberating."

I remembered how fast he'd left me when those elevator doors opened. "Will you go back to Paris now?" I asked, steeling myself for a blow. "Find a beautiful woman and have an affair?"

"That's not what I want," he said. "You know what I want. The problem is, I never know what *you* want and I'm sick of searching for smoke signals over this."

"I'm sorry."

"No, that's the easy way out. This time I want you to say it. Tell me what you want."

I dug my fingers into the blanket and leaped. "You might've decided that you're out of patience for whatever we are or could be, that it's not worth it. I wouldn't blame you if you didn't want to try. But I'd like it if . . ." I hugged my knees to my chest, tried not to shake.

His brows hunkered low. "If you think you owe me—"

"It's not about owing anyone anything, Noel. I liked our kiss." The words came out slush-tumble, shy and vulnerable, a truth spoken without the aid of a cold stone mouth while remembering the warmth of his real one. "I liked it very much."

"But?" he asked quietly.

"I need time to get used to this. You might think I've had enough time, all the time in the world, too much time, time after time, and I'm not trying to be a tease, I'm just . . . I'm just . . ."

"Familiar words, *just, just,*" he said. "I picked them apart more ways that you can guess. *Just, just,* it's not personal. *Just, just,* wait for me. *Just, just,* I'll never be ready. *Just, just,* I'm not into you, but I'll spare your feelings."

I flinched. "It was never that. I mean, I'd never want to hurt you, but there was more. I wasn't only trying to be nice."

"That word, *nice.* I hate it. *Nice* has carved my guts up."

The room fan shut off, and my words sounded loud in the newborn quiet. "Then maybe you're right to stay away from me."

"That's not what I mean."

"Then what do you mean?"

He hesitated, then sat on the end of my bed. "Do you remember the first time we met?"

"You mean in the French class I kicked your butt in?"

He smiled back at me. "That one. I sat beside you because you were the most gorgeous creature there."

I snorted. "You'll look good in glasses. Some wire rims—"

"You're the one who needs her eyes examined. But here's what you didn't know. I'd seen you before."

"When?"

"That summer—your first, I think. You sat in the music room with headphones, your eyes closed and the most complex expression on your face. You were crying. Not sobbing, just tears leaking out of you, just . . ."

I remembered that occasion, because I'd visited the music room only once. Liszt had played through those headphones, and I'd cried for hours, envisioning Moira as she'd wanted to be. The experience landed me in the ER with the only migraine I've ever had and Kit hovering, so worried that even she threw up.

My relationship with music changed after that. Already it'd been months since music had come to me as a new song, since I'd sunk my saxophone in the bay. I recognized then that music might be poison for me. And while I knew melody and song would always be there— in stores and in elevators, on TV and blaring through other students' earphones—I wouldn't immerse myself in it if I could help it.

Not long after that, sounds churned in me again; but it wasn't my music, the music I'd once heard on the wind. These notes were piano, and I felt them like thorns thrust in my temples. I shut my mind against them, the same way I used to block my sister. It drained me in the same way, too.

"That was a complicated time," I said on a shiver.

"I thought it might be. What I'm trying to say, Maeve, is that I'm not afraid of your complexity. Just the opposite. But I can't deny my complexity anymore. I'm more than a nice guy. I'm a man who's attracted to you." His voice lowered. "I'm a man who wants you."

I pulled the covers higher, then realized he might read that the wrong way—or the right way—and put them down a little. Frankly, I didn't know what I wanted anymore. His lips twisted as he watched me.

"Do you get these nightmares at home?" he asked.

I nodded, relieved at the turn of subject. "They've been worse lately. More intense."

"Do you think they're tied with that *daydream*, for lack of a better word? You know, with the bus?"

"Maybe." I wove my fingers together and stared at my blanket-cloaked knees. "Kit wants to open my cranium and make sure everything's properly oiled, all gears in place, you know. The complexity you mentioned, there might be more to that than you bargained for. Things happen with me, crazy things sometimes. I'm pretty much a mess."

"I've always liked a good mess."

I raised my eyes to see that his emanated sincerity. How many times had I walked into his studio to find him in madman mode? Sketching. Painting. Sculpting. Paint all over his hands. Why had I wasted so much time?

"Still cold?" he asked as my molars rattled together.

"Freezing."

"Do you trust me?"

I paused. "Yes."

"Then lie down. Come on," he said when my eyes widened.

I did, though my heart skittered like a live fish on the bottom of a boat. He walked away, and the light cut out from the other room. He returned with blankets, put them over me, around me. I felt a depression on the bed.

"Noel?"

"Trust. Show that you can." He urged me onto my side, then lay behind me. Though covers clumped between us, he wrapped an arm around my middle. I shifted, shook.

"Kit told me about shivers and fevers once," he said.

"I'm not sick."

"She said you shiver when your body needs to raise its core temperature. With a fever, the body needs to cool down, but because of the sickness, signals get crossed and the message is that the body's too cold. Effed-up signals equal shivers, see?"

"But I don't have a fever. I'm not sick. I'm freezing."

"Yes, we've already established that." He rubbed a hand over my arm. "Tell me more about these dreams."

I told him about the ever-present door and water. I even mentioned Ermanno's role in my most recent nightmare. Mistake.

"Guy's getting to you, Maeve. You need to stay away from those apartments."

Any thoughts I'd had about revealing Ermanno's actual presence at the jazz club vanished at the tone of Noel's voice, the way his arms spasmed around me. A fantasy duel was one thing, but *helpless damsel in distress* was not a role I'd ever be comfortable with in reality.

To derail him, I talked more about my dream, added each remembered detail—which ended up derailing me, too.

"Being left by all those other skulls wasn't what bothered me so much." I stared into the darkness. "This will sound dumb."

"Go ahead and sound dumb. I'm too tired to notice."

"I had no light. It was like something Garrick said once about soul bonds—"

"Here we go."

"—and my soul was smothered. I had no soul."

"You're right, it's dumb. You definitely have soul."

"But I was just a head, you know? I was trapped with no way out, like being buried alive and—"

"Maeve—"

"—like the dark, dank, cold covered me at some point—"

"Maeve—"

"—and I didn't even scream, because I'd pulled the dirt down on myself."

"Without arms, too. And, yeah, you screamed."

"Now he laughs at me." I elbowed him as well as I could through the blankets.

"No laughing," he said. "It's just that you're alive and free. You're here, not stuck at all."

I tried to look at him but couldn't, mummified as I was in covers. "I am so stuck. Help me." His arms lifted, and I shifted around until I faced him in the shadow. "You think I'm being overly dramatic. I am." I nodded. "It's one of my flaws."

"Flaws, charms, whatever."

"Noel."

"Here's what I think. You do have legs—I've seen them, petite and gorgeous. So kick the dirt off. Be what you want to be. Be whole."

"How do you kick when it's all in your mind?" My voice caught, and Noel maneuvered me until my head lay against his chest. "I'm not weak," I said.

"I know you're not."

"And I'm not afraid. Not of most things."

"You're one of the strongest women I know."

"Will you still think that if I ask you to stay here tonight? Maybe you'll keep the nightmares away."

"I'll always think it," he said, and kissed my head.

I flashed on my mother for a moment. What would she say if she knew her daughter—her twenty-five-year-old grown woman of a daughter—slept huddled beside a man? *You're a disgrace! How could you do it? How could you?* She wouldn't believe it was with a wad of blankets between us. I almost wished she could see.

Noel's arms loosened as the minutes passed, and then I recognized in him the first deep breath of sleep.

"I need you, Noel," I whispered. "You're my shore."

Even though this truth frightened me, I embraced it. And when another tremor shook me, I smiled and welcomed that, too. Because I knew I'd grown warmer at the core and that my light burned a little brighter because of it all.

I WOKE TO Noel watching me from my bed's close counterpart, propped on one arm. I didn't even feel self-conscious about that or what had transpired the night before. Progress.

"Good morning," I said, and he smiled, right before a crack of thunder shook the air. My heart leaped. "Wow."

"You slept through the worst of it."

"Really?"

"Tired girl."

"I must've been." Lightning filled the room as I sat up. "No sightseeing today, huh?"

"The forecast's bad for the next five days. I thought that maybe . . ."

"What?"

"Listen, Maeve, about your *empu*. I was there again yesterday—that makes four trips for me. Whatever I think, and whatever Ermanno's problem is, Putra's never there."

"I was told that he's dealing with an illness," I said, remembering. "He must be at his apartment sometimes, though—he's left those notes."

Noel grunted. "If he'd wanted to meet you, don't you think he would've contacted you by now?"

"Maybe so." Though he never would if Ermanno told him I'd sold the *keris*. Why had I found it necessary to confront the *empu's* brother and lie like that? *Stupida!* I rose and stared out the window, at a black sky.

"So I was thinking you should take a break," he said.

"A break?"

"Abandon the *empu* hunt for now. Come with me to Paris."

I spun around. "Paris?"

"I have things to take care of before I can go back to New York. You can meet Ellen and humble me with your French. I'll show you the sights and introduce you to that mannequin. You'll have more to tell your students. You can—"

"All right, already, I'll go with you to Paris if I must!" Could cheeks crack from smiling too wide? "But let's see the Pantheon today. It's supposed to look incredible in the rain."

"The Pantheon, in the rain, with the red woman. I think I can handle that."

My face warmed. I was the red woman, all right.

"We'll have to take a cab," he said. "Are you up for it?"

I considered. "Can we pay him extra to drive slowly?"

"We can try that." He took my hands. I stepped on tiptoes and kissed him. Gently. He wrapped his arms around me. I sensed a shiver.

"Do you feel cold?" I asked.

"No," he said. "I feel hope."

NOEL LEFT LATER that morning to make arrangements, and I packed. It didn't take long to fill my bags, and then I reached into the safe for my *keris*. My hand met only chill metal.

I reopened every dresser drawer. Empty. Empty. Empty except for a Bible. I remembered my search at home during my father's visit, when the *keris* had been in my saxophone case, but this disappearance couldn't be blamed on some mysterious mental lapse. I hadn't risen in the middle of the night and retrieved it from the safe. Not when Noel had been with me, his arms around me, the entire time.

I checked the floor, under the beds and covers. I'd nearly convinced myself the blade had been stolen when—

The pillow. Check.

Memories of skulls and frozen water and muddy hills assaulted me as I recalled Garrick's words: *Put the blade beneath your pillow. If you have a nightmare, the* keris *is bad.*

I swatted at the pillow, flipped it to reveal the *keris* beside its sheath, like a snake shed of its skin. Felt the convulsive swallowing of a fearful person and recognized the person as me.

It has an intention. A will.

A will to spur nightmares and make me question my sanity?

It removes inhibitions. That's how it works.

My convictions fell apart. Maybe I'd been manipulated by the *keris* from the beginning. Chasing an *empu* to Rome? I should be in my apartment, sorting papers with Sam on my lap and preparing for classes. I remembered my beloved sax and the kiss I'd delivered its Roman cousin last night in a fit of aggravated passion, and realized, yes, I'd lost control. And Noel . . . ?

My hand shook as I lifted the *keris*. It felt hot and gleamed dark in my grip, the blood line such an angry red it seemed the blade should drip crimson onto my sheets.

My vision overflowed with gray, then white.

Eling.

I smelled the earth, the must of our shed, as Moira pondered her scabs.

"Now we'll always be joined, no matter what."

I heard her laugh, felt her hand slip, and held tighter.

"Wait, we have to say the words."

Her eyes grew huge. "Till death do us part? This is silly!"

"No, it's not good enough." I pushed our small bleeding fingers together. "I know! 'Even if I die, I'll be with you for always.' Say it."

"Even if I die, I'll be with you for always."

Color returned as I came back to the present, though I doubt I had any in my face. I looked at my finger, healed for over fourteen years, and felt it throb.

I didn't think. Just stuffed the sheath over the blade, thrust on my shoes, left. I saw Giovanni in the lobby.

"Mio Dio!" he said. "What is the matter?"

The Last Will of Moira Leahy

I wished I knew the Italian word for *pawnshop*. "I need to find a place where they'll buy this from me. Someplace close. Anywhere but Trastevere, Giovanni." Anywhere Ermanno wouldn't get his hands on it—or me. The irony that I was now doing what I told him I'd already done was not lost on me. "Is there a place?"

"*Sì*," he said after a moment. "There is a place."

Out of Time

Castine, Maine
NOVEMBER 2000
Moira and Maeve are sixteen

Moira stood frozen beside her bedroom window and watched as Maeve walked next door. Ian would be home soon, and he couldn't see Maeve just now—not after the argument.

Why did you blow me off today at school? Why didn't you just take my hand? You think you're too good for me, don't you?

Moira hadn't known how to react to that. He'd obviously walked up to Maeve and reached for her. Acid rose in her throat at the thought.

You still want to hide it all? It's been three weeks!

She'd called on the original excuse: *My sister—*

But Ian wanted no part of that tired line. *Your sister will have to deal.*

Kit emerged from her house and followed Maeve to the backyard, then sat in the hammock. Maeve paced before her, her hands flying through the air. She flung hair over her shoulder with a jerk of her head, then feigned ripping it out. When she stomped the ground, like she would the bleachers at a school rally, Kit laughed. Moira relaxed a little; Maeve must not have been talking about Ian and Moira.

Moira abandoned the window and stepped before the mirror. She arched her head and pretended to laugh. She tried to fling her hair over her shoulder, though it took three attempts to get it right. She used Maeve's hairbrush and noticed the rougher bristles made her strands more like her sister's, a little wild. She studied her reflection as she widened her eyes, lifted her hands, and made them flutter as Maeve did when she described an event. She paced, then stepped back before the mirror with flushed cheeks.

Passionate, she thought. *I look passionate.*

The Last Will of Moira Leahy

A car door slammed. She rushed to the window to see Ian stride up the drive. His last words rung in her head.

I'm sick of the game. I'll tell Moira myself, I swear it.

Please don't let him see her, Moira thought, but Kit sat alone on the hammock.

"What are you doing?" Maeve's face appeared near Moira's in the glass.

Moira whirled around, her hand over her chest. "How long have you been in here?"

Long enough, Maeve's eyes said.

"Are you ever going to tell me what's going on?"

"Are you ever going to lay off?"

Moira thought she sensed her twin's hurt feelings, the way she used to sense all her emotions, but that was impossible now. Maybe the sorrow was Moira's. She *was* sorry. Sorry for so much.

"You regret something you did," Maeve said. "I can feel it."

Moira threw down the brush. "How many times do I have to say this? You're not welcome in my mind! Leave me to my life!"

"I thought I was your life. I thought you were mine."

Tears pooled like a fast leak in Maeve's eyes. Moira thought she could count on one hand the number of times she'd seen her sister cry. She felt wretched to see it now, to know she'd caused it.

"I don't know you anymore," Maeve said.

"Don't say that." Moira swallowed her own tears.

"This is what you want, fine. I'll never come to your mind again." Maeve dashed tears from her cheeks as her features hardened. "You know, Moira, I think I figured something out about why you could never sense things like I do, why you never heard the music, and why you never would've been good at the sax. You're afraid of everything. We're supposed to be so alike, but we're not. Because I'm not afraid, Moira. I'm not afraid to let go."

Cold emptiness pervaded Moira's senses as Maeve walked away. She thought she'd been blocking her twin for weeks, but a bond must still have dangled between them, must always have been there. And she'd never meant for the distance to last forever. This, now, felt irrevocable. Unbearable.

She heard the front door open, close.

"Maeve!" November air stung Moira's eyes when she lifted the window. "Maeve!"

Ian stood in the grass with Kit, his eyes on Moira. For a second, she thought he recognized the swinging pendant she wore, but then he turned to her sister, who'd stepped onto the walk.

"Maeve!" he shouted.

But Maeve didn't turn. Not for Moira. Not for Ian.

"Leave me alone!" she said, and ran off. Kit followed.

Ian kicked at the fallen leaves, then went inside. The door crashed shut behind him.

Moira closed the window and wrapped her arms around herself; it hurt to breathe. Soon everything would come out, all of her deceptions. And at what cost? She removed the saxophone necklace and left it on the dresser. She used her own brush and pulled her hair back into a ponytail. And then she dropped her barriers against Maeve.

Come back to me, she thought. *Come back.*

She went downstairs and sat on the piano bench but couldn't summon the desire to play.

"I haven't seen you there in a long while." Her father leaned against the doorjamb. "Everything all right, sweetheart?"

"Not really, Daddy."

"Well," he said, "do you know how to fix it?"

She had broken the bond with her sister. Was there glue for that? She had lied to Ian. He would hate her when he learned the truth. Even her parents would despise what she'd become and that it had all begun with jealousy. Moira despised herself, too—for the choices she'd made and the damage she'd done, the damage her lies would still do. Maybe hating herself had made it easier, somehow, to do it all in the first place—actions that required no pride or sense of self-worth.

"I don't know how to fix this, Daddy."

He nodded. "I'm going off this weekend to fix the Hobsons' old boat. Need some stabilizers—wood and glue—and to find the weaknesses. I'll patch what I can, reinforce, and heed the leaks. That's important," he said. "Never ignore the leaks, Moira."

Long after Daddy left, Moira stayed in her room, thinking.

The Last Will of Moira Leahy

There'd been no sign of her sister or Ian, but she couldn't imagine facing them with what needed to be said anyway. Finally, she sat down at her desk and withdrew a sheet of stationery. She touched it—a fragile, thin serving of wood—unsure whether it could truly patch this leak, but ready to try just the same.

CHAPTER SIXTEEN
ABIN BLOO

*D*rizzle spit at me as I strode over slick stone, past cars and people. I heard no music, not on the streets, not in my mind. Not then.

"Scusi," a man said, because I'd stalled before a brick façade. I stared at the sign. This was it—the pawnshop. The *keris* burned against my chest.

I walked on until I found a public fountain and bench. I sat and pushed wet hair off my face, wiped my nose with the back of my hand. A woman with two children approached, but she took a look at me—and maybe the blade sticking out of my coat—and turned away to find another place to sit or drink. Smart woman, good mother.

Eling.

I remembered leaving Castine, the effort it took to pack my things, say good-bye to my father, my mother's straight back. To leave Moira. That had been the hardest thing I'd ever done. But this I knew: Sometimes you had to cut out a piece of your heart in order to save the greater part of yourself from annihilation.

Some things were inhibited for a reason. Some things should remain buried. Whether the *keris* held power or it was all in my sick

200

head didn't really matter; what mattered was that the blade had become interwoven with the bones of all my skeletons.

And *eling* would kill me.

I stood, resolved, and walked back to the pawnshop.

Merchandise lined a long and narrow room, but I was blind to
specifics. I had something to sell, I told the woman behind the
counter. I showed her the *keris*. I knew the amount she offered was
far below the blade's worth, but it didn't matter. She tucked a yellow
euro in my hand and it was done.

Back outside, I leaned against the brick and sucked cold air
through my mouth. My head filled with noise, lost words—*Vinah
way pleshee myna*—and dissonant notes that made me light-headed. I
stumbled further from the shop. People stared.

Abin fanto. Abin rextin.

The voice grew dim as I wandered unknown streets, mapless and
bereft. Minutes passed, hours.

Abin fanto.

I remembered arms around me. Moira's.

Abin fanto.

I realized with a jolt what the words meant.

Abin fanto: Good-bye, love.

Abin rextin. Rextin. This was my name. The name my sister called
me. And she was Bloo.

Abin, Rextin. Abin, Bloo.

Good-bye, sister.

I redirected myself, started back the way I'd come. How could I
have sold the *keris*—something that reminded me of good times, of
adventures with Moira when we'd been whole and happy? How
could I think to give it up, to cave in to some ridiculous fear? How
could I blame it for nightmares I'd had all along? I'd get it back. I
would. But the mazelike streets I'd ensnarled myself on seemed to
have other plans, and a thick fog descended on the city. *Game over,*
nature seemed to say. *All is lost.*

I wouldn't accept it.

I demanded right-of-way as I ran through intersections and
across roads. I felt myself soaked through, skin to bone, when the
sky opened again. No cab stopped for me.

In the end, my father's homing genes saved me. I returned to the pawnshop and told the woman I wanted my *keris* back. I thrust two yellow euros at her. She handed me the blade, then asked me to leave; I'd dripped all over her wood floor.

I SAT FOR hours on the polished granite-and-marble inside the famed Pantheon, while a freefall of rain stormed through the opening in the high dome. The great eye that was the oculus, its iris a mosaic, seemed to weep.

"It's mind-boggling to think people stood here two thousand years ago and watched rainfall just like this."

Noel, impossibly, stood behind me.

"How did you find me?"

"I have superhero powers. I thought we'd established that." He paused, studied me. "We talked about it this morning."

"Oh. I forgot."

He sat. Our knees touched. "You all right?"

"This place was supposedly the temple for all the gods," I said. "The gods' messenger was the goddess of rainbows. Her name was Iris." I pointed to the oculus.

"Interesting," he said. "But I asked about you."

"The root of the word *iris* is Greek for rainbow. I wonder if they thought about that. I wonder if you can see a rainbow in here when the sun shines through a storm."

"Maeve."

"What?"

"Let me in. Tell me."

"There's nothing to tell."

"You're here alone, crying on the floor. I think there's something to tell."

Crying? I wiped at my face, at the sea salt on my cheek.

"What happened?"

The *keris* flared under my coat.

Vinah way pleshee myna. Bloo.

I couldn't shake the sense of her. Moira was everywhere: in the storm, in my head, my blood. "I had a sister, Noel."

202

"Yes, I know. Moira."

"We were twins."

"Twins?"

I nodded.

"What happened to your twin?" He asked it quietly, like he might, with a quick inhalation, take the query back.

I'd never told anyone, but now I found myself transported back and back. I was no longer in Rome; I was in Castine. It was not December; it was November, nine years past. And I was not After Maeve; I was Before Maeve.

But not for long.

I'D HAD A knack for foretelling disaster with the people I loved. I'd sense it creep along the back of my neck or trek through my marrow to kick at my ribs. I'd felt for a long while that something was wrong with my sister. Are you okay? *I'd ask her, and she'd nod.* Yes, Goose. *I felt in her a kind of restlessness I could only identify with music, with wanting to play and not having enough time for it, yet I saw her at the piano less and less.*

When we turned sixteen, our sick poppy gave us passports, and my soul cheered, because our future—full of travel and music and each other— loomed so close. But Moira became a stranger to me, almost overnight. She'd leave the house and get defensive when I asked questions. She closed herself to me, though sometimes I felt a new happiness in her, along with a new grief.

One night, Kit handed me an envelope from her brother. I evaded her questions pretty handily, acted like I didn't care about the letter. The truth was, I had a crush on Ian—everyone did—but I didn't want anyone to know about it, or the kiss he'd given me on my birthday. Especially Moira.

I read the note.

Maeve, meet me at the lighthouse this time.

I read it again.

this time.

Out of Time

"Girls? Someone, come here."

Moira fumbled the knife again, then lay it down and wiped her hands on a kitchen towel. "Be right there!"

She'd been making dinner, a salad to go with the chicken-and-rice casserole already in the oven, but she'd had a hard time performing even simple tasks tonight. She knew what she had to do—face Ian and Maeve, tell the truth. If only she could do that without losing them both.

Maeve was right—she was afraid of everything.

She went upstairs. "Mom?"

"In here." Her mother stood over Poppy in his room, her hands clasped over her mouth. "He won't answer again. He's barely moved all day. He won't eat. I wish your father was here, but he can't afford to turn away jobs right now, even if it means working up the coast on a weekend."

Ben Hobson's boat. Moira had forgotten.

She sat beside her grandfather and put her palm against his cool face. "You look tired, Pops. Did you sleep okay last night?" She searched for an answer from his mouth or in his eyes, but none came. "Should we call the doctor?"

"It's Saturday. They'll just send us to the ER and we'll have another bill in the mail next week that we can't pay. No." Her mother gathered platefuls of untouched food, put them on a tray. "We can do what they do for him and better."

Moira looked at Poppy again, his pale skin. "Can you call Ben Hobson and have him tell Daddy? Tell him to come home."

"What's going on?"

Maeve. Her presence in the doorway had an instantaneous affect on Moira's body, did something to her blood—turned it to ice water or curdled it in her veins, maybe. They hadn't spoken since their argument the previous day. Moira stole a glimpse of her twin and spied runaway hairs sticking out from the hood of her sweatshirt.

"Where have you been?" their mother asked. "Poppy's bad again."

"Sorry, I didn't know." Maeve sat on the bed opposite Moira and stroked their grandfather's cheek as Moira had done seconds before. "I'm sorry you're sick today, Pops." She waited a beat, lowered her voice. "Don't *you* wonder where I've been, Moira?"

Moira hesitated, her anxiety quickening. "Yes."

"I went walking," Maeve replied. "I have a lot to figure—"

Their mother interrupted with a sharp question. "What in God's name is this?" She held a folded sheet of notebook paper.

"That's mine." Maeve stood and opened her hand. "It must've fallen out of my pocket."

"Your poppy's sick, and you plan secret meetings? Who's this note from?"

Maeve said nothing.

"Is this from a boy?"

Waves of nausea rippled through Moira at Maeve's continued silence.

"How dare you, Maeve Leahy! How dare you do this now? I don't have time for this! What've you done to encourage him?"

"I haven't done anything." Maeve glanced at Moira.

No. Oh, no, no, no! Ian had sent a note. Moira tried to read the words crumpled in her mother's hand, but it was impossible except for the word *Maeve*.

"Who is he?"

Please don't tell her.

Maeve shook her head. "No one."

Her mother focused eyes on Maeve that would've made Moira recoil, but Maeve didn't flinch. "You're not to leave this house unless it's for school or lessons." She tossed the note on her tray. "Not even to walk around the yard."

"That's not fair!"

"Until you tell me the name of that boy, you're grounded. Stay with Poppy." She left the room with the tray. Dishes rattled as she walked down the stairs.

Maeve turned to Moira. "Explain it," she said evenly.

With great effort, Moira looked into Maeve's eyes—eyes swimming with questions and the slim hope that she hadn't been dealt a deep betrayal. She wished she had the note she'd written earlier, that she could hand it to Maeve and be done with it. She was grateful for her mother's shout—"Moira, this chicken is burning!"—and stood quickly.

Maeve grabbed her arm. "What have you done?"

"I can't talk about this now," Moira said. She'd give her the note. Tomorrow. Tonight, she had to find Ian. She walked away from her sister and down the stairs. And though she never once looked back, she felt Maeve's eyes on her the entire time.

CHAPTER SEVENTEEN
THE DARKEST STORM

 tried to call Ian to ask about the note, but our phone seemed dead. My mother had probably taken it off the hook. I skipped dinner. Instead, I waited at my window until dark.

A light went on in Ian's bedroom. I watched his pacing shadow form until the room went black again. Gone. To meet me, or to meet her. I had to know. I waited until he stepped from the house, then I reached for my window. The wood stuck. I watched as he got into his car and started it. Mrs. Bronya yelled at him from the door. He drove away.

I forced opened the window. The chill November air tasted like rain. Our coats were downstairs, but I found an old satin marching-band jacket in my closet. Not ideal, but I pulled it over my sweatshirt and moved back to the window to assess the tree.

The big oak had arms I'd linked with many times before, but never from my bedroom window. My father had promised a lash to my backside if I ever tried. It was an easy reach to the closest limb. I threw myself onto it, come what may, and swayed there for a second like a monkey. Then I hoisted my legs onto the thickest part of the branch and shimmied down until I sat in the crook of the tree. The first drops of rain bled into the satin as my feet touched the ground.

I ran past my home, and up the hill toward the lighthouse. The sky *was exceptionally dark, apart from the occasional bolt of lightning, but I knew these roads. I ran past a few more houses and their dim-light offerings, ran until I met the woods. Branches snagged my hair as I followed a path.*

By the time I made out the black column that was the lighthouse, my wet coat felt like a straitjacket. I stopped, listened. Heard only the percussive sound of hard rain on dead leaves.

It happened fast. I fell. Someone had grabbed me and pulled me down, pinned me against the ground. Ian. His lips covered mine, devoured. Rain beat around us as thunder detonated overhead. I should've stopped him. Maybe I could have, then. But I was young and I liked him, and this kiss was like no kiss I'd ever known. Every part of me rose up to meet him, and my hands tracked his body.

He said something, the word car, *but I shook my head as he put his mouth back on mine, found my tongue. When he pulled back, his words sputtered at me like the hard rain. "Ignoring . . . Cold . . . How would you like? . . . Answer? . . . Answer!"*

He shook my shoulders once, but I had no answer.

He kissed me again, harder. I felt his hand beneath my shirt, but it wasn't until I felt wet leaves against my hips that I tore my mouth away.

"Stop," I said, but I couldn't hear my voice over the surging staccato of the rain. I tried again—"Ian, stop, wait"—as thunder screamed again, too.

He stopped. I thought he'd heard me. But then I felt the tug of my pants.

I struggled to sit, yell. Struggled with my body, to pull up, move him off, get control. But everything was confused. He sunk me back into the ground, and then I couldn't even fight anymore, because I was drowning in an emotional seiche as the strongest sense of foreboding I'd ever felt rolled over me. I was lost in its wake. I dimly registered that the wind had changed, that the raindrops fell sideways.

As Ian spread my legs, I opened my thoughts to my twin, let them pour out of me in a flood of disgust.

You own this, Moira, *I thought.* Whatever comes of this is because of you. I hate you.

I thought for a moment I felt my sister and her horror, but then all I could feel was my own.

Please, no. Please. Don't.

I closed my eyes and went away in my mind, up through the swell of a

November storm, the explosion of expanding air, light and loud, and past the clouds, in search of the sun.

But it, too, seemed lost.

"MY GOD, MAEVE. My God."

I couldn't look at Noel. His raw voice said it all. But the story, for all its horror, wasn't nearly finished.

"You don't have to—" he began, but I didn't stop. The dam in my mind cracked wider.

I DON'T REMEMBER walking. I don't remember how I made it home wearing only the drenched satin jacket and my unbuttoned pants. I remember my mother, though, her ragged face as she opened the door. I remember the slap she delivered to my immobile cheek and mute mouth with her palm, and that she yanked at my pants to prove a man had been there, had left evidence of that mixed with my blood. I remember what she said—that I was a slut, that I'd desecrated our home with my filth.

"Poppy died while you did this!" she screamed.

I couldn't process that. I wanted to fall into the floor beside my pants, be absorbed by the walls, evaporate.

"You've all left me, left me with—"

She fell to her knees, her shoulders shaking, her hands over her face. I remember thinking the way the light fell on her made her look fractured, and that if I touched her she would break into tiny pieces.

"Where is your sister?" She lifted her head to glare at me.

Sister? I knew the word. Sister.

"Moira's missing and I know you can find her, so find her! Poppy's dead, do you hear me?" She scrambled to her feet and shook me. "Find her! Find her!"

She shook and shook, but I felt nothing but the crystal edges in my chest, a blanket of icy molecules. There was no trace of the soul thread that had always connected me to Moira, her to me. There was only the bob of my body as I floated in the abyss, clinging to the stump of an umbilical cord and hearing the final echoes of a clarion connection.

Somewhere in the distance a clock chimed twelve.

Out of Time

Castine, Maine
NOVEMBER 2000
Moira and Maeve are sixteen

Moira peered out the living room window at eleven o'clock, desperate for any sign of Ian. He'd probably wanted to meet now, but where? She had checked every garbage can in the house and hadn't been able to find his note, and she couldn't face Maeve to ask about those lost details. Tomorrow she'd tell her the truth, and she'd tell Ian, too. For tonight, she needed to be with him and feel his skin beside hers one more time. She'd savor every second, in case he never kissed her again.

"Moira?" Her mother approached, her eyes all but lost in the bags beneath. "I'm going to check on Poppy again, then go to bed. I put the chicken pan in the sink to soak. Can you clean it and lock up?"

"Sure. How's Poppy? Does he seem comfortable at least?"

"He's asleep, last I checked."

"How about you, Mom? Can I get you anything?"

She hugged Moira. "You're a good girl, Moira Leahy." Her voice sounded choked, but Moira couldn't tell if she cried, because her mother turned and went upstairs.

A good girl? Could she ever believe that of herself again?

She replaced the phone on its hook and, despite the hour, dialed the familiar number.

"Hello," Kit said.

Moira hung up. She rubbed her temples as rain beat against the eaves. At least they'd have a little shelter at the lighthouse. That's where he'd be, she knew it.

She opened the hall closet and chose the purple jacket that had been a gift from her mother's cousin who was from away. *Never use that in the boat,* her father had said. *You'd never be seen in the water with it.* She pulled it on, though the sleeves didn't reach her wrists and the buttons wouldn't close over her chest.

The Last Will of Moira Leahy

The wind surprised her with its strength when she went outside. She struggled to close the door quietly, then stepped around puddles collected on the walk to Ian's house. His car, she realized, wasn't in the drive. Had he managed to sneak past his parents and take it? Was he waiting for her on the road? That would be . . . brilliant! They'd be dry, warm; they'd have a place to be together, and later to talk. She pulled her bike from the shed and made her way onto the road, anxious to find Ian as soon as possible.

Lightning flashed as she pedaled uphill, struggling to see the road in the heavy downpour, despite her bike light. Finally, she reached the fork, and stopped. One path would take her to the lighthouse; its hill was a challenging ride even in good weather. The adjacent road was flatter but lead only to more homes. She hoped for headlights, any sign of Ian's car, but a dozen minutes passed, and still she stood at the crossroads as rain pooled in the front of her hood and streamed before her like a falls.

He'll find me, she thought, as her skin rippled with gooseflesh and her clothes grew sodden through gaps in her coat. Lightning filled the sky again, followed by a giant clap of thunder. A great sense of opening came upon her then. Maeve. Maeve had come back to her. She even heard her voice.

You own this, Moira. Whatever comes of this is because of you. I hate you.

The lighthouse. They were there. She knew it with numbing certainty. Rain pelted her eyes and cheeks as she pointed her bike uphill once more. She pumped furiously at her pedals. Her wheels spun.

Please, no. Please. Don't.

She teetered, lost momentum, fell. Left her bike. Ran. The road seemed an endless stretch of black, until pain made her stop. Moira felt herself torn open for a second time and knew what it meant, her shadow sense keen and raw. The unimaginable. Ian and Maeve. Maeve, oh, Maeve.

She vomited in the road, then stumbled blindly back to her bike. Lost. Wanting home. Safety. Out of the nightmare. But she couldn't bring herself to leave. She angled her face to the sky and wailed. It sounded, eerily, like the wind, like music. Her sister was innocent. She had to stop them, even now. She had to tell them the truth. She was the only one who could.

A calmness of mind filled Moira as she faced the lighthouse, even

211

as the storm grew more violent. She found her seat again and began the slow trek uphill on the bike—determined, more sure of herself than she'd been in a long time.

Headlights blinded her when she rounded the steepest part of the bend. She shielded her eyes at first, but then she waved, hoping with everything in her that it had all been a mistake: that the shadow sense had been wrong; that her sister was at home, asleep; that Ian had come for her after all, to wrap her in his arms and warm her and forgive her and love her; that the car would stop.

But the car did not stop.

THE DRIVER—A drunk on his way to getting drunker—didn't realize he'd hit something as he swerved past, though he thought he'd seen a large, purple butterfly cross his windshield. He didn't know that he'd tossed a young woman into a ditch filled with reeds the color of smashed pumpkins—and he probably wouldn't have cared just then if he had.

Later, he'd find a piece of a bike's handlebar jammed in his fender and wonder about that Leahy girl from Castine, the one everyone was talking about. He'd never tell a soul.

CHAPTER SEVENTEEN
(SUSTAINED)

ain continued to spatter onto the marble floor of the Pantheon, and at me. The storm seemed relentless.

"My mother wouldn't let me in the house until I found my sister," I said. "I stood in the shed all night. I didn't even hear when the car came to take Poppy to the morgue. The next morning, Kit found Moira in a ditch. She'd been hit by a car."

Noel said the words over and over: *So sorry.* What else was there?

"I used to trust my feelings the way I trust the sun will rise and set. They told me when to be careful and gave me music. They prevented disaster at least once. But for the most significant event of my life, my feelings failed, because I blocked her. I blocked her to punish her."

"No," he said.

"Yes, I did, to punish her because she liked the same guy that I liked and because I thought she might be seeing him and because she'd shut me out." I rocked a little, wanted to curl up on the floor. "I didn't come close to understanding the depth of it all—her feelings or her lies, that she'd taken my name, or how far they'd gone."

"You couldn't have known."

"I could've kept a link to her or at least kept my barriers up at the end. But I wanted her to know what she'd caused, and feel my pain and hatred."

"Maybe she didn't. You can't know what she felt."

"I do know. I made her feel it," I said as rain spit at me. "I wonder if she still feels it."

"Don't do that. You're here. You're still alive."

I looked at the oculus, but there were no rainbows—just the storm and a cluster of birds that flew in, out again. "So is she. She's been in a coma for nine years. She's brain-dead."

WE SAT SIDE by side until the rain stopped. Noel held my hand, rubbed my skin, mumbled kindnesses. What could he say? Mine was not an ancient history littered with beautiful relics. Nothing could be done to save Moira. There would be no miracle. There was what there was: A bitter mother who believed life cruel for stealing her good daughter, a lost father, and me.

WE BOUGHT SANDWICHES at the bar to eat in Noel's room. I tore into my food, but Noel just sat, expressionless.

"Aren't you going to eat?" I asked.

"What about music?"

"What about it?"

"Is Moira why you don't play?"

I took a sip of water and remembered when I saw Ian for the first time *after*. I didn't like to think about this, the lost look of him. I didn't like to think about him at all. But I still recall how the wind blew his too-long hair into his eyes, covered them like the veil my mother wore to Poppy's funeral.

"Ian came to me after the accident. He'd figured something out—that the woman he'd had sex with that night wasn't the woman he'd *been* having sex with. 'I think I accidentally had sex with Moira before the crash,' he said. I'll never forget that: *accidental sex*."

"Christ. What a blow to that guy."

"Don't feel sorry for him," I snapped.

Noel said nothing, but his eyes held tight to mine.

I took a deep breath. "I told him that Moira had been his lover all along. I was just the girl he'd raped."

Noel winced. Ian's reaction had been much stronger.

Rape? How can you say that? It was incredible, beautiful even—the storm, you, all of it. I love you, Maeve. You know it!

Incredible? Beautiful? Love? I wanted to be sick. He made me doubt myself, though. I'd liked him, had kissed him back at first. Maybe I hadn't struggled enough. Hadn't said no enough. Had just lain there and let him . . .

Had it really been rape? But it had. It had.

"He wouldn't believe he'd been with Moira all along."

Why are you lying? You don't think I know you? I could pick you out of a thousand identical people. You're just different, Maeve.

"He must've felt some doubt though," I said, "because he listed things he thought proved him right. His evidence."

What about the necklace you wore, the one I gave you?

What necklace?

The saxophone stone! And what about the time you played for me in the grass? That was real!

Moira never played the saxophone for you. She couldn't have, because she couldn't play.

You pretended to! he said. *But it was all there in the touch of your hands. No, you're lying,* he repeated, and his eyes grew wide. *Moira, Moira,* he said in a crazy, escalating chant.

What a twist. He'd thought I was pretending to be my sister.

You're not Maeve, he said, *but you're letting them believe it because you want to be her. Jealous bitch! You're Moira!* he shouted. *Maeve's the one fighting for her life in a hospital right now, and you stole her name because you're weak! Don't think I won't know! I'll know when you never play the saxophone again! I'll know because you'll be too chickenshit to do anything with your life but sit in your garden with a book and play that fucking piano!*

"Maeve?"

I lay my shredded napkin on the table. "Ian thought I was Moira after the accident. I considered the idea for a while—that I was her and I'd just lost my mind somewhere along the way.

"A few days later I went out onto the Penobscot with my sax. I didn't care that it wasn't safe to be on the water anymore, I just had to get away from everything and everyone on the land. And I think I needed that communion, you know, to play my music and feel that I was me, Maeve. But when I tried, I couldn't—" I choked on the words. "I couldn't catch my breath. I felt like I'd lost a lung."

I'll know when you never play the saxophone again.

Random pieces of life fell into place there on the water. Ian watching me with his telescope, listening to me play in his boat. Ian making me a saxophone necklace that I'd never seen. Ian asking Moira to play for him. Ian asking Kit when my album would come out, if I'd really tour Europe someday, when I'd leave for good. Ian telling me I might just be the one to get out of Maine, a spark of grudging admiration in his eyes right before he kissed me on my birthday. The piano music I'd seen flung around the room. Moira's desire to learn the sax. Moira's anger, the way she'd blocked me out.

"Moira had loved Ian, and he'd loved the idea, I guess, of someone who'd have a big career outside of Castine. How could I ever find joy in music again when it was at the center of so much jealousy and pain, and the greatest loss I'll ever know? I tipped my sax over the side."

It had been quick, the sea's claiming of my instrument. The bell had filled with water, bobbled and toppled and sunk below the surface. Gone.

"It wasn't your fault, Maeve."

"Well, not just mine."

He shoved his plate aside. "It wasn't your music's, either. It wasn't even Moira's or Ian's."

"How can you—"

"Hang on, hang on," he said as I gritted my teeth. "It was bad luck."

"Bad luck?" I almost laughed.

"A string of circumstances that ended in tragedy. None of you are bad people." I glared at him. "Does Ian still think . . . ?"

"That I'm my sister?" I shook my head. "Reality kicked in after a few weeks. He tried to apologize."

I'm sorry. I'm sorry for everything.

I'd said nothing. Just left him where he'd found me, standing on the stone beach to stare at the sea.

Later, I'd gone to Bangor to see my sister. I went every day at first, then less often when they transferred her to a long-term facility closer to home. Each trip scored me like a fresh cut to my heart, so much worse than anything I'd seen with Poppy. No smile or glimmer of light from her, no feeling. Even her face began to lose its natural shape, the dips and valleys filling into roundness.

Dead. Brain-dead. My sister was dead inside. She was no longer in the bed, I'd tell myself, she was . . . elsewhere.

I couldn't have imagined anything worse, until the day I overheard my sister's doctor speaking with my father. He'd run some tests, he explained, because of abnormalities in Moira's cycle, and they'd discovered something called a missed miscarriage. Moira had been pregnant. When my father noticed my presence in the doorway, he set the rules.

We won't tell your mother about this. She doesn't need to know about another lost child. We'll never speak of this again—not to another soul, not even to each other.

I might have gone crazy, if not for Kit. Something happened to her when I grew somber and careful: She asserted herself like never before. I suppose she recognized that no one, including me, was taking care of me—though my dad tried, when he wasn't working all hours—so she decided to take up the cause.

"Kit and I had both applied for early graduation and made it through the hoops. She pushed me to stick to that plan, told me it'd be good to leave Maine and start over in a new place. And I'd realized something. Hard work made the days move faster and unfocused my mind on everything I'd lost."

How easy it had been to submerge myself in language instead.

Vinah way pleshee myna.

"You know the rest. We were accepted at Betheny U. I haven't been back to Castine in years. It's just too hard. End of story."

After we finished eating, I gathered our dinnerware to return to the bar and caught him staring at me in that way that meant he was trying to puzzle something out.

"What?"

"Who—Forget it."

"Go ahead. Ask." I'd made my soggy pages available for viewing. He could turn them if he wished.

"Moira's been brain-dead for almost a decade. What about closure? Wouldn't everyone like it? Have your parents considered taking her off life support?"

"They did. They took her off four years ago." I rubbed my arms; this particular ache never lessened. "Moira's case is a medical anomaly," I said. "She kept breathing without any help at all. No one understands why."

Out of Time

Castine, Maine
MAY 1992
Moira and Maeve are seven

"It was the summer of 1779," said Mrs. Markey. She stood in the field with all of Maeve and Moira's first-grade classmates. It was a familiar field, home to ball games and sometimes long walks. Moira watched a cricket leap around a patch of grass until she heard the word *ghost*. "The story goes that a ghost lives here, down deep in a cavern beneath the bricks. Castine's drummer boy died during a battle in the Revolution, which is very sad, isn't it, boys and girls?"

They all nodded, quiet.

"Some people used to say you could hear the boy pound on his drum at midnight. That's kind of scary, isn't it?"

They nodded again, and Mrs. Markey smiled a little. Moira took Maeve's hand and squeezed.

"But we don't really believe in ghosts, do we?"

Moira shook her head so hard, she gave herself a headache.

"Legend says the ghost decided to leave the field where he'd died to come here to the dungeon of Fort George." She pointed at a brick-and-cement structure that didn't seem much longer than Daddy was tall. "Are there any questions?"

No one seemed to have any.

"Then we're off to Fort Madison. Come along, class."

Maeve grabbed Moira's arm, which made her trip a little. "Why do you think he went?"

Moira screwed up her face. "What do you mean?"

"The ghost boy. Why would he leave a big field and go into a tiny dungeon?"

She didn't know; she shook her head.

"It doesn't seem very smart."

Moira agreed with her that it didn't, then picked a dandelion and blew white fluff in Maeve's face, happy to be free of ghosts and dungeons and all things that go bump in the night.

The Third Will

MOIRA

SEVERAL TIMES DURING THE NIGHT I WAS AWAKENED BY THE TOUCH OF THE WIND STIRRING THROUGH THE SLEEPING TREES, WHISPERING GENTLY IN MY EAR A THOUSAND REMINDERS OF YESTERDAY'S DREAMS. STAY A MOMENT, I ASKED, BUT BEFORE I COULD OPEN MY EYES THE FRAGRANCE WAS GONE, AS A BIRD IN WILD FLIGHT.

—NOYES CAPEHART LONG,
FROM HIS PAINTING *WHISPERER*

CHAPTER EIGHTEEN
SECOND CHANCES

"I have something to tell you," Noel said the next morning. We had turned the settee in my room toward the window and sat watching raindrops smear over our reflections. "I hate to bring it up after yesterday."

I couldn't take any more pity. Not from either of us.

"It was sad for me, remembering," I said, "but I'm okay. Moira's accident happened years ago. It's not my now." Or it wasn't, usually. I propped my feet against the window's wooden framework. "Shoot."

He leaned back, appraised me for a second. "I called my grandfather last night to say we'd be home soon. He wasn't happy."

This threw me. "He misses you, I know it."

"He wants me to stay and hand those notes over to Jakes."

"Okay, this might be a stupid question," I said, drumming my fingers over my thighs, "but why didn't he send everything to Jakes himself?"

"Because he promised my mother that any search would go through me. The risk would have to be mine."

"Risk?"

"Evocative word, isn't it? I heard it for the first time yesterday. He

223

threw in some guilt, too." Noel's accent thickened to Garrick levels: " 'You don't know what it's like to want something and have no choice but to wait with hope?' " His look took on a new significance and lassoed me in.

"The risk," I said, after a hard swallow. "What did he mean?"

"On my eighteenth birthday, he gave me a letter from my mother—something she'd written years before. I wouldn't read it. That letter was in the first FedEx."

"Jesus, Noel! You never opened it?"

"I didn't want her excuses."

My feet hit the floor. "You have a window to the past! You can finally understand! If you won't, then give it to me and I'll—"

"I opened it last night. After."

After my meltdown. After he'd found me in the rain. After we'd talked about *After*.

"What you told me, it made me think . . ."

"Good," I said. "If any part of my history inspired you to take real action now, then I'm nothing but glad."

"I don't know if I am."

His mother's letter, he explained, had been far from a sweet bedtime tale. She'd written of a man who beat a woman, who broke her nose and ribs, shoved her down an elevator shaft. A woman who ran but was always found, who was threatened with a gun and death. A woman who became pregnant and ran harder, hid better. Who landed in an asylum.

"That's where I was born, in a nuthouse, and then I was shipped off to my grandfather. They kept her for another five years, until she stopped insisting my father hid behind every closed door with a gun," he said, as I dug my nails into my palms. "She lived with us for a while. I remember a skinny woman. Bedraggled with a crooked nose. Big brown eyes. Ticklish feet."

I imagined this: a child pulling off socks, making a tattered woman smile and laugh. "Why didn't she stay?"

"She said she felt him out there searching and had to go before he found her, and me. Her paranoia made her leave."

"Maybe she did feel him. How do you know she didn't?" Suddenly, I felt a kinship with this woman. "Does she know your father died years ago? Does she know he's gone?" A terrible thought: "Did she kill him?"

Noel gripped his skull, closed in on himself a little. "Nothing's what I thought. My father's alive, Maeve. He doesn't know I exist. Wareham isn't a family name, and neither is Ryan. Those names were changed because she insisted I could be stolen or hurt if he learned about me and found us. So my grandfather isolated us in a little town. Kept me out of public school. Didn't let me walk more than a block from the shop without him, Christ, for the longest time. But I had a roomful of art supplies, didn't I? It's a miracle he ever gave me that motorcycle. She wanted me kept."

"Kept safe. She was afraid for you."

"She could've taken me with her."

"She didn't want you to be hurt."

"I could've helped."

"You were a child."

"Not always a child." He rose and clutched the curtain. I stood, too, squeezed his tense arm.

"She left that letter, Noel. Wasn't that her way of inviting you into her life, when you were ready to search?"

"I don't know. She could be anywhere. In an asylum, bloody well off her rocker. Dead. Or still hiding, scared." His expression bled desperation and regret.

What would a man capable of beating his wife do to learn she'd hidden a child from him, changed his name? What would he do, him, the worst kind of monster? *Like Ian,* a part of me cried, while another said, *No, no, not like him.* Noel's father was far more dangerous, far more conscious of his decisions.

"What are you going to do?"

"The only thing I can. Find her."

Find her! You have to find her!

Maybe I was living vicariously through Noel, but I ached for him to succeed and find peace. Because it was still possible.

"I faxed everything to Jakes, including the letters in the second package. They weren't from her," he said, answering the question before I asked. "A next-of-kin notice that she'd checked out of a hospital in Lucerne, another note from a safe house in Purbeck,

that sort of thing. Now that he has it all, things could move quickly."

"Should you leave for Paris today?" I asked, as a cold wind leaked through the window seams.

"He said I should wait until he knows which side of the continent she's on, if she's here at all. So I need to stay. More than that, I want to. Effing weird, eh?"

"Not weird. She's your mother." I smiled as reassuringly as I could and stifled what I knew to be true: Life made no guarantees when it came to closure.

THE WEATHER, LOYAL to the forecast, stayed wretched all day. Noel and I didn't do much. Played cards. Watched TV. Waited for the phone to ring. I lay on the bed at one point with my legs straight up against the headboard and wall.

"What're you doing?" Noel asked.

"Imagining life as a ceiling creature. See that lamp there?" I pointed at the scoop-bowl light above me. "A ceiling creature could sit in that."

"A ceiling creature would burn its ass on the bulb."

"It's why all ceiling creatures have hot asses," I said, gratified by his snort of laughter. No better time to tell him what was on my mind. "I want to go to Sri Putra's again."

His upside-down grin flatlined. "Why am I not surprised?"

"Because you sense I'm a diehard adventuress." Truth was, my need to understand the *keris* had been resuscitated over the last twenty-four hours. What had happened when I'd seen those white lights and had that vivid memory of blood and promise? My mind, playing tricks, maybe. Walking me over the ceiling.

Something new had occurred to me, too. Ermanno, who clearly had no qualms about reading the notes Sri Putra left for me, might never have given my contact information to his brother. Somehow, I had to find a way to leave a private note for the *empu*—tell him where I was and that I still had the blade. At least then I'd have tried everything, dug as hard as possible for answers before packing my questions and leaving Rome. My poppy would've done no less.

Noel remained silent.

"Maybe he's back," I said, "or maybe he's left another note." I righted myself and leaned closer to the meager glow coming in through the window. There was a spot in my vision from the lamp. "You don't have to come."

"Funny," he said. "Let's get it over with."

NOEL CARRIED A big umbrella borrowed from the hotel, but I veered out from under it and let the sky drizzle on my hat. Once, when I slipped on the slick stones, he grabbed me up, and I took the opportunity to lock his hand with mine and keep it there. He smiled when I did this and shifted our hands to interlace a finger with my pinkie.

We walked with squeaky-sole sounds down the deserted hall of Putra's apartment, prepared for anything: Putra away, Putra at home, Ermanno stalking about. No one could've predicted what we found.

The *keris* with bold ovals that the *empu* had purchased from Time After Time protruded from his door—a door now covered in the same red *X* marks I'd seen in my dream. The note I'd written for the *empu* slipped from my hand, onto the floor.

Noel rocked the blade free. Dropped it. The corridor still echoed with sound when he held my likeness before me—the photograph stolen from his wallet. I hadn't even registered that it was there, impaled by the blade. Ermanno had cleaved my face in two.

Shuffling sounds registered. Putra's neighbor, Mrs. Fiori, plodded down the other side of the hall as if up to her thighs in water. She wore black. Her words raised my skin.

"Death lives here. There is death."

The illness she'd mentioned . . . had Sri Putra died?

"Never again, Maeve," Noel said, his voice vibrating with anger. "Never again. Say it."

"Never again."

He kicked the ruined blade, and I saw it from the corner of my eye—my fallen note fluttered and flapped, then sailed right under the *empu*'s door. I crouched, pressed my cheek against the linoleum and peered through the sizeable gap between the floor and the wood. And there was my note—just out of my reach.

• • •

FURY POURED OFF Noel as we walked to the hotel. I felt something else: vulnerability. I didn't like it.

"Go back to Betheny," he said at one point.

I stopped. He did, too.

"Why?"

"A psychopath just stabbed your picture."

"You want me to go?"

"Yes," he said. "I want you to go."

"What if I'm not willing to leave town because of some guy with anger-management issues? What about your mother?"

"I don't know what's going on with this investigation, Maeve. It could be days or months before I hear anything. You can't hold my hand the whole time."

"And what if I could? Would you want me to?"

He surprised me with a rich laugh, then took my hand and squeezed. "I'd never turn down this hand. Not ever."

A different kind of defenselessness rose up in me. It hurt, felt good, like the piecing together of broken glass. I smiled and hoped nothing would shatter. He stared at my face and mouth, and I wished he'd kiss me. And he did. A gentle kiss. Safe. Too safe. Maybe now that he knew everything about my past, he'd decided it was best not to love me. Maybe no one, not even Noel, would look for comfort in glass arms.

The rain came harder. He opened the umbrella.

"Tomorrow's New Year's Eve," he said. "Let's have that. Then we'll see what happens."

"All right," I said. "We'll see what happens."

I DRESSED FOR New Year's Eve in wool gabardine trousers and a top I'd been suckered into buying at Mariella's. The blouse skimmed my body and dipped low in a V, framing my garnet necklace in a perfect color match.

"You're beautiful," Noel said when I opened the door to him later.

"Oh, no," I said. "You're much finer." He sported a rich brown suit and green dress shirt. Italian, all the way.

"We can stand here and argue about it all night or . . ."

"Or?"

He pulled a rose out from behind his back, kissed the bloom, handed it to me.

Well. I have to admit that the romantic in me—and yes there was one, even if it was slight—swooned a bit. I inhaled the flower's berry essence and felt my insides turn warm as a *keris*. I bit my lip, unbit it, struggling with the foreign role of woman-on-a-date.

"It's up to you, but Giovanni said we could borrow his bike. The restaurant's a little far for walking, and finding a cab might be difficult. I think it's safe. Giovanni said the old Roman tradition of throwing things out of windows on New Year's Eve is a thing of the past, though his uncle apparently tossed a refrigerator from a second-story apartment in 2006."

"That'd make for an interesting hangover," I said, but that's not why I smiled. "So you'll drive us?"

He tipped his head. "Do you trust me?"

My insides quivered as I nodded.

"Do you want a ride, pretty lady?"

Noel. Flying. How could I resist? "You bet I do."

ONE EXHILARATING RIDE later, we stepped inside a dungeonesque space illuminated with flickering torches and lit hearths. Romance oozed from every quarter, yet I took my seat. I glanced at Noel, away, back again, fluttered my lashes. Realized I was a pathetic flirter. Hopefully, my blush was lost to the fireglow.

Dinner came: thick cuts of lamb and pumpkin risotto dotted with globs of mozzarella. The rice filled my mouth, sweet, tangy, and buttery. A strolling violinist smiled between us as if sharing lovers' secrets, as his bow keened and strings cried. How I wanted to be that lover, then.

"You never replaced your sax?" Noel asked, when the musician left to greet other guests.

"I couldn't."

"It's your paper and paint, you know."

"Maybe it is."

"You never hunger for it?"

"Hunger?" I dragged my hand under the table and played a harmonic melody to accompany the violinist right there on my lap. "Yes," I said. "I do."

Reach up. Kick the dirt off.

"You must be hungry then. A lot."

Hungry. Tired. Ready to move on.

"I want to get past it, Noel. I'm ready to be free."

"So decide it," he said. "Make it happen."

"I want . . ."

Reach. Just do it.

"What do you want?" Noel asked, as whispers of risk and possibility played over me like the kiss of a bow over taut strings.

"I want . . ."

Reach.

And I did. I stood and reached across the table, touched the strong bones of Noel's cheek and jaw, knowing the skull beneath shone full of light. Then I put my butter-tang mouth on his and hoped he tasted my solidity.

Someone's voice cleared behind me. Our waiter, with a message from Giovanni, who'd made the reservation for us. We were needed back at the hotel. *Emergenza*, he'd said.

Noel's mother had been found.

THE BIKE'S SLICK power and the way the wind whipped at me as we turned down another street reminded me of a ride on the Penobscot. Even the sound of fireworks seemed swallowed whole by the engine's throaty growl. People bundled in mufflers and heavy coats lined the streets as we sped past. Even more gathered in the piazzas, dancing to the buskers' music and drinking. Families sat on folding chairs and ate from kettle pots. Teenagers lit earsplitting bottle rockets. Children played with sparklers and spray cans of string. Old women sang. The smell of roasting chestnuts permeated the air.

I tucked my hands under Noel's jacket and nestled my face against his back. I let my fingers wander a little—easy enough to blame on the bump of a tire against cobblestones or the need for a better grip. But the moment rained magic, the sky aflame. I found a place between his shirt buttons and grazed his skin. He hunched his shoulders and pressed against my cheek. I kissed him through his jacket.

"I wish you didn't have to go," I said, knowing my words would be flung safely away.

Car horns blared as we neared our hotel, and firecrackers split the air as we rushed through the door.

"*Dio mio!* I have looked for travel for you to leave right away," Giovanni told Noel. "Your hunt man—"

"Jakes?"

"—he said you should go tonight to London."

"So it's England," Noel said.

"You say you do not like to fly in planes," Giovanni said. "There is a train leaving Termini station in a few hours. It is a slow train to Milano in the night, but you will be there by morning. From there, you can go on to Paris and London."

Noel turned to me as the sulfurous scent of explosives filled my nostrils. "Come with me," he said. "You thought you might like to before."

I smiled, so happy he'd asked; and though part of me tingled at the whisper of *avventura*, I shook my head. "That was when it was about packing up an apartment, seeing Ellen's shorts, and thanking a mannequin. This is your mother. Your journey."

He nodded, and I knew he understood. "Giovanni, can you look into flights for tomorrow? Put me on a red-eye to London?"

"You're sure?" I asked.

"I can't leave you now." He took both of my hands, raised them to his chest. "Let's have midnight."

I smiled, and for the first time in my life, felt a little like Cinderella. In a piratey kind of way.

CHAPTER NINETEEN
ON PASSION
AND PURGATORY

ow do you know when the time's right, when you feel safe enough, when you're willing to take the chance? These are questions I'd asked myself over the years, when I'd said no to a date or turned my head to avoid a love scene in a film. When I'd clung to *just, just.* Now I knew the answer: You know because the time's right, and you feel safe enough, and you're willing to take the chance. Because you're with the right person.

Noel and I stepped into my room, and I locked the door behind us, leaned against the wood. He said my name, and I turned but couldn't look at him.

"I hope you don't think—" he started. "What's in your head?"

"I don't know. I don't—" I met his eyes. "You said once that you loved me. Do you still? Do you want me at all?"

"Of course I still love you." His eyes went dark. "Of course I want you."

Tension unraveled in me—*thank you, thank you.*

"But I'd never want to be one of your regrets," he said.

The words hurt for a second, but then I realized that he didn't know what I'd come to understand. Time to remedy that. I put my hands on his face.

"I love you, Noel. I love you and want you, and I'm not made of glass, damn it." I couldn't read the complex play of emotions over his face, but then his hands settled on my waist.

"Christ," he said. "The woman of my dreams is throwing herself at me—"

"Well, I wouldn't say throwing—"

"—and I can't believe I'm saying this—"

"So don't."

"—but maybe you need more time. You've been through hell." He stared beyond me, at the door.

"Noel Ryan, you look at *me* now." I tried for a witchy glare when his eyes met mine. "Are you telling me what I need?"

"No, just—"

"Let me rephrase." I arched against him. "Don't tell me what I need. I need you. And I demand your compliance,"—I couldn't help myself—"pirate."

He raised a brow. "Let me get this straight. I'm at your command? I have to listen to you?"

"Absolutely."

His hands spread over my back. "Then who am I to resist, lowly wretch that I am?"

"I'm glad you finally know your place." I stood tall and kissed his mouth, felt his hesitation and was almost grateful for it. *Yes,* I thought, *let me do everything, let me be able to.*

I wanted to prove it to myself, and somehow I did that night. I possessed a flame, a passion that grew and twisted into a knotting ache of desire. The need my actions impelled frightened me a little, but not enough to stop.

"I love you," he murmured, and kissed my neck, our bodies pressed together. "I adore you."

How could I have gone without this? Why did I?

It's how it should've been.

Slow. Kisses to face and lips, ears and neck, that melted away the chill inside of me. Fingers on eyelids, feathering lashes, playing over cheeks, making music there. My mind swelled with a rich inventive melody as I reached for Noel's buttons, peeled off his jacket and shirt, touched flesh I'd seen a few times in person, more often in my dreams.

"You're so beautiful." He held my chin when I tried to turn away. "I'm almost afraid to touch you."

"Don't be." I pulled my blouse over my head, let it fall to the floor. "I'm not afraid," I said, though I felt a hint of nerves when I recognized the depth of his desire. But Noel was not Ian. Then was not now. There was no storm here, and I would not shut down. I wanted this moment. I moved into his arms. "I trust you."

We lay together and spoke love words, creating incandescent moments I'd remember all my life: when he traced over my skin as if I were a piece of precious marble and called me beautiful—until I believed him; when he kissed me until every thought toppled from my head and my body bowed to sensation; when he linked his fingers with mine and kept his gaze on mine as we joined together, finally, so different from what I'd known; when he whispered words—pianissimo, incomprehensible—in a language that was foreign to me but that I learned bit by bit as the minutes passed; when we twined close, after, and both trembled.

"Are you cold?" he asked.

"I don't think I'll ever be cold again."

Yet, despite the warmth within me, the light I knew had grown so much, and the exhilaration of newfound freedom and triumph and love, something was wrong. The music in my mind had turned dissonant—a crash of sounds that didn't belong together, like the splinter and hiss of burning ice. I pushed the noises back and kissed his chest.

"*Buon Anno*, Noel Ryan."

"Happy New Year, Maeve Leahy."

"*Auguri.*" I settled against him and tried to sleep. Still, I couldn't shake the disconcerting emotion that lurked close, like a faceless presence just outside a darkened windowpane.

NOEL WAS GONE when I woke, already on a red-eye flight to London. He'd left something on the pillow beside me: a miniature replica of that unfinished work I'd stumbled upon in his studio weeks ago. Finished now. Full of color and depth. Ardor shone on my face as my lips pressed against a saxophone, and a crimson wash covered it all. The red woman, he'd said. Not made of glass at all, but warm, passionate, alive.

He'd written a chant on the page.

I love you, Maeve Leahy.
I love you
I love you
I love you
I love you

NOEL'S WASN'T THE only note I received that morning. Another had been tucked under my door.

Visit Museo delle Anime del Purgatorio

Proprio in tempo! My mind filled with a new composition, a *Rocky*-esque song of achievement. Sri Putra was not only alive, he'd found my note and, through it, me—not to mention a way around his brother's prying eyes. But why did he want me to visit a museum of purgatory? I headed down to the lobby; Giovanni was more informative than any guidebook.

"Museo delle Anime del Purgatorio is a small and beautiful museum near Piazza dei Tribunali," he said, straightening papers behind the front desk. "Sometimes the dead in purgatory leave a mark before they go to heaven. The museum shows this. If you like that, there is also a place called Santa Maria della Concezione. There are . . ." He thumped his head.

"Heads?"

He frowned. "The bone."

"Skulls?"

"*Sì.* There are skulls and bones all over, even in the walls. You should go and say hello to them. It is a beautiful crypt."

"A crypt?" I rolled my shoulders. "Who wants to be surrounded by death? I try not to think about it, Giovanni."

"You are in the wrong city, then."

He had a point.

"There is heaven, angels," he said, spraying cleanser on his desk. "Heaven, it makes death great. Yes?"

"*Sì.* If you believe in that sort of thing."

"You do not believe?"

I had to laugh at his scandalized expression. I supposed everyone in Rome, or at least most everyone, was Catholic. "I'm glad you believe, Giovanni."

"Life is good," he said. "Death is part of that, so death is good, no?"

"I'd like to think so."

He waved a paper towel in the air. "Then you should think so."

I WAS ABOUT to head out to see if the museum of death-gone-wrong was closed for the holiday when Noel called. I could barely hear him over the clamor coming through the line.

"I'm using Jakes's iPhone—and no comments about that," he said as I laughed. "We're on a train that's about to leave London for Wareham. Can you believe it? Wareham's a town near Purbeck." Wareham as in Garrick Wareham. "And my mother's last name, she changed it to match mine: Ryan. Faith Ryan."

My heart raced for him. "You must be so excited!"

"And missing you, remembering you," he said with a tone that brought to mind the taste of his skin. I wished I could kiss him, run my hands down his back; I told him so. He groaned, said, "Have you made plans yet?"

"I may stick around a while longer. There's more I'd like to see and . . ." Museo delle Anime del Purgatorio stared up at me from a scrap of paper, and despite a pang of apprehension, I decided to tell him the truth. "I found another note this morning, slipped under my door this time."

He paused. "Did Giovanni see who left it at the desk?"

"No one left it. I asked. It must've been delivered to me directly." Hush. "Noel?"

"I'm trying to figure out if I can get off the train. We just started moving. It might be possible—"

"Hang on, listen!" I told him about the note I'd dropped at Putra's place, the one that jetted beneath his door. Surely, he'd found it—and me, because of it.

"Sit down, Maeve, there's something you need to know."

"I am sitting." My fingers splayed out like a five-pronged anchor over the cool sheets.

"I don't know why I kept this to myself. Maybe I wanted to prove it first so that you wouldn't accuse me of overreacting again, or maybe I didn't want to scare you—but now you need a little fear. I want you to change your room, or better yet go back to Betheny. I can't protect you when I'm nine hundred miles away." Protection again. But it was hard to feel outraged when he sounded so urgent. "Take out your notes," he said. "Lay them out, side by side."

I gathered them, minus the business card Ermanno had liberated the day we'd met: two notes in my jacket, three in a drawer, today's on the side table. I put them on my bed.

"Look at the note that invited you to Rome, the one with Putra's address," he said. "Compare the handwriting in the first line to the writing in the address."

Visit with me in the New Year.
There is much I wish to tell you.
Via della Scala ____, No. 47
Trastevere

I noticed nothing, and told him so.

"Compare that to any of your others then," he said. "Any that use the word *visit*."

Visit Santa Maria in Cosmedin
Visit Il Sotto Abbasso
Visit Villa Borghese
Visit Museo delle Anime del Purgatorio

"The *V* is different," I said. Of course Noel would pick up on that.

"It's not just the *V*," he said, as the difference in the *N*'s leaped out at me, too. "That's just the easiest to see. There's an openness to the first line of that invitation, and the last three lines don't have that—

in fact, they read like the work of someone trying hard to replicate something but not quite able to get away with it."

"Wait, I don't—"

"It's a theory," he said, "but I'm pretty sure I'm right. My grandfather swears he met the *empu*, so it's probably true that Putra wrote part —— note ——" The line broke up as I registered his suspicion. The invitation had two authors? "Still there?"

"I hear you," I said. "Keep talking."

"The business card Ermanno took that first day—Putra wrote on that in front of my grandfather. Studying it would've been telling, so I went to Ermanno and tried to get it back. He said it was impossible, that he was an expert at making things disappear permanently. Then he asked about you."

No wonder Noel had been so annoyingly overprotective.

"I think Ermanno was with Putra in Betheny," he continued. "Siblings traveling together—it's not unlikely."

Maeve, let's travel someday on a train.

Yes, maybe it'll come off the track, and then we can go wherever we want, drive it across the sea and over to Europe—

"I think Ermanno wrote part of that invitation, Maeve, and I think he left all those other notes, too. He knew you had the *keris*, and he's the only brother we've seen."

"But that's exactly why it can't be him!" I said. "He's seen me in person. Why leave notes? And why would Sri Putra leave a note that asks me to visit him without leaving an address?"

"Who knows? Effing notes have been as irrational as Ermanno. The only thing I've learned about that guy is he's obsessed with your *keris*."

This, I knew.

"The first time I saw him alone, when I went back to get that note, he said the *keris* would harm you and I should give it to him. I told——go——hell——threat——wallet vanish. I need you to—— what——listen——Maeve, can you hear me?"

"It's the phone line. I'm losing you."

"Promise——stupid——notes——Ermanno—promise——"

"I promise to stay away from Ermanno, Noel. Don't worry. I'll forget about the notes." The connection died. I hoped he'd heard my reassurances.

I studied the notes again; how could I have missed those *V*'s? What else had I overlooked?

I remembered *Old Gypsy Madge's Fortune Teller and the Witches Key to Lucky Dreams*, gifted to Ned Baker by someone looking for something stronger than love spells. Perhaps someone obsessed with *magia nera*.

Remembered Ermanno's faltering expression—recognition, maybe—when he saw me. *You should be looking for me. Not him. Me.* Had Ermanno intended to masquerade as an *empu*, all for the *keris*? Had he developed a new plan after his first one failed?

Remembered Ermanno's hand in my purse and his purple face at Il Sotto Abbasso.

Remembered that Ermanno, as temporary landlord, had keys to every apartment. If he'd found the note I'd meant for his brother, he'd know that I still had the *keris* after all. What could he do? Go to my room. Try the handle. Lure me away from the blade with another note. Or maybe he just wanted to turn me into another half-baked burn mark in the museum of purgatory.

Maybe I should go to the museum. Maybe Ermanno would be there and I could confront him, one last time. But I'd promised Noel—promised—and I didn't want him to ever wonder if he should've jumped from that train and into the English Channel to get back to me.

"IF NOEL'S GONE and the *empu* guy's gone, why not come home?" Kit asked for the third time when we spoke that night. I'd called to explain why I'd registered under a new name—Betheny Castine—and that I hadn't had a psychotic break. "I'm worried about you, and your cat misses you," she said as I unpacked in my new room. The layout was the same, but the colors were darker— coffee brown and sapphire blue.

"I'm not coming home yet because I have more to see," I told her. "And I refuse to let Ermanno chase me away."

"Who's Ermanno?"

My resistance was down. I told her everything: that a guy with a love of black magic had been following me around Betheny, leaving me notes; that Noel was convinced Ermanno had lured me to Rome and was continuing to lead me around on a chase fit for a goose; that Ermanno had developed a fascination with my *keris* and seemed determined to get it; that his tenants spoke of the trickster's butter-coated, skeleton-key fingers; that I didn't trust him to keep those fingers away from my hotel door; that he was the reason I'd changed my location—and my name.

"Wait a minute," Kit said. "He's wanted the *keris* for weeks? That's why he was in Betheny, following you around? And he has a history of breaking and entering?"

"Well"—I tried to close the drawer I'd filled; it stuck—"I can't be sure, but—"

"Maeve, was that *keris* hidden or something the day our apartment was left open? The day the dog got out?"

I abandoned the drawer. "No, I had it with me." At the university, then Time After Time. "Why?"

"I didn't leave our apartment unlocked."

"Yes, you—"

"I wasn't home until that night, when I ran into your father and helped him bring that boat table inside."

"Kit, are you sure?"

"Yes, I'm sure," she said, as I sat heavily on the floor. "I didn't say anything because I thought you'd done it and you'd forgotten, and I didn't want to make you feel . . . Well, and then your dad had that ticket to Rome, and a vacation seemed like the perfect chance for you to get your health back. Could you have left the door unlocked, Maeve? Is it possible?"

"No," I said, remembering Sparky's little face as we'd left that day, her distress at being the one left behind. Remembered, too, finding her barking madly on the lawn, coated with ice. Upset because she'd known a fox had been close, sniffing around.

He'd been there. Ermanno had been inside my apartment.

"Come home."

"No. Like I said, I won't let Ermanno chase me away."

For several minutes, I tried to convince her not to worry, but my limbs trembled in the sheets when I lay down and I couldn't bring myself to turn off the lamp. I kept the *keris* by my side, hating Ermanno for making me so fearful—especially after all I'd gone through, after all I'd accomplished.

240

Purgatory. Purge. Out with the old, in with the new. I thought of timeworn appliances flung from windows to land on the stones below, like dead crows dropped from the sky. Purge. Purify. Pure. Fresh. Free of corruption. Absolute. Cleansed.

I fell asleep like that: the lights on, slurred chords in my head. And I woke the next day with it all still there, and rose, and headed out, without stopping for coffee—and without fear—to visit Museo delle Anime del Purgatorio.

THOUGH I'D ANTICIPATED the museum of purgatory to be an exhibition of the bizarrely morbid—as in crawling skeletons glued to the walls—I found an understated museum just off a Gothic church, housed in a little room that smelled of soup. A few people milled around inside, including a nun who smiled at me when I entered. No sign of Ermanno. I hugged my purse a little closer.

Behind a locked case, a scatter of frames held papers, documents. One bore a smudge purported to be the scorch mark of a hand, though it looked more like the print of a dove to me.

The nun stepped beside me. "What a miracle," she said, in English.

"Do you really think so?"

"Oh! You're American!" She giggled, covered her mouth with her hand. "I should've paid more attention to my languages. I can barely speak a word of Italian."

"So many here speak English," I told her. "You'll be fine."

"Yes, people have been kind." She regarded the case again. "What a wonderful way to remind us of the power of prayer."

"How do you mean?"

"All of these requests sent from those poor in-between souls in purgatory, asking for masses. Without prayer, these people never would've made it into heaven." She smiled. "I'm sure they're there now. These pleas were made long ago and many prayers were surely said. But I'll pray for them all, just in case."

"You believe in purgatory?"

Flecks of orange danced in the brown tint around her dilated pupils. "Oh, yes! All of the dead need our prayers, dear. So many do."

What silliness. I looked again at the objects and their scars. Singed fingerprints on a book. Scorch marks on pillowcases and

shirtsleeves, on nightcaps and other papers. More burned hand-prints on a table. Requests for prayers, for help? How easy these items would be to create. Why should anyone believe? What did it prove to trust in any of it?

"Sister Lynn. It's time, dear."

Another nun stood at the door, much older than the one beside me, and much sterner of face.

"Yes, sister. I'm coming." Sister Lynn turned to me with a fur-rowed brow. "That woman never takes a break," she muttered, then added, louder, "It was nice speaking with you."

"You, too," I said.

Alone in the room now, I read an account: *21 December 1838*. The night a hand became imprinted on a page. Reports of a presence, chill air, and hearing the voice of the dead—of a brother who asked for help to end his suffering in purgatory.

I thought of Moira, all that I used to share of her feelings. Not dead. Not dead. But . . .

Idée fixe, I could not shake the thought. What would it be like to be in a coma? What would it be like to die and still breathe and breathe and breathe? My vision flashed white, to an image of me or Moira—one of us—seconds away from stabbing her shadow, and I knew even as my throat coated with acid.

Like purgatory.

"THERE IS A message," Giovanni said when I returned to the hotel. He reached behind the counter, handed me a note.

> Maeve Leahy, let us meet
> Via della Scala ___, No. 47
> I will stay through January 6
> Salam
> Empu Putra

So Ermanno had finally come right out and claimed his brother's identity. Little did he know his *V*'s gave him away. I wasn't afraid this time. I was angry.

"The man who left this—you didn't tell him I was still here, did you?" We'd talked about this yesterday. My parents, Kit, and Noel were the only people allowed access to me.

"A boy ran in and put this on the counter," Giovanni said. "We did not see any man."

Later that night, I heard from Noel with news that made my heart race for the right reasons: He'd found his mother. She'd been afraid to answer her door at first, then sobbed after realizing who he was. They'd talked for hours.

"We were both nervous. God, I told the worst jokes," he said, as I remembered the boy he was, the child who'd tickled her feet. "She's a potter. She's going to show me her studio tomorrow." She'd promised not to run.

I couldn't have been happier for him and told him so, then reassured him that I was safe and not planning anything stupid. I didn't mention my trip to the museum or the new beckoning note. I wouldn't let him worry about me when he was dealing with something as singular and life altering as reconnecting with Faith Ryan, trying to oil her rusty smile.

I told him that I loved him. He said he loved me, too. But when I hung up, I recognized the feeling that sometimes ran wild in my blood with presentient assuredness. It would be a long time before I'd see Noel Ryan again.

I SPENT THE next seventy-two hours trying to ignore the approach of January 6, even though "Harlem Nocturne" looped through me continuously. During the day, I traversed the city. I finally saw the Forum, the Colosseum, and Michelangelo's dome, and ate my fill of tiramisu and gelato. I watched a puppet show. At night, I stayed in, ate at the bar, spoke with Noel.

I was particularly restless on the fifth. I took a tour of Rome's famous bridges, and even stepped over the one that led to Ermanno's apartments. If he was there, hiding in the cool bulb at the top of a lamppost, I didn't see him, but I could almost feel the growing momentum of that second shoe—the one that was about to drop.

That night, as I filled the sink with hot water to wash a few things, I found something theory-shattering in the pocket of a pair of jeans.

Visit Il Sotto Abbasso

This was the extra note I'd picked up about the jazz club—not the note Noel had found first. I'd forgotten all about it. Though their messages had been identical, their styles were not; this one was written with the same *V* as the initial invitation to Trastevere.

I leaned against the countertop and stared at myself in the mirror. The jazz club was the only place I'd seen Ermanno outside of the apartment building. Was there something special—?

It's only open Sunday nights. He didn't know if he'd see you again at the apartments; he'd hoped to catch you at the club.

To persuade me—or frighten me—into giving him the *keris*. But why two notes?

Insurance. He saw Noel take the first one and didn't trust him to pass it on. He thought it could be his last chance.

If that was true—if Ermanno had left *this* note—this loopy, flourishy note—and was one of the two authors of the note left for me in Betheny, then he'd written the first line: *Visit with me in the New Year.* Why?

Because he knew his brother would be gone by then, and he wanted you—and the keris—*all to himself.*

Suddenly Ermanno's words made a more perfect sense. *Never enough speed, never enough luck. You should be looking for me. Not him. Me.*

Noel was right. Ermanno had been in Betheny. He'd followed me and broken into my home. He'd duplicated one note and altered another. He'd meant to intimidate me.

Noel was also wrong. Whatever the bounds of the Italian's obsession with the *keris*, whatever its root, Sri Putra had been behind the directives. *He* had sent me to Santa Maria in Cosmedin, Villa Borghese, and Museo delle Anime del Purgatorio, and had left one of the notes about Il Sotto Abbasso. He was alive. Safe. Escaped from his brother's sleeve. And tomorrow was January 6—our last chance to meet.

Things weren't always what they seemed. How could I have forgotten?

In the morning, I would walk to Sri Putra's home. One last time.

CHAPTER TWENTY
THE EMPU

I rose early and dressed in clothes Giovanni would not approve of—khakis and a button-down cotton shirt. I was prepared to defend my comfortable choice when I stepped into the lobby, but I found he'd donned something a little more casual as well: a hat, white wig, wire-rim glasses, plaid skirt, black shawl, and apron. His face looked covered in soot, and he stood beside a broom as he passed gifts to two children.

"Are you a good witch or a bad witch?" I asked him when the boys, who looked to be about three and five, sat before us to open their presents.

"I am good, like Santa. You have not heard of Befana?" he asked, and I shook my head. "It is the holiday Epiphany today and we like to please the guests." He mouthed, "My mama."

I smiled as the older boy ripped off the wrappings to reveal a panettone box. He seemed less than pleased; he sprang up, knocked Giovanni's faux glasses onto the floor, then raced to the bar. "Mama, Mama!" he cried, as his brother continued to work at his tape.

"Who could not like panettone?" Giovanni said with a frown. "We ran out of knicky knacks two hours ago." He picked up his glasses and settled them back on his face.

"You're a good man, Giovanni Benedetto Chioli," I said.

"That is right. A good man." He smoothed his skirt.

My mood degraded a bit as I walked to meet with the mysterious Sri Putra. He and Ermanno were brothers—*half* brothers. Were they alike or not? I'd once said, in an attempt to silence my father, that chasing the *empu* might find me chopped into bits and left in a suitcase. Truth was, I *had* followed a stranger to a foreign land. Anything could happen. Anything might. I continued on, though I hoped I wasn't treading my own personal plank.

The familiar flag of Italy slapped back at the wind as I stepped under it and into the apartment building. I pulled the *keris* from my bag, walked the hall with light steps. There was no movement here, no life. No sound either, until I lifted my hand to knock on Putra's battered door and a thud emanated from the overcast end of the hall. I knew a stairway lurked in the darkness there—knew who used it, too.

I'd just unsheathed the *keris* when the door beside me opened. A man stood there. Not Ermanno. In fact, this man couldn't have been more than five feet tall. His face bore deep creases, and he dressed all in black, including that funny hat I'd seen just once before.

"Good. You are brave," he said with a light, melodic accent. Indonesian.

"You're really real." I shook my head, tried again. "You're Sri Putra."

"You are Maeve Leahy." He smiled, and I saw that the lines on his face were forged from these smiles. "I am sorry to miss you before now. Come then. Enter."

He left the door open, but disappeared back into the room. I stood there as that familiar scent slithered into my nose and mouth, down my spine. What was it?

"Frankincense," said Sri Putra's voice from within.

"Excuse me?" The aroma strung me along, until I teetered on the threshold. No sign of Ermanno.

"The smell is frankincense. You are safe here," he said, and I realized I still held the *keris* out before me. Was the man psychic? I'd never experienced anything like that outside of my own blood. I lowered the weapon and stepped into the apartment.

All of my questions, even my apprehensions, vanished when I saw the ruin. The puppets that had charmed me weeks ago now dangled by their necks, their legs ripped off, cut off, burned, their brass tubes bent. Some were strung up by their feet, beheaded altogether. The shelves were emptied, hacked up, and splayed at haphazard splintery angles on the floor. Chimes that had once tinkled beneath the vent were torn down; a single strand hung alone now, never to make music again.

I walked farther into the room, past walls marked with large red X's, to find the elaborate relief panels had suffered an active war—queens and forest animals defiled, smeared over with something I hoped was only soot. Chopped wooden figurines sat mounded on the floor along with the skinny-pot instrument I couldn't name before—its strings pulled out, its neck broken.

"You are a musician. Why do you not make music?"

I rounded on him. "What do you know about me? Why did you go to Betheny and leave that book and the notes and pound nails into my door? What's wrong with you people?"

"I did not do this." He indicated the wreckage.

"Then what's wrong with your brother?"

"Ermanno is broken, so he likes to break." The words felt like a shrug.

"You accept this?"

"It is a sorrow, but I am still whole." He folded his hands. "Are you whole, Maeve Leahy, or are you broken?"

He couldn't know about Moira, though I had the sense he did know, that he knew everything. The idea twined through me like ivy, until I felt choked by it. "I don't know how to answer that," I said, "and even if I did, you haven't answered my questions yet."

"Come then. Let us speak together."

I followed him to a nook just beyond the door, where rumpled purple pillows lay scattered on the floor beside several large unlit candles. Natural light filtered in from two adjoining rooms, though the red-X-ed walls were cast in shadow. I peered beyond to a small kitchen where pots hung from the ceiling, a scene strongly reminiscent of Time After Time.

Feathers lifted from the ground as Sri Putra sat on a cushion. I sat as well and crossed my legs, then sheathed the *keris* with some reluctance. Around us, several fabric shells lay deflated—slashed and emptied.

"I have many left to repair," he said. "The table is destroyed. Are you uncomfortable?"

"I'm fine." I imagined him on his knees, searching for feathers, stuffing them back inside their sleeves and stitching edges together. But I didn't want to feel sorry for Putra just then. I wanted answers.

"Ask your questions," he said. "I will answer."

The man had an eerie knack. "Why were you in Betheny?"

"That is where many dreams took me," he said, "so I went."

I wouldn't focus on Ermanno and his poisonous behavior, but this much I wanted to know—it would be a test of the *empu*'s forthrightness and my assumptions. "Was your brother in those dreams, too? Was he in Betheny?"

"Ermanno was there, it is true. I should not have stayed so long with him, but I wanted to know you were the one for the *keris*."

This made no sense to me. "How's that your place to say?" I argued. "I won it at an auction. I paid for it."

"I would have given it to you, but that is how it happened after I brought it there."

My eyes bugged, kicked open at last. "You brought it to the auction? It was yours? But you bid on it!"

"I did," he said with a hint of a smile. "I admit I doubted fate. I had to make sure there would be only one who wanted it enough to fight."

"There was more than one, though," I said. "Your brother wanted it. He still wants it. Why didn't you give it to him?"

The *empu* nodded. "I believed that Ermanno understood the *keris* would choose its fate and that it was not meant for him. He knew that I had seen a woman in my dreams, and he said that he also wanted to see the *keris* find you. It was because I recognized you at the auction that I let you win."

"*Let* me?" He obviously didn't know the power of Irish resolve. "Look," I said, "don't get me wrong. I'm glad I won the *keris*, but it could just as easily have been anyone else. It was a fluke I even went out that night."

"I believe you are wrong. There is one meant for this *keris*. That is you. This at least you must believe."

"Why must I?"

"You feel no kinship with it?"

"Kinship? I admired it, so I wanted it."

Loved it at first glance.

"I'm glad I have it," I continued.

Felt sick when it was lost.

But these feelings, bound with memory, proved nothing.

It's changed you.

"Has it changed you?" he asked, like a shadow sound with the power to stab. "Have you walked a bolder path since the *keris* found you?"

His wording rattled me. "*I* found *it* on a table with a bunch of other things people didn't want anymore."

Like music.

"I liked it," I said. "I bid on it, I wrote a check for it, I took it home. All actions I controlled."

"Your mind and actions are always your own with no strings or wires." He indicated the myriad puppets around us, their broken parts useful now only for analogy. "The *keris* would wish to help you on your true life path and that is all."

Despite the frown on my face, his smile didn't turn. He pulled several candles close, then lit them one by one until the shadows crept back into the creases of the wall. I noticed for the first time that the corners of the ceiling bore a scattering of sapphire blue stars.

"So you wanted me to know about the *keris*," I said. "You left a book for me, and your address in Trastevere, but why not just tell me where I could find you while you were in Betheny?"

"I left a note for you with the book," he said. "You were to let me know how it went with the *keris* and ask any questions you might have had. I left the phone number for my hotel."

"I received only the book."

"Only?" Sri Putra glanced at an empty cushion shell and blew out the match. I knew his thoughts: Ermanno had taken the note, buying himself time and ensuring my confusion. I had the feeling that

Sri Putra had known little to nothing about his brother's machinations. Time for illumination.

"This is everything I have." I pulled out seven notes: six from him and one from Ermanno. I set those down for him to see, then handed him an eighth—the note with his address that Ermanno had altered, the one that had lured me here. Sri Putra almost seemed to age as he studied the defiled invitation, then the extra note that had led me to the jazz bar.

"This went further than I knew," he said. "I am sorry. My mind has been elsewhere."

The X-marked walls featured prominently in my peripheral vision, and I remembered the illness he'd been attending to. Had someone died?

"Ermanno's mother died."

"I'm sorry for your loss," I mumbled automatically, and he inclined his head.

"I have stayed beside her these last days as she slept the deepest sleep of near death. Her sickness began a year ago, and so I moved here to be close. The *keris* came to me shortly after that." He focused on a flame. "Perhaps I should not have stayed. Ermanno was intrigued by the *keris* and my way of finding you. I should not have told him as much as I did or let him travel with me, but I still have guilt."

"Guilt?"

He regarded me. "Let us speak more of Ermanno later," he said. "Focus now on what is in your hands. Your fate. Your questions."

My fingers contracted around the *keris* in my lap. "Why did you travel all the way from Rome to a little upstate New York town over a dream and a *keris*?"

"Why have you come so far to talk about it?" he countered.

"I lost my mind," I said, then, "My father forced me." Still, another response rose above the others.

Avventura.

Yes, I'd had that during my trip to Rome. I'd played an instrument again and reconnected with my music. I'd accepted love. I'd taken a picture of a woman hanging laundry on a line.

I flashed to a memory of Moira and me in our boat, young and dressed as pirates, as sure of our futures as my grip on a *keris*. Maybe I'd wanted unwavering confidence again, to be Alvilda for a while or just have the balls Ian used to say I had. Maybe that's why I'd bought the *keris* and come to Rome.

"I don't know why I came," I said.

He studied me with an intensity I thought only Noel possessed. "What have you learned? Consider your journey to know the will of the *keris*. Did you bow to the truth, the past, the present?"

His words struck hard, reverberated through me like a gong.

Truth: the Mouth of Truth, where I'd acknowledged some of my core self.

Past: the Etruscan Museum, and Borghese Gallery and the rape statue, where I'd remembered what I'd lost.

Present: Il Sotto Abbasso, where I'd reconnected with a piece of my soul, my music.

So what was the Museum of Purgatory? Moira's present? Her future? Mine?

It's what you fear. All of it.

"What do you fear?" he asked.

I drew a sharp breath. How could he, this small man, this outsider, probe with such precision through layers of skin and muscle and bone, to see the secrets lodged inside of me? How could he know what my experience had been? There'd only been one who could ever do that, only one who ever should.

"I didn't come here to talk about me," I said, angry now. "I want to know about the *keris* and its *luks*. I want to know what it was made for, because I'm curious. More than anything, I want to understand why you came to Betheny and sold the blade to George Lansing, and why you and your brother followed me. I want to know why you left those notes for me here in Trastevere, and how you knew I'd come. And I don't want to hear anything other than fact and truth."

Water dripped somewhere, magnified in the silence. Putra's black eyes seemed to spark a little in the candlelight. "I have explained myself for much of my life, and for this I grow weary. I am Putra. What has been has been. What will come will come. You would like truth, but only truth you understand."

251

"That's wrong. That's not how it is."

It's not how it used *to be.*

"You are afraid to trust in fate, as most are," he said.

"I'm not afraid. I just choose not to believe in things that don't exist. Santa Claus. The tooth fairy. Angels. Fate." How could anyone believe in such a concept when terror could rise with the flash of one black wing, one raging storm? "I don't understand why anyone would trust so blindly."

He bunched his dark lips. "If I did not trust, if I did not listen to fate and the will of the metal, I would make a poor *empu*. This gift of listening came from my father and his father before him, back hundreds of years."

"Listen to metal, to iron and steel and pieces of meteors?" The whole thing sounded crazy.

"Many think as you do. Many no longer believe in my work or the *keris*. But this I know: Sometimes you have to step beyond sense to follow instinct."

Eling.

The word slapped out at me. I remembered with painful clarity the connection I once shared with Moira. Knowing her feelings and sometimes her thoughts. Flying high on life because the sense of her bolstered me like a brace to bone.

Eling.

I thought of my twin in a hospital bed in Maine, sustained, somehow, by her own breath. The truth of why beyond me.

Eling.

Music surged through me, silvery and serene. I closed my eyes and saw Moira and me dancing on the beach in Castine, our hands clasped and bodies tuned to the wind. My mouth watered as I tasted notes, as memory spun light and joy from the shadowed seams of my mind.

Eling.

Who was I to say what was true for other people, to define their experience as real or holy or freakish or anything else? Maybe Putra heard the will of the metal the way I used to hear the will of music on the air. Maybe I'd become closed to possibility. Closed the way my mother always had been.

I opened my eyes, looked again at the scatter of feathers around us, the stars on the ceiling, Sri Putra's piercing gaze. "I'm sorry, Empu Putra," I said, and lay the *keris* between us.

"You understand."

My lips curled in reluctant humor. "Not everything in life can be measured or accounted for by the five known senses."

"Good. We have much to talk about."

EMPU PUTRA BROUGHT out a tray and set it on the floor between us. I added two slices of ginger to a plain white mug of tea and then suspended my inclination for disbelief as he told his improbable tale.

The will of the *keris* and its desire for a journey had grown over many months, he said. He meditated over the pull he felt, and dreamed the name *Betheny*. At first he thought this referred to a woman the *keris* sought, and then he looked through the Third Eye—his name for the hole in the blade—and saw Betheny, New York, on a map.

"The *keris* had needs that I felt"—he clasped his arms over his chest and hit his hands against his shoulders twice—"every day. I knew I had to go."

He used the Third Eye again and found the auction house, then he gave the *keris* to George Lansing to sell. This explained George's exasperation over Putra's competitive bidding that night.

"You took a lot of risks," I said.

"To me they were not risks." He dragged four additional unlit candles close to us and pulled out his matchbook. "I wanted to speak with you after the sale, but I could not find you. My brother learned your name and that you worked at the university from a woman at the auction house. I left the book, my business card, and the note."

A card and a note I'd never received. Ermanno again. But I wouldn't be diverted. "That book left more questions than answers."

He struck a match, and his smile glowed in its light. "I knew this. I hoped you would call to speak of the *keris*. I understand now why you did not." He lit the remaining wicks. Yellow light danced over the walls and turned the red *X*'s orange.

"You left a note for me about *eling.*" Remember. "Why?"

"I knew the *keris* would need you open to affect you. I thought this a good clue. I thought everything would work, until one day I went to a store and found you."

"Time After Time? You didn't follow me there?"

"No," he said. "I thought it was kismet, and that I was led there because you were going to sell the *keris*. I'd felt certain you were the one, but that day I wondered if you might be a holder as I had been. After all I had done and believed to be true, I was curious. Later, I met the man from that store and learned you had kept the *keris*. He said he knew you. I asked him to contact me if you ever did sell him the *keris*. We heard earlier that day that Ermanno's mother had grown sicker and we were needed." *Emergenza.* "I wrote a last message for you and we left."

I fingered the note Ermanno had tampered with—*Visit with me in the New Year*—and this time couldn't hold back my tongue. "Your brother's less subtle than you are."

"He does not trust fate. And he was not ready to leave."

"Why?"

"Ermanno had a strong desire as a boy in Java to gain our father's attention and acceptance. He was very young when I became an *empu*, and he spoke often of becoming one of us. My father would not hear of this; he called Ermanno *ora pati Jawa*—half a Javanese."

"That's unfair," I said, hardly believing I would stand up for Ermanno but bothered just the same. "Just because he wasn't pure Javanese shouldn't mean he couldn't become an *empu*."

"The problem was not the blood. Ermanno would not listen to learn. He was hasty. He could not look outside of himself. My father despised his selfishness, so he would not teach him what Ermanno and his mother called our work: *magia.*"

Magic.

"When my father died, Ermanno's mother brought him here to Rome, and I stayed behind, a grown man. I learned later that he was not accepted by his friends because of his differences, or because he tried black magic." The *empu* bowed his head as if shamed. "To capture magic is what he wants most. He does not understand the true nature of our work or that some things cannot be bound."

"I still don't understand why he didn't take the *keris* from you when he could have—*before* the auction."

"It was after the *keris* proved itself by finding you that he fully realized its power," Sri Putra said. "Ermanno has hundreds of *kerises* of his own but their subtlety is lost to him. The will of your *keris* is too strong for even a closed mind to miss."

I lifted my mug to take a sip and noticed something floating in my drink. A feather. I slid the bit of plumage up the side of the mug with my finger, then lifted it out and set it on my knee. I caught Putra smiling at me. "How many *luks* does my *keris* have?"

"Twelve," he said.

"But it's supposed to be odd—always odd."

"Who says always odd?"

"The book you gave me, first of all, the Internet, and friends of mine—people who work at the antiques shop you visited. They know a lot about old weapons and myths."

Sri Putra gestured to the *keris* that lay between us on the floor—could he touch it? Yes, I nodded. He unsheathed it, then turned the blade over and fingered the stain. But before I could tell him about that, he said, "It is rare to have twelve *luks*, but it happens. The number twelve is a sign of unity, of harmony despite difference."

"Are you sure it isn't just a flaw?"

"There is no flaw," he said. "No bit of pandan leaf will hang from the end of this *keris*. It was made well, and it was made to protect."

I wouldn't even ask what pandan leaf was. I felt confused enough. "I thought it was made for unity."

"It was made for unity and to protect and more." He stroked the uppermost crosspiece of the sheath. "This *wrangka* is shaped like a boat, for freedom. This is a very strong *keris*. It is no surprise that it grew restless."

"Unity, protection, freedom, and restlessness. Okay." I remembered my promise to hold his point of view, though speaking as if the *keris* had a will of its own still stretched my limits.

"There is no blood or heart in this *keris*, but power moves through it. You have felt it, I am sure." He set the blade back on the floor, pushed it toward me. "Find your proof."

"But—"

"I sense you still doubt." Creases formed dark lines at the bridge of his nose. "Come."

I settled my fingertips on the metal. The sensation of energy, of heat, radiated through my digits, up into my arms. "It's very warm," I admitted. Possibly warmer than ever before.

"What else have you felt? What has the *keris* done?"

There was no point withholding information, aside from not wanting to sound like a crazy person—a concern that seemed almost farcical now, all things considered. I took a deep breath and let loose. "I found it in a closed case under my bed back home even though I'd left it on a table, and just a few days ago it landed under my pillow when I'd had it in a safe. A friend of mine thinks I have PTSD, though, so maybe I—"

He raised his hand and I stopped jabbering. "The *keris* can move. That can happen," he said. "It wants to be close to you."

A broken sound came from me, not quite a laugh. "And I had something like a hallucination while holding it the other day. I saw a white light. Does that happen, too?"

"Yes, yes, the waking vision. Good."

"That's good? It made me remember something, it re-created a moment when I'd cut my finger. I felt it all over again, like I was there—really there."

Even if I die, I'll be with you for always.

"Ah." He touched the blade with all of his fingers. "There is more here than metal, and that is why."

"What are you talking about?"

"Do you seek truth?"

"What do you mean? What truth?"

He pinned me with his gaze. "This metal is not warm."

"It is," I said, ready to square off over it. "This metal is. It is right now. You must feel it."

"It speaks only to you this way. It is warm only to you."

I shook my head, but I knew it was true. No one else seemed to feel the curious heat. "Why?"

"That is not the *keris*," he said. "It is the *hantu*."

The foreign word churned through me, as I broke it down: *Hantu.* Haunting. "Ghosts?"

"You do not believe?"

Believe, believe.

Like Giovanni and Sister Lynn, their urgings to believe, just believe, in acknowledging old bones, in purgatory and a silvery afterlife.

"No." I rubbed at my breastbone, the sudden ache there. "I don't believe in ghosts."

"To believe is your choice," he said. "They are still there. One is here." He tapped the blade. "It is the *hantu* that wanted you. It is the *hantu* that woke this *keris*. It is the *hantu* that gives this blade such power and increases its will. It is the *hantu* that made it all happen."

My laugh sounded maniacal even to me. Because this was impossible. There was no room left in me for whatever story he wanted to tell. I brushed the feather off my leg, onto the floor, and then I stood. Wanted out. Out of that room, that building, out of the idea he was trying to back me into.

I left the *keris* where it was and stepped away. "Thank you and good-bye," I said.

Putra's gaze lingered on the space I'd already vacated. I waited, unsettled by his silence. Finally, I turned and walked from the room, to the door. I'd just turned the handle when he spoke.

"You can accept it or not. Though I must tell you that it is better for her if you do."

CHAPTER TWENTY-ONE
UNBOUNDED

"er?" My hand dropped from the door handle. I turned to face Putra, who'd followed me into the room. "Who is 'her'?"

Bloo. Sister. Bloo. Bloo.

"No. No."

Maeve, believe.

"No. She's not dead!"

Rextin. Believe.

"Stop it! I don't believe in this, I'll never accept it, I don't!" Music swelled in my head—a crescendo of raw emotion beyond labels of dread and shock. I put my hands over my ears. "Who's the *hantu*?" I shouted. "Who?"

"I cannot know." I thought he, too, shouted, though I couldn't be sure when my head contained a monsoon. "Open without struggle and your mind will quiet."

I rebelled against the idea utterly, and applied all of my will to silence the music and a voice I'd never thought could be anyone's but mine. Sweat gathered on my face, beneath my lip, as I pushed and pushed.

And then . . . quiet.

I collapsed to the floor, curled against the door, wept.

"You will have no peace with that heaviness inside."

"Why did—Why did you—do this?" I said between sobs. "Why would anyone want—anyone else—to be—haunted?"

"It is not as you say."

There was no denying it—the presence in my skull. Why hadn't I realized before? I grasped at my hair, my scalp. "Get out!" I yelled at whatever lurked inside of me. "Leave me alone!" If a priest had been in the room, I would've given him leave to exorcize it. But there was no priest, only Sri Putra. He sat beside me.

"I believe the *hantu* is of good spirit," he said.

I shook my head violently. Don't tell me. Don't tell me anymore.

"The *hantu* is a woman. Most *hantu* are women. I can never know who it is, but I sense she knows you and is new to her metal home," he said. "I know you do not want to believe, but I wish you to listen. Listen and hear this truth."

My teeth rattled as I rocked my body like a cradle.

"The *hantu* needs the *keris* to remove inhibitions. They bond for greater power," he said. "The *keris* was once revered by men and kings. It was so honored because it could fly to protect its owner, fly even into the hands of gods. Pretend you are such a willful *keris* today, when no one believes you are more than a pretty knife. Then someone who believes, who needs you, calls for you. Will you go?"

"But I—"

"Will you help?"

Another sob wracked my throat. "Yes!"

His eyes brightened even as mine continued to fill. "Because just as the *hantu* wants to affect the world again, so does the *keris* itself. Just as the *hantu* wants to touch the past, so does the *keris* itself. They need each other to be heard." He leaned closer. "You tell me now. Who is the *hantu*?"

"No, I can't—I don't know."

"A friend who has died? A loved one?"

"She's not dead!"

"Who is not dead that you speak of?"

"My sister!"

He pressed his thick lips together. "*Hantu Pusaka*. A family spirit can use the *keris* to make contact. With defenses low, the spirit can touch the living—"

"She's not dead!" I screamed.

His long quiet look unraveled me again, and again I sobbed, my face pressed against the door. I would leave the *keris* and its *hantu*— some awful rogue spirit who posed as my sister, who meant to pry into my mind and drive me mad.

But how could it know our secret language?

How could it know our names for one another?

Doubt scored me. If I left the *keris*, if Moira's spirit truly lived in the blade, if it was meant for me because of her—

Not dead, not dead! Impossible!

What could she want from me? To haunt me eternally? To punish me for not hearing her that night, for what happened with Ian, for hating her then, for her coma? Her purgatory? But I couldn't leave her. Not again. Not when I knew—might know—I hit my forehead against the door. Not when I could touch her, not when I could hear. And the voice had been kind. If it was her, maybe—

I unfolded myself with careful movements, propped my back against the door. I faced Sri Putra. "I'm not afraid," I said, though of course I was. "Moira's my twin. She's in a coma. She's brain-dead."

"She is on machines?"

"She breathes without them." I thought of her in a hospital bed, my mother beside her, reading a book. I hadn't looked on Moira's face in years, her warped features, blue-pale skin, or thatch of dulled rag-doll hair. I hadn't even been there when the doctors unplugged her machines, because I couldn't bear to see her die, just as I couldn't bear to see her live.

"It would be a blessing for her to go," I said softly. "I wish she'd just drift off." Die. Just die.

Let me, came a returning whisper along with faint strains of music.

I pushed it all back again and held firm. Fatigue covered me like a thick blanket.

"This hurts you, this thing you do," the *empu* said. "It will continue to hurt you."

260

Fresh tears burned my eyes as I hugged myself, crossed arms over chest. "There's a force in me . . ." How to explain? "There's so much inside. Music. A voice."

"Is the voice your sister's?"

"I don't know. Maybe. It's not tonal. It's just a voice within my head, like when you think through your own thoughts."

"Do you dream of her?"

"Sometimes I dream and know someone in the dream is meant to be her"—I thought of the child, the girl with the red hair—"but I never see my sister. I never see Moira as she was."

"Never?"

"Not since her accident. That was almost a decade ago."

His forehead bunched. "Do you have bad memories?"

"Things didn't end well between us." So many lies, such deception. Hateful words and blood and terror.

"She may seek healing."

Could it be that easy? "What can I do?"

"Invite her to your dreams. Hear what she will say."

I thought of the door, the water. I would drown.

"Come," he said. "I would like to show you something."

I rose slowly, feeling older, and followed him back to the pillows. He picked up the *keris*, then ran his finger down the dark stain.

"This mark," he said. "You see it?"

"It's blood. I cut myself and wasn't able to clean it off."

"That is the mark of the *hantu* saying she has found the one. I believe she will stay until you hear her. She may stay beyond that. But I must tell you that, despite her will, I sense her spirit has grown thin."

I took a shallow breath. "What do you mean?"

"She fights against the pull to leave this world. It is her choice how long to continue, but she may not move on until you hear her. Why not listen after all she has done to reach you?"

My fear doubled when I had a vision of my sister afloat in the Penobscot, lost and alone and calling to me, losing consciousness along with hope.

"Your sister's light will continue," Sri Putra said. "No light needs a body to move through space and time."

"I've dreamed of light," I told him, "and skulls. Everyone's skull shone with bright light, but mine was just a speck."

He nodded, quiet for a moment. "Perhaps that is why she stays."

WE SAT ON deflated purple pillows, and drank tea, and talked about dreams and death and light and life for hours. He told such stories; I hoped I would remember them all long enough to share with Garrick. He asked me to stay for dinner. We ate fried tofu and noodles with our fingers, and talked some more, until the candles burned down to stubs and midnight loomed. Time to go.

"You'll leave tomorrow?" I asked.

"Sometime tomorrow, yes. Ermanno's mother is gone now and so is my reason for staying. Ermanno will inherit the building and does not want me here, as you can see." He gave a wry smile and glanced around us at the wreckage. "I have nothing much to pack."

"I'm shocked at this," I told him. "He's so destructive."

"It is sad, but Ermanno destroys nothing better than himself. I try to understand. If I were not able to touch the *keris* and feel its will, it would hurt me as well."

I hugged the *keris* to my chest. "Where will you go? You have no other family?"

"My wife died of cancer long ago," he said. "There were no children."

I remembered something. "Garrick said you're looking for work at a university. Will you teach?"

"*Empus* are not in demand so much anymore, but fate will decide." He held out a business card like the one he'd given Garrick. "I believe you did not receive my Javanese address when last I left it for you."

"No, I didn't." Of course Ermanno would've taken his brother's card, limiting my knowledge and leading me to only one place: directly to him in Trastevere.

"No matter where I go, this is always my home and I will always return. Will you write? I would like to know how things go. I would like to write a paper to say, 'Here is a *keris* full of will that you cannot doubt. See what it has done?'"

"A paper? You don't think the story's worthy of a book?"

He smiled back at me, and I took the card. We walked to the door.

"I believe love is the purpose of all knowledge. Sometimes knowledge comes to us through books, but also it comes through suffering," he said. "I can see you have suffered, Maeve Leahy. Now you may live a better life."

"Thank you, Empu Putra, for everything," I said, stepping into the hall.

"Open yourself to your loved ones and they will not have to resort to such measures to get your attention."

"I'll try."

He nodded and closed the door.

I WAS OVERWHELMED with information to contemplate and digest. But as I walked away from the meeting with Sri Putra, I realized that I did believe it: My sister's spirit resided in the *keris* in my hand. I didn't know what it would all mean, but as I traveled in the dark, I felt lighter of heart than I had in a long while. Moira was, after all, my dearest love, my twin, the other half of me for better and for worse and for always.

I'd walked halfway across the bridge leading to my hotel when the *keris* gave a great flare of heat. Someone ran close. I stopped, turned as Ermanno charged out of the dark and rammed into me. I tried to catch my fall, and the *keris* clattered to the ground.

"That is what I should have done long ago."

I couldn't catch my breath to respond.

"Now that you know what my *game* is"—his smile burned white in the glow of the street lamps—"I will take what should be mine."

I scrambled to get there first, but he grabbed the *keris* ahead of me. My hands and knees trembled on the cold stone as I crouched before him. "Please, please give it back," I said. "The *keris* is precious to me, Ermanno."

"Now you beg?"

"I said 'please.' "

"You will beg more." He smiled with a slashed mouth.

"I won't."

"You will." He grazed the *keris* across my breast.

"No."

"You forget I saw you at Il Sotto Abbasso. Women like you don't say no. Very—what is the word?" He spat on me when I held out my hand. "Slutty. I did not know you were a *puttana*."

"No!" I shouted as he tossed the *keris* up into the air. I felt the ascent of it, the descent, in my organs. He caught it.

"You want it?" he said. "Then you will beg."

When I refused again, he tossed the blade higher. I screamed when he nearly missed catching it one-handed.

He held the *keris* in his fist. "Beg," he said, like a growl.

"Give it to her, Ermanno. It will never be anything to you." Sri Putra stood on the bridge.

Ermanno turned and scowled at the man who was his half brother and so wholly different from him. "I have heard enough on this, and I will not listen anymore. Go to Java! Leave!"

"Not yet," Sri Putra said, as I leaped to my feet and onto Ermanno's back.

"Let it go, Ermanno!"

He tried to buck me off, grabbed my arms, hollered, swore, called me crazy.

"I'm crazy? I don't frighten old ladies with spells and voodoo dolls!" I tightened the grip of my legs around his waist, my arms across his neck.

"I will hurt you," he said. "Do not think that I won't!"

"I'm not afraid of you," I told him, and meant it.

We were beside the edge of the bridge when I realized his intent. The steep fall, the pitch-dark waters. I hung on—"No!"—but felt the burn and twist of my flesh as he tried to pry me loose. He yanked again, brutally hard, and one of my arms came free of him. I fluttered there for a second before dropping inelegantly to my feet, and then I leaned my hips against the bridge's safety wall, panting, and waited for his next move.

Sri Putra stepped up and stood beside me. "This is very wrong, Ermanno."

Ermanno laughed. Ermanno bowed. His hands drew up as they had the day we'd first met, until the *keris* was over his head.

It happened in an instant: Ermanno screamed, gripping his hand. The blade was gone. I heard, faintly, the splash of water, and turned to look over the side, my nails scratching at the brick. The *keris* had fallen into the Tiber River.

How far would it be swept overnight? How deep was the water? In all likelihood, even in tomorrow's light, I would never find it. I would never see it again.

I was vaguely aware of the arguing brothers, Ermanno's angry red hand, when I decided, called out in my mind:

Bloo! Moira! Where are you?

I let go each and every one of the barriers I'd erected to safeguard myself, and almost fell to my knees as the tumble of emotions rolled over me. Grief and dread, desperation and need and love. And then, the voice.

Come quick. I'm here.

I BARELY RECALL finding stairs, the endless trek down them. I remember the water, though; the chill of it stabbed my bones like a hundred daggers.

Come now. Hurry.

I followed the voice like a compass, let loose my breath, and felt my body sink. My hands found stone.

Here.

Where are you?

Here. Here. You're close.

I moved hand over hand along the bottom of the Tiber.

Now, grab.

I did. My hand burned. The *keris*, its sheath gone, sliced deep into my flesh. I tried to pull back, couldn't.

It's time.

The water became a rushing, feral force. I kicked, suddenly desperate for air, but I couldn't lift to find the surface.

Open the door. Do it now.

The door from my dreams stood, unbelievably, before me. Closed. Submerged. Spitting even more water.

Use your will and mine. It's now or never. Open it.

Now or never. The words flayed my reservations.

I reached out, felt the handle, grasped, turned. The door was too heavy.

Pull. Pull hard.

I felt it give, just a little at first. And then roiling waves crashed out at me as it flew open. I would die.

Don't struggle so, like a wild frantic bird that is rending its own plumage in its desperation.

I knew then I wasn't crazy. Who but Moira would quote *Jane Eyre* at such a moment?

Breathe. Breathe deep and listen.

My lungs, desperate and without options, sucked in the seething water. The force whirled inside of me, but soon I found I could exhale, inhale, as if I were a fish with gills.

It's not your fault, Maeve. It's not your fault.

The *keris* disappeared from my hand just as I felt it inside my chest—hot, slicing. I thrashed, tried to pull away.

Stop. This won't hurt you, and I'm not here to hurt you. I don't have much time, so listen. Listen.

I felt myself nod.

I don't blame you for what happened, Maeve. Believe that. You'd just learned I was meeting with Ian. You were worried about me and what I'd been doing, so you went to see him. That was good and right.

No, it wasn't good. It wasn't right. I wanted to hurt you.

No, you wanted to know the truth, and you deserved to know the truth.

Another tug, another slash of heat, and I felt the heavy ache of extension, like a frozen joint pried open.

I'd stolen your identity, your light. I deceived you. Another rip. *I deceived Mom and Dad. I deceived Ian. I deceived myself.*

I shouldn't have blocked you.

I blocked you first. We both suffered.

I shouldn't have opened to you the way I did later. I shouldn't have tried to hurt you like that or make you feel—

I heard her weep.

I'm sorry for that. I'm sorry you were damaged that night, in so many ways. I'm sorry my lies cost you so much life.

Me? Who cares about me? It cost *you* everything. At least I'm here. I'm okay. You're in some empty, in-between place. You need to go, Moira, move on. Find peace.

I care, Maeve, and you're not okay, you're not. Yes, you're good at what you do—great even—but you've let go too much. Take yourself back. Stop thinking of your soul's desires as guilty pleasures. They're who you are! So keep your language, but take your music. Take Castine. Take avventura. *Take Noel. I like him, by the way, and you're right—he could've been like someone out of* Jane Eyre, *but he's much more stable than poor Mr. Rochester.*

I laughed through my tears.

I need you to forgive me, Maeve.

I forgive you. God, Moira, of course.

No, I need you to forgive me by letting go. And forgiving yourself. And forgiving Ian. And by helping him to forgive me, too. Please.

Moira.

Please.

Each word stripped something away, brought a new expansion and a deeper, cleaner breath.

I love you, Maeve, and I want you to live.

I tried not to buckle under the awesome sense of decompression as something inside me, invisible bindings, fell away and melted into a cocooning ocean along with my tears.

Why did this feel like grief?

Because you're letting go.

Something ethereal brushed my hand and the swirling slowed, the water cleared. Moira drifted there, like a water angel with a billowing ruby halo, her hand over mine and eyes locked with mine in the warm womb of the strange sea. I stared at first, then touched her face. Real. Solid. My sister.

Oh, Moira, I've missed you. I've missed you so much.

I've missed you. Never block me, not ever again.

I'm so sorry about the music—

Never be sorry about your music.

Your music, Moira. Yours. I'm sorry you were so unhappy. I wish I'd understood. I could've helped. I should've realized.

Stop, Maeve. Let's not waste any more time with regrets.

We swam close and held tight to one another, the sense of wonder

just as keen and intense as it'd ever been. Since before we were born. You're so beautiful, I thought, feeling her light within all parts of me.

A strained look crossed my sister's face when we stopped our dance—a look both sad and triumphant.

Remember, Maeve, if you owe me anything, it's a full life. Music and love and avventura. *Don't neglect those things ever again. Don't punish yourself anymore. Just move on. I'm here. I'll always be.*

She kissed my mouth.

I can fly now. I can fly.

I felt her threadbare spirit lighten further as my lungs reawakened to a burn. Wait, I thought. Her face grew haunted as she shook her head. And then she kissed me again.

You're free.

Her fingers slipped away. My body lifted through the water.

No! I love you! Don't go!

Hands wedged in my armpits, dragged at me. My head breached the surface of the Tiber. I took a startled gasp. "Not yet, not yet. Wait!"

The *keris* was in my hand.

I tried to go back. There was so much to say. How could she go now when there was still so much to say? But whoever pulled at me was stronger than I was, and as soon as I heard the voice I recognized Sri Putra.

"Are you all right?" he asked.

I continued to struggle as he towed my body to the edge, up onto the land.

"You cannot go back," he said as I leaned against the muddy earth and coughed river droplets.

"It was Moira," I managed to say. "She's the *hantu.*"

"Do you need a doctor? You were down for a long time, and you are cut," he said. Blood seeped from my hand, dripped onto the soil. Blood flowed from him as well, from a cut near his eye, a gash in his check.

"What did he do to you?"

"It is no matter," the *empu* said. "It is over now. Ermanno will not bother you again. He followed you into the waters and has seen truth."

"He's seen what? My sister? Then he knows that the *keris* holds power. He won't quit now, he never will." I held more tightly to the blade.

"It is over," he repeated. "Ermanno was attracted to the promise of power in your *keris*. He was attracted because of the *hantu*. He saw the *hantu* as true magic."

"But nothing has—" *It is over. It is over. Was. Was. Saw.* Past tense. Something had happened, snapped inside me, gone . . . empty. I focused on the sense for a moment, tried to understand it.

"Oh, no." Found my feet. "No, no. I've got to go."

I wanted to run through the streets, but I could barely stand. Within minutes, the *empu* found me a cab.

"Be well," he said. "Be strong."

My eyes stayed on him even after he shut the door, but my words were for the cabdriver. *"Avanti! Scappi! Scappi! Ancora, ancora, ancora di più!"* I said. "Fly!"

"PICK UP. SOMEONE, come on, pick up!" I held the receiver hard against my ear—three rings, four, six, eight. "Oh, God!" I hung up the phone and went through the sequence again, entered codes, waited. "Please, hurry."

"Just one moment," said the crisp voice of a male operator.

Several minutes later, the line connected. One ring, two.

"Moira Leahy's room," I said to the receptionist when she picked up. "Hurry, please."

The phone rang at the station near my sister's room.

"Judy speaking," said a voice.

"Moira Leahy," I said. "I need to know if she's all right."

"Are you family, ma'am?"

"I'm her sister, her twin."

"Just a moment," she said, and put me on hold.

"Come on!" I shouted.

Torturous minutes later, she returned to the line. "I'm sorry, but I can't tell you anything at this time."

"What does that mean? Are my parents there? Is my mother? Please, can I speak to one of them if they're there?"

"Can you call back in a little while?"

"Please, isn't there a nurse I can speak with?"

"Not at this time. I'm sorry. Please call back."

"Can you just look—" I said as the line went dead.

I sat, frozen, on my bed as my hand bled onto the sheets.

The call came an hour later, almost to the minute. "I'm sorry, Mayfly," my father said. "So sorry, sweetheart."

But I already knew. The *keris* had grown cold.

Yet the bloodline remained.

"YOU SHOULD SEE a doctor."

"I have to get home, Giovanni," I said as he tucked the end of a long white strip of gauze around my injured hand. We stood in a room off the hotel's kitchen, full of buckets, a neat desk, and a large first-aid kit.

"It will scar. The cuts, they are—"

"Yes, deep. I don't care." I stood. "My flight's in five hours. I can't take time right now for anything but getting to the airport. I won't miss my plane."

"You will not miss it," he said, his lips pressed in a line. "I will take you there myself."

"Believe me, Hercules won't fit on your bike." His eyebrows did their funny dance, and it hit me how much I'd miss him. "You'll tell Noel when he calls that I had to go home to Maine, not New York?"

"*Sì*, I will do that if you promise to come back. I will throw a coin in the Trevi Fountain for you." He pulled a yellow box from one of the wire shelves behind him and handed it to me.

"Another panettone?"

"They *riprodursi*," he said, "like bunnies."

I left my Bugs Bunny sweatshirt on the bed in my room with his name on it. Somehow I thought he'd appreciate it. I knew where I'd find another one.

Will Reborn

MAEVE

YOU CAN TRY TO ESCAPE IT, BUT THE TIDE ALWAYS
CATCHES YOU, IN THE END.

—ALVILDA

CHAPTER TWENTY-TWO

GHOSTS OF
CASTINE

It had been years since I'd seen the house I grew up in, or a tall elm's bark dusted in snow. Evidence of the most recent nor'easter swept across the walk. I would go outside later that afternoon and clear it—to be helpful, to give myself something to do, to allow the shutdown of my mind. Mrs. Bronya peered out at me from a window as I emerged from my rental car. She raised a hand, and I read her meaning even from a distance: *I'm sorry for your loss.*

Inside, I set down my bags, pulled off my boots and left them on the rug, hung my coat in the closet. I stood in the entry for a minute with my eyes closed and listened to the quiet, breathed in the scent of home—indescribable and familiar and missed more than I'd realized.

I found my father in the living room asleep on the couch with Sparky, who gave a single bark when she saw me, then put her head back by my father's side.

"Maeve." He rubbed at his eyes. "It is you."

"Of course it's me, Daddy." I knelt beside him on the rug and grasped his hand. "Are you all right?"

"Just tired." He looked bone-weary, world-worn.

"You should sleep then," I said. "We'll talk later."

273

I left to find my mother. Not in the kitchen or the laundry room. I walked upstairs. Not in Poppy's room, which had been turned into a tidy office. My mother sat in her bedroom, in the rocking chair beside the window. She didn't turn when I called her name, just stared out at the snow. I sat on the edge of her bed for twenty minutes at least, then made my way to my own room, the room I'd shared with my sister.

It looked just as I remembered it, only neater. I put the bag on my bed and pulled out the *keris*. And then I walked to my sister's bed and lay the blade atop her quilt.

"I don't ever think I said—" The words felt thick in my throat. "Thank you."

I lay myself down beside the *keris*, felt the cool cotton beneath my cheek, and slept without dreams.

THE SERVICE FOR Moira was simple, held right at the funeral home, and with most of Castine in attendance. My mother looked as though she would fall down at any minute, her face covered in black like an old-world widow, her frame slight. My father stood by her side and held her elbow.

A hand found my own.

"Sweetie," Kit said, beside me. "I'm so sorry."

I nodded, looking at my sister's flaccid face as the minister spoke words I could not hear. Yesterday I'd lined her casket in music— sheets from her piano bench, favorite tapes, and the box I'd purchased at the auction for the little girl. My mother had watched in silence. She'd yet to speak to me.

My breath came sharp as the minister closed the casket, and it took a lot of will not to push him aside, lift the lid again, and shake Moira by her shoulders, to yell, "Okay now, enough, it's time to wake up!"

I stood there with Kit and waited until my parents pulled away from the flower-covered box. Finally, I stepped up myself, put my hand atop the cold wood and tried to say good-bye.

Wisest angel, I said in my mind, envisioning Moira's face as I'd last seen it, her hair billowing out behind her. *I'm glad you're free of your purgatory. I hope that you're happy.* I imagined her smile. *But we made an oath. Don't think I will ever, ever forget it.*

I put a bloodred rose atop her coffin.

"I'll be with you for always."

"WHAT CAN I do?" Kit stood beside me as others paid their respects, filtered away from the ceremony.

"Nothing," I said. "There aren't pills or tests for this."

She scanned my face. "There are medications," she said. "Things you can take short term to help you over the hump."

"Kit, I don't need drugs."

She sighed. "There's a doctor in Bangor I think you should see. He's supposed to be very good."

Right. About the sights and sounds, the waking dreams, the voice in my head. All Moira's doing. Because I wouldn't listen and wouldn't remember and wouldn't let go. Because I'd landed us both in purgatory.

"I already made the appointment," she admitted.

"All right, Kit, but I think everything will be okay now. I really do."

"But you'll see the doctor?"

"I'll see the doctor."

She studied me. "I talked to Noel yesterday."

"Oh." I clasped my hands together. "Did he seem all right? I know he wanted to be here, but I just couldn't . . ."

"He's worried about you. Why didn't you let him come? You need support right now. Don't block him out."

Block. No. I didn't mean to block him. I'd learned my lesson about that.

"He's still in Wareham with his mother," I said. "And I just can't handle everything at once. I need time with my parents alone and to fall apart if I'm going to."

"You should," she said, her tone vehement. "Let it all out. Fall a-frickin-part already. Don't hold things in or you really will need drugs."

"Kit? Mom wants to know if you'll stay for dinner."

My spine straightened at the voice, both familiar and foreign to my ears. Ian Bronya stood right behind me.

"I'll be there," she told him, then turned to me. "Unless you need me, Maeve. I'm happy to—"

"No, I'm fine," I said. "We certainly have enough to eat." Lobster pies claimed every square inch of our freezer.

"Can I have a minute?" Ian asked.

I took a step away from them, but Kit grasped my arm, leaned in, and whispered, "No, Maeve, he wants to talk to you. He wants to pay his respects."

"No," I said. "Don't go."

"It'll be okay, just give him a minute. I'll call you later. I won't leave without saying good-bye." For a moment, she stared past me at her brother, but then she walked out the door. Only a few people remained, including my parents.

I steadied my breath and turned around. Ian's eyes were as blue as ever, just as I remembered, and though his hair looked darker, hints of sunshine still shone in streaks. How was it that it was now, looking at him, when I felt closest to tears?

"I wanted to tell you how sorry I am," he said.

"You're sorry for my loss?"

"Yes." He searched my face. "I'm very sorry for your loss."

For which loss? I wondered. The loss of my sister? Of my virginity? My naive worldview? The last decade of my life? Which of these losses are you sorriest for? But despite my knee-jerk response to him, I knew these thoughts weren't quite fair and couldn't summon any true anger.

We stood there, awkwardly, not sure what to do, where to look. Maybe he wanted to say something meaningful, to acknowledge that this horrible, shameful thing involving all three of us so intimately was finally over—or maybe he hoped I'd be the one to express it. But I was having a hard time finding words, just then. I remembered Moira's request—*help him to forgive me*—but still I could do no more than walk away, out the door, out of the building. I only breathed again once my feet tread over the snow-covered path that would take me home.

• • •

The Last Will of Moira Leahy

AT SOME POINT over the years, my parents had added a screened-in porch to the back of our house. After the service, I sat out there with a kerosene heater and watched as sleet fell, the wet crystalline mess of nature splat-sticking to the wire.

"Maeve?"

Kit's face appeared beyond the mesh door. I motioned her in. She sat beside me on the bench.

"He told me," she said without preamble. "Ian told me he raped you."

My stomach fell as she put her hand on my head. Rape. What an ugly word, what an ugly act. I didn't want to think of it, not ever again.

"Maeve, oh, Maeve, why didn't you ever tell me?"

"How could I? He's your brother. You love him."

"I should've known what he was capable of." The tears in her eyes were angry ones, I knew. "I could've helped you!"

"You couldn't have. You shouldn't even know."

"I can't believe this! I think he wanted me to *absolve* him. I don't know if I'll ever be able to speak to him again."

"Kit, don't," I said sternly. "It's not about you, and it happened a long time ago."

Tears streaked down her face now. "But how could you not tell me? Why didn't you trust me?"

"He's your brother."

"And?"

I felt the room shift as I stood and walked to the screen. "He didn't know it was me."

"Wha—How do you—"

"He didn't know it was me," I said, with conviction this time. "He thought I was Moira. They'd been lovers. It was an accident."

"Rape is rape, Maeve. Did you say no?"

"Yes, but—"

"No 'buts'! You sound like you're defending him!"

I did. How unlikely was that? "I've hated him for a long time for what happened, but he didn't act in a vacuum. I just . . . I just don't think we should blame Ian for everything."

Silence.

"He thought you were Moira."

"He thought I was Moira. And he thought Moira was me."

"Oh, God."

We stood together for a long time in the cold, until the dark came and I made Kit go home, back to the warmth and to her brother. Better to face the things that make you want to shrivel up. Always better.

I remembered the Ghost of Castine and thought I finally understood why the drummer boy had left his field for a dungeon.

"It feels safe there, doesn't it, little boy?" I said to the night. "Safe, closed off from those reminders of pain and suffering. It seems easier not to face the blood field."

I listened to the rhythmic pelting against the screen, so very much like drumbeats.

"I MISS YOU," Noel said when he called a short while later. "I wish you'd let me come."

"I'm sorry." I sat on my bed and felt the weight of the day sink me low. "It has nothing to do with you. It's me. I just have to be in this world for a little while."

"Can't I pay my respects to that world? Sorry," he said before I could respond. "I just want to hold your hand."

He had returned to Paris that afternoon, and he was ready to pack his things and make his way to Betheny. His time with his mother hadn't been easy; he'd learned hard details about her life, what she'd been through. But they'd reconciled themselves to the lives they'd had and focused on the lives they still had to lead. Lives they would be a part of, each with the other—though she planned to stay in England.

"Give her time to face her fears," I advised him. "You planted the seed. Leave it awhile. And if that doesn't work, you can always start haunting her dreams."

"Sense of humor still intact, I see." He wasn't laughing, though; I felt his desire and need even over the phone.

Oh, Noel. I can't. I just can't. Though I hadn't fallen apart, I felt depleted. How could I give more?

"I'm here for you," he said. "Remember that I'm here."

I stared up at the bare ceiling. "I won't forget."

The Last Will of Moira Leahy

• • •

MY MOTHER FINALLY spoke to me the day after the funeral.

"Would you like some lasagna?" she asked. "I'm sick of chowder and lobster pie."

"Yes, I'd love that," I said, surprised. "Can I help in the kitchen?"

"Don't trouble yourself," she said, and left.

That night, she asked me to pass her the salt. Two minutes later, she asked me to pass her the pepper. I thought I caught the hint of my father's smile.

DAYS LATER, THE sun made an appearance and tempted me down to the beach. I sat on a boulder the color of elephant skin and looked out at the great blue-gray and beyond. I knew Moira was out there, somewhere, playing our music on the sea. She was there, calling for me with Poppy, bobbing in the water. She was there, picking rocks from a distant shore—smooth ones, pebbles of the darkest berry blue—and laughing at the stupidity of boys. She was there, she was there, I reminded myself, even though I couldn't hear her anymore. She was there, she was there. I had to believe it.

"Maeve?"

"Mom. Careful," I said as she picked her way down the stairs leading to the beach. Wind had stripped the steps of their snow, but sometimes ice covered the wood.

I waited, curious and alarmed, for her to approach. She'd grown so thin, her hair long and unkempt and streaked with gray. I knew her days had been filled with Moira—caring for Moira, reading to Moira, crying over Moira. And I'd been jealous of that attention once, the attention she'd paid to my comatose sister.

She sat beside me and looked out at the sea. I looked at her for a while, then turned my face toward the water as well. I'd stopped waiting for words when they finally came.

"I dream of her," she said. "Maybe it's not Moira, but I think it is. She's just a little girl. Looks like both of you and neither of you at the same time."

My eyes watered. "What does she want?"

"I think she wants to play," she said, and it occurred to me, as we

279

both laughed and cried, that maybe this girl who seemed like Moira yet wasn't her was still our family. The baby my mother had lost, maybe, or my sister's tiny child—Ian's daughter, the one my mother didn't even know about. I remembered what Sri Putra had told me: No light was ever lost.

"I'm glad you dream of her."

"I found something," she said. "It's been so long since Moira's been sick." Sick. Like a cold, the flu, a bout of fever. "It was time to tidy a little, donate some of her old clothes."

I nodded, could see the therapeutic value in this for my mother even as part of me rebelled against the idea of her throwing out anything of Moira's. *Let me go through things,* I thought. *Let me take pieces of her. Her stuffed bear. The laughing stone with the silly face she'd found on this beach. The T-shirt with her name on it. That wooden bird she'd carved with Daddy. Don't throw her away.*

"A whale," my mother said, pointing out at the bay. I looked in time to see a fin disappear into the water. "I forget sometimes how deep the Penobscot is. I spend so much time beside it that I don't come out here to sit and look or think about what's under it all. I should do that more often."

I watched the complicated turn of her expressions, unsure exactly what to say.

"I found this," she said, and pulled an envelope from her pocket. Moira's tabby-cat stationery. My lungs deflated as she pressed the letter into my gloved hand, held there for a prolonged moment before letting go. "Read it when you can. When you have time." She waited a few beats before standing, then laid her hand on my shoulder and squeezed. "It'll be all right."

I nodded, mute.

"It's freezing out here," she said, casting one last look at the sea, breathing it in. "I'm going to head back."

"Be careful." I watched her walk up the stairs, all the while consumed with one fact: I had a letter in my hand from my sister. A letter. Once my mother was out of view, I opened the envelope's already unstuck flap and pulled out the paper.

Dear Ian,

The Last Will of Moira Leahy

My insides sank a bit. I'd hoped the letter would be for me—words from the grave, of illumination and everlasting love. Still, I read on.

Dear Ian,

This is the hardest thing I've ever had to do.

I need to tell you something that may make you hate me, but I have to take the chance. Things aren't what you think they are. In fact, things are very different than you think they are. Before I tell you what is different, I want you to know what is true about us. I know that sounds terrible, and I guess you'd be right to be scared about that sentence, because so much isn't true. But let me start with the good stuff.

We have shared so much together. You have taught me a lot about who I am and what I want to be. I admire you so much. I love you, Ian. That is true, and I hope that no matter what you believe about me after you read this, that you realize my love for you was always real. One of the most real things in my life. Along with the love I feel for my sister, Maeve. Yes, you read that right, my sister is Maeve.

You see, Ian, I am Moira. The girl you've been kissing and meeting with, the girl you've been loving and who's been loving you back is Moira. The boring sister. I don't have a good excuse to give you. Why did I do it? Why did I take the saxophone stone that day and let you believe I was Maeve? Why did I meet with you and let you think you were kissing her? I guess the answer is that I wanted to kiss you, and I thought if you got to know me—no matter what my name was—that you could love me, too. But that doesn't make what I did right.

I know you love Maeve. Maybe you love me, too. Maybe you love us both. I hope so. But I know you love her because of her cool personality and the way she runs off with you and Michael to dig up treasure and play football and stuff. And I know you love that she's going to get a recording contract and leave Castine someday. I wish I could play the sax, but my mother wouldn't let me try. Oh, well. I wish you liked the piano, but I guess not everyone does, huh?

What I'm trying to say, Ian, is that I love my sister, too. And I love you. And this lie is getting too big for me. I don't want to hurt any of us, including me. I don't want to hate my sister for being someone you like. It hurts me. And it hurts her. And I feel that hurt in a way I could never explain.

So I'm sorry, Ian. If you love Maeve, you should just tell her and see what happens. I'll try to stay out of your way. If you can forgive me, and you think you love me, then I will be the happiest girl in the world. I would like that more than anything. You and me. Ian and Moira. I'd be proud to hold your hand at school or anywhere else. And we can look for a new stone together—one shaped like a piano this time.

I love you. I hope you can forgive me someday.

Love, Moira

I shattered. Broke like I'd never cried before. A thousand glass-shard tears filled my eyes, and I bled them out. Oh, Moira! Why didn't you send it?

I stumbled up the walk and slid twice on the stairs, caught myself with the rail. Once on flat land, I ran over the path. Ian stood there in the drive, packing his car.

"Maeve," he said, noticing my approach. "What's wrong?"

"Read it."

He stared at me as I staggered before him, drunk on grief and regret, and then looked at the paper I'd thrust into his hand. I waited until I saw the words hit home. The admission that she'd pretended to be me. That she loved him. That she loved me. That she hoped he loved her. That she was sorry for all of it.

Misery scarred his features as well. "Jesus. You just found this?"

I nodded.

"Come here," he said, and I let his arms encircle me. What strange war comrades we made. What a strange war it had been. "I'm sorry, Maeve. Believe me, I'm so horribly sorry."

I pulled away, gripped his arm. "Forgive her."

"What?"

"You need to forgive Moira. It's important. Forgive her."

"I forgive her," he said. "I forgave her a long time ago." The wind ruffled his hair as fine lines grew around his lips. "Can you ever

282

forgive me? Would she? Not a day goes by that I don't regret . . . everything."

He looked me straight in the eye, and I didn't look away.

"You hurt me, Ian, and you hurt Moira. But I know you didn't set out to hurt either one of us. I think we've all suffered, more than enough."

Open the door, said the voice of my memory.

"Ayuh. I forgive you." I heard the caw of a bird and finally understood. "*We* forgive you."

CHAPTER TWENTY-THREE
ALPHA AND OMEGA

took a leave from the university, over the objections of the dean of my department, several of my colleagues, and Kit. My parents nodded when I told them, seemed to understand, though my father took me aside later and asked if I was sure, if I was all right, if I needed to talk.

"I just want to stay, Dad. Not forever. Just for a while longer." I had the most overpowering urge to see flowers in bloom again here, to be around for the moment the snow would clear away at last, the rains would come in earnest, and the trees would ripen with flowery fruits.

Noel also seemed to understand. I couldn't bring myself to speak with him for long or even often—once a week, maybe twice. It was a step back for us, this silent *wait for me, wait* request I made of him again, and I didn't always know that either of us would stay true to it. I had a difficult time seeing beyond Castine.

I did keep my appointment with the neurologist in Bangor. Dr. Philip Heath ran tests, gave me an MRI, took my blood, and made me fill out endless paperwork. In the end, he proclaimed me fit and well—though he asked that I call his office immediately if I ever experienced another waking dream or heard abnormal sounds. I agreed that I would, but I knew his definition of *abnormal* would differ from mine.

284

One day, I walked to the corner store for some essentials—milk and eggs, some coffee. Before I left, a package of glow-in-the-dark stars caught my eye. "With Adhesive! Guaranteed!" the sticker promised. I added it to my pile of goods and left for home.

I worked that day to cover my bedroom ceiling with those stars. Sure, I'd nicked the idea from Sri Putra, but I wasn't a complete copycat. I made constellations: Cygnus, Corvus, Orion, Gemini. Over my sister's bed I made Virgo, for our birth month.

At night, I'd drift off to sleep with my eye on those stars. Moira, I'd think. Bloo. Are you there, riding Delphinus's back? Where is your light? Where have you gone?

In my worst moments, I grieved over the wasted years when she'd lain comatose, when I might've felt her spirit join mine if I hadn't been so fearful and closed. Now my mind was home only to my thoughts and my voice.

But I dreamed of Moira every night.

There were no doors, no water, just her and me. Usually in the sunshine, sitting in the grass, playing our music or looking at the clouds. Sometimes we were young, sometimes old—with white hair and sagging breasts and false teeth that we would pluck out of our skulls and laugh over. Sometimes we would speak our language, and I would grasp it for a second as I woke, then lose its meaning again, like a slick eel diving back into the deep. But that was all right. I knew I'd catch it again.

THE SUN BEGAN to show itself on a more regular basis and wake me early in the morning. The snow did melt. Birds returned from their hideaways. Buds appeared as white-speck life on the otherwise bare and winter-ravaged branches. And Moira's roses, my grandmother's old yellow blossoms, tight and closed at first, unfurled in the warm rays.

One afternoon, I felt particularly restless. I retrieved the *keris* from its place beneath my pillow. (My mother no longer asked why I did this unusual and seemingly perilous thing.) I went onto the front porch and sat in a splintery rocking chair with the blade on my lap. The thin white scar lines on my palm reminded me that the *keris* was a true weapon, so I took care with it, sheathless as it was.

I rocked and studied the new spring colors as my fingers traced over the curves of the blade and the resilient blood mark—something I'd done so often, I could probably do it in the dark. I'd just lifted the *keris* and looked through the aperture when the mailman approached our door with a package in both hands.

"A big one," he said, and asked me to sign for it.

My pulse leaped a little when I saw my name on the box, but it wasn't until I was alone with it that I realized it came from Noel, postmarked Betheny, New York.

I hurried to the kitchen and grabbed a pair of scissors, then went back to the porch and scored along the edges of the box. I tore and cut at some difficult tape before managing to open an end. Beneath wrappings of silver lay a beautiful wooden case. Waves of shock eroded something in me as I took it in, what it was, and what it meant. And then I flipped open the duet of latches and looked at the instrument that sat like a golden moon against a thick pile of midnight velvet.

Noel had sent me a saxophone.

I stroked the smooth mother-of-pearl keys with the tip of my finger and took in the engraved lettering of the brand-new Selmer. I opened the note.

Dear Maeve,

Call me selfish. I want to hear you play your instrument again sometime soon. Everyone needs their paper and paint—especially a red woman like you.

Yours, Noel

p.s. No throwing this in the ocean.

It was the closest he ever came to pressuring me back.

I HAD THE most fantastical dream that night. A man, very like Sri Putra in appearance, sat on a dirt floor near a great stone hearth and blazing fire. In his hand he held metal tongs and worked something—a blade, I realized—hot, alive, over the flame. His arms curled and wrists bent as he muttered words I could not understand.

This *keris* he then passed on, and so it went from man to man. Finally, a young Sri Putra gave this blade to a man with a straw hat and sunburned skin. The man was Poppy.

"Thank you for saving my wife," Sri Putra said, and Poppy nodded before the scene changed again.

Moira and I played Alvilda, the *keris* in my hand and raised to the sky, just moments before being lost in the sea. I saw the blade covered in seaweed, caught in a lobster trap.

Time slurred. I saw an aperture form in the blade's metal and knew, somehow, that the *keris* meant for this to happen. The Third Eye. The *keris* needed it to find its way back.

I saw the blade ascend through the water and lift into hands. Saw it pass from a man with a fishing cap to another in a great wool coat. It traveled in a boat and then an airplane. It lived awhile with a thin woman and a Pekingese.

Two times more it changed hands before finding Sri Putra in Rome. The *empu* held the *keris* and knew it for his kin's own creation— the *keris* he'd given to my poppy for saving his wife after the explosion of a young volcano, long before the cancer had taken hold.

And then the uncanniest part: Sri Putra looked straight at me in my dream. "I am a professor now," he said. "Found. We will see each other again. I have made a new sheath."

I didn't forget any part of this odd tale, and so the next day, as my mother worked soil in the garden, I told my father about the dream.

"Interesting," he said as I set a plate of eggs before him.

I raised my brow in a way I believed would make Giovanni proud. "That's it? Interesting? How about plausible?"

"It was a dream." He shrugged and took a bite of egg.

Yes, it had been a dream. But I knew dreams. They held answers. Sometimes questions. Challenges. Puzzles.

"I'll never forget that Alvilda business, though," he said, wiping his mouth with his sleeve.

"Well, we were crazy then." I handed him a napkin. He took it without looking remotely abashed.

"Queen Alvilda, piratess of the sea. Even she settled down for her king eventually."

"Even she did, huh? Are you trying to say something, Dad?" I smiled. "Want to get rid of me?"

"Oh, no. No. Just saying that after all her war and craziness, even she found peace in the end. And she loved him, after all. That's all I'm saying. Nothing but that."

THE DAY CAME when my father proclaimed it safe to go out onto the Penobscot again, and so I trudged down to the dock where he'd uncovered our motorboat and set it in the water. I relieved it of its ropy confines and started the engine. Wind whipped my cheeks and ears, and made my hair come loose from its short ponytail. I steered out of the mouth of the bay, just a bit, then shut off the engine and sat. The air was cold still and the water choppy, but the sun shone.

Of course I missed my sister acutely in these moments—there was one now where there were once two—but I wasn't alone in the boat. I opened the wooden box beside me and pulled out the new saxophone. I tucked a reed in my mouth, then fitted pieces of the instrument together. I attached the neck strap and looped it over my head, set the reed into place and secured the ligature. I put the sax's neck on its body and tightened the screw, feeling tighter still in my chest.

Déjà vu. The last time I'd been here with a sax, I'd dropped it in the bay. So much had happened since then.

You have suffered, Sri Putra had said.

I knew this to be true.

I forgive you, Moira had said.

I felt the truth in that as well.

No throwing this in the ocean, Noel had said.

I didn't want to.

I closed my eyes and lifted the mouthpiece, felt the cold press against my lips, took a breath, and played a long note, held it until my lungs ached. I opened myself—every part and bit—and out poured a song of anguish and love and acceptance and hope. I felt, quite strongly, that Moira came through in that song, that she'd handpicked every note herself; and when I finished, when I put the saxophone down on my lap and wept, I thought I heard her voice.

Don't be afraid of death. It's so much like birth.

I shivered long and violent, and felt a shift along all of my faults as the greater part of me gave way to that, believed it. I held a vivid image in my head of my old saxophone at the bottom of the sea, shifting as well, displacing sand and weed, then lifting, rising beyond the sea's sky, and releasing a bubble of air and a single solemn note.

And it was like death.

And it was like birth.

EPILOGUE

*T*hree days after playing my soulful tune, after not chucking my new sax into the sea, I picked up a box of Sunset Sky and dyed my hair as close to its natural color as I could make it. Then I packed up my few belongings, hugged my parents good-bye, and made my way back to Betheny.

I knew I should go to my apartment first, get a clean change of clothes, visit with my cat, see if Kit might be at home, and then call the university. Instead, I drove to Time After Time.

I pulled into the small lot and emerged from my car. The season had progressed here. The trees bloomed full, and the air smelled sweet. A bee flew by my face, lingered for a moment, then buzzed away.

Outside the shop door sat several large boxes and a six-foot tiki tower. How fierce the wooden man's grimace, but I marched up to him nonetheless.

"Maeve? Is that you?"

I craned my head to see Noel peering from a second-story window. He wore a red bandanna for a cap and looked every bit a pirate with his long hair poking out from beneath it.

He grinned. "Why didn't you tell me you were coming? The shop's a bloody mess with inventory—so am I."

"I've always loved a good mess."

"Christ, you look fantastic! It's really you?"

"Really who? I'm Alvilda the fearless, back from my adventures. Are you of royal blood, mate?"

My smile turned to a frown as I realized he'd ducked back from the window, but then I heard feet pounding on the stairs. I didn't wait for him to do it for me. I opened the door myself, and stepped inside.

AUTHOR'S NOTE

Dyce Head Lighthouse in Castine, Maine, probably wouldn't have been an ideal spot for Moira and Ian to meet for all its surrounding buildings, though I've tried to take advantage of some historical facts. Though the lighthouse itself had been defunct for years, a keeper's house abutting it had been occupied for all but a brief period during which time a fire destroyed some of the house and a reconstruction took place. This timeframe coincides with Moira and Ian's trysts.

Dyce Head Lighthouse was relit in 2008 and is once again a functional lighthouse in Castine.

ABOUT THE AUTHOR

THERESE WALSH has a master's degree in psychology. She lives in upstate New York with her husband and two children. This is her first novel. Visit her at ThereseWalsh.com or WriterUnboxed.com.

ABOUT THE TYPE

THE TEXT of this book was set in Bell, a Transitional typeface created for Monotype in 1931 and originally cut by Richard Austin in 1788 for John Bell's type foundry. When Bell's foundry closed down, the font migrated for decades under different names: "English Copperplate" at the American Riverside Press in 1792, then "Brimmer," and later "Mountjoye," until font designer Stanley Morrison restored the name again in 1931. Unique to Bell is its break from tradition for numerals: They are two thirds the height of the font's capitals and sit evenly on the line.